THEY CAME TO A VALLEY

THEY CAME TO A VALLEY

Bill Gulick

Caxton Press
Caldwell, Idaho
2002

All of the characters in this book are ficticious, and any resemblance to actual persons, living or dead, is purely coincidental.

Copyright © 1966 By Grover C. Gulick

All rights reserved. No part of this book may be reproduced in any manner without the express written consent of the publisher, except in the case of brief excerpts in critical reviews and articles. All inquiries should be addressed to: Caxton Press, 312 Main Street, Caldwell, ID 83605.

First Caxton printing March, 2001
Second Caxton printing July, 2002

ISBN 0-87004-420-6

Originally published in 1966 by Doubleday & Company, Inc.
Reprinted by arrangement with the author.

Printed and bound in the United States of America
CAXTON PRESS
Caldwell, Idaho
168747

Part One

The Journey

CHAPTER ONE

As he rode past the cannon at the far end of the Fort Laramie parade ground, Matt Miller noted that the corporal he had seen chained there earlier in the day was gone. A hell of way to punish a man for drinking, stealing, fighting, or whatever it was he'd done, the old guide mused. Tie him up like a sheep-chasing dog. Put him on public view on a Sunday where officers, enlisted men, wives, emigrants, Injuns, kids—all strolling around in their Sunday best—could see him in his shame.

What kind of thoughts run through a soldier's head when he's chained up that way? Does he repent of his sins? Not likely. Does he vow not to do again whatever he's done to put himself in such a fix? Probably not. But it teaches him a lesson. Sure. It teaches him not to get caught next time.

Light spilling through the windows and doorways of the laundry huts and teamster shacks showed Matt Miller the trail as he rode through the outlying settlement fringing the military post. To his nostrils came the smell of the lumber yard, of horses stabled nearby, of dust and soap and newly washed clothes. Nobody needed to punish *him* for his sins; his battered old body tended to that. Right now, in spite of the two belly-easing drinks he'd just had with the colonel, his furred tongue and aching back were telling him in no uncertain terms he'd had too much whisky and too little sleep last night. Sure, he'd been entitled to a spree after the monotonous dry weeks on the trail out from Council Bluffs. But he wasn't young no more. Repent, said his kidneys; that was gospel a man his age had to listen to.

His horse's shod hoofs echoed hollowly on the worn planks of the bridge spanning Laramie River, then there came to him the clean, pungent, sage smell of the open plains and the acrid woodsmoke of valley campfires. Through the dark he could see the circled wagons of the Iowa train now, vague blobs in the night, the lowered tongue of one chained to a rear wheel of the next like dogs sniffing one another. A guard watching over the grazing livestock outside the circle was whiling away the slow-passing time with a song, singing it not fast and sprightly like it was meant to be sung, but slow, sad, and sweet, like a lover's lament:

Oh, he left his sweetheart crying
Where the red, red rose is dying;
And she'll linger there a yearning
While she waits for his returning . . .

Yes, he's gone to save his country
For Abe Lincoln and for liberty . . .

People were damn fools, Matt thought. They ran away from the war but they couldn't leave the war at home. They had to drag it along with them, like an iron ball on the end of a chain; they had to think about it, talk about it, argue about it, fight any man that disagreed with them at the drop of a meaningless slogan. It was always talk made the trouble. And ideas. And slogans. Nowadays you didn't get mad at a man and jump him because he personally had done you dirt, which was the only sensible way to behave; you just up and clobbered him because of what he said or professed to believe.

Like last year. Matt brooded, when I guided that train of New Englanders out to California and they got in such a ruckus in the Mormon settlements near Salt Lake over the Saints having more than one wife. Why should that matter to them? And that wild-eyed Irishman I run into out in San Francisco who was such a rabid England-hater. If he was so set on fighting the English, why didn't he stay home? But, no, he comes over here and starts organizing a secret society which he says is going to kill all the Britishers and set Ireland free.

He's a red-hot freedom-lover, he claims, and brags long and loud about being an American citizen and a good Democrat. Yet he damns the North. He says the Yankees got no goddam business telling Southerners they can't own slaves. And he hates Injuns. Says a bounty ought to be placed on their scalps. Hates the Chinese, too. Says they ain't fit to live. Gets drunk one night and cries like a baby over the poor, oppressed people of Ireland, six thousand miles away, but God help the Injun, Chink, or nigger that crosses his path.

Look here, I says, just to get a rise out of him, what's the difference 'tween a poor, oppressed Irishman in your country and a poor, oppressed Injun, Chink, or nigger in mine? How come you cry over one and spit on the other? Where's the logic to that?

Come at me with a whisky bottle, the bastard did. But I showed him *that* kind of argument didn't shine with me . . .

Unsaddling his horse, Matt turned it in with the rest of the guarded stock and carried his bridle, saddle, and blanket into the wagon enclosure. Daniel Lynn, the wagon captain, looked up at him as he dropped his gear nearby, smiled a knowing smile and said, "Get all your business done at the fort?"

"Yeah."

"You look beat. Have a lumpy bed last night?"

Not troubling to answer, Matt hunkered on his heels, took the simmering coffeepot off the fire and helped himself. Lynn had the family Bible open on his knees; he made it a custom to read a few chapters to his youngsters each Sunday evening, as their mother used to do. Sally was mending socks, Henry repairing a bridle. Sally gave Matt a smile.

"Have you had your supper?"

"Coffee's all I want."

"I put something aside for you. It will take only a minute to heat it up."

"Thanks, I ain't hungry."

Henry kept his eyes fixed on his work. Watching the boy awkwardly try to worry a hole through the leather bridle strap, Matt took a small whetstone out of his pocket and grunted, "You got a dull awl there, boy. Best touch it up a mite."

"It's sharp enough."

The boy was peeved about something, no doubt about that. Watching him turn red in the face as he dug, twisted, and shoved, Matt tried to recall what it was he had promised Henry he would do and then hadn't done. Let's see, we made camp yesterday noon; I said I had some business to tend to at the fort; he wanted to tag along; his pa said no; then I said I'd come back and pick him up this morning and show him around the fort and the Injun camps . . .

Oh, hell, I *must* be getting old! Awl pierced leather, making a ragged, too-big hole. Hurt eyes burning in his flushed face, Henry looked up triumphantly.

"See?"

"Boy, I'm plumb sorry," Matt said, putting down his cup. "I got tied up and couldn't get back."

"Who cares?"

"Henry, mind your manners!" Lynn said sternly.

"Well, what I meant was I went over to the fort and saw it by myself. You ask me, it ain't much."

"Did you see the colonel's pet deer?" Matt asked.

"Yeah. Sorriest-looking deer I ever saw. Looked like it had the mange."

"That'll be enough out of you, young man," Lynn said, closing the Bible. He looked at Matt. "What did you find out?"

"The colonel says it's a bad year for Injuns. They been raisin' cain 'tween here and Bear River."

"Will he give us an escort?"

"Only as far as Platte Bridge, which is just a hundred miles. He don't have enough men to patrol the trail any farther than that. He says twenty-five wagons ain't enough. To be safe, he says, we'd ought to join up with somebody else headin' our way an' make up a train of at least fifty wagons."

"Somebody like those cursed Missourians camped next to us?"

"That was his notion, yeah."

A frown came to Daniel Lynn's square, solid face as he gazed out into the darkness. Faintly through the eddying currents of night air came the sound of singing from the emigrant camp a quarter mile away:

> *Shall we gather at the river?*
> *The beautiful, the beautiful river . . .*

The voices were sweet and true; the beat strong and rhythmic. They sing almost as good as darkies do, Matt mused. Tell 'em that an' they'd knock your head off, of course. But it's true.

Lynn shook his head. "I'd as soon throw in with a bunch of Mormons as that crowd of backwoods ridge-runners."

"We ain't got no choice, Daniel. They're headed for Oregon an' so are we. Time's runnin' on. Lord knows when a train of your kind of people will come through."

"They're all Rebel sympathizers, I'd bet."

"We ain't fightin' the war out here."

"A couple of them came calling yesterday afternoon. A pompous little jaybird named Cornelius Belford and a big bear of a young fellow named Will Starr. Belford invited us over to the preaching this morning."

"Did you go?"

"A few of us, yes." Lynn cast a look at his daughter. "Sally made me take her. That fool Belford sure runs off at the mouth once he gets himself wound up. He preached for two solid hours."

"Oh?" Matt said, giving Sally a wink. "An' did he convert you, Daniel?"

"Pa is already a good Christian," Sally said with a laugh. "But Mr. Belford did preach a fine sermon. You could tell he believed every word he said,"

"And he said every word ten times over," Lynn muttered sourly. "Who would be fool enough to trust a man like that?"

"You've got to make allowances for preachers," Matt said. "From what I've seen of the breed, it runs to wind."

"Belford's no preacher, he's just a talker. He told me he worked at the carpenter trade back home. But he thinks it's his right to tell people how to live whenever he gets the chance."

"What brand of religion does he hold to?"

"He didn't say. But it's a red-hot one."

It would be, Matt mused. Ridge-runners liked their pork high-flavored, their whisky raw and their preaching salty. Sin and backslide all week. Catch hell for it on Sunday. Wipe the slate clean with a real orgy of preaching, hymn-singing, repenting, rolling in the dust and speaking in tongues. A service like that made a man feel cleansed and ready for Monday.

"How did the rest of them Missourians strike you?"

"Seedy, Matt. Just plain seedy."

"Oh, Pa, that's an awful thing, to say!" Sally exclaimed indignantly. 'They're poor, maybe, but they can't help that. They're suspicious of strangers—but who wouldn't be after all the things they've gone through?"

"How do you know what they've gone through?"

"Mrs. Shelby told me."

"Who's she?"

"A woman I talked to this morning. Ruth Shelby. You just can't imagine what she and her family have gone through since the war started. It's the most pitiful story I ever heard. Now she's about to have a baby and they've got no doctor with them. I promised to help her—"

"What can I do with her, Matt?" Lynn said, giving the old guide a weary look. "Sixteen years old—and already she's taking other people's problems on her shoulders, just like her mother did."

"I told her we had a doctor with us," Sally said serenely. "She wants to talk to him. I asked Dr. Riley to go over and see her but he wouldn't do it." Sally smiled at her father. "You'll make him go, won't you. Pa?"

"I can't make anybody do anything."

"You're wagon captain. People have to do what you tell them to."

"Not unless they feel like it."

"But you will tell him, won't you, Pa?"

"All right, I'll tell him," Lynn said impatiently. He gazed out into the dark in the direction of the Missourian camp. Matt could guess what was running through his mind. He'd already lost two sons in the war, fighting for the Union cause, and had seen their mother waste away and die from grief. Because he wanted to take his remaining son and daughter as far away from the war as he could get them, he had sold a good farm, pulled up roots of a lifetime and set out for a new land at an age when most men were done with moving. Though he seldom let his bitterness show, it was only natural that he blame something, hate somebody, for the things the war had done to him.

"How much of a risk would we be taking, Matt, if we did go on with just our twenty-five wagons?"

"All I know is what the colonel told me. He said it would be considerable. He had no reason to lie."

"We're not cowards, any of us."

"No," Matt said slowly, glancing at Sally and then away, "an' neither was them people in the Otter train, which was set on an' massacred by the Snake Injuns a few years back. I seen the leavin's of that fracas, Daniel, an' they wa'n't puny. I recollect findin' a yellow-haired gal—what was left of her, anyways—who must've been about Sally's age . . ."

Daniel Lynn's jaw worked and he interrupted curtly, "All right, Matt, you can spare me the details. Let's go over and talk to them."

Henry leaped to his feet and said eagerly, "Can I go with you?"

"No."

"Aw, Pa—!"

"Let the boy come along," Matt said, getting to his feet and patting Henry on the shoulder with a smile. "He won't be in the way."

"Well, I suppose there's no harm—"

"I'll go saddle my horse," Henry cut in. "Want me to saddle yours, too, Pa?"

"We'll walk," Lynn said. "It ain't far."

Chapter Two

As they crossed the dark flat between the two camps, Matt could hear the singing grow louder, its rhythm more compelling:

> *Where bright angel feet have trod . . .*
> *Yes, we'll gather at the river*
> *The beautiful, the beautiful river . . .*

He remembered a trapper he'd known, years ago, who'd come from the Missouri hill country. What a mean booger *he* had been! I seen him kill a horse with a club one time. No reason for it. Just felt mean and ornery, the horse balked on him, so he beat it to death with a club. I seen him beat a squaw nigh onto death, too. No reason for that, either; he just felt like beating a squaw so he did.

Which ain't to say all Missoury ridge-runners are as mean, wild and vicious as that booger was. But they're a breed bears watching. Something about that backwoods hill country air seems to make 'em feel they can be a law to theirselves; something plagues 'em, the only way they know to get it out of their system is to start clubbing, cutting, or shooting.

I mind what happened to that ornery trapper booger. Took on too much alky one night, decided he had to beat on somebody, picked the wrong man. Well, none of us mourned or missed him . . .

The singing stopped as they entered the circle of firelight; faces turned toward them; unsmiling eyes regarded them suspiciously. Standing on the lowered tailgate of a wagon, Cornelius Belford was in shirtsleeves, his tie loosened, his collar unbuttoned. He was an unusually short man—barely five feet, Matt guessed—and slight of build, but his eyes and manner held an intensity of purpose that clearly indicated he did not intend to be ignored. Seeing them, he hopped nimbly to the ground and hurried toward them through the crowd, trailed by the dark-haired giant, Will Starr, and a girl of eighteen or so, whom Matt supposed to be his daughter.

"Gentlemen, this is a pleasure!" Belford exclaimed, pumping first Lynn's hand, then Matt's. He smiled at Henry, who was almost as tall as he was. "This is your son, Mr. Lynn?"

"Yes. Henry, shake hands with Mr. Belford."

"How do you do," Henry mumbled.

"This is my daughter, Melinda," Belford said. "And I believe you've already met my young friend, Will Starr."

Though Matt himself topped six feet by an inch or so, he had to crane his head back and look up at a sharp angle to see Starr's face as they shook hands. "Glad to know you," the old guide said. "How's the weather up there?"

Will Starr grinned amiably, as if long accustomed to such jokes, and said it was fine. Melinda Belford, the top of whose head barely reached Starr's armpits, was staring curiously at Henry Lynn; she was small-boned, fine-featured like her father, strikingly pretty, and even the modestly cut, coarse-woven dress she wore could not conceal her ripe, well-rounded figure. Unused to such close feminine scrutiny, Henry Lynn scuffed the dust with a toe, trying to pretend that the condition of the soil was the only thing in life that interested him just now.

"I saw a number of your people at the morning service," Belford said as he fastened his collar and adjusted his tie. "I was hoping more of them would come over again tonight."

"They're tired," Lynn said, making a visible effort to be agreeable. "Not that they didn't enjoy the preaching this morning." He hesitated a moment, then said with his accustomed directness, "Mr. Belford, I'll make this short and sweet. You're headed for Oregon, I hear, same as us."

"That's right."

"Matt went over to the fort and asked the colonel how the Indians are behaving in the country west of here. The colonel says they're acting up bad. He says no wagon train of less than fifty wagons should risk traveling beyond Fort Laramie. You've got thirty wagons in your train, we've got twenty-five. So it seems plain what we ought to do."

Belford let Will Starr help him into his coat, put on his hat, took a handkerchief out of his pocket and carefully dusted his sleeves and trouser legs. "You're suggesting that we combine our trains, Mr. Lynn?"

"Ain't that the sensible thing to do?"

"It would seem so, yes. But joining our groups would raise a number of problems, Mr. Lynn. We should try to solve them in advance, don't you think?"

"We came here to talk."

"Melinda," Belford said, turning to his daughter, "tell Armand Kimball and Andrew Hale I want to see them at once."

"Where will I find them?"

"They're around someplace. Hurry, now!"

The girl turned to go, then paused. "Do you want to see Levi, too?"

"Who?"

"You know—Mr. Hale's friend—the Indian."

Belford frowned. "I made it clear to Andrew Hale we were hiring him alone. We have no use for his dirty Indian friend."

"Levi is still with him, just the same. I saw them eating supper together."

"Very well, I'll settle that matter later," Belford said impatiently. "But tell them to come at once, please."

The coquettish way Melinda tossed her head and gave Henry a superior smile as she turned to go made Matt figure her to be something of a tease. Not a very experienced one, either, else she'd not waste her time making a twelve-year-old boy feel ill at ease. Raised strict, likely. Watched close by her parents. Which was not a bad idea, he'd say, judging from the way she acted.

"The guide who brought us out to Fort Laramie was a crotchety, stupid old fool," Belford explained. "I was forced to discharge him a few days ago. This new man I've hired, Andrew Hale, came to me highly recommended. He's young—so young, in fact, I was reluctant to take him on—but after talking to him a while I became convinced that he knows his business. Are you acquainted with him, Mr. Miller?"

Matt nodded. He knew Andy Hale, all right, and he guessed that if any guide could put up with the contrariness of these Missoury ridgerunners Andy could do the job—because he was hill-raised himself. Eastern Kentucky or some such place. But Matt was also acquainted with the guide Belford had said he'd fired; in fact, Matt had done a bit of drinking with him last night. And the way *he'd* told it, he'd got so disgusted with this crowd he'd just up and quit them. But that had no bearing on the problem to be solved now, so there was no point in mentioning it.

"Sure, I know Andy," Matt said. "He's a good man. Far as that goes, they don't make men much better than his Injun sidekick, Levi."

Belford made a gesture of distaste. "I've never yet met an Indian I had the slightest use for, Mr. Miller."

"Levi is a Delaware."

"So? His skin is red, isn't it?"

Matt shrugged and made no reply. Convincing an Injun-hating white man that there was as much difference between an intelligent, educated, religious-minded Delaware and a wild Plains Indian as there was, say, between a white Boston preacher and a Texas horse thief was a chore which experience had taught him he couldn't handle.

Melinda returned with the three men she'd been sent to fetch and introductions were made around. Giving young Andy Hale and the quiet-mannered Delaware, Levi, a brief nod, Matt concentrated his attention on Armand Kimball, who appeared to be a different sort than the crowd of lanky, cold-eyed, poorly clothed hill men and women silently pressing in from all sides.

From his clothes and manners, Armand Kimball looked to be a city man, thirty-five or so, well-fed, prosperous, good-humored, but shrewd. A merchant, maybe, from St. Louis. Matt wondered how such a man had gotten mixed up with this crowd.

"The first thing to be decided," Cornelius Belford said, after briefly outlining Lynn's proposal to the newcomers, "is how the combined train will be managed. Tell me, Mr. Lynn, how is your group organized?"

"What do you mean?"

"What are your rules? Who gives your order of travel? Who sets the watches? Who disciplines rule infractions and what are the penalties?"

"Why, we just sort of work things out as we go along," Lynn answered, looking a bit irritated. "Before we left Council Bluffs, the folks held a meeting and elected me wagon captain. I didn't much want the job but somebody had to take it. We hired Matt here to guide us. So far, we ain't had no trouble to speak of."

"You have had trouble, though?"

"Sure we have. When you get a bunch of families traveling together, things are bound to come up that rub somebody the wrong way. That's just human nature."

"I can see that you'd have trouble, being so loosely organized. Well, we'll soon cure that. I have written down a list of rules, Mr. Lynn, that have worked most efficiently for us. I shall have copies made and distributed to your people—"

"Just a minute, Mr. Belford," Lynn said, his jaw tightening. "What do these rules amount to?"

"They're quite simple and explicit. No firearms to be discharged within half a mile of the train. No profane language. No drinking. No traveling on the Sabbath—"

"Not even when it's needful?"

"It is never needful, Mr. Lynn! God lays a curse on any group that profanes His day by traveling on the Sabbath. 'Six days shalt thou labor, and on the seventh—'"

"I've read the Bible, Mr. Belford. And I'm just as religious as the next man. But the Bible says if your ox falls in a ditch on the Sabbath, you've got a right to labor to get it out. It may be needful to travel on Sunday."

"Your religious precepts are looser than mine, Mr. Lynn."

"Well, I sure don't let my religion make a fool of me."

"Are you implying that I do?"

"All I'm saying is that when plain common sense tells us we've got to travel on Sunday, we travel," Lynn answered doggedly. "But let's skip that point for the time being. Read the rest of your rules."

As Belford went through the list, Matt could see Lynn's scowl deepening. Some of the rules made sense, Matt conceded, but a lot of them were pure hogwash, obviously thought up by a self-important man who had studied a mess of emigrant guidebooks that were as much fancy as fact. There had been a lot of that kind of junk published and sold since the first wagons had headed West thirty years ago. Not that Matt himself had ever read any of the stuff—reading was an art he'd never had the time or opportunity to acquire—but in every party he'd ever guided to Oregon or California there'd always been at least one scholarly, opinionated, self-appointed expert who made his life miserable by quoting him outlandish advice set down by Hall Kelley, Lansford Hastings, John Frémont, or some other fool.

Kelley had been crazy as a bedbug, of course, and had never crossed the country by the overland route; Hastings' bad advice had been responsible for the Donner party disaster; and Frémont, from what Matt personally knew of him, had been a sight more interested in glory than in facts. Sure, there had been *some* truth in what all of them had written, but, human nature being the contrary thing it was, greenhorn travelers invariably accepted the chaff of fiction and left the grain of fact behind for the birds.

"Obviously, the combined train will need only one guide," Belford was saying. "The fair thing to do, it seems to me, is to decide by a vote of all our people whether that guide shall be Mr. Miller or Mr. Hale. We will, of course, share equally in the expense of his wages."

"Your bunch outnumbers ours by five wagons," Lynn protested. "If brought to a vote, your man would be bound to win."

"We have to be fair, don't we?"

"Sure, but we've got to be reasonable, too. Your man may suit you fine, but I'll be blessed if I'll trust the safety of my twenty-five families to a youngster I've just met when I've got an experienced old hand like Matt here, who's led us out from Council Bluffs with no trouble to speak of."

"Andy knows what he's doin', Daniel," Matt said soothingly. "Don't you never doubt that."

"I ain't doubting it. All I'm saying is, this is no voting matter—you're going to be *our* guide all the way."

Armand Kimball, who had been listening intently, spoke for the first time. "It seems to me that the more experienced men we have with us the better." His smile included them all. "Why don't we keep both guides? You pay yours, Mr. Lynn, and we'll pay ours. Wouldn't that work out, Cornelius?"

"Well, yes. But I still think—"

"You and Andy can get along, can't you?" Kimball said, looking questioningly at Matt.

"No reason why not."

"Andy?"

"Sure."

"Then that's settled."

"All right, I'll accept it," Belford said. "But I must insist on one point. A division of authority would be disastrous. Either your guide or ours must be in charge. We'll put it to a vote—"

"No, we won't!" Lynn interrupted angrily. "If one of them has to be in charge, the logical man is Matt. He's more experienced. He's older—"

"Isn't it possible he's *too* old?" Belford said curtly. "The guide I discharged was about Mr. Miller's age. He was so stupid and set in his ways nobody could get along with him."

"That's not the way I heard it, Mr. Belford," Lynn said. "I was told he found you people so quarrelsome and hard to get along with, he just up and quit."

"That's a lie! Isn't it, Armand?"

Staring bleakly down at the ground, Matt drew absent designs in the dust as he hunkered on his heels. Christ on a crutch! Lynn is a mule and Belford is a terrier and between the one's balking and the other's yipping we'll be fighting all the way to Oregon, should we ever get around to starting out. Look, you damn fools, he wanted to say, only two things count: Sticking together and covering miles. Keep them two things in mind, everything else will work out fine. Forget 'em—like you're doing now—and nothing will.

But he kept his thoughts to himself. Maybe a fight to the finish now would clear the air.

Again Armand Kimball played the role of peacemaker. "It's really immaterial why we parted company. The point is, we did. What I'd like to hear now is how Matt and Andy feel on this matter of divided responsibility. Andy, what is your opinion?"

"Matt said we'd get along. We will."

"Matt?"

"We'll make out fine."

"Now that that's out of the way," Lynn said, giving Belford a triumphant look, "is there anything else we disagree on?"

"I'm not satisfied that it *is* out of the way," Belford answered, looking a bit nettled, "but I'll let it pass. Now then—our most important problem is how the combined train will be governed. These are the terms which I feel we must all accept: First, every person must promise to abide by the rules of conduct which I've outlined to you. Second, you shall act as captain of your group, Mr. Kimball of ours. Third, each group shall elect six members to a board which shall be the over-all ruling council for the combined train. I shall serve as its president. By simple majority vote, the council shall have the power to enforce all discipline for infractions of the rules. It shall also have the power to override any decisions made by the guides or wagon captains."

"Will you have a vote on the council?" Lynn asked.

"Certainly."

Lynn gave a snort of disgust. "Just what I thought!"

"Inferring what, Mr. Lynn?"

"The majority will always be on your side. You'll be bossing the whole train."

"Authority has to be given to someone, doesn't it? After all, our group *does* outnumber yours. And you must remember, Mr. Lynn, it was you who came to us suggesting we join forces, not us who came to you."

Daniel Lynn smiled disarmingly. "You need one more rule, Mr. Belford."

"What's that?"

"That when a man needs to ease his bladder, he's got to get permission in writing from you."

In the strained silence, Henry Lynn's sudden peal of nervous laughter was as out of place as a shout at the close of a prayer in church. Not that Matt blamed the boy. It *had* been comical, damned comical, the way Daniel Lynn's earthy remark had let the wind out of Belford. But the rage in the eyes of the slight-statured Missourian made it plain he could not endure being laughed at by a twelve-year-old boy.

"You impudent little devil!" he exclaimed, taking a step forward and cuffing Henry sharply on the side of the face with an open hand. "I'll teach you to respect your elders!"

Daniel Lynn lunged at Belford; Matt leaped forward to keep them apart; Will Starr, Andy Hale, and Armand Kimball joined the scuffle; and during the general jostling Henry Lynn managed to land a brisk kick on Belford's shin. Letting out a howl of pain, Belford crow-hopped around, holding his bruised shin with both hands, while Henry massaged his stinging cheek and made sniffling sounds that were more indignant than hurt.

Breathing hard, Daniel Lynn thrust off the hands restraining him. "Don't worry, gents—I ain't going to hurt him. He ain't big enough to be hit by a man—or to hit one. "

Belford's face was pale. "I'm sorry, Mr. Lynn—deeply sorry. But he laughed at me. And he kicked me."

"I know he did." Lynn seized his son by the arm. "Apologize to Mr. Belford, Henry."

"For laughing at him?" Henry asked sullenly. "Or for kicking him?"

"Both."

"I apologizes Mr. Belford."

"So do I, Henry."

Lynn jerked his head at Matt. "Come on, let's go back to camp."

"Please don't be hasty, Mr. Lynn," Armand Kimball said. "This has been a most unfortunate thing to have happen, but it has nothing to do with the problem we were discussing. I suggest we meet again in the morning and try to work out our differences—"

"No," Lynn said. "I won't discuss anything with a bunch of people led by a fool."

As Lynn, Henry, and Matt left the enclosure, none of the Missourians moved or spoke. They appeared to be stunned by the fact that a serious discussion of a big problem had been broken up by such a petty incident. Well, Matt brooded, this ain't the first time a big powwow has been busted up by a gnat. I mind a fracas a bunch of us trappers got into with a band of suspicious Crow bucks, years ago, out in the Wind River country. We'd met and was talking sweet as you please, then absentmindedly-like I reached for my butt to scratch a fleabite that was pestering me, and one of them fool Injuns taken the notion I was fixing to pull a knife on him. And the ball begun . . .

"Pa," Henry said hesitantly, "I'm awful sorry."

"Never mind, son. It wouldn't have worked out anyway."

"What'll we do now?"

"I don't know. Matt, you got any ideas?"

Sure, lots of ideas. But this ain't the time to spill 'em to you, Daniel, because you're too hot under the collar to listen. For instance, if I told you that Armand Kimball, Andy Hale and the menfolk of them scared Missoury families will be putting a sight of pressure on Belford to forget his stupid rules and take to the trail about the same time we do, you'd just say you don't care a good goddam what they do. You tried, you'd say. You went to them and proposed to join the two trains. Maybe that was a mistake, because Belford strikes me as a tough man to trade mules with when he thinks it's *his* mule you want. But the shoe's on the other foot now; next time, he'll be forced to come to you. And you ain't no slouch as a mule-trader yourself, Daniel, when it's *your* mule the other fella is after."

"We got a bit of repair work an' outfittin' to do," Matt said. "One more day should wind it up. Come Tuesday mornin', I'd say, we'd ought to head out."

"With just the twenty-five wagons?"

"Yeah."

"And the risk?"

"Won't be none to speak of 'tween here and Platte Bridge. Beyond there—well, we'll see."

Chapter Three

Standing in the shadows between two parked wagons, Ruth Shelby ceased whispering the prayer she had been fervently breathing. God is dead, she thought bitterly. Or does not care. No, she must not blame God for what had happened. A vain, self-centered man, who put having his own way above the dictates of common sense, had been responsible for it. Yet Cornelius Belford had the conceit to call himself a leader!

Among the Missourians there had been talk for days about the wisdom of joining forces with another Oregon-bound train. When Daniel Lynn had come over tonight, excitement had spread quickly and she had shared in it. She had desperately wanted to go to the conference with her husband, Benjamin, his younger brother, Isaac, and their father, Obidiah, but she had not dared. This meant too much to her; she would not be able to control her trembling, she knew, and that would worry Benjamin.

Pleading weariness, she had left the menfolk, gone back to her husband's wagon, made sure that little Naomi was sleeping soundly, then had circled around through the dark outside the enclosure to this spot where she could watch and listen without being seen. What she had observed and heard dismayed her.

Now she tried to pull herself together. She must get back to the wagon before the menfolk returned. Clumsy and awkward with the unborn child she was carrying, she ran through the dark, half-climbed, half-fell over the wagon tongue, then paused to lean against the wagon's inner side. Her breath came in painful gasps. She should get into the wagon and go to bed. It would be dark there and Benjamin would not be able to see her face when he told her the bad news. But for the moment she did not have the strength to move.

Hearing voices raised in heated discussion, she lifted her head and forced a smile as Benjamin, Isaac, and Grandpa Shelby came up. "Is it settled?"

Something her husband saw in her face made him hurry to her side and take her by the elbow. "Ruth! I thought you were going to bed."

"There were things to do."

"You're pale as a ghost. Don't you feel well?"

"I'm a little tired, that's all."

"You shouldn't be up so late. Come on, I'll help you into the wagon."

She was aware of the worry in her husband's face, the concern in Grandpa Shelby's eyes, the sympathetic yet embarrassed way Isaac stared at her, as if he wanted to do something for her but did not dare try. Benjamin aided her toward the rear of the wagon and the fact that he had not troubled to answer her question told her that her act had been a poor one. Suddenly a strange gurgling, cooing sound from the direction of Grandpa Shelby's wagon, which was parked directly in front of theirs, made Benjamin stop and stare at her in surprise.

"Is that Naomi?"

"Of course not! She's in bed."

"It sure sounds like her."

Isaac and Grandpa Shelby hurried toward the other wagon. Benjamin climbed up on the tailgate of their own wagon, pushed the canvas aside, shined a lantern around the interior, then looked down at her in panic. "She isn't here!"

"She must be!" Ruth cried, her heart climbing into her throat. "I tucked her in not fifteen minutes ago . . ."

"Hey!" Grandpa Shelby shouted. "Take a look at this!"

Running forward, Ruth found Grandpa Shelby down on his hands and knees, whooping with laughter, as Isaac dragged a squirming, feather-covered object vaguely recognizable as a child out of the shadows underneath the neighboring wagon. Ruth squealed in horror. The child was Naomi. The chubby, golden-haired toddler was barefoot, clad in a long pink flannel nightgown that had been clean a few minutes ago but now was hopelessly soiled; her hands, arms, and face were smeared with a dark, sticky substance and were so covered with feathers that she looked more like a bird than a child.

Dropping to her knees with a shriek, Ruth grabbed up the little girl, then let go of her in disgust. "For Heaven's sake! What *has* she gotten into?"

"Molasses!" Grandpa Shelby chortled. "She had a whole blamed jarful under there! She had a feather pillow, too. Danged if she didn't go and pick it plumb to pieces! Ain't she a sight, though!"

"'Lasses!" Naomi cooed, reaching for her mother with a cherubically innocent smile on her round face. "Got 'lasses!"

"Well, I never!" Ruth laughed hysterically. "Turn your back on that child for two seconds and she's into something! How will we ever clean her up?"

"Easy as pie," Grandpa Shelby chuckled. "Jest bile some water, scald her from crop to tail, then pluck her like a chicken. She's jest the right size fer fryin', I 'low!"

It took a good half hour of scrubbing and feather-picking to get

Naomi in shape to be put to bed again, which gave Ruth time to compose herself. Though he had every right to do so, Benjamin did not scold his wife for letting the child get into mischief. That was not his way. He never belabored the obvious, never said what did not need to be said. He knew just as well as she did that the seventeen-month-old toddler had a perfect genius for getting into trouble and finding dangerous playthings.

A butcher knife temporarily laid aside, a pot of hot coffee simmering on a fire, a skilletful of frying bacon, inevitably attracted Naomi's never-still inquisitiveness. None of her dolls held the fascination for her that a filthy dishrag did; let one be put down in her sight, and immediately she would be washing her face with it, chewing on it or gleefully swishing it into a bucket of fresh drinking water that Benjamin or Isaac had just set down after going some distance to fetch it.

She feared neither animal nor man. Heavy-footed oxen, fractious horses, balky mules, surly dogs—all were pets to be played with to her. So were the Indians that were continually coming into camp to beg, steal, or bully things out of the Missourians; the dirtier, smellier, more lice-ridden they were, the better she seemed to like them. It had amused Ruth and her menfolk at first to see how quickly little Naomi had learned to imitate the Indian grunts of greeting. To watch that curly golden head bobbing, the round face beaming, the chubby right arm upraised as the child toddled toward a dark, blanket-wrapped savage crying "How!" made one laugh till the tears came.

But as the settlements fell behind, as the Indians grew bolder, more arrogant and more hostile, Ruth began to have second thoughts as to the wisdom of letting the little girl treat every savage she met like a favorite uncle. Yet how did one go about substituting caution and fear for trust and friendliness in a child that age?

Naomi took the scrubbing with her usual sunny good nature. By the time she was ready for bed, she had fallen sound asleep in her father's arms. Isaac and Grandpa Shelby said good night and retired to their wagon. Benjamin tucked Naomi in, helped Ruth up, kissed her gently and lay down beside her. She had thought herself so exhausted that she would fall asleep the instant her head touched the pillow. Indeed, for a while she did seem to be dropping swiftly down into the blessed forgetfulness of unconsciousness; then the descent slowed, stopped, her numbed mind came alive again and presently she found herself lying wide-eyed and tense as she stared up into the confined darkness.

The camp slept. Near her she could hear the steady breathing of her husband and child. In the next wagon, she could hear Grandpa Shelby snoring. Canvas made a poor wall, she had learned, and in the night stillness any sound louder than a whisper carried a long way, a fact that sometimes proved amusing, more often embarrassing.

Far off, a wolf howled at the stars. Life is a long grieving, she thought. I had no right to unburden myself to poor little Sally Lynn as I did this morning. She's had her own griefs, too, and more to come as she grows older. But a body has to talk to somebody. And I was just her age when my griefs began . . .

No, she thought fiercely, she would not let her mind dwell on such things. Her lost parents, her lost first-born son buried on the lost green hillside of her lost home, her lost friends, the lost peace and happiness of her youth, the lost roots. The decision to leave the strife-torn Missouri hill country which had been their home had been as much hers as her menfolks' and they had known losses and griefs, too. They had not complained. So she had no right to complain.

In a sense, she was caught in a trap of her own setting. Because she had steeled herself against tears and any outward show of panic, her menfolk assumed her to be a calm-minded, sensible woman, who could take whatever trials came without breaking down. How strange, she thought, that they could live with me four years and not know what is really in my heart, that they could mistake the paralysis of fright for calm, the indecisiveness of weakness for good sense. But it happened. So no matter what fears torment me now, I dare not ease my soul by unburdening myself to them.

A sudden stab of pain in her left side made her catch her breath. Was it beginning now? No, it could not be. She had a month left, she was sure. Where would the wagon train be then? In the mountains far from any settlement? In the awful desert whose terrors they all dreaded so? Making a stand against hostile Indians?

She wanted to scream out in terror. She wanted to seize Benjamin, shake him awake and tell him what a coward she really was. She wanted—oh, God, she wanted to be a child again, secure in her own home in her own land, asleep in her mother's arms!

Beside her, she heard Benjamin stir in the darkness. The regularity of his breathing altered and she suddenly realized that he was awake. She did not move, did not speak. She felt his weight shift on the mattress under them and knew that he had raised himself up on one elbow and was staring down at her. She heard him whisper very softly, "Ruth . . ."

"Yes?"

"Did I wake you up?"

"No. I was just lying here, thinking."

"About what?"

"Oh, Oregon, the baby, you, us . . . lots of things."

"You asked me if it was settled."

"What?"

"Joining trains."

"Well, is it?"

"No. Belford spoiled it. He slapped Lynn's boy."

"Whatever for?"

"Because the boy laughed at him. He deserved being laughed at, God knows, but it was a fool thing for a grown man to do. Lynn walked off in a huff—but the point is, the trains ain't joining up."

"You think they should?"

"What I think doesn't matter a hang to a fool like Belford. Pa and I talked it over. These people ain't our kind, Ruth, even if they do come from our part of the country—no more than a lot of our neighbors were our kind after the war started."

"I know."

"Pa and I talked with Lynn this morning. He seems like a sensible man. And I saw you talking with his daughter."

"Yes," Ruth said, hardly daring to breathe, to hope. "Sally is a sweet girl."

"Did she tell you they have a doctor in their train?"

"Why, I believe she did mention it, yes."

"Pa says we've got a perfect right to join up with them Iowans, if we want to—no matter what Belford and his crowd does."

"You know what's best, Benjamin."

"Well, considering that they *do* have a doctor—I know you ain't worried about having the baby, Ruth, but why take chances? Belford and his crowd don't like our politics, our religion, our feelings toward the war or nothing about us. Sure, we've got a few friends in this train—but mighty few. Why don't we just tell Belford and his crowd to go to the devil, pull our wagons over to the other camp and join up with people we stand a chance of getting along with?"

"Will they have us?"

"Lynn told us this morning we'd be more than welcome." She forced her voice to remain low and calm. "If that's your best judgment, Ben, then I agree it's the thing to do."

"It is. It truly is, Ruth."

"Then let's do it."

He chuckled good-humoredly. Leaning toward her, he nuzzled her cheek with his nose. "You know something? You're the easiest woman to get along with I ever married. Calm and sensible, no matter what happens."

"With you to lean on, what do I have to worry me?"

"Good night, honey. Sorry I woke you up." Gently he kissed her. "We'll move our wagons first thing in the morning."

"Good night, Ben," she whispered.

Not until his steady breathing told her he had fallen asleep did her tears come; they were silent tears, bathing her closed eyes in a sweet, relaxing warmth as she dropped down into the deepest, most restful sleep she had known for a long while.

Chapter Four

Watching the Iowa wagon train break camp and pull out shortly after daybreak Tuesday morning, Andy Hale listened sympathetically to the grumblings of the Missourians but shrugged noncommittally when they asked him if he thought it had been a mistake not to merge the two trains. That had been Belford's doing, not his, and he did not intend to get off on the wrong foot with these people by telling them that their leader had acted the fool. Nor did he intend to ruffle their feathers by pointing out that they hadn't behaved too well themselves.

Even though they had reached Fort Laramie two days ahead of the Iowans, the Missourians still had a good day's work to do before their train would be ready to take to the trail. Like the Iowans, they had had sick and lame animals that must be traded for sound ones, loose iron wheel rims that must be heated and refitted, wagons that must be repaired, stores of supplies that must be replenished. The hardheaded Iowans had undertaken these chores at once and had wasted neither time nor energy complaining about prices, which were high because of the war and the isolation of the settlement. But the Missourians had screamed in outrage.

Trade two lame oxen for a sound one and still give boot? Not on your life! Pay a dollar-fifty for heating and refitting a wheel rim? Hell, man, that's only a four-bit job back home! Fifty cents a pound for beans? Mister, you'd ought to wear a mask and carry a gun!

The first two days after reaching Fort Laramie the Missourians did no trading, buying, or contracting for repair work, spending the daylight hours prowling suspiciously about the settlement, pricing things, and the evenings bitterly comparing notes as to which of the merchants, traders, or blacksmiths seemed inclined to cheat them the least. Sunday, they refused to do a lick of work of any kind. Monday, they at last started doing the things that had to be done, reluctantly accepting the same trades offered them and the same prices quoted them on Friday, though they made sure the tradespeople knew that *they* knew they were being robbed. Tuesday, sight of the Iowa group pulling out spurred them to a feverish pitch of activity, but by then there was no making up the time they had lost.

"Don't worry, we'll catch up!" Belford said. "Just wait and see!"

"We'll pass 'em inside of a week!" Will Starr said enthusiastically, siding with Belford as he always did, lending his strong back and willing hands wherever needed, as was his habit. "Won't we, Andy?"

"Likely," Andy said with a nod and a smile.

But he knew better. It was a long way to Oregon, sure, but time was gold and the prize went not to the swift but to the steady. *Cover ground and keep together; a day lost is lost forever.* A train could travel no farther in a day than the strength of its poorest teams permitted. Say you made six miles one day, ten the next, eight the day after. Those miles were miles put behind you. But fritter away a day in camp and there was no way in God's green world you could up your daily mileage for the next week to seven instead of six, eleven instead of ten, nine instead of eight, without puffing your stock in such poor shape that presently it wouldn't be able to travel at all.

He did not tell the Missourians that. He was a guide, not a sheep dog, and he knew that you didn't hustle this breed of people along by nipping at their heels. The guide Belford had fired had tried that and gained nothing by it. Keep your mouth shut, Andy told himself; give no advice till it's asked for; don't force-feed the flock; just scatter your grains of wisdom around on the ground careless-like and let them scratch for them; that way, they'll digest them better.

Tuesday afternoon, Andy and Levi rode over to the sutler's store at the fort. The day was hot; the dust, dry air, and burning sun had combined to give them both a thirst which plain water could not begin to quench. Levi bought a can of tomatoes, from which he alternately sipped juice and speared tomato chunks mouthward on the point of his skinning knife as he leaned against the jamb of the open doorway, gazing impassively into the heat-hazed distance. Andy lounged on the wooden counter, reflectively munching on an oversized dill pickle. The sutler, a fat, florid-faced man who looked as if he had no use for plain water as a thirst-quencher either, considered the Delaware disapprovingly, squinted sourly at the half-eaten pickle in Andy's hand, then spat a stream of tobacco juice in the general direction of the brass spittoon at the end of the counter.

"Them ridge-runners figure to pull out tomorrow?"

"Yeah."

"How come they didn't join up with that Iowa train?"

"Didn't hit it off, somehow."

"A man'd think people could forgit politics and the war long enough to git through the Injun country."

"What a man thinks people ought to do and what they do do are two different things."

"That's Gospel, I guess."

Armand Kimball came into the store, nodding politely to Levi as he passed him. Smiling genially at Andy, he took off his hat and mopped his sweat-beaded forehead with a clean white handkerchief. "Hot, isn't it?"

"Warmish, yeah."

"Would a shot of whisky make a man feel better or worse?"

"Try a pickle."

Kimball made a wry face. "No thanks, I'd rather take my chances with whisky. Will you join me?"

"And break a camp rule?" Andy said, lifting his eyebrows in mock horror. "I'm surprised at you, Mr. Kimball, even suggesting such a thing."

"It's not my rule," Kimball said with a trace of irritation. "Anyhow, we're not in camp at the moment. Will you join me?"

"Drinking alone spoils a man's character, they say. I'd hate to be responsible for spoiling yours."

The sutler set out a bottle, two glasses, and a stone crock of water with a tin dipper suspended from its rim. "Help yourselves, gents, but go easy on the water. It'll rust your guts."

Kimball glanced at the doorway; hesitated, then lowered his voice. "What about your friend?"

"Levi? He doesn't drink"

"Well, I suppose that is best," Kimball said, looking relieved. "From what I've heard—" Breaking off, he motioned at the bottle. "After you, sir."

"What have you heard?" Andy asked curiously.

"That Indians and whisky don't mix," Kimball answered, looking embarrassed. "Something in their makeup—"

Levi tossed the empty tomato can away, wiped his knife on the seat of his pants, sheathed it and padded quietly over to the counter. There was no sign of expression on his dark, smoothskinned face, but his black eyes were twinkling. He tossed half a dollar on the counter.

"Gimme a glass."

The sutler took a small glass from the shelf behind him, set it on the counter and reached for the half dollar. Levi's quick fingers caught his wrist. "That's a two-bit glass. When I drink with white men, I want white man measure."

Scowling angrily, the sutler replaced the small glass with another twice its size. Levi poured it level full, raised it, looked over its rim unblinkingly at Armand Kimball, then downed the whisky to the last drop. Setting the empty glass down, he bowed with dignity.

"Scuse me, Mr. Kimball. I'm gonna go out and scalp a couple of soldiers."

Turning on his heel, he padded silently out of the store.

Andy threw back his head and laughed heartily. Kimball said in an aggrieved voice, "You told me he didn't drink."

"He has his pride."

"I didn't intend to hurt his feelings." Kimball's face grew suddenly anxious. "Will he be all right?"

"Sure. His head and stomach are as strong as yours."

Kimball poured their drinks. From their first meeting he had impressed Andy as an intelligent man with a talent for making himself liked. He appeared to have money, for his wagon was new, his oxen good ones, and he had hired an eighteen-year-old son of one of the Missourians to drive them for him. He seldom disputed Belford's decisions or took sides in arguments; when pressed to do so, he invariably took refuge behind the fact that he was a city man, out of his element, and was only too happy to go along with whatever the majority wanted to do. Thus, his approval was sought by all, even Cornelius Belford.

"About Levi," he said, then paused.

"Yeah?"

"I know he's your friend, Andy. The fact that you vouch for him is good enough for me. But Cornelius has prejudices."

"So I've noticed."

"Suppose he insists that Levi be left behind. What will you do?"

"Quit you."

"You feel that strongly about him?"

"We've been friends for a long time, Armand. Under his skin, Levi is the whitest man I've ever known."

Kimball took a swallow of his drink. "I was sure you felt that way. In fact, I told Cornelius as much."

"He asked you to sound me out?"

"He put it more bluntly than that. I was to tell you that Levi could not come along." Raising a hand as Andy started to speak, he added hastily, "I'm not telling you that, understand. But I was told to."

"Why didn't Belford speak for himself?"

"Because I pointed out to him that if you defied him to his face, he would be forced to discharge you. He doesn't want to do that. But with me acting as a buffer—well, let's say that when there is no direct confrontation between disputing parties a compromise can usually be arranged."

"That sounds like lawyer talk to me."

"You've found me out, Andy. The law is my profession."

"I won't see Levi mistreated."

"He won't be, I assure you. I'll smooth things over with Cornelius somehow."

"You seem to be good at that."

Kimball laughed sardonically. "I've had enough practice, God knows." His face sobered. "Cornelius Belford is not a completely unreasonable man, Andy, even though he may appear to be so at times. You've got to forgive him a few mistakes. He has a great responsibility on his shoulders."

"Sure."

"Tell me something. Do you feel we should have joined forces with the Iowa train?"

"Yes and no."

"Now *there's* lawyer talk!"

"Put it this way. When there's only one bed, the worst of enemies can sleep together in it if sleep is what they're after. But if they're going to fight all night, they're better off apart on the *floor.*"

"Do you anticipate Indian trouble west of Laramie?"

"Between here and Platte Bridge, no. Beyond there, a small train can expect the worst."

"Cornelius swears we'll catch and pass the Iowa train."

"I know," Andy said, nodding. "But we'd be the worst kind of fools if we made a race of it. They've got better stock than we have, better wagons and a guide who knows his business. They've got a full day's start. If they push ahead at their best pace, we won't get close enough to them to see their dust."

"Will they push the pace?"

"Search me."

Armand Kimball refilled their glasses. "You're a difficult young man to pin down, Andy. But I think you know more about their plans than you're telling me. Didn't I see you talking to Matt Miller yesterday afternoon?"

"We passed the time of day, yeah."

"Reaching what conclusion?"

"If you must know," Andy said with a laugh, "Matt said it seemed a great pity that two wagon trains heading the same way only a day or two apart couldn't stay close enough together to join forces should real trouble threaten. He said sometimes things work out better accidentally than when they're planned. He said they had a pregnant woman with them who just might slow them down some when her time came. And I believe he said something about things looking different when Lynn and Belford had cooled off a bit."

"To all of which you agreed, I trust?"

"He's a wise old coon, Matt is," Andy answered. "Me, I don't argue with my elders."

Chapter Five

Will Starr had fascinated Melinda Belford from the moment she first laid eyes on him. Beyond what little information he himself had volunteered, nobody knew who he was or where he came from. One day two months ago when the Belford wagon had mired fast in a mudhole on the road between the home they had just left and Independence, he had appeared out of nowhere, a big, powerful man on a big black horse, frightening Melinda and her mother half out of their wits, and causing Melinda's father—who had been coaxing, commanding, pleading with and raging at the oxen until reduced to a state of trembling incoherency—to murmur to his wife, "He may be a bushwhacker. You and Mellie go over to the wagon and get in. My pistol is under the seat. When I come over, slip it to me."

Before Melinda or her mother could move, the huge stranger smiled in a friendly fashion and said, "Looks like you're stuck."

"Yes," Melinda's father snapped peevishly, "we're stuck."

"Maybe I can help you."

Swinging off his horse, the stranger politely touched his hat brim. "You'd best stand back, ladies. There's apt to be some mud flying."

Melinda, her mother, and her father moved back and watched helplessly as the big stranger walked around the wagon, intently studying the rear wheels, which were sunk hub-deep in the soft, sticky mud, paused at the front of the wagon to check the yokes and chains, and ran a huge hand soothingly along the necks of the weary, panting oxen. Melinda could hear him talking to the animals and the gentleness of his voice amazed her. Completing his circle, he picked up the bullwhip which Melinda's father had thrown aside in disgust and handed it to him.

"Let's try 'em again. Seesaw your pull, working 'em first one way, then the other. That'll free the front wheels. I'll give a boost from behind."

Melinda's father was too exhausted to argue. The big stranger waded into the mud at the rear of the wagon, put his back to it, gripped the underside of the bed with both hands, then said, Now."

The whip cracked, the oxen lunged, the stranger heaved— and the wagon moved. Though her father did not believe her when she told him about it later, Melinda was sure she saw both rear wheels lifted clear of the ground for a moment.

At her father's invitation, the stranger traveled with them the rest of that day. His name was Will Starr, he said; he spoke vaguely of having spent some time down in Texas and the Indian Nations; he said he was on his way to Independence to look for a job with a freighting outfit. Because they were traveling alone through a country overrun by lawless men, Melinda's father was anxious to have all the friendly company he could get, so when they stopped for the night he invited Will Starr to take supper and camp with them, which Starr seemed pleased to do. He had stayed with them ever since.

Physical strength was a quality her father had always envied, Melinda knew, for it was one which he sadly lacked himself. His admiration for this amiable young giant knew no bounds, and, having accepted him as almost a member of the family, he took great delight in showing him off. Despite his immense size, Will Starr was far from clumsy. His hands were sure and quick, his coordination good, his movements supple and graceful. In the impromptu contests staged to while away the time while the train was being organized in Independence, he proved that few men could equal his skill with a rifle, pistol, or knife; no two men teamed together could throw him wrestling, and, most surprising of all, not a man or boy in camp could outrun him at any distance longer than two hundred paces.

"Takes Will a spell to hit his stride," one of the Missourians said with a chuckle, "but once he gits to moving, nothin' 'cept a race horse kin ketch him!"

If he had been anything but soft-spoken and modest about his physical capabilities, men would have hated and feared him. But there was nothing of the bully in him. He had a way with animals. He was extremely shy around women and never spoke to them except in a manner of great respect, no matter how outrageously they tried to flirt with him—as some did, to Melinda's great disgust. He was never out of temper, willingly lent a hand to any task that needed doing, and made himself so agreeable and useful that he had not an enemy in camp.

In a sense, it was Will Starr's doing that Melinda's father was elected president of the wagon train's Ruling Council. Most of the emigrant families flocking to Independence that spring were strangers to one another, and, because of the war, were extremely suspicious of people whose views might differ from theirs. There was a great deal of visiting around, of sizing up, of argument, of talk. Melinda's father talked as convincingly as did half a dozen other men who were trying to organize the train, but his small stature was a great handicap. Will Starr helped him overcome that. Curious men came for a look at this young Samson; when they found him constantly at the side of Cornelius Belford, respecting him, nodding agreement to everything he said, quietly backing him, they could not help but be impressed.

In troubled times, like clings to like. Except for Armand Kimball, who was too self-contained and diplomatic ever to express his true politics and loyalties openly, and the Shelby family, whose Union leanings did not at once emerge, all the families that joined the train were in sympathy with the Rebel cause. Most came from the hill country of southern Missouri; most had suffered so many indignities at the hands of their biased, pro-Union neighbors that they could no longer tolerate life in Missouri and had determined to seek a newer and freer land in whose laws they could have some voice.

Melinda had long been aware of her father's passion for pushing himself into a position of leadership. "Your pa likes to run things," her mother had once told her wearily. "'Why, I do believe he'd rather run things than be rich. Guess that's what comes of him being such a runt." She had looked frightened, then, as if amazed that her long-held secret resentment had found voice, and hastily added, "Don't never tell him I said that, Mellie! He's mighty picky about his size."

Melinda was conscious of that. Even wearing his Sunday shoes, which he'd had made with built-up heels, her father stood barely five feet. She knew that because she herself was five-two and could, on those rare occasions when he stood toe to toe with her, gaze down into his eyes. Whenever possible, he avoided such direct comparisons of height with his wife and daughter. On the village streets, he always walked a stride ahead of them, never at their side. When they stood, he sat; when they sat, he stood; when they approached, he moved away. It was a silly vanity for a man to possess, Melinda felt, but it was one she had never dared to ridicule.

Only once in her life had she ever heard her father swear. That had been long ago, as a child, when she chanced to be in the barn loft and he had led a tall, rawboned horse out into the yard and tried to mount it. Having only a short ride to the pasture to fetch in the cows and being in a hurry, he had slipped a bridle on the horse but had not bothered to saddle it. Three times she watched him place his hands on the horse's withers, vault upward, fall short of reaching its back, and slide to the ground. He looked so completely ridiculous that she had to clap her hand over her mouth to stifle her giggles. She could see his lips moving, his face darkening, but she could not make out what he was saying until, after his third failure to mount the animal, he led it over beside the chopping block, stepped atop the block, shook a defiant fist at the sky and cried aloud in utter agony, "God damn it, I wish I were ten feet tall!"

Though she feared her father, she had long since ceased to respect him. She obeyed him because there was nothing else she could do, but secretly there burned in her a sullen, rebellious resentment. For as long as she could remember the family had been poor. There had been a succession of moves from one leaky-roofed, run-down, shabby cabin to another, and the soil of each plot of land her father tried to till seemed always to be too rocky, too thin, too inclined to wash, too tired and worn out to produce a decent living, even if he had been inclined to give it his full attention—which he never did.

He frankly admitted that he was an indifferent farmer. His heart simply was not in farming, he said bitterly. Though he was a good carpenter when he chose to work at that trade, the people who could afford to pay him cash wages for his labors invariably were merchants, well-off townspeople or farmers more prosperous than himself. He resented taking orders from such people; he was sure they called him "poor white trash" behind his back; he violently disagreed with their conservatism in religion and politics; thus, he seldom lasted long on any job.

Among the poorer people who believed as he did, he had built up quite a reputation as an orator, a debater, and a preacher. Put him on a platform raised above the level of the crowd, where he could command its undivided attention, and he became a man transformed. His sincerity, his fire, his truly excellent voice, and the extensive vocabulary he had acquired from intensive readings of the Bible and every other piece of good literature he could get his hands on, combined to give him dignity and power.

"Cornelius Belford would make his mark in the State House," his friends said time and again. "Or in Congress, for that matter —if only he could get himself elected."

That, indeed, was the problem. Not an election came along but what he was running for some county or state office, desperately trying to get one foot on a lower rung of the ladder leading to political success. But always he lost by a narrow margin, for it was his misfortune to live in a county and a district in which his party was slightly outnumbered. A man less forceful in stating where he stood on issues might well have had his perseverance rewarded in time by drawing a few votes from disgruntled members of the opposition party or perhaps might have eased into office because of the lethargy of the opposition voters in not going to the polls on a rainy day. But because he had long since shown himself to be an extremely vocal and positive man, no one ignored him. If you were against him, you made sure your vote was recorded—whatever the weather.

Melinda did not know exactly what part her father had played in the event that had caused the family to leave the community so hastily. Certainly it had not been a direct one, for, violent though his antagonisms were, she could not imagine him killing in cold blood. Oh, there had been meetings, she knew, of a society which he had organized and led—open meetings, at first, then, as the war wore on and feelings in the divided community became more bitter, secret ones. The sympathies of the society's members were with the South; that was well known. A pro-Union man was found dead on a backwoods trail not far from the Belford cabin, his body riddled with buckshot. It was remembered that he and Cornelius Belford had exchanged harsh words on the village street a few days previously; a grand jury made up of Union men was called into session; the rumor spread that Belford was to be indicted and tried; a friend brought a midnight warning; and by dawn Cornelius Belford had loaded his family and their portable possessions into a wagon and was heading north.

Melinda had been happy to go. Though in her younger years her father had gone to some pains to make sure she acquired a good knowledge of reading and writing, she had had little formal schooling. All she knew of geography was that Oregon lay somewhere to the west. She had never owned a store-bought dress in her life. She had been to a few church socials and neighborhood parties but had never learned how to dance. She had never gone anywhere alone with a boy. All her parents had ever told her of the basic facts of life had been her father's stern but vague warning: "If I ever catch you misbehaving with a boy, Melinda, I'll horsewhip you!" and her mother's equally vague advice: "Always remember, Mellie, there's only one thing a boy wants from a girl—and he ain't to have it till you're married."

Her curiosity thus whetted, Melinda had managed to learn from secret, giggling conferences with older female acquaintances what it was one did when one misbehaved with a boy and what the one thing was that a boy wanted of a girl but must not have without marriage. That the two things turned out to be one and the same did not greatly surprise her, but as yet she had not been seriously tempted nor had she had the opportunity to satisfy her still lively curiosity on the subject. She wasn't sure she even wanted to. Still, lately she had begun to look at Will Starr and wonder .

She was beginning to realize that she was attractive. Back home, she had suspected as much, but a mirror was a cold voiceless thing compared to what a girl could see reflected in man's eyes. And not in just one man's eyes. She had learned that she could see her image in the eyes of almost every man she met, whether he be a boy of twelve or a grandfather of fifty, simply by walking in a certain way, tossing her head in certain way, smiling in a certain way. More than that, by covertly watching other girls as they walked, tossed their head or smiled at those same men, she could tell how they compared to her in the mirror-eyes of men. And now she knew what she had merely suspected before.

She was attractive to men. Most attractive.

It was a wonderful piece of knowledge to possess. Just how she would put it to use, she had not as yet decided . . .

The wagons of the Missourians were ready to roll. Sunrise was two hours past, but the early morning chill of the high plains still had a bite to it. Her mother was already in the wagon, impatiently calling to her to get in. But she waited, for she had seen Will Starr's big black horse loping across the dusty flat toward her father's wagon. She pretended not to see him. She fussed with her sunbonnet, untying and retying the bow under her chin, and then, timing her move just right, she put a hand on the wagon wheel and lifted a foot to the step.

"Can I give you a hand, Miss Mellie?"

"Why, thank you, Will," she said, turning her head to smile up at him as he leaned out of the saddle, letting her weight go back on her elbow, which was lost in his broad, strong palm. He gave her a boost; out of the corner of her eye, she noted that he was keeping his gaze discreetly high, well removed from the inch of her calf exposed above her high shoetop. "You're very kind, Will."

"Don't mention it.

His white, even teeth flashed in an embarrassed smile as he touched his hat brim and turned to ride away. Suddenly she called, "Will!"

The big horse, the big man, instantly whirled back to her.

"Yes, Miss Mellie?"

"Never mind. It's not important."

"What is it, Miss Mellie? Is there something you wanted to tell me?"

"Yes, but it will keep. Run along now, Will."

Like a knight dismissed by a queen, Will Starr reined his horse about and rode away, looking troubled, looking puzzled, looking forward no doubt to the moment when she might choose to tell him whatever it was she had started to tell him now but hadn't. She giggled.

Truth was, she had had nothing at all to tell him; she had just been experimenting, amusing herself by seeing how quickly he would respond to her slightest whim.

From far ahead, came the cry to roll out.

I'll think of something to tell him this evening, she mused.

The wagon lurched into motion.

Chapter Six

Much to Henry Lynn's disgust, his father had bought a whole raft of schoolbooks before they left home and had told him that just because they were going to Oregon he needn't think he'd be permitted to run wild and neglect his learning. There'd be lots of spare time on the trail, his father said, and Henry would have nothing to do but cut wood and carry water for his sister and give his father a hand with the stock now and then, so he might as well put in a couple of hours a day cultivating his mind.

That was a pet phrase of his father's which Henry heartily detested. The way his father talked, a body would think that a boy's mind was a field of ground, which must be plowed, harrowed, sown, weeded, and then harvested when the crop got ripe. What kind of crop grew in the mind? Henry never bothered to ask his father that, for he knew good and well what his father would have answered.

"Grains of truth, son. Kernels of wisdom."

Maybe so. But from what Henry had seen of the world the market for that sort of crop was mighty limited. Sure, a fellow had ought to know how to read, write and do sums. And he did know. Any further mind-cultivating seemed to him an awful waste of time.

His father left it to Sally to make sure he studied. She was a mighty tough proposition to get around. Back home, she'd had ambitions to be a schoolteacher, and from the way she bore down on him he guessed she'd have made a good one. Every day when the wagon train made its noon halt she'd set him down where she could keep an eye on him, put a book in his hands, and would make sure he stayed there until the wagons were ready to roll again. In the evening after supper she'd give him the same shabby treatment. There was no faking with her. Each noon she would lay out a definite lesson for him to master, just as his father back home used to block out a certain section of garden for him to hoe; and each evening she'd check to make sure he'd weeded his educational patch clean. If he hadn't, she kept him at it as long as daylight lasted—and at this time of year the days were almighty long.

Matt Miller approved. Mind-cultivating was a fine thing, he said, and danged if he didn't wish he'd done more of it himself when he'd been a boy.

"How much schooling did you have, Mr. Miller?" Sally asked the old guide one evening.

"Oh, not a whole lot," he answered evasively.

"Did you finish grammar school?"

"Feard I didn't."

"How many years did you go?"

"Not many."

"Four?" she persisted. "Three? Two?"

"Wal, if you jest got to know the truth, gal," Matt said giving her a sheepish grin, "I went to school 'zactly three days. Teacher tried to whup me. 'Stead, I whupped him. When I got home, Pa said if fightin' was all I was goin' to learn in school him an' my brothers could give me my fill of that, so I might as well stay home."

"How did you learn to read and write?"

"Never did, I'm ashamed to say. Always wished I had though. It'd be a way to entertain myself, now I'm gittin' old."

Sally smiled sympathetically. "You're never too old to learn, Mr. Miller. I'd be happy to teach you."

Matt shook his head. "It'd jest be a waste of time, Sally." Grinning, he reached down and tousled Henry's hair. "But you learn this young sprout real good, hear me? Hone him to a sharp edge. Time'll come when he'll thank you fer it."

Right now, Henry was in no more of a mood to feel grateful to his sister for breaking up the clods of ignorance in mind than he was to feel friendly toward Matt for backing it up. Wasn't Matt himself a perfect example of the uselessness of book-learning? What if he couldn't read or write? He sure wasn't stupid. Every man in the train looked up to him, sought his advice, respected his judgment, and accepted whatever he said as Gospel truth. If there was a thing worth knowing about the West, you could bet your boots he knew it.

Henry spent long hours riding at the old guide's side as the wagons rolled across the monotonous sagebrush flats flanking the windings of the Platte; and it was a rare day when he didn't glean any number of unique, useful grains of fact from the old mountain man's seemingly inexhaustible supply of wilderness lore. For instance, one day they got to talking about cattle, and Matt said, "Funny thing, but cows won't eat salt once they git west of Laramie."

"Why not?"

"Ask a cow. But they won't. Here's another funny thing: West of Laramie, people don't come down with cholera."

"Why not?"

"Dunno that, neither. But it's so."

"Seems like there ought to be a reason."

"Shore, boy, thar's a reason fer everything that happens in this queer old world. But what's the sense of you an' me frettin' about reasons? It's what happens that counts, not why. Time you git as old as I am, you'll come to appreciate that."

For days on end the tall mountain called Laramie Peak stayed in sight, first ahead of them, then to their left, later behind them. Because it was the first mountain Henry had ever seen that looked like he'd always imagined a mountain had ought to look—remote, mysterious, somber in its aloofness from the surrounding plains—it fascinated the boy. He asked Matt if he'd ever climbed it.

"Shore. Many's the time I've cut timber, hunted an' trapped on the old gal. She's quite a mole-hill, boy. But I only clumb clean to the top once." A reflective gleam came into his eyes. "That was when I first laid eyes on her, thirty years ago. 'Course, she was a lot smaller then—not hardly half as high as she is now."

"Aw, I don't believe that! Can you see a long ways from the top?"

"Halfway round the world, seems like."

"How high is it?"

"Why, I never got around to measurin' her with a yardstick myself," Matt said, "but a guv'mint survey fella that did told me she tops ten thousand feet."

"How do you measure a mountain?"

The leathery sun-wrinkles around the old guide's eyes deepened in the ghost of a smile. "Oh, they's several ways. Fer instance, you kin dig a hole straight down from the top till you hit salt water—"

"Aw, Matt! I really want to know!"

"—which is the hard way, of course. Then another way is to build a fire and see how long it takes water to come to a bile. I ain't exactly shore how that works. But the general idee seems to be the higher you git the quicker your water biles. I was with an Army fella up in the Wind River country once and seen him try it. Frémont, his name was."

"Did it work?"

"Wal, Cap'n Frémont, he calc'lated this here mountain we was on topped out twenty thousand feet. I told him twelve was more likely. 'Course, he'd gone at it scientific, whilst I was jest goin' at it by signs any ignoramus could read."

"Like what?"

"Like how far we was above timberline, the color of the sky, how hard it was to breathe—stupid things like that."

"How high *was* the mountain?"

Matt's eyes twinkled. "Guv'mint survey fella that come along later made it out to be twelve thousand er so."

"How did *he* measure it?"

"Why, with his mountain-measurin' thingamajig, how else?" Matt said, scowling impatiently as he always did when pestered more than he cared to be. "You see, Cap'n Frémont had busted his'n, which was how come he tried the water-bilin' trick."

"But he was wrong and you were right."

"That ain't the point, boy. The point was, he went at it scientific, whilst I was jest guessin'. So the map-makers taken his word fer it till an even more scientific fella come along. You wouldn't expect 'em to believe an ignorant old coot like me, would you?"

Usually the wagons avoided the dusty stage road, traveling parallel to it and a ways removed from it along the many trails made by the countless wagons that had passed this way over the past thirty summers. A strong, hot, dry wind blew from the southwest most days, and when Henry asked Matt if the wind always blew like that here, the old guide said, "The weather's mighty dependable in this part of the country, boy. Summers, you kin depend on it bein' too hot; winters, you kin depend on it bein' too cold. Both seasons, it's too windy. When it rains, it rains too much; when it don't, it stays dry too long. Yes sir, the weather's mighty dependable—all bad."

Always the stock craved water and much of the time the river was out of reach. Standing pools occasionally were found on the plain but often they were so heavily impregnated with alkali that one dared not let an animal drink from them. Again, pools would be found whose water was perfectly sweet. Frequently the pools appeared in unexpected places, hidden by tall sagebrush. The oxen pulling the wagons and the loose milk cows and horses being herded along beside the train would smell the water at a distance and bolt toward it if not forcibly restrained.

Whether Matt remembered the location of every pool or actually had a more keenly developed sense of smell than the animals did, Henry did not know, but seldom did the old guide fail to spot the pools before the livestock did. Time and again as they rode along at the head of the train Henry saw Matt suddenly raise his head, wrinkle his nose like a dog testing the wind, peer suspiciously into the distance, then grunt, "Water ahead. Hustle back, boy, 'fore I give you a silver dollar, and tell the herders to mind their stock."

When he knew the water ahead to be bad, Matt would swing the train to the windward side of the pool so that the animals would not scent it. When he was in doubt, as he sometimes was, he would ride

IDAHO TERRITORY 1863

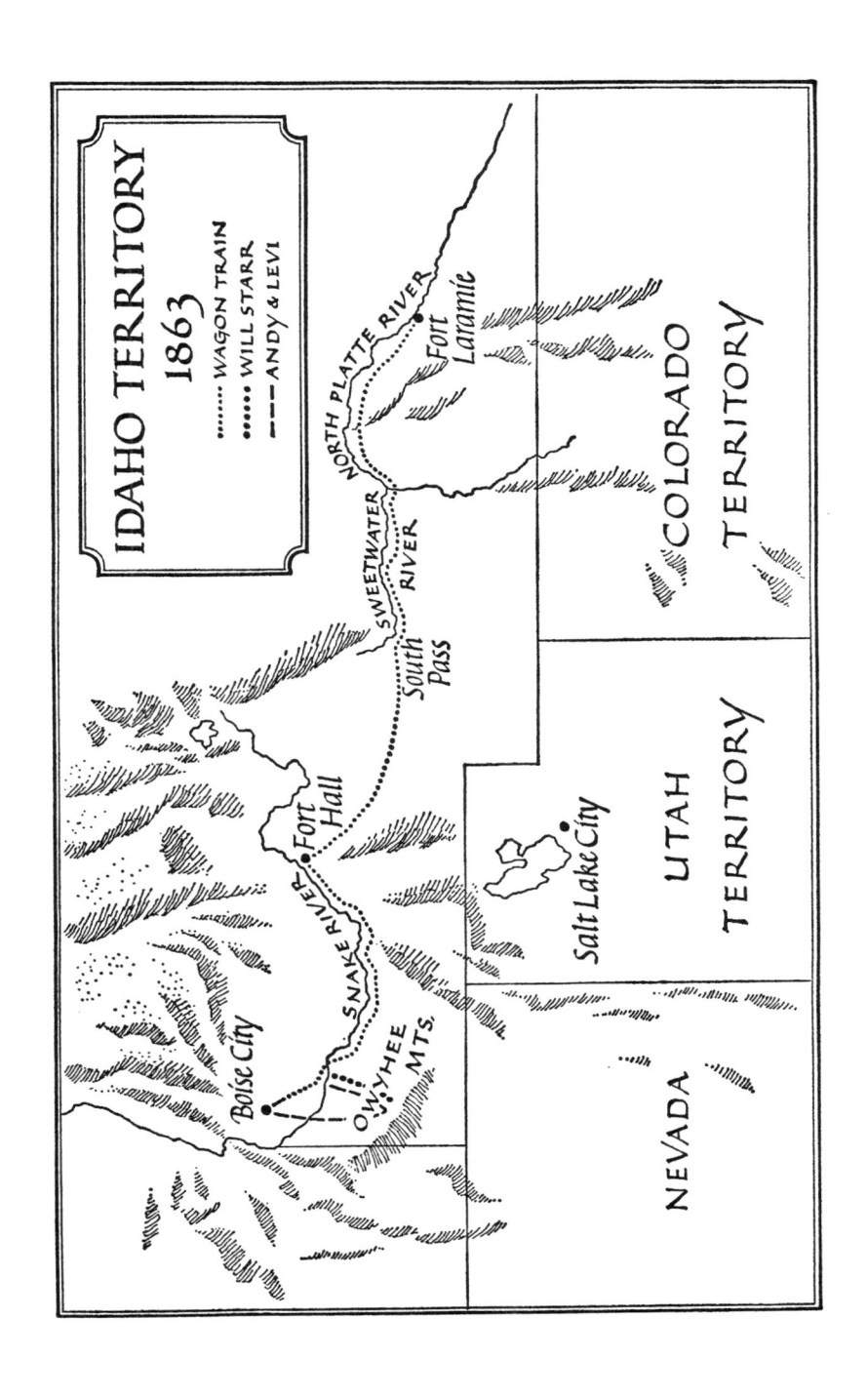

- ······ WAGON TRAIN
- ••••• WILL STARR
- ——— ANDY & LEVI

ahead and check the pool, and on several occasions he let Henry go with him. Usually the pools containing poisonous water were crusted with white deposits around their rims, but this warning sign was not always present. At pools which looked perfectly safe to Henry, Matt would dismount, sniff, cautiously taste, then shake his head and mutter, "No good." At others, which to Henry looked green, slimy, and repulsive, Matt would not even bother to get off his horse, grunting after the briefest of glances, "It's all right."

"How can you tell without tasting it?"

"Use your eyes, boy! Can't you see it's got mosquitoes in it?"

"It looks awful."

"Shore it does. But mosquitoes can't live in alkali water. An' cows ain't as finicky as you are. Far as that goes, when a man gits thirsty or hungry enough he forgits to be dainty. Why, the things I've seen men drink an' eat . . ."

Back at Fort Laramie, Henry had had the notion that it would be the jumping-off place, the last civilized settlement they would see until they got to Oregon. He had expected the country west of Laramie to be a lonely, empty wilderness inhabited by no living beings except howling Indians in full war-paint, and he had looked eagerly forward to seeing the plains black with immense herds of buffalo. But the only buffalo he had seen so far had been a tame one at the fort, though the ground across which the wagons now were traveling was dotted with dried dung which it was his chore to gather for cooking fires. And daily they met people on the move.

Eastbound Mormon freighters; parties of gold-seekers headed for places he'd never heard of; soldiers patrolling the road; Indians—but never in war-paint. Each day the westbound California stage overtook them and the eastbound Omaha stage met them and he marveled at the news that the continent now could be spanned in a mere twenty-four days.

One evening a squad of soldiers headed for Fort Laramie took supper with them and Matt sat far into the night talking to a man in civilian dress who was traveling with them. The man appeared to be about Matt's own age; his face was weather-marked and deeply lined; his eyes were keen, his manner of expression rough and dryly humorous. Although Henry had heard him introduced to his father as Major Bridger, Matt kept calling him "Gabe," and as the two old friends hunkered before the fire they seemed to be exchanging their thoughts in a special language all their own, using hand signs, Indian fashion, almost as frequently as they used words. Henry had never heard Matt laugh so much.

Next day, the old guide appeared to be unusually moody, riding for long periods of time without seeming to be aware of Henry's presence beside him. Though he knew that Matt disliked having his thoughts interrupted, Henry could bear the quiet no longer.

"Have you known Major Bridger quite a while?"

"A long spell, yeah."

"Did you work with him?"

"Gabe an' me trapped together off and on."

"What did you trap?"

"Beaver."

"Was there a lot of money in it?"

"Fer some men I reckon thar was. But none of it stuck to my fingers."

"Why did you quit?"

Matt gave him an exasperated look. "You're the dangdest sprout fer askin' 'why?'"

"Well, I was just curious, that's all."

"Oh, it ain't that I mind your questions particularly. It's jest that I ain't interested much no more in why things happen. 'Cuz they're gonna happen, boy, whether you know why ox don't, so why trouble your mind with things you can't change?" Peering into the distance, Matt rode in silence for a time, then said, "It was a measly worm done me in, an' that's a fact."

"Aw, you're joshing me again!"

"No, I ain't, boy. Used to be, no gent which *was* a gent would step out of his house 'less'n he was wearin' a genuine beaver hat made out of pelts trapped by fools like Old Gabe an' me. Then along come the silkworm—an' beaver was done."

"What did you do when you quit trapping?"

"A little of everything."

"Did you ever prospect for gold?"

"Yeah."

"Ever find any?"

"Not to speak of."

"Ever drive a stagecoach?"

"Couple of years."

"Ever get held up?"

"Lots of times. Out in Californy, where I was drivin', road agents was thick as fleas on an Injun dog, them days."

"What did you do when you got held up?"

"The same thing any sensible man does when he finds himself starin' down the barr'l of a gun. I reached fer the sky."

"Didn't you ever shoot it out with a road agent—not *ever?*"

"Come to think on it," Matt said, giving Henry a sidelong glance, "I did try to once."

"What happened?" Henry asked eagerly.

"Got my head blowed off with a charge of buckshot."

"Aw, Matt!"

"Fact, boy. But as luck would have it they was a female seamstress ridin' the stage. She taken a needle an' thread an' sewed my head on again. But in the excitement she put it on backwards. Since then, I ain't been shore whether I was comin' er goin'."

A week out of Fort Laramie a passing Army patrol gave them the news that the Missouri train had pulled out a day after they had, and from then on Henry found it an exciting game to keep close check on the relative position of the two trains. It was easy to do. If no horseback traveler chanced to overtake them and pass on word of where and when he had seen the other party, a visit to a telegraph station quickly obtained the desired information.

To Matt, the transcontinental telegraph line was a trifling, newfangled invention of no practical value, but to Henry it was the marvel of the day. The operators in the lonely, isolated stations were a bored, gossipy lot with little to do but listen to the messages being exchanged between San Francisco and Omaha, and usually they welcomed his visits. When he asked them what the wires were saying, they would tease him and tell him outrageous lies, but so long as he took it good-naturedly they would eventually get around to telling him what he wanted to know. Fascinated, he would watch an unshaven, tobacco-chewing, sardonic operator reach nonchalantly for the key and tap it with a rapid, careless *rat-tat-rat-a-tat-tat-tat*, wait, tap it again, and presently the rat-a-tat-tat answer would come over the sounder, the operator would hit his key, spit a stream of tobacco juice, and say, "They camped at Horse Shoe Crick last night."

Henry soon learned better than to ask the operators how far it was from one place to another in terms of miles or hours of travel. They neither knew nor cared. Their world was the sounder, the key, and the long hours of boredom in a land they hated and feared. As long as the sounder crackled, they were at ease, but when it went silent fear rose in their throats. Maybe the silence meant only that fire, flood, or landslide had broken a section of the line or that a buffalo using a pole as a scratching post had pushed it down; maybe a station call unanswered meant only that its operator had stepped outside to the privy, was peacefully taking a snooze, or blissfully drunk. But with bands of hostile Indians constantly roaming the country, a silence could mean grimmer things, so why trouble your mind with how far it was from here to there in terms of miles or hours of travel when you knew it was way too far for help to reach you in time when you needed it?

Matt knew distances, of course, but always he spoke in terms of days of traveling time rather than miles. The Missourians were a day and a half behind, three days, two. Once after Henry had climbed atop a rocky ridge in late afternoon and spotted a dust-trail far to the east and had told Matt how it lined up with the river's windings and distinctive landmarks which Matt had pointed out to him earlier, the old guide nodded and said, "Yeah, likely that's them. Way I figger, that's where they'd be by now."

"How far behind us are they?"

"Couple of days."

"Two days!" Henry exclaimed. "You mean I saw *that* far?"

"We git atop the Blue Mountains, out Oregon way," Matt said with a laugh, "I'll show you a spot where you kin see farther in one look than we kin travel in *ten* days."

Henry carved his name on Independence Rock, scrambling all over the pile of rounded gray granite stones jutting up out of the flat sage plain trying to find the marks Matt told him he'd made thirty years ago, but he could not locate them. He viewed the wonders called Split Rock and Devil's Gate. He looked for poison spiders along Poison Spider Creek but found none, though Matt swore there used to be oodles of them, big as dinner plates. He tasted the water of Sweetwater River to see if it was sweet and was disappointed to discover it wasn't; Matt said he guessed Sugar Rock, which used to sweeten the river, had melted plumb away.

As the land began to rise and timber appeared, he pestered Matt until the old guide said, yeah, likely there was a spot atop the divide where a body could stand with one foot on the Pacific slope and the other on the Atlantic, spit twice without hardly moving his head, and one spit would add to the waters of one ocean while the second increased the volume of the other.

"'Course they's a law agin it," Matt warned him.

"Aw, there isn't!"

"Fact. The people livin' in Californy an' Louisiana made the guv'mint pass it. We get into the middle of South Pass you'll see a sign painted on the side of a bluff, which says: 'Do not spit in our oceans—it's unsanitary.'"

"Is South Pass narrow?"

"Jest like the eye of a needle, boy. But don't worry. Back at Laramie

I measured your pa's wagon to make shore it could git through. He's lucky—it'll clear with an inch and a half to spare on each side."

Now of early morning and late evening the air had an autumn-like chill to it, which struck Henry as strange, for July was near at hand. His horse tried to bite him as he bridled it one morning—an unheard of thing. Even more startling, the fat, placid gray mare which his father sometimes rode suddenly laid back her ears and narrowly missed kicking his father's brains out. The oxen had begun acting queer, too, raising a fuss over nothing, fighting their yokes and chains as they had not done since the days when they were first being broken to work.

"It's the altitude, I reckon," Matt said. "Somethin' in this high mountain air makes 'em go off their heads."

"How high are we?"

"The Pass is upwards of seventy-five hundred feet, they tell me."

"Isn't it hard to climb?"

"Shucks, boy, we've done clumb it already."

"Where did we start?"

"This side of the Missoury River from Council Bluffs. We been goin' uphill ever since."

Henry felt cheated. If the pass that crossed the continent's backbone and separated the waters of the Atlantic from those of the Pacific weren't going to amount to anything, what mountain pass would? For years he had read and dreamed about painted wild Indians but the only Indians he'd seen this trip had been tame ones. All he'd seen of buffalo had been bones, chips, and the soldiers' pet back at Fort Laramie. He had heard a lot of tales from Matt about fighting, scalping, and great deeds done by hero-sized men, but all he himself had done had been travel, go to bed, get up, help with the chores, and study. Nothing exciting had happened; nothing at all.

Oh, sure, there had been talk of hostile Indians and still was. There had been the quarrel between his father and Mr. Belford back at Laramie. There had been a mild kind of pleasure in keeping track of the other train. Among the Iowans, there had been some petty arguments and bickerings, and once there had been a fist fight, which ended almost before it began. But outside of that, nothing had happened; nothing at all. He was beginning to believe that nothing would.

The train was moving now through a wide, flat trough covered with sagebrush. To the left loomed high, bare buttes which appeared to be very close at hand when you looked directly at their tops but which you came to realize were miles away when you dropped your eyes to the expanse of ground lying between you and their base. To the right the country rose still higher and was covered with stands of pine; now and again, way off to the northwest, you could see the jagged, snow-capped peaks of what appeared to be real, honest-to-God mountains. Much to Henry's disappointment, Matt said that the train would not pass through that range, for the trail stayed well to the south.

"Used to be good beaver country up there," Matt said reflectively. "Good country to lose your hair in, too. Them Crows are a tricky breed."

"Are the Crows the worst Indians you've known?"

"Not quite. Got to give the Blackfeet the prize there. An' the Snakes are almost as bad."

"Which Indians are the best?"

"Nez Perce, I'd say."

"Which tribe has the best horses?"

"You got to give that to the Nez Perces, too."

"Do all Indians understand sign language?"

"Yeah."

"How come?"

"Dunno. But they do."

"Did you ever get bit by a rattler, Matt?"

"Boy, don't you *never* run out of questions?" Matt said with a chuckle. "Shore, I been bit by a rattler."

"Where?"

"Out in the Bear River country."

"Where on you, I mean?"

"On the butt. I sat on the fool thing."

"What happened?"

"Why, I got up in a hurry."

"Very sick?"

"Sickest dang snake you ever seen," Matt said, nodding solemnly. "Fact, it up an' died."

"Didn't you feel bad?"

"Wal, yeah, I *did* feel kind of sorry fer the pore thing, but after all I didn't go to sit on it—"

"Weren't *you* sick?"

"Wal, I rode standin' up fer a few days. Truth is, that rattler didn't bite very deep into the meat. What hurt me was my partner taken his knife and slashed the fang marks to make the blood come and then seared me good with a hot iron to steam out the poison. Worked first rate, too, but it ain't a treatment I'd recommend." Jerking his head at a low ridge directly to the west, which looked to Henry no different than any of the other ridges they had seen that day, the old mountain man said casually, "Lookee yonder, boy. That's the top of South Pass."

Gazing ahead, Henry decided he would never again believe a thing Matt told him. For South Pass was a good sixteen miles wide, if it was an inch, and as flat as the Iowa farm back home . . .

They made camp in early afternoon on a small stream at the base of the hills to the right, where the grass was good and timber near at hand. Matt persuaded Daniel Lynn it would be a good idea to lay over here for a day or two. The desert lay ahead, he pointed out, and the people and stock were tired. Besides, Doc Riley had told him he thought Mrs. Shelby's time was close at hand.

Chapter Seven

It was three o'clock in the afternoon when the first pains came. The train stopped shortly thereafter. Dr. Riley climbed into the Benjamin Shelby wagon—in which Ruth had taken to bed at her husband's insistence even though she had not felt in the least like lying down—checked her pulse, looked at her tongue, rolled back her eyelids with a none-too-clean thumb, peered nearsightedly at her pupils through his steel-rimmed glasses, and felt gingerly of her swollen abdomen.

"Um-hmm!" he said. "Um-hmm!"

She gazed anxiously up at him, seeking reassurance in his face. She did not find it. Dr. Riley was a timid-appearing, vague little man in his late forties, usually in need of a shave, with a habit of laughing nervously and swallowing his words when asked a direct question. Her voice was sharper than she intended it to be.

"Well, Doctor?"

He took his gold-cased watch out of his pocket, reached for her wrist, then, recalling that he had already taken her pulse, scowled intently down at the face of the watch. Assured that it was still running, he snapped its cover shut and fumbled the timepiece back into his pocket. "You've—ah—had two children, Mrs. Shelby?"

"Yes."

"How was it—ah—with them?"

"I had a bad time with the first. The second came easier."

"Um-hmm! Um-hmm! Well, you'll—ah—be all right, Mrs. Shelby. You'll—ah, be all right. Just lie still and rest."

After Dr. Riley left the wagon, Grandpa Shelby stuck his head in and cheerfully told her not to worry about Naomi, for Sally Lynn had volunteered to take care of her. Isaac stuck his head in, smiled at her self-consciously, and told her not to worry about the family's supper; he would fix it. Benjamin asked her if she would like him to roll up the canvas on the sides of the wagon so that she could see what a pretty spot they were camped in.

"Please do."

It was a lovely spot, she agreed after he had rolled up the canvas so that she could see out in both directions. To the north rose hills much like those back home, save for the fact that the trees were pine rather than oak. The grass on the floor of the open meadow nearby seemed thicker than the grass back home and of a darker shade of green. The mountain wildflowers were blooming now, and they seemed much more profuse and more vivid in color than any wildflowers she had ever seen back home.

"I wish I could go for a walk," she said wistfully.

"It's best you rest."

"I know. But I can't help wishing."

A clear, sparkling creek wandered across the meadow. Some of the men and older boys were fishing; she could hear their shouts of triumph as they jerked flopping trout out of the water. The younger children were wading, casting pebbles, laughing with glee. To the south and slightly below the camp, she could see the gray-green monotony of sagebrush, and, far beyond, high, grim, lonely buttes standing stark against the sharp blue of the sky.

"We're right in the heart of South Pass," Benjamin said. "I don't reckon many babies have the luck to be born astride a continent."

"No, I suppose not."

"Have you thought of a name?"

She gave him a weary smile. "No, have you?"

"People have been joshing me. They say it ought to be a different kind of name. Like Continental Divide. Or Constance Divide."

"Good Heavens! Who'd ever saddle a child with such names?"

"Well, they were only joshing."

She slept poorly that night. Save for an occasional intestinal cramp or twinge that she was sure meant nothing, she felt no pains. She was not particularly uncomfortable. But a restlessness kept her tossing and turning in her lonely bed long after the camp had gone to sleep. She missed Naomi, whom Sally had taken into the Lynn wagon; she missed Benjamin, who had spread his blankets on the ground outside on the assumption that she would rest better with the bed all to herself. And each time she did manage to quiet her mind and nerves to a point where she was about to fall asleep, a milk cow would moo, an ox would bellow, or a horse would whinny within the wagon enclosure, into which the animals had been brought for the night, and she would be wide awake again.

It was not uncommon for the stock to make an occasional disturbance, but tonight the same restlessness, the same uneasiness that troubled her seemed to affect them, too. Hearing the animals constantly moving about, feeling the wagon shake as some beast blundered against it in the dark, hearing bawl answered by bawl, first individually, then in deafening chorus as the long hours dragged on, she felt suddenly afraid. She knew—or thought she knew—why her own nerves were on edge. But what ailed the livestock? Did they smell something in the night wind? Did they sense something beyond human capacity to sense? Did their beast instinct warn them of impending danger?

No, it was foolish to think such things! She closed her eyes and tried to force herself to sleep. But for the rest of the night she dozed only in fitful snatches.

Dawn came, the morning passed, and still the pains did not return. Sally brought her some breakfast and chatted with her for a while. Dr. Riley looked in on her just before noon, mumbled vaguely, and went away. Benjamin climbed into the wagon and sat down beside her.

"How do you feel, dear?"

"A little tired. I didn't sleep much last night."

"Nobody did. The cattle were raising too much of a racket. What did Dr. Riley say?"

"He just mumbled."

"When does he think it will be?"

"Pretty soon. That's all he will say." Her voice grew exasperated. "He isn't much of a doctor, Ben." Seeing the worried look that shadowed her husband's eyes, she tried to make light of it. "Why, I'll bet a pretty he's never even had a baby before."

Benjamin's smile was wan. "Be odd if he had, him a man and all."

"You know what I mean. He's never helped a woman have a baby before. Oh, I suppose he's fixed broken arms and legs and dosed people. But he doesn't know beans about babies. I can tell that by the way he acts."

"Well," Benjamin said, a helpless look coming into his eyes as he took her by the hand. "Well, you try to rest, dear."

"But I feel so guilty, Ben. These people have been so nice to us. The minute I felt a little pain—which for all I know is only gas—they stop and say they're going to lay by till the baby comes. Suppose it doesn't come for days?"

"Don't you fret about that. Lynn says everybody can do with a rest. So does Matt." He patted her hand. "Think you could take a nap if I left you be?"

"Stay a while. Please stay."

"Sure, if you want me to."

A noontime hush lay over the camp. As soon as daylight had come, the livestock had been let out of the enclosure and driven onto good meadow grass a mile or so away in hopes that they would eat and drink their fill and be quieter tonight. But it was not only their bellowing that was missing, Ruth mused. Another sound that she had long been accustomed to, a cheerful, pleasant sound, was hushed, too. Listening for it, she grew tense, but she did not hear it. Suddenly she was frightened.

"Ben! The meadow larks aren't singing!"

"Too hot for 'em, I guess."

"But they always sing. I've heard them every day since we left home. Why aren't they singing now?"

He smiled uncertainly. "A meadow lark only sings when he feels like it, Ruth. Ain't you never noticed that? Sure, he'll sing fine in the cool of the morning and evening. But he won't sing a lick when it's raining or when it's too hot or cold to suit him."

"Are you sure?"

"Guess I've heard enough of 'em to know. Mr. Meadow Lark is a fair-weather bird, if ever there was one."

She tried to believe that. "I suppose we should be grateful he doesn't sing at night like our stock do. What on earth ailed them last night?"

"Matt says they just got spooky."

"At what?"

"Change of water or grass, maybe. Or it could be the altitude, he says. He's seen stock spook for no reason at all in this high country, he says, but never as bad as last night. 'Course some of the people are saying the stock smell—well, smell something."

"Indians?" Ruth said, watching his face.

"Yeah," he answered, and his lips were compressed.

"But we haven't seen an Indian for days—and they were friendly."

"Well, you know how some people are. They say not seeing hostile Indians is a sure sign they're around, watching us. But don't you worry. People get just as spooky as stock do, with no more reason." He leaned down and kissed her on the cheek. "You try to get some rest. I'll put down the canvas."

After he had gone, she closed her eyes and did manage to doze off for an hour or so. Presently she became aware of voices outside—a boy's and a man's—which by some freak of terrain or breeze were carrying to the wagon in which she lay much more clearly than the speakers could have intended. Recognizing them as belonging to Henry Lynn and his father, she guessed that they must be standing outside the wagon enclosure, probably in the shade of the pine trees at the base of the nearby hills.

"... and Matt said I could keep it!" Henry was saying excitedly. "But I was to get you off alone first and tell you where we found it!"

"Wait a minute, son. Slow down. Where did you say you and Matt went?"

"That way. Back up in the timber. We made a half circle, beginning down in the meadow and working our way around through the high country, looking for sign—"

"What did Matt think he was going to find?"

"All he said was maybe the stock spooked at nothing last night. But if something real scared 'em, it'd leave sign and he intended to find it."

"Did he?"

"No, but he's still looking. He told me you might get to wondering where we were and I'd better come back to camp."

"All right. Now about that scalp—"

"It's Indian, Matt says. He ain't sure what tribe. Crow, maybe. Or Shoshone. He says it's hard to tell unless you've seen the hair growing on the Indian—"

"Skip the details, son. Where did you find it?"

"It'd be maybe five or six miles back in the hills. North. It was an old camp—at least a month old, Matt said. Some of the lodgepoles were still standing and there was Indian junk scattered all around, like somebody had left in a hurry. There wasn't anything worth keeping, though, except this. We found it under an old rotten hide. I asked Matt if I could have it and he said sure, 'long as I didn't go scaring people with it. So I came to you first—"

"I'd have tanned you good if you hadn't!"

"Ain't it something, Pa? Look how it's stretched over a willow frame with a kind of handle on it. Matt says that's so you can wave it around when you do the scalp dance."

"Which you'd better not try, believe me!"

"Oh, I won't! But I can keep it, can't I, Pa?"

"What do you want with a dirty old Indian scalp?"

"I just want it, that's all. None of the other kids have one—"

"Now you listen to me, Henry. If you show that scalp to a living soul, if you breathe so much as a whisper to anybody— even Sally— that you've seen an Indian camp, you'll answer to me in a way you'll never forget. Do you understand?"

"Sure, Pa. I promised Matt I wouldn't spook nobody. But can I keep it?"

"Whatever for?"

"Oh, I don't know. Maybe to show to my grandchildren someday— if I ever have any."

Ruth heard Daniel Lynn laugh. "All right, son, as long as your grandchildren are the only ones you show it to. Give it to me. I'll put it away in a safe place. Now you remember what I said about not talking . . ."

The voices faded away. Ruth felt sick. A sudden impulse came to her to cry out to Benjamin and ask him to make sure Naomi had not strayed away from the camp, but with an effort of will she restrained it. Naomi was all right. Sally was a dependable girl and would watch her closely. And if she told Benjamin that she had been frightened by something she had overheard, he would insist on knowing what it was, and would become angry at the Lynns. It was nothing, really. A month-old camp. Nothing at all.

She closed her eyes and tried to go to sleep. Deliberately she forced her mind to close all doors to the future and present and look only toward the past . . .

She had been an only child. Until a few months ago, she had never journeyed outside the borders of the county in which she had been born. Until she reached the age of sixteen, four years ago, her life had been as peaceful and tranquil as that of a person traveling as a passenger in a boat over the still surface of a quiet lake. Her world had consisted of the plain but comfortably furnished cabin in which she had been born, the eighty-acre farm which her father tilled, the timbered hills and the cleared valleys of the immediate neighborhood, and the village five miles away. She had her school, her church, her cousins, aunts and uncles. She had her playmates and friends. As she grew older, a neighbor boy began courting her and she began to think of marriage. In proper season, all the things that were a part of growing up had come to her, and her world seemed solid and unshakable.

One day her mother complained of feeling poorly . . .

The boat had reached the lake's outlet.

Both her father and mother were dead within two weeks, taken off by the virulent epidemic of smallpox that had counted toll in almost every household in that section of Missouri. On the adjoining farm, the Shelbys lost the mother, the eldest son, and the infant daughter. Left were the stunned father, Obidiah, the eighteen-year-old son, Benjamin, and the fourteen-year-old son, Isaac.

Although Benjamin had been courting Ruth for almost a year, they had not yet reached the point of an understanding. Now he declared his intentions, and she knew she must make her decision quickly. The farm was a good one but she could not work it alone. A prosperous uncle offered to take it over and let her come live with his family; a less prosperous cousin suggested that he take it over and move his family in with her. Neither offer appealed to her, for she knew what her position would be with either set of relatives: that of an unmarried female in another woman's home. And that she could not face.

So she married Benjamin Shelby, which angered both sets of relatives, and with his and his father's help successfully fought for and held onto the property so jealously coveted by her kinfolk. At a time when her whole nature yearned to give in to weakness, circumstances forced her to be strong. Religiously raised, sheltered against the facts of adult life, totally ignorant of the physical and emotional aspects of the relationship between the sexes, she was given little time to adjust herself to living with her new husband. She and Benamin spent the week immediately following their marriage in her parents' cabin, then he loaded all her personal possessions into a wagon, moved her to his father's cabin, and she became wife, daughter, sister, and mother to three men—all of whom were relative strangers to her.

Never by word or deed did she let Grandpa Shelby, Benjamin, or Isaac know how frightened of them she was. She went about her chores with a smile on her face, was agreeable, did the cooking, bed-making, washing, mending—did all the things that the menfolk of a family have a right to expect of a woman. But she was not a woman; she was only a girl. And daily she walked in terror.

To balance Benjamin's demands upon her as a bride against Grandpa Shelby's grief-inspired assumption that she would do for him exactly as his dead wife had done and Isaac's fear that she would treat him as a younger brother or try to raise him as a son, required a wisdom and maturity she did not possess. But she did the best she could and did it with such good will that eventually all three men came to respect her. They never knew that all the while her mind had been glazed with fear.

Her first child, a boy, had been born within the year. By then, the Shelby menfolk had changed the fence lines and turned the two farms into one. With Ruth's reluctant approval, they wrecked the house in which she had been born and used the best of its timbers and floor boards to add two rooms to the Shelby cabin.

"Going to need 'em, I'm guessing," Grandpa Shelby said with a wink at Ruth, and Benjamin laughed and agreed.

The child lived but two months.

Naomi came along a year later. The Rebellion had begun by then. That the war would have any effect on this backwoods corner of Missouri at first seemed highly unlikely. No one in the county kept slaves. Ruth's father had never believed in slavery. Neither had

Obidiah Shelby and his sons. Tilling their own land, proud of their self-sufficiency, they went their way beholden to no man and wanted no man beholden to them.

Corn was their cash crop. They kept a few cattle for milk and beef. Well-tended bottom land garden patches supplied the household with vegetables; a couple of acres of orchard and berries with fruit. They let their hogs roam the rocky, timbered hillsides, rooting out a living on pecans, acorns, snakes, or whatever else appealed to their omnivorous appetites, save for the weeks prior to butchering time when they were penned up and fattened on corn. A plot of flax for linen; a few sheep for wool; an occasional early-morning or late-evening prowl through the woods with a gun in search of squirrel, possum, rabbit, deer, or bear for wild game—these were enough for the family to live on.

It was not a lazy man's life. Lazy men let their wives and children cultivate the corn, weed the garden, and tend to the orchard. Lazy men scrounged up a boiler, copper tubing, mash and sugar, built cautious fires in remote corners of the hills, and set themselves up in business. When their product was ready for market, they advertised that fact discreetly, and, when the customers came, showed what good fellows they were by drinking with them, telling yarns, arguing States' Rights, Secession, Slavery, Hard Times, the Rebellion, and bragging about what *they* would do to cure the nation's ills if given half a chance.

Obe Shelby's attitude toward such men coincided with his sentiments toward slavery. If a man would rather drink and talk than work, that was his business. If he wanted to own and work niggers, that was his affair, too. Obe Shelby did not hold with either; but he would no more dream of tipping off a Government Revenue agent to the location of a neighbor's whisky still than he would join a rabid Abolitionist on a platform shouting down the evils of slavery. Let those who objected to what their neighbors did tackle the job of reforming them. He had his own work to do. All he asked was that he be let alone to do it.

The realization that this was to be a war in which no one could be neutral did not come to Ruth at once. No battles were fought in the county. No columns of Union or Rebel troops marched along the winding roads. No cannon boomed. Outwardly the oak-covered hills and the stream-filled hollows showed the same peaceful face to the sky that they had showed every day of her life. But there came a time between the day she laid the boy-child in his grave and the day she brought the girl-child into the world when she recognized the terrifying fact that she was living in the midst of a battleground.

That it was emotional, rather than actual, made it no less real. There had been an unconscious choosing of sides. You had to take one or the other now, for the area lying between had gradually shrunk to a sharp-drawn line. How did people know that one family's sympathies lay with the Union cause, another with the Rebel? No one could say. But they knew. Before long it was as if the head of each household had painted a sign proclaiming his sentiments and hung it on his front door. Remarks made by a man months ago—even years ago—came back to plague him. Because Obe Shelby had once expressed a favorable opinion of Abe Lincoln, because he once had said he would not lift a finger to defend any man's right to own slaves, the sign on the Shelby door read UNION.

During those anxious weeks early in the war when the state of Missouri wavered between casting its fortune with South or North, Obe Shelby was troubled, Ruth knew. When the news came that Missouri intended to stick with the Union, he nodded approval, said that settled the question once and for all, and Ruth sighed in relief. There would be stability and peace in this part of the country, at least, no matter how fiercely the war raged elsewhere. And peace in her own immediate world was all that mattered to her.

But Obe Shelby had been wrong. The question was far from settled. Ruth was hurt to discover as the weeks passed that more and more of her close friends and relatives were avoiding her when she saw them on the village streets. Others, with whom she had never been close, now went out of their way to greet her cordially. Always the first group was known to be pro-Rebel; the second pro-Union.

People began to take care what they said and to whom they said it. Strange new words came into use. Guerrilla. Bushwhacker. Copperhead. In a community that had seldom been troubled with petty theft or malicious damage to property, seemingly senseless outrages began to occur almost nightly. A haystack would be set afire, a rail fence would be torn down so that stock could get into a cornfield, a horse would be stolen, a hog killed, an outhouse tipped over. At first these happenings puzzled everyone, but as time passed the pattern of the mischief began to emerge.

Families that had prospered, that by thrift and hard work had raised their store of worldly goods above that of the average, usually held pro-Union sentiments. It was natural that they should. Why destroy a way of life that had been good to them? They were the substantial citizens of the community. Their taxes and tithes supported the schools, the law, the churches. It seemed only reasonable to them that if they stood solidly behind their state and federal governments, order would prevail. But they overlooked two things: These were not reasonable times; and in this particular district they were in the minority. And it was they who suffered now.

Appeals to the sheriff proved useless. He was a Democrat, a Rebel sympathizer, a poor man with ambitions to be rich, and shrewd enough to see which side of the bread his political butter was on. He talked glibly, investigated each complaint, ate a lot of free meals and drank a lot of free drinks served him by aggrieved farmers and village folk, but the only person he ever arrested was harmless old Sammy Fish, the village drunk, who habitually staggered to the jail and turned himself in at least once a month anyway.

In the beginning the mischief had been simple spite-work, one group of drink-emboldened men taking advantage of troubled times to settle old grudges against another. But as it became apparent that the law intended to let matters run their course, when news began to filter into the county that the desperate Rebels were paying good prices for horses, meat, and guns, when it became known that elsewhere in the Border country men were riding under cover of darkness and Southern patriotism, the acts of violence took on a grimmer tone. Steal a Union man's stock, burn a Union man's cabin, rape a Union man's wife—well, this was war, wasn't it?

Panic gripped the land. Men who had tried to be neutral dropped all their Union friends and proclaimed their sympathy toward the Rebels. Others hastily loaded their families and belongings into wagons and fled the county. What stubborn, propertied Unionists were left organized in self-defense. Among them were the Shelby menfolk.

The organization called itself the Enrolled Militia, or the Home Guard. The State of Missouri and the United States government officially blessed it and made vague promises to back it. The men met and marched and drilled, furnishing their own rifles, ammunition, and uniforms. They elected officers. They made their show of force, riding in squads, platoons, and companies over the hills, into the hollows, and along the streets of the county villages. They met no enemy, save for an occasional tavern drunk who would hoot at them as they rode past; they fired no shots; they fought no battles. And the State of Missouri and the United States government stood in back of them as promised.

"Way, way in back," was the way Obe Shelby sardonically put it, for no help other than words was ever forthcoming.

And on dark nights, their households continued to suffer.

One evening Benjamin was shot at while walking from the barn to the house. Another, a flaming torch was hurled through a cabin window. No woman dared go anywhere without a man along, these days, and always the man went armed. Some of the rasher souls in the Home Guard argued that it was high time they fought fire with fire and did some night-riding of their own. Obe Shelby said that was fools' talk and he'd have no part of it; but he admitted that something drastic would have to be done soon.

As the increasingly bitter war went into its third year with no end in sight, the nervous strain under which they were living began to affect Ruth's health. She slept badly, had little appetite, and became so apprehensive that the bark of a dog or the fall of a dead tree limb in the night would set her to trembling uncontrollably. Would she never know peace again?

What was going to become of them? She was pregnant again. Naomi, a year old now, was beginning to crawl around and was as hard to keep up with as a curiosity-filled kitten. Worrying about the child to be, the lively child that was, the safety of her menfolk and her own failing health, Ruth knew that she was nearing a breaking point.

One cold January evening she paused on the threshold between the kitchen and the living room as she heard Benjamin say: ". . . get away . . ."

Her heart stopped. Benjamin and his father were sitting with their backs toward her, their shoes off, their stockinged feet extended toward the warmth of the open fire. On a low stool to one side of the stone fireplace, Isaac, sensing her presence, glanced up at her, then made a sign with his hand to his older brother. With a guilty start, Benjamin got to his feet and turned to face her.

"Done with the dishes, Ruth?"

"Yes."

"You look tired. Come in and sit down."

She did not move. "Who's going to get away?"

He hesitated just long enough to reveal to her that his mind was framing a lie. "The Ransoms. They've decided to leave."

"You told me that yesterday, Benjamin. But you weren't talking about the Ransoms just now. You were talking about us, weren't you?"

He dropped his eyes. "It was just talk, Ruth."

"Don't you think you should include me in it?"

Benjamin exchanged glances with his father, who nodded and said, "She's right, Ben."

Benjamin led her to a chair by the fire and gently rested a hand on her shoulder. "The way things are going, getting away seems like the sensible thing to do."

"Where would we go?"

"West. California, maybe. Or Oregon."

"We'd sell the farm?"

"We'd have to. Traveling takes money. There's no telling how the war will end—or when. Maybe there won't be anything for us to come back to here."

"When would we go?"

"That's what we've got to decide. We can't leave until after the baby comes, of course."

"That won't be until July."

"I know. Say we figure to pull out in August. That'll be too late to head west this year. But we could go up to Independence or Council Bluffs, winter there, and be set to move out with the first train come the next spring."

"What would you and Isaac do?"

"Oh, I guess we could find jobs."

She did not ask where they would live during the long months of waiting, for the answer to that question was obvious. They would have to rent a house or take rooms in a cheap lodging place. She would be among strangers with a new baby on her hands and Naomi to keep up with. Winter would end travel and farm work and the town would be full of teamsters and common laborers with nothing to do but drink, gamble, fight, and compete for odd jobs. Merely to exist would take a lot of money, which would buy them nothing but time. The dreary prospect of months of idleness appalled her.

"If we did that, it would be a year and a half before we even started west."

Benjamin nodded, a bleak misery in his eyes. "It's that or stay here until next spring. I'm afraid if we wait—"

"Oh, Ben!" she exclaimed, seizing his hand, "if we're going to get away, let's do it as soon as we can! Not next spring, not this summer—but now—this spring!"

He stared down at her. "What about the baby, Ruth?"

"Let it come when and where it will!"

"You want to get away that bad?"

"I want peace, Ben, peace—wherever we have to go to find it!"

Grandpa Shelby sold the farm to a Rebel sympathizer for three hundred dollars in cash, two new wagons and sixteen head of unbroken draft oxen. They laid in a good supply of bacon, flour, corn meal, and molasses, but there was little dried fruit or beans to be had. Traveling would be hard on dishes, Grandpa Shelby said, but the only tinware Ruth could find in the village store was a pair of tin cups, so she resigned herself to using her good delftware, though she feared little of it would survive the trip. They decided to take along two cows for fresh milk. The menfolk bought a plentiful supply of ammunition for their rifles, shotguns, and pistols. Viewing the veritable arsenal spread out on the cabin floor, Ruth said, "My goodness, do we need all that?"

"We ain't leaving here with much," Grandpa Shelby said grimly. "But what we've got we aim to keep."

He was not thinking merely of Indians, Ruth knew. He was thinking of a neighbor, an outspoken Union man, who had sold out and headed north a year ago, only to be overtaken and robbed of everything he possessed before he'd even gotten out of the county. Bushwhackers from Arkansas had officially been blamed for the deed; but rumor placed the blame closer to home.

Few friends and relatives came to say goodbye, for in addition to a reluctance toward being identified with Union people they feared what might happen to their homes and property in their absence. The night before leaving, Grandpa Shelby, Benjamin, and Isaac argued heatedly over whether it would be wiser to wear their blue Home Guard uniforms while traveling or dress in everyday clothes. Grandpa and Isaac were for wearing uniforms, Benjamin against.

"We're not soldiers," Benjamin said. "We're a family traveling."

"'Tain't so," Grandpa disagreed. "We got a paper from the government which says we're being transferred to the California Militia, ain't we? So we got a right to wear our uniforms."

It was true that they had the paper, officially transferring them from the Missouri Home Guard to the California Militia, but they knew and Ruth knew that the paper meant nothing. They were not headed for California; they were heading for Oregon. And once safely out of Missouri, none of them intended ever to bear arms in any cause but that of their own self-protection.

"Let's make it clear who we are and what we stand for," Grandpa Shelby persisted. "If it comes to a fight and we have to kill or be killed, there'll be no question which side we're on."

That she could calmly listen to talk of killing and feel no emotion was an indication of the numbness that filled her mind and soul. Looking back for the last time, next morning, at the cabin, at the graves on the greening hillside, she felt a vague, wordless grief, but she shed no tears. Benjamin, who had stopped the wagon to give her this last look, said gently, "Ready to go on now, Ruth?"

"Yes."

He put his hand on hers and his voice was thick with emotion. "I'm proud of you, honey. I just can't tell you how proud."

And the wagon moved . . .

How far we have come since then, she mused. And how far we have yet to go. The early afternoon heat was making her drowsy. As she drifted into the vague borderland that lies between waking and sleeping, her thoughts became disjointed.

Strange that we've seen no buffalo . . . I looked forward to that. But there have been antelope. Such pretty animals! So swift, so graceful, with their quick turns, their long leaps, their twitching white tails. Like flags. Isaac listened so intently when Matt told him all a hunter had to do to lure them within gunshot range was to tie a red rag on a stick and crawl toward them, waving the stick, whetting their curiosity. They would run away, Matt said, then turn for another look. Lie still, then. Wave the red flag. Presently they would come mincing back. When they got in range, you fired.

Isaac had tried it. She giggled aloud. How silly he had looked, wriggling forward on his stomach, waving the red flag, pausing, moving forward again—and it hadn't worked at all . . .

"Reckon antelope are smarter, these days," Matt said, a twinkle in his eyes.

"Or people dumber," Grandpa Shelby chuckled.

Isaac had been mad at Matt for a week, sure that he'd been hoorawed . . .

Fort Laramie. She'd not soon forget that Irish sergeant's eyes. So blue, so friendly. Yet cold as steel when he'd found that group of bullying, threatening Sioux trying to wheedle food, tobacco, or money out of the Shelbys, to whom a practical joker in the train had sent them with the cruel lie that the Shelbys were rich and giving fine gifts to all the Indians they met.

"Away with yez!" Sergeant Blue Eyes had yelled. "Away with yez! These people got nothin' to spare for beggars! Git, I say, or b' Jeesus, I'll drown the lot of yez!"

Sergeant Blue Eyes stayed for supper and lingered a long while afterward, talking, cheering them up, giving them good advice. She had seen a shadow on his face, knew that something was troubling him, and finally had asked him what it was. Then it came pouring out.

He was leaving Fort Laramie next week, being transferred East. His wife and three children were here, he said, but he could not take them with him. He was worried about the children. Such bright little boogers they were, and they ought to be in school getting a proper education. He'd been thinking, he'd been wondering—well, ma'am, if only some family headed for Oregon would take them along and put them in a good mission school . . .

A mission school? Yes ma'am. My woman is an Indian, you see—a Sioux—and she'll be going back to live with her own people. But half the blood in the youngsters is mine, ma'am, and when they're dressed up they hardly look Indian at all. I love the boogers, ma'am, so I was thinking, wondering, hoping . . .

She hadn't said no. She hadn't needed to. He had looked at her, lowered his head and murmured, "It's too much to ask. I know. May the Saints bless you, ma'am, you're a good woman with troubles enough of your own . . ."

She had cried that night out of pity for Sergeant Blue Eyes; she wept for him now; the tears eased her and she slept. No, she was not sleeping; she was awake. Isaac was hunting antelope. She was sure that the young man was Isaac, though she could not see him clearly through the tall sagebrush, for above the sagebrush a red flag on a stick was waving back and forth, back and forth. Foolish, eager Isaac. He'll get cactus spines in his chest. We'll have to pluck them out; we'll have to strip him, scald him, pluck him like a chicken. He'll be all over feathers stuck tight to his pink little cheeks and arms. However did he find that jar of molasses . . .

No, it isn't Isaac hunting, isn't Isaac waving the flag. *I* am hunting, *I* am waving the flag. I have a gun and I am waiting, waving the flag. Whatever are you going to do with all those guns, Grandpa Shelby? ". . . and they said it was bushwhackers, but the colonel said. . ." How beautiful the antelope are! And so close! Brown eyes . . . no, blue. Why, it isn't an antelope at all! It's Naomi! She's toddling through the sagebrush, her golden hair rumpled by the wind; she's laughing, holding up a chubby arm, crying: "How!"

She's close to the flag now. She reaches for it. A huge Indian rises up, seizes her by the hair, his knife flashes in the sun . . .

Ruth Shelby screamed in terror. Raising her body up rigid on her elbows, she screamed again and again. When full awareness came to her, she did not know whether she had screamed aloud or only in her dream. But suddenly she realized that it did not matter. No one could have heard her. For the stillness of mid-afternoon had been broken by a tumult of noise outside. Oxen were bawling, horses whinnying, dogs barking, men shouting, children wailing, and over the bedlam she could hear the clank of chains, the screech of wheels, and the creaking of wagons in motion.

She tried to get up, but a sudden tearing pain in her abdomen took her breath and strength from her. Weakly she sank back on her bed.

After a moment she managed to roll over on her side and inch her way toward the canvas, determined to lift it and see what was going on outside. But again searing pain gripped her and she fell back, bathed in cold sweat.

After what seemed a long while, a face appeared in the opening at the rear of the wagon and a voice said, "Are you awake, Ruth?"

"How could I be anything else? What on earth is happening?"

"Ben thought you might be wondering," Isaac answered. "He said not to disturb you, but if you were awake to tell you."

"Tell me what?"

"Old Corny Belford and his bunch have caught up with us. They're fixing to make camp."

"I should have known!" Ruth groaned. "All those dogs and howling children! Well, I suppose they'll be going on first thing in the morning and we'll be rid of them."

"They ain't inclined to," Isaac said, shaking his head. "They're a mighty scared bunch. They seen some Indians—or thought they did—and they want to join up with us. Mr. Lynn is raising an awful fuss. He don't want 'em camping anywheres near us. He's drawn a deadline and is threatening to shoot the first person that crosses it."

"Has he gone out of his mind?"

"Pretty near. And he ain't the only one, Ruth. All our womenfolk are upset. You see, every last kid in Corny Belford's train has come down with the whooping cough."

Chapter Eight

Through the waning afternoon, Ruth Shelby lay listening to the turmoil outside. From time to time one or another of the Iowa women dropped by to see how she was feeling, and, finding her anxious to know what was going on, told her what they had seen and heard. Yes, the Missourians really were scared. No, they hadn't actually *seen* any hostile Indians, but two days ago they had crossed the trail of what Andy Hale said was a sizable party of Shoshones, which *might* be hostile. It had frightened them so badly that they had traveled from early dawn until late dark ever since in an effort to catch up with the Iowans.

Their oxen and horses were acting crazy, too. Nobody knew why. Some of the men said the animals must be eating a poison weed or berry that affected their brains. Others theorized that the air circulating up the Pacific slope of the divide was different from that they had been breathing and was making them act like fighting drunks. Matt insisted that the altitude was to blame. But whatever the cause, one thing was clear: the livestock had gone crazy as bedbugs.

Sally Lynn stopped by for a visit. She seemed reluctant to talk at first, and Ruth suspected that her father had given her strict orders to say nothing that might upset her, but under Ruth's persistent questioning she became more informative.

"Mr. Belford says we've got to stick together. Pa didn't like the idea at all—particularly after he found out so many of their children have come down with the whooping cough. But now he agrees that joining the trains is the only sensible thing to do."

"I hope he makes them keep their distance."

"Oh, he intends to. The men are re-forming the wagon circle now. Our wagons will stay on this side and theirs on the other. No one is to cross the dead-line between. Pa even warned them to tie up their dogs."

"Did they?"

"Well, they raised quite a fuss about it. Particularly when Pa said he was posting guards with orders to shoot any dog they saw running loose. One of their men got mad and said—" Sally suddenly bit her lip and broke off. "Oh, I shouldn't be telling you this! It'll only make you fret."

"Land's sake, girl," Ruth said in exasperation, "if there's one sure thing that'll take a body's mind off her own troubles, it's hearing about somebody else's! What *did* the man say?"

"That anybody that shot *his* dog would get shot himself. Just then, a fight started between one of their dogs and one of ours. Mr. Shelby jumped in to stop it—"

"My husband?" Ruth interrupted.

"No, his father. Pa caught hold of our dog and held it. The other dog bit Mr. Shelby and he kicked it." Sally giggled. "Henry said he kicked it at least ten feet. The Missouri man that owned the dog picked up an ax and came at Mr. Shelby—" Sally gave her a stricken look. "Oh, now I *am* upsetting you!"

"And I'll *stay* upset until I find out what happened next! What did Grandpa Shelby do?"

"Well, he grabbed the man and they wrestled for the ax. Then Pa stepped in, took the ax away from the man and knocked him down. Two other Missouri men made for Pa. Mr. Belford was yelling, 'Stop it, stop it!' but they weren't paying him any mind. Then all of a sudden, Henry said, Will Starr jumped in, grabbed a man in each hand by the back of their necks and lifted them right off the ground. He told them if they didn't simmer down he'd knock their heads together. Henry said they simmered down right away."

"Goodness me! What a disgraceful way to behave! What's causing all the racket outside now?"

"The men are driving the livestock inside the circle for the night. Pa didn't want to do it—there's close to four hundred head, he says—but Matt and Andy say it's best. Particularly if there really *are* Indians around." Sally smiled as she prepared to leave. "I've got to go start supper. Is there anything special you'd like, Mrs. Shelby?"

"No, dear. But please bring Naomi over as soon as you've fed her. I want her to sleep with me tonight."

"She's no trouble, really. If you sleep better alone—"

"That's just it, I don't. Please bring her, dear."

"Of course I will. I'll bring you some supper, too. Now you get some rest, Mrs. Shelby."

Rest? Ruth felt a sudden desire to laugh out loud. Dog fights, man fights, whooping children, crazy livestock, a baby due any hour, an ignorant doctor, Indians on the prowl—and all anyone can think of to say to me is get some rest! Well, she supposed that was all there was to say.

Benjamin put Naomi to bed beside her shortly after dark and kissed them both good night. He would not be going to bed for a while himself, he said, but either Grandpa Shelby or Isaac would be sleeping on the ground just outside the wagon and would hear her if she called. She gazed at him anxiously.

"What will you be doing? Where will you be?"

"We decided it would be best to leave openings at each end of the wagon circle, just in case we can't control the stock. Matt thinks that will be safer than trying to pen them in too tight. But we'll have men on horseback guarding the openings. I'm to stand guard until midnight. Now go to sleep, dear, and don't worry.

The camp settled down to relative quiet. From the wagons on the far side of the enclosure Ruth could hear a constant fretful crying of babies, a never-ending convulsive whooping and coughing of sick children, and her heart went out to the mothers whom she knew were awake and doing what little they could to ease the terrifying spasms. *Oh, God, spare Naomi this!* Somewhere outside the circle a wolf howled. A dog tied to a wagon wheel bayed an angry, frustrated reply. The wolf howled in a different tone, mocking him. Now all the other dogs in camp joined in the contest of voices—growling, barking, yipping, baying.

"God damn you, shut up!" a man cried hoarsely.

A mule brayed. A horse whinnied near at hand and was answered, far off, by half a dozen of his kind. Ruth heard an ox low. No, she thought wearily, "low" certainly was not a properly descriptive word, for there was nothing low about this sound. Dark though it was, she could picture the beast throwing back its head until the cords along the underside of its neck stretched taut, filling its great lungs with air, opening its mouth, then forcing out a wailing blast of strained, anguished sound, while its eyes bulged half out of its head.

Children were waking on the Iowa side of the circle now. Whimpering, Naomi crawled into her arms and she held the child close, murmuring soothingly, "Hush, child, hush!"

She sensed that all the livestock were on their feet, moving restlessly about, and now and then over the din she could hear the guards shouting to one another. Several times the wagon rocked as animals brushed against it, and she recognized the wisdom of Matt's decision to leave gaps in the enclosure. If the beasts chose to run, no barrier would hold them.

The smell of the animals became suddenly rank and strong in her nostrils. She sensed that they were afraid. Of what? She did not know; but suddenly she was frightened, too. It was not simply her imagination working overtime, she knew; this was something as tangible as smoke, as threatening as humid, electricity-charged August air prior to the breaking of a violent thunderstorm.

Wood crashed. A man shouted a warning. Then there came a low rumble, as if the very earth itself were beginning to move. Somewhere a woman's shrill scream of terror split the night, followed by a man's frenzied yell, "Indians! Indians!"

And the stampede was on . . .

It was mid-morning, next day, before Benjamin climbed wearily into the wagon and told her that as far as anybody could make out there had been no logical reason for the stampede. No Indians had been seen anywhere near the camp, he said, nor had Matt, Andy, or Levi come across any Indian sign other than the month-old remains of a camp Matt had found in the hills to the north yesterday.

"The stock spooked—that's all we know. Nobody got hurt, thank God, and we've rounded up all the cattle and horses we're apt to find."

"Does Matt think they'll stampede again tonight?"

"Likely they will, he says. He says it might be a good idea if we tried to travel a few miles today. But Lynn won't turn a wheel unless you feel up to it." He eyed her apprehensively. "Do you?"

"Anything is better than this. Let's travel."

"Have you felt any more pains?"

"They come and go."

"Well, the minute you're sure it's really beginning, we'll stop."

"For Heaven's sake, Ben, will you quit fussing over me and tell Mr. Lynn to get the wagons started? The sooner we leave this awful place, the better we'll all feel."

Naomi was playing outside and wanted to stay there, but Ruth insisted that Benjamin lift her into the wagon where she would be out of the way while the men yoked up the oxen. The child had a strongly developed will of her own and fretted and squirmed as she tried to get away from her mother. Outside, the normally placid oxen and draft horses fought, kicked and pitched, and normally even-tempered men shouted and cursed as they tugged the yokes, chains, and harness into place. It took the combined efforts of all three Shelby men to yoke each pair of oxen and maneuver them into their positions at the front of the wagon, and Ruth, silently praying that no one would get hurt, knew that never again would she think of cattle as being phlegmatic animals.

As she wrestled wearily with Naomi, trying to divert the child's attention to her favorite doll, Ruth saw a procession of men and women walking slowly toward a lone pine tree on a knoll a short distance outside the wagon enclosure. Her throat swelled with pity as she noticed that two men were waiting there, heads bared, shovels in hand, and a mound of fresh dirt at their feet. She saw the procession stop. The distance was too great for her to recognize faces, but the stature and gestures of the man speaking at the graveside told her that he was Cornelius Belford, and the smallness of the blanket-wrapped figure presently lowered into the grave told her that the child being buried was very young. Presently she saw the people turn and walk away. As the two men with shovels started filling the grave, Benjamin came to the rear of the wagon.

"We're ready to roll, Ruth."

"Oh, Ben, look!" she murmured, her eyes still on the knoll. He did not turn his head, but his face was gray and haggard as he nodded. "I know. A baby died last night."

"Who was its mother?"

"One of the Missouri women. She—"

Without warning, the wagon lurched into motion. Caught off balance, Benjamin tumbled to the ground. Outside, she heard Grandpa Shelby yell. Naomi toppled toward the sideboards, Ruth barely managing to catch her by one arm in time to save her from falling through the canvas, the lower edge of which was not yet lashed down. The child screamed in fright.

Ruth knew from the terrific pace at which the wagon was lurching along that the oxen were running away uncontrolled and there was nothing she could do to stop them. Sooner or later, she realized, the clumsy vehicle would turn over, and she thrust Naomi flat on the mattress, awkwardly rolled over, and, with arms widespread and hands braced against the sideboards of the narrow wagon bed, covered the soft, small young body with her own.

Then she closed her eyes and fervently prayed.

In times of stress, odd thoughts pop into a person's mind. Waiting for the wagon to capsize, bracing herself for it, hearing the shouts of the men and the screams of the women outside as the wagon careened through the camping grounds, Ruth thought hysterically: *I never knew oxen could run so fast! If they keep up this gait, we'll get to Oregon in a week!*

Somewhere ahead, wood splintered. The wagon slowed perceptibly, though it still was moving at a dangerously rapid pace. She heard the tattoo of a horse's hoofs, then a dull thud, then another. And then, unbelievably, the wagon came to a halt. She rolled over on her side. Naomi, half smothered and extremely red in the face, gave her a look of violent indignation, opened her mouth to suck in all the air her lungs could hold, and kept it open as she put the air to use in a piercing squawl.

"There, there, child!" Ruth murmured, tears of laughter and relief streaming from her own eyes as freely as tears of anger and hurt coursed down Naomi's cheeks. "Hush, now, hush!"

A smiling, dark-eyed face appeared in the opening at the rear of the wagon as a mounted man paused there. Touching his hat brim politely, Will Starr said, "Are you all right, ma'am?"

"Oh, yes, I'm fine! Are you the one who—?"

"That's good," he said, and vanished.

She heard running footsteps outside, heard Will Starr speak briefly to Benjamin and Isaac, then Benjamin climbed into the wagon, his face white as chalk. His hands shook uncontrollably as he put his arms around Naomi and stared down at Ruth.

"Are you hurt? Are you all right?"

"Of course I'm all right!" she snapped peevishly. "I wish people would quit asking me that! All I want to know is, what happened?"

"The oxen ran away."

"I gathered that. But what stopped them?"

"The lead team broke its yoke and bolted. That slowed up the others. Then Will Starr rode alongside and knocked the second pair down."

She stared at her husband in amazement. "He *what*?"

"Just what I said. He knocked them fool oxen down."

"With his bare fist?"

Benjamin laughed. "No, with the barrel of his pistol. But he could've done it with his bare fist if he'd had to. Honest to God, Ruth, I never seen a man move so fast in all my life!"

"Well, I hope you thanked him."

"You can bet your sweet life I did! But he just laughed and passed it off like it was a thing anybody could do. He says it's easy to knock an ox down if you know where to hit him. He's showing Isaac how right now. And from now on, honey, Isaac is going to be walking on one side of that lead pair and I'm going to be walking on the other. We'll be carrying clubs and if either of us sees an ox take a deep breath and *look* like it wants to run, we'll knock its brains out."

There had been a time when such talk would have horrified Ruth, for she had always been fond of animals and felt that they should be treated gently. But now she just nodded and said with complete approval, "Good! I hope you do!"

Though none of the draft animals were as tractable as they formerly had been, the combined trains managed to travel a few miles before making the noontime halt. Usually this was a two-hour stop, with the oxen, mules, and horses being unharnessed and permitted to rest and graze. But when Matt said it would be best to leave the stock hitched up and cut the nooning to an hour, not a single voice was raised in dissent. The train pressed on five miles further during the afternoon, which took considerable starch out of the now tired stock. Shortly after camp was made, Isaac—who had a bad habit of speaking before he thought—stuck his head into the wagon and said to Benjamin, who was at Ruth's side, "Did you hear the news, Ben? Matt seen some Indians!"

Benjamin looked irritated, but there was no point in silencing his younger brother now.

"Where?"

"Near last night's camp. Matt and Henry Lynn rode back this afternoon to look for a strayed cow. They trailed her to our camp and ran smack into a couple of Indians. They looked like Shoshones, Matt said. They'd found the grave where the baby was buried and dug into it—"

"Oh, no!" Ruth exclaimed.

"Isaac, ain't you got a lick of sense?" Benjamin said angrily. "With Ruth in her condition—"

A shamed look reddened Isaac's face. "I'm sorry, Ben. I just didn't think."

"You never do."

"Don't scold him, Ben," Ruth said. "Finish your story, Isaac. What did Matt do?"

"Well, one of the Indians took a shot at him, then they both hopped on their horses and beat it. Matt was pretty mad, I guess. He said he'd have gone after them if Henry hadn't been along and he hadn't figured they had friends close by. He said he's going to leave some blankets used by them kids with whooping cough behind where the Indians will find them and he hopes they all take sick and die. He said he buried the baby again as decent as he could."

"I hope its mother doesn't know, poor soul."

"I ain't going to tell her, that's for sure."

Ruth had finished her supper and was lying watching the approach of evening when she heard a cheerful voice inquiring for her outside. A moment later the sky was blotted out as a bulky, smiling woman climbed laboriously into the wagon and said, "How are you, dear? Ain't you had that baby yet?"

Ruth's heart leaped with pleasure. "Beth Duncan! Am I ever glad to see you!"

"Thought you might be, honey. Just thought you might be." She chuckled. "You should have heard the fuss Daniel Lynn raised when I told him I was going to cross his silly old deadline whether he liked it or not."

Of all the women in the Missouri train, Elizabeth Duncan was the only one that Ruth really felt close to. She was in her early thirties, a plump, not at all pretty woman, blunt of speech and manner, and the most open, outgiving woman Ruth had ever known. It did not surprise Ruth in the least that she had crossed the line in defiance of Daniel Lynn's orders, for when she decided to do a thing she did it and no mere man was going to stop her. In fact, she seemed to hold all men in contempt, except for her husband, Phil, whom she loved wholeheartedly and never found fault with despite the fact that he was generally recognized to be lazy, weak, and much fonder of whisky and bragging talk than he was of work.

"Brought you a jar of wild plum jam, 'case your sweet tooth gits to achin'," she said with a smile. "Ben tells me your appetite ain't too perky."

"That was awfully nice of you."

Beth Duncan eyed her shrewdly. "I hear Doc Riley's a fool."

Ruth laughed. "How *do* these things get around?"

"People talk. And I've seen him. But don't you worry none, dear. I've borne three babies myself and helped more women bring theirs into the world than Doc Riley ever seen. When your time comes, I'll be handy."

"Beth, you don't know how good that makes me feel. I've been frightened half out of my mind."

"Fiddlesticks! You ain't scared, just a little nervous. That's only natural."

"How are your children?"

"Oh, they all come down with the whooping cough. They're still barking a blue streak, but they'll be all right."

"The baby caught it, too?"

"Sure. But he's fine now." Gently she patted Ruth's hand. "Get some rest, dear. I'll tell Ben all he needs to do is whistle and I'll come running. Between you and me, we'll teach that dumb sawbones a thing or two."

When Beth Duncan had gone, Isaac stuck his head into the wagon and said, "Does she know?"

"Know what?" Ruth said with a frown.

"About the Indians opening her baby's grave. Everybody's been trying to keep it from her."

Ruth closed her eyes and silently wept. *Dear Lord,* she prayed, *among a people who seem to have no secrets from one another, let this one small secret be kept from her. Strong as she is, this might be more than she could bear.*

The pains awakened Ruth at ten o'clock that night, and this time they were the real thing. Beth Duncan came and so did Dr. Riley; at five minutes past midnight by the doctor's gold-cased watch a husky, blue-eyed boy uttered his first gasping cry. It was a good omen, Ben said, that his first breath should be drawn on the Pacific side of the divide, for the air he would breathe for the rest of his life would be freer than any his parents had ever known. And if Dr. Riley's watch were right, the date of his birth must be recorded as the Fourth of July.

"I suppose people will insist we give him a patriotic name,"

Ben said with a smile. "How would it be if we called him Independence Day Continental Divide Shelby?"

"No," Ruth whispered, just before she fell asleep. "No, Ben. We'll simply call him David."

Chapter Nine

Out of consideration for Mrs. Shelby, the train remained in camp next day. Daniel Lynn would have preferred traveling. The oxen and horses were still hard to handle, there was solid evidence now that hostile Indians were nearby, the Missourians were becoming increasingly resentful of the quarantine imposed upon them, and idle time would be bound to breed trouble. But the Iowa womenfolk insisted that Mrs. Shelby was entitled to a day's rest—fractious livestock, skulking Indians, and sullen Missourians notwithstanding—and that settled that. Already the women were busy washing clothes, baking, and doing the other tasks which could not be accomplished while on the move.

"When a woman sets her mind to do a thing," Lynn complained to Matt, "how's a man to change it? She won't listen to reason. Facts don't impress her. She won't scare. What's a man to do?"

"Jest what you're doin'," Matt said. "Nothin'."

From the Missouri side of camp came the sound of rifles and pistols being fired into the air, followed by a great din of pounding on pots and pans, wild yells and whoops of laughter. Gazing across the enclosure, Lynn could see a crowd of men and boys milling around just beyond the parked wagons. He scowled.

"What's going on over there?"

"Reckon them ridge-runners are startin' their celebration."

"What celebration?"

"Ain't you heard? They're plannin' a big Fourth of July to-do to show what patriotic citizens they are."

"Patriotic?" Lynn said contemptuously. "That bunch of Democrats and Copperheads? They don't know the meaning of the word!" Listening to the racket, he said suspiciously, "Sounds to me like some of them are getting their snoots wet."

"Wouldn't be surprised. They bought a couple of barrels of whisky back at Platte Bridge, I hear tell."

"What happened to Belford's rule against drinking?"

"Reckon it'll git bent considerable today."

Lynn gave a snort of disgust. "Well, they'd better stay out of our hair."

As the morning wore on, the Missourians became increasingly

noisy and rowdy. Rifles and pistols crackled incessantly as men engaged in shooting matches. Wrestling bouts degenerated into rough and tumble fights. Men argued, hoorawed one another and played practical jokes. A pair of dogs were pitted against each other in a fight that drew a crowd of yelling, jostling, betting men, ending up in a quarrel between owners, who drew knives and carved each other up so badly Dr. Riley had to be sent for to come over and repair the damage.

Despite all the guards could do to stop them, a number of curiosity-filled Iowans wandered over to see what the excitement was all about and some of them stayed to partake of the whisky and fun. The Missourians decided that if the Iowans could cross the quarantine line, so could they, and did. By noon, the quarantine had broken down completely and both groups were mingling freely, their political differences forgotten, Iowan and Missourian strolling about arm in arm, laughing, chatting, and frequently pausing to add more liquid to the mortar of their newly cemented friendship.

Matt agreed with Lynn that there was nothing to be done. These were grown up men, and any attempt to use force would only make matters worse. "Let 'em git acquainted," Matt said dryly. "Maybe we'll all end up one big, happy family."

"God forbid!"

Immediately following the noon meal, Lynn observed a large group of Missourians gathered around a wagon, where one of their number was making a speech. It went on for some time, frequently interrupted by enthusiastic handclapping, whistles, and cheers of approval. Presently it broke up, and he saw half a dozen of the men, jovially drunk from the way they walked, crossing the enclosure in the direction of his own wagon. Henry, unhappy because his father had strictly forbidden him to go over to the Missouri side of camp, sat in the shade pretending to study. Ashamed of being caught even making a pretense of pursuing knowledge, he hastily closed the book and thrust it behind him, but Sally, washing dishes nearby, saw the move and scolded him sharply.

"Henry! Get back to work!"

"Aw, it's a holiday."

"Not for you it isn't."

Muttering resentfully, the boy retrieved the book and opened it on his knees.

Phil Duncan was leading the group. Grinning and snickering, the Missourians paused, and Duncan said, "We been a-talkin', Daniel. We been a-discussin' important matters."

"Oh?" Lynn said, eying him coldly.

"We have. An' we come to the conclusion we gotta organize."

"Organize what?"

"Ever'thin'!" Duncan said, waving a hand vaguely to include the entire camp. "Ever' goddam thin' there is!"

Phil Duncan had a receding chin, washed-out blue eyes that never quite focused on the person he was addressing and a weak-spined amiability that made him a favorite butt for practical jokes. No one took him anywhere near as seriously as he took himself and he possessed but one asset that Lynn was inclined to respect—his wife, Beth. She seemed to love the fool—God knew why! —but sorry as Lynn felt for her in her recent grief and grateful as he was to her for what she had done for Mrs. Shelby, there was a limit to what he would take off her clownish husband.

"Whatever you've got to say to me, Phil, say it without swearing."

Phil Duncan cast a sheepish sidelong glance at Sally. "I 'pologize. Truly, I do." He swayed back on his heels, peering at Lynn. "Point is, we've decided to have a general meetin' at two o'clock. Gonna hold an 'lection. Want all you Iowa people to come."

"Just what do you intend to elect?"

"Gonna 'lect a pres'dint an' a council an' two wagon cap'ns an' four loo'ten'ts, that's what. Gonna make a mess of rules how things'll be run from now on. Gonna organize ever'thin'. If you Iowa people want any say-so, you better be there."

"Now you listen to me, Phil Duncan. We threshed this out a month ago back at Laramie. I made it clear to Belford then how I felt, and I feel the same way now. We're not coming to your meeting. Furthermore, we won't pay the slightest attention to any rules you make. Is that clear?"

"You jus' better come," Duncan said sullenly.

"Well, we're *not* coming. And now you'd better go."

Drawing himself up in drunken dignity, Phil Duncan muttered, "We'll see, Daniel Lynn! We'll jus' see! C'mon, boys, we got a lot of 'lectioneerin' to do."

When they had gone, Lynn said to Matt, "What do you make of that?"

"Maybe they were jest funnin' him. Proddin' him into makin' a fool of himself."

"He doesn't need prodding to do that."

"Well, we'll know shortly," Matt said, jerking his head at another group of men heading their way. "Yonder comes Belford."

With the Missouri wagon captain, Lynn saw, were Armand

Kimball, Will Starr, and Andy Hale. Cornelius Belford looked worried.

"You talked to Phil Duncan."

"Yes. And we're not coming to his fool meeting."

"Mr. Lynn, I confess I don't approve of a lot of things that have happened today," Belford said. "But you must try to understand. My people are frightened. They're worried about their children, their stock, and the danger of Indian attack. They're used to doing things in a democratic way—"

"I'm a Republican, myself."

"Why bring politics into this? I was using the word in its broader sense."

"Has it got one?"

"Mr. Lynn, if you insist on being sarcastic, we'll get nowhere," Belford said testily. "I merely wished to point out that my people are used to talking things over in open meetings, putting them to a vote, then abiding by the decisions made by the majority."

"Then why don't they stay sober?"

"Why did your people cross the quarantine line?"

"They're human."

"Exactly! And so are mine." In a more patient tone, Belford said, "For safety's sake, we've agreed to travel together. My people feel we should have some sort of joint leadership. Can't you at least make a pretense of going along with that?"

"What do you mean 'pretense'?" Lynn asked suspiciously. Belford nodded to Armand Kimball. "It was your idea, Armand. You explain it to him."

Kimball smiled disarmingly. "It strikes me, Mr. Lynn, that the only serious point of disagreement between you and Mr. Belford is that you insist on running your train and he insists on running his. True?"

"Yes."

"Then let's leave it that way. But to satisfy the demand of our people for joint leadership, why couldn't we elect an overall council of twelve men and a president to oversee the combined trains? They would have only advisory powers, of course—"

"Then why bother?"

"Because that's what our people seem to want."

"In other words," Lynn said, "just because a loud-mouthed, drunken rabble howls at the moon, you say we should toss them a bone to chew on and keep them happy, whether it's got any meat on it or not?"

"That's one way of putting it. But I prefer to call it a practical compromise."

"Who would we run for president of the council?"

"For the sake of peace, I would stand for the office. And I assure you I would not interfere in any way with either you or Mr. Belford."

"He would be elected without opposition," Belford said. "I'm positive of that. Particularly if both you and I swung our influence behind him."

Lynn studied Armand Kimball thoughtfully. The man appeared to be sincere, and he felt a grudging admiration for Kimball's willingness to take on what was bound to be a thankless chore. He guessed that Kimball was diplomatic enough to maneuver Belford a bit, if it came to that. But he mistrusted sham of any kind, even under the name of practical compromise. He shook his head.

"Gentlemen, it won't wash. I'll have no part of it."

"Why not?" Belford demanded.

"Because I won't. That's reason enough."

"You're a stubborn man, Mr. Lynn. You can see only *your* side of things—like every other bull-headed Republican I've ever met."

"Well, now that *you've* brought politics into the argument," Lynn said heatedly, "let me tell you what kind of people you Democrats are. You're great ones for talk. You love to hold meetings, make speeches, and lay down high-sounding rules, but when it comes to behaving yourselves as individuals you do just as you please. If your people had stayed sober today, if you had come to me with a common-sense, open, and above board proposition, I might have listened—just as I was willing to listen back at Laramie. But you played Mr. High-and-Mighty then and you're playing the same game now. I'll have no part of it."

Belford's eyes smoldered. "Very well, Mr. Lynn. If that's going to be your attitude, I refuse to be responsible for anything that happens at the meeting. Good day."

Andy Hale, who had had nothing to say, lingered behind after Belford, Kimball, and Will Starr had gone. Sally called cheerfully, "I've made a pot of fresh coffee. Who wants a cup?"

Matt, Andy, and Daniel Lynn squatted silently on their heels by the fire while she poured. Andy glanced over at Henry and grinned.

"Good book?"

"Terrible."

"Not enough action to suit you?"

"It's a schoolbook. Arithmetic."

"I've got some paperback novels I'll lend you. Great yarns. A killing on every page and not a word of truth in 'em."

Handing Andy his coffee, Sally said disapprovingly, "Then why do you waste your time on them?"

"Happen to like 'em, that's all."

"You'll never develop your mind reading trash."

Andy gave her a puzzled look, as if that thought had never occurred to him. Henry said jeeringly, "Don't pay her no mind, Andy. She wants to be a schoolteacher. She's all the time lecturing people—"

"Pa, make Henry stop talking like that!" Sally exclaimed, coloring under Andy's smiling scrutiny.

"That'll be enough out of both of you," Lynn said impatiently. He eyed Andy. "What do you suppose those ridge-runners will do?"

"They've been drinking some."

"Drunks don't scare me."

"And talking considerable."

"Talk don't scare me, either."

"No, but the point is they're scared, mad, and drunk. That's a mighty potent mix, Mr. Lynn. They've got to work off their steam one way or another. The best thing for your people to do is not to cross them."

"There's a limit to what we'll take."

"Sure. But what's to be gained arguing or fighting with drunks? The shape some of them are in, even a little scuffle might turn into something nasty."

"You're suggesting," Lynn said, "that no matter what they do, we turn the other cheek?"

"For today, yeah."

Lynn looked at Matt, who nodded and grunted, "Makes sense, Daniel."

"All right," Lynn said reluctantly. "I'll pass the word around. But if they go too far . . ."

The meeting was held at two o'clock and great was the sound and fury thereof. Despite Lynn's advice that they stay on their own side of the circle, a number of curious Iowa men attended, and, because the whisky still flowed freely, the tales they brought back were an odd mixture of fact and fancy.

Four Iowans and eight Missourians had been elected to the ruling council, with Cornelius Belford to be its president. One of the new wagon lieutenants was an Iowan, the other three Missourians, among them Phil Duncan. It had been proposed that all the food, firearms, and livestock be pooled and redistributed so that each wagon would be equipped the same; that a committee be appointed to see to this; that any person disagreeing with anything the majority voted to do be brought to summary trial before the council, with the penalty for conviction to be at the least a cash fine, at the most expulsion from the train.

Nobody was sure which, if any, of these proposals actually had been brought to a vote, passed, rejected or been tabled, but the very fact that they had been discussed threw the Iowa side of the camp into turmoil. When the rumor spread that someone had overheard a group of Missouri hot-heads violently arguing the proposition that what they should do was arm themselves, march over to the Iowa side of camp and "show them damn black Republicans who's running things *now*," Lynn had all he could do to keep his people from preparing to meet force with force.

The entire camp was in bedlam. Disgusted with the behavior of their traveling companions, four families of sober Missounans hitched up their teams and crossed their wagons to the Iowa side of the circle. Two tipsy Iowa family heads decided that they would be happier with the Missourians, and, despite the anguished protests of their wives, crossed their wagons in the opposite direction.

Adam Schramm, a cantankerous old Iowa bachelor who did unpredictable things when he got a few drinks under his belt, harnessed his two teams of horses to his wagon, jumped aboard and drove recklessly through the camp, shouting, "To hell with everybody! Oregon, here I come!"

Nobody paid him any mind in the excitement; but he did cause quite a stir an hour or so later when he came running back into the enclosure afoot, wild-eyed and disheveled, crying, "Indians! Indians!"

Matt, Andy, and Levi rode out to investigate. When they returned with his wagon and three of his horses, Matt told Lynn, "Wa'n't no Injuns. Found his wagon tipped over, his rifle layin' on the ground an' one of his horses dead. Shot right behind the ear."

"Who shot it?"

"Schramm himself, I reckon. Guess the old fool mistook the critter fer an Injun."

Phil Duncan and one of his cronies, both very drunk, came over to the Iowa side of the enclosure and went from wagon to wagon with a bucket of red paint and a brush, painting a number on the side of each wagon cover. Officiously Duncan informed the Iowans that each wagon had been assigned a position in the line of march and must keep it, with the lead wagon one day dropping back to the rear the next. If he had been less tipsy, Lynn did not doubt that one of the Iowans would have carried out the grumbling threat to make Duncan eat paint, brush, bucket, and all, but, seeing the shape he was in and mindful of Lynn's warning, they let him be.

Catastrophe struck two hours before sunset when the last whisky barrel—still a quarter full—fell off the tailgate of a wagon and ruptured. There was heated talk, Lynn heard, of bringing the miserable wretch who had caused the disaster to immediate trial for conduct unbecoming a Missourian, a patriot, and a Democrat, but mercy—and the inescapable fact that drumming the rascal out of camp would allay nobody's thirst—prevailed.

As twilight approached, the camp began to quiet down. One of the Missouri families that had crossed to the Iowa side got into an argument with their new neighbors, hitched up and recrossed the enclosure in a huff. Both Iowa families returned to their own crowd, the wives red-eyed and grim from one cause, their husbands from another.

Lighting his after-supper pipe, Matt looked across the fire at Daniel Lynn and grinned. "Been quite a Fourth of July, ain't it?"

There was no humor left in Lynn. "Suppose they try to make their rules stick tomorrow?"

"We'll ignore 'em."

"And if they persist?"

"My notion is, there'll be some big heads an' sour bellies on their side of camp, come mornin'," Matt said calmly. "So let's git up real early . . ."

CHAPTER TEN

Dawn was only a faintly perceptible paling of the eastern sky when the Iowa side of camp began to stir. Moving from wagon to wagon to make sure no laggard overslept, Matt was grimly amused at the zest with which the men piled out and the haste with which the women threw breakfast together. Last evening, he'd known that these people would heartily welcome an opportunity to repay the Missourians for the indignities inflicted upon them, but never had he seen a party of emigrants get ready to take to the trail with so little lost motion.

The din was terrific. Mindful of the aching heads, queasy stomachs and raw-edged nerves among the drugged sleepers on the far side of the enclosure, the Iowans overlooked no possibility for making noise. Skillets clanged, kettles banged, children hollered, men and women shouted at one another—all with the greatest of cheerfulness, for the groans and curses heard from the waking Missouri wagons made it evident that the more early morning gaiety that could be stirred up on this side of camp, the more misery would be suffered on the other. No revenge could have been sweeter.

Sluggishly the Missourians came alive. Dogs barked, sick children cried and whooped, oxen, horses, and mules bellowed, whinnied, and brayed. As the light grew and the Missourians saw that already the Iowans were finishing breakfast, loading their wagons and hitching up their teams, panic seized them. Above all else, they feared being left behind. Phil Duncan, red-eyed and shaky, came running across the enclosure and vainly tried to catch the attention of first one and then another of the busy Iowans, pleading, "You got to wait for us, now—you got to wait for us!"

No one paid him the slightest heed.

Hastily the Missourians brought in their stock and started hitching up, willing to sacrifice breakfast rather than be deserted. But their draft animals were not inclined to be cooperative, and watching the struggles between beasts and men put the Iowans in the best of spirits. Helpfully they shouted bits of advice across the enclosure and were roundly cursed in reply.

"We're set to roll," Lynn said as Matt rode up.

The rising sun had barely cleared the gray line of horizon to the east. Matt grinned down at the wagon captain.

"Shall we line 'em out by the numbers?"

"No sir! Put Mrs. Shelby's wagon up front out of the dust."

"The rest can fall in behind wherever it pleases them to."

Whips popped, men shouted, wheels turned. Angry cries from the Missouri section of camp were answered by triumphant jeers from the moving wagons. Phil Duncan, who had been scurrying frenziedly back and forth across the enclosure, trotted alongside the line like a worried sheep dog, shouting vainly, "Fall back there, you! Now you move up! Make way there, you!"

The Iowans cheered him on.

"You tell 'em, Phil!"

"Hey, Phil, can you read my number this mornin'?"

"Ain't your wagon number six, Phil? How come it ain't up there where it's supposed to be?"

"Don't let the Injuns git you, Phil! There's a mess of 'em just over the ridge yonder waitin' to clean up on our leavin's!"

Utterly exhausted and frustrated, Phil Duncan fell behind and dragged himself back toward the camp of the Missourians, a few of whose wagons now were beginning to straggle after those of the Iowa party. It would be at least half an hour, Matt guessed, before the last of the Missourians would be ready to roll. By then, the lead wagons of the train would have traveled a mile or more and the party would be so strung out across the sagebrush plain that it would take it quite a while to corral in case of Indian attack. Gazing back along the widely spaced line, Daniel Lynn looked troubled.

"You sure it's safe, Matt?"

"Andy and Levi rode a wide circle yesterday afternoon."

There ain't an Injun in miles."

"What'll those ridge-runners do to Andy if they find out he connived with you on this?"

Matt grinned. "Hang him, I reckon. But they ain't goin' to find out, Daniel. Our agreement was we'd put all the blame on you. Anybody's neck stretches, it'll be your'n."

"I'll take my chances," Lynn grunted. "Do you think we ought to slow down and let them catch up?"

"Not fer a while. It won't hurt the stock to push 'em hard fer a spell. An' it'll do them ridge-runners a sight of good, I'm thinkin'."

Two days of hard traveling cured both the animals and the Missourians of a lot of bad habits, Matt noted. He heard no more talk about organization, rules, and order of march. When the train halted for its nooning and evening camps, Beth Duncan came over to see how Mrs. Shelby and the baby were getting along, Dr. Riley went among the wagons of the Missourians and did what he could for the sick children, and now and again Daniel Lynn, Cornelius Belford, and Armand Kimball discussed matters of mutual concern in a polite, restrained way. It was a loose sort of arrangement, but to Matt's practical mind it had one shining virtue—it worked.

As the train took to the trail the third morning, he walked his horse alongside Benjamin Shelby, who was keeping close watch on his oxen, and asked, "How's the wife today?"

"Feeling some better."

"Young 'un fat an' sassy?"

"He ain't regulated very good yet. Sleeps all day while the wagon's moving and stays awake all night when it's stopped."

"Wal," Matt chuckled, "so long as he ain't howlin'."

"Oh, he don't cry much except when he's hungry," Ben Shelby said. "But feeding him is a problem. My wife don't have enough milk for him. We can't give him cows' milk 'cause the cows that ain't gone dry are giving milk so bitter it ain't fit for an adult to drink, let alone a baby."

"Cows git that way west of Laramie. Too much alkali in the soil, I reckon. What are you feedin' the cub?"

"Beth Duncan is nursing him."

"*Phil's* wife?"

"Yeah. She's got milk a-plenty—and with her own baby dead . . ." Ben Shelby looked up at the old guide, a troubled, tormented light in his eyes. "Sure, I know what you're thinking. Beth Duncan laid her baby in its grave, dead from the whooping cough, and brought mine into the world only a day later and the same breast that fed one is feeding the other. But what else could we do, Matt? What else could we do?"

"God knows," Matt said gently, and meant exactly that.

In the confusion of circling the wagons preparatory to making camp in late afternoon, Matt heard the cry, "Indians! Indians!" Deserting their teams, Missourian and Iowan alike ran to their wagons, frantically calling for their womenfolk to hand out their guns. Well aware that whether the alarm proved real or false, first things must come first, Matt rode among them, shouting, "Mind your teams and make your corral! Make your corral! Make your corral!"

When the first wave of panic had subsided and the wagons had been formed into a reasonably tight circle, he turned his attention to the reported Indians and found that Levi, who customarily acted as an outrider, had the situation well in hand. The Delaware had intercepted a family of three bucks, two squaws, and a passel of button-eyed kids on the plain a few hundred yards from the camping grounds and was talking with the head of the household. Matt rode out and joined him.

"Bannocks," Levi said. "Got some dried salmon they want to trade for powder and lead."

Matt looked them over and found them a sorry lot, ragged, dirty, and poorly mounted. The grandfather had watery, festered eyes and wanted some white man's medicine to heal them. They had but two guns among them, one a thirty-year-old Hawken that looked like it had never been cleaned, the other a short-barreled, big-bored, ancient Hudson's Bay Company fusil made especially for the Indian trade and as likely to do as much damage to the person firing it as to its target. The squaws and one of the younger bucks wanted to come into the camp of the whites and trade, but Matt, making hand-talk, told them there was a bad disease in camp, that if they caught it their children would have coughing fits and die.

No matter, the young buck replied. The squaws and children would remain here. *He* was not a child nor was he afraid of the coughing fits. He had a charm which protected him against all disease. Even bullets could not kill him, he boasted, for he had been in the Bear River battle with General Connor last winter and had survived. Of course, *he* was a good Indian, he hastened to add, and a friend of the whites. He had a paper to prove it. Proudly he took a stained, greasy piece of paper out of his medicine bag and handed it to Matt.

"My eyes ain't much good fer close work," Matt said, passing the paper on to Levi. "What does it say?"

"'This is to certify that the bearer ain't no worse than he looks,'" Levi read. "'He ain't never been caught stealing nothing he couldn't carry, drive off, eat or ride, nor drinking anything he couldn't swallow. You can trust him just as far as you can trust any Indian.'" Levi paused. "It's signed: 'A. Lincoln, California Volunteers.' Then it says: 'P.S. If the bastard looks cross-eyed at you, shoot him. He fought us at Bear River.'"

Handing the paper back to the Indian, Matt said he was pleased to hear that he was such a good friend of the whites. The Bannock beamed and carefully put the paper away. His family had much dried salmon, he said, but they yearned for meat with red blood in it and lacked powder and lead with which to kill game. If only he were permitted to come into camp and trade . . .

A number of curiosity-filled Missouri and Iowa men had come out from the parked wagons. One of the Iowans, Cal Weaver, nudged Matt. "What's he sayin'?"

"He's got some dried salmon he wants to trade for powder an' lead."

"By golly, I've heard about salmon all my life and I've yet to taste it. Tell him I'll trade with him."

Cornelius Belford was eying the Indians dubiously. "Is it wise, Matt, to give these savages ammunition?"

"It's damn foolishness, I say!" Zeke Pence, a Missourian, declared. "Where's your brains, Weaver?"

"You just mind your own business."

"I figger this *is* my business."

"Well, I figure it ain't! All I want is a taste of salmon."

"Tell you what *I* think," another Missourian broke in. "*I* think we ought to give these damn Injuns all the ammunition they deserve—a charge of powder an' a ball of lead right between their eyes! The murderin' bastards—!"

"Simmer down, boys," Matt said wearily. "Trade if you want to, Cal. Clothes, trinkets, anything except ammunition. I'll tell 'em they ain't to come into camp and are to be gone from here by sundown—"

"I say we ought to kill 'em," Zeke Pence grumbled. "After the way they dug up Beth Duncan's baby—"

"Christ on a crutch!" Matt exploded. "That happened miles from here. An' the Injuns that done it weren't Bannocks, they was Shoshones!"

"What's the difference? An Injun's an Injun."

Matt gave a snort of disgust but did not trouble to answer. Grumbling, the Missourians went back to camp. After trading several pounds of dried salmon to Cal Weaver for an old shirt and a broken-pointed pocket knife, the Bannocks went on their way—also grumbling. And when Mrs. Weaver saw the blackened, filthy-looking chunks of fish her husband had wagged home and instructed her to boil for supper, Matt heard her do a sight of grumbling, too.

Next morning, Matt asked Cal Weaver, "How'd you like your first taste of salmon?"

"Terrible! My stomach grumbled all night!"

Wal, that was the way things went, Matt brooded. Some days, a man jest couldn't please nobody.

It was always a bad mistake, Matt knew, to tell greenhorns there was a choice of routes, because sure as God made green apples they wouldn't let their total ignorance of the country keep them from arguing over which was the best to take. He'd warned Andy about that and he knew that the younger guide had kept his lip buttoned. He'd talked it over with Lynn, too, and the Iowa wagon captain had said, "You're the guide, Matt. We'll do whatever you say."

"Wal, the cut-off's safe enough. Thing is, there's bound to be an argument if them ridge-runners find out there *is* another way, so let's keep it to ourselves."

But the word got out; how, Matt never learned. Maybe from gossip picked up from eastbound travelers met along the way, from soldiers, from trading-post talk. But in some manner, the Missourians *did* find out, and the fat was in the fire. The evening the train made camp on the Sandy, a delegation led by Cornelius Belford came over and questioned Matt about it.

Yes, he admitted, the trail did fork here. Trains bound for Salt Lake or California swung southwest and followed the Sandy till they hit Green River, crossed it, traveled on southwesterly for a piece till they struck Black's Fork, then stuck to that stream till they came to Fort Bridger.

"Used to be, trains bound for Oregon went thataway, too," Matt said, "but there's no sense in us doin' it. The stock's in good shape. We can take the cut-off."

"What do you mean 'cut-off'?"

Fort Bridger lay a considerable distance to the south, Matt explained, and all those miles had to be made back in a northerly direction to the Bear River Valley, while the cut-off route bore directly west from here. Belford frowned.

"If that's so, why did wagon trains *ever* go by way of Fort Bridger?"

"Wal, there's good grass and water on that trail. Takin' the cut-off, we'll cross a mite of dry country."

"Desert country?"

"Call it that."

"How much time does the cut-off save?"

"A week, more or less."

"But if it's desert country . . ."

Truth was, Matt had learned long ago, the word "desert" scared the pants off of Missourians. They were used to green, grass-covered, tree-covered hills, whose frequent rains made water no problem. Flat, open country made them feel ill at ease. Even on the high plains west of Fort Laramie, where creeks, rivers, and timbered bottom lands had always been in sight, they had felt edgy, naked, exposed. Now the thought of striking out across a seemingly endless wasteland, where for days on end a man would not see a tree or a live stream, where he knew there would not be a drop of water for himself or his animals save what he carried with him, filled them with dread.

"What's a week?" the Missourians argued. "Let's take the long way and play it safe."

The Iowans, plains-raised and used to open country, ridiculed their fears, taking a perverse delight in favoring the cut-off route simply because the Missourians opposed it. Lynn said bluntly, "No use arguing, Cornelius—we're taking the cut-off."

"What if a wagon breaks down?"

"Why, we'll fix it if it's fixable—just as we would anywhere else. If it's not, we'll switch its load to another."

"What if the stock can't stand it?"

"They can."

"What if we have an accident and lose some of our water?"

"We'll go thirsty. But we'll get through."

"I think it should be put to a vote. After all, our lives and property are at stake."

"So far as I'm concerned, Matt's word is enough for me," Lynn said testily. "He says the cut-off is safe. We're taking it. Your people can do as they please."

When the Iowa wagons set out, next morning, the Missourians followed, expecting the worst. They were not completely disappointed. Three oxen and two horses died. One of the Missouri wagons broke down and had to be left behind. Several of the water barrels sprang leaks in the hot, dry wind and blistering sun, and, during the last half day of travel, animals and humans alike suffered intensely from thirst. But the crossing was made; the week was saved.

For a couple of days after the train struck the well-watered valley of the Bear River, Matt let it ease along, giving the stock time to regain their lost flesh and strength on the fine bottom land grass. This had always been one of his favorite spots in the West, he told Lynn as the wagons followed the windings of the river in a general northwesterly direction, and he'd long wondered why it hadn't been settled by land-hungry emigrants from the East.

"What would a man do here?" Lynn asked.

"Farm, raise cattle, build towns."

Studying the valley with his shrewd dirt-farmer eyes, Lynn shook his head. "It doesn't appeal to me."

"What's wrong with it?"

"The soil's off-color."

"Off-color from what—Iowa soil?"

"I doubt you could grow corn here with the nights so cool."

"How can you tell till you try?"

"It's too dry. Just look how deep the dust lies in the trail ruts. Why, I'll bet it hasn't rained here this summer."

"There's lots of water in the river. A man could irrigate like the Mormons do down at Salt Lake."

"It takes rain and black soil to raise corn," Lynn said with a tolerant smile. "Any farmer knows that. Back in Iowa—"

"Damn it to hell, that's jest my point!" Matt said in sudden exasperation. "What're you pilgrims headin' West *fer,* anyways, if it ain't to find a new an' different country? This ain't Iowa an' it ain't Missoury—it's Idaho Territory. And any man that tries to do things out here the same way he done 'em back home is bound to fail. He's got to learn new ways."

"Well, I'm not too old to learn new ways," Lynn said good-humoredly. "But I certainly don't want to settle in the middle of nowhere. This country is too far from civilization to suit me."

"It ain't as far as it once was," Matt muttered vaguely. "Not near."

Chapter Eleven

Bear River swung south presently and the train climbed out of its fertile valley and traveled for several days across a plain strewn with the cinder-black rubble of an old lava flow. One evening shortly after the wagons had made their circle, a ragged, dark-complexioned stranger rode into the Missouri side of camp. Zeke Pence, mistaking him for a half-breed with mischief in mind, stopped him at rifle point.

"Where in the hell d'ye think you're goin'?"

The stranger pushed back his gray slouch hat and grinned down at him. "Why, I hear tell you folks are from Missoury. Happen to hail from there myself, so I thought I'd stop by and say howdy."

"You live out here?"

"Sure do. Run a ferry and tradin' post on Snake River a ways west of Fort Hall."

"Where you bound now?"

"Salt Lake City."

"You a dirty Mormon?"

The stranger laughed heartily. "No sir! I'm a washed and scrubbed Baptist—leastways, I used to be. What's more, I'm a Democrat, a Yankee-hater and a ridge-runner born and bred."

Zeke Pence lowered his rifle. "What part of Missoury do you hail from?"

"Taney County."

"The hell you say! Why, I come from Taney County myself!" Zeke studied the stranger with a more friendly interest.

"What might your name be?"

"Lafe Perrin"

Zeke introduced himself and shook hands as Lafe Perrin dismounted. "You wouldn't be related to old Frank Perrin, the miller, by any chance?"

"We'd be second cousins, I reckon. You know old Frank?"

"Well, I just guess I do!" Zeke said with a broad grin. "I done married one of his daughters."

Lafe Perrin took supper with Zeke and his family. Soon it was all over camp how close Zeke had come to shooting one of his wife's relations—which would have been a prime joke on her, everyone agreed. Knowing Lafe to be a garrulous, boastful man and wanting neither to cramp his style nor hear more of his bragging, Andy Hale stayed clear of the circle of curious Missourians that congregated around him that evening, asking him questions about Salt Lake City, Idaho Territory, and why he had settled where he had. But he knew that Lafe's stories had given them considerable food for thought, because for days afterward first one and then another of the Missourians came to him seeking confirmation of marvels Lafe Perrin had told them.

Yes, Andy said, it was true that the Latter-day Saints called all non-Mormons "Gentiles." No, he hadn't heard Lafe's story about how old Brigham Young had undertaken to run all the "Gentile" merchants out of Salt Lake City and how the first three businessmen to be given the boot had been named Cohen, Goldstein, and Liebowitz. Yes, the Snake Indians had massacred thirty emigrants out in western Idaho three summers ago, but that tragedy had happened south of the river and the Missourians and Iowans would be taking the northerly branch of the trail, which meant crossing the Snake twice but was shorter and safer.

Lafe had boastfully passed around a buckskin sack of gold dust, Andy knew, and had bragged about a big new strike recently made in the Boise Basin diggings of southwestern Idaho Territory, which he said was "bound to beat Californy and Nevada all hollow." The Missourians had been impressed. Even Armand Kimball shared the general excitement.

"Lafe says there are twenty thousand prospectors in the Boise district now and the mines are producing a million dollars' worth of gold a month. Do you believe that, Andy?"

"He's a talker. But it's a big strike, I've heard."

Cornelius Belford's interest in the newly created Territory of Idaho had been stimulated, too, though in a different way. "He says Governor Wallace is a Republican, and so are the federal judges and the secretary. But Idaho hasn't elected a legislature and a delegate to Congress yet. There are a lot of Democrats and Southern sympathizers in Idaho, he says, and his guess is the Democrats will make a clean sweep of the elective offices this fall. Do you think he's right, Andy?"

"I couldn't say. The boom was just starting when I came through that country last fall."

"How long will it take us to reach the Boise district?"

"Three or four weeks."

"I'm mighty curious to see it."

"Thinking of turning prospector?"

"Heavens, no! But from what I've heard, Oregon is full of Yankees. If Idaho's really booming and filling up with *our* kind of people . . ."

During his ten years in the West, Lafe Perrin had tried his hand at mining, farming, running pack-strings and keeping store in many places; when asked, he'd been only too glad to give the Missourians his opinion of each region.

"Californy? Well, I don't reckon you folks would like it down there. Good land's all taken, gold's mostly gone and a white man can't earn a decent wage—not with the country full of Chinks that'll work twelve hours a day for a handful of rice."

"What about western Oregon?"

"Why, it used to be they was some fine farm land out there. But the best of it's been claimed. 'Course, they's lots of timber land left but clearin' off them big trees is a chore, believe me. And it rains there nine months out of the year."

"What about Washington Territory?"

"Well, west of the Cascades it's too damned wet, east it's too damned dry, and both sides of the mountains they's too many Union-lovers to suit me. But here in Idaho, now . . ."

Here in Idaho, now, there was gold, water, unclaimed land, and the kind of people a ridge-runner could get along with. Here the winters were short and relatively mild. Sure, Idaho was a long way from any-wheres, he admitted, but its isolation was an advantage rather than a drawback. Miners had to eat; food supplies were scarce and dear. All the gold strikes so far had been made in mountainous country where the nights were too cold and the soil too poor to raise much in the way of garden truck, but down in the low country along the valleys of the Payette, Boise, and Snake rivers there was lots of good soil for farming, endless supplies of irrigation water and wild bunchgrass a-plenty on the benches for milk cows, beef cattle, or sheep.

"Why, if I didn't already have all the business I could handle with my ferry and trading post," Lafe declared enthusiastically, "damned if I wouldn't turn to farming or ranching out in the Boise country myself!"

The Missourians listened with the reserved skepticism which was second nature to them—but they listened, Andy noticed. In past years, the emigrants he had guided west had always regarded the country lying between the Continental Divide and the foot of the Blue Mountains of eastern Oregon as a desert to be crossed as quickly as possible, a bleak, endless stretch of nothingness whose heat, dust, and wind must be endured while the slow miles reeled out behind and travel-wearied minds yearned for the distant green land of western Oregon. But since Lafe Perrin's visit, he noticed that people were looking around them with a certain cautious curiosity. They were not favorably impressed with what they saw. But they were looking. And, like Armand Kimball and Cornelius Belford, they were wondering . . .

Andy was beginning to do some wondering himself. Camped in the valley of the Portneuf the evening before the train reached Fort Hall, he said to Levi, who was hunkered on his heels nearby, "Be about the third week in September when we hit the Willamette Valley, wouldn't you say?"

"If the weather holds."

"Then what'll we do?"

Levi drew designs in the dust with a stick. "Maybe I'll go back to Kansas. I been thinkin' about it."

"For good?"

"My people are there. I been thinkin' maybe I'd find me a woman and settle down on a little farm."

Levi had been married once, Andy knew, but his wife was long dead and they had had no children. Somehow he could not picture the Delaware turning dirt-farmer and putting down roots in a country as settled as Kansas.

"I got a better idea."

"What?"

Before Andy could elaborate, Melinda Belford and Will Starr approached through the growing dusk. Both seemed greatly excited.

"We want your advice," Melinda said.

"Well, I can spare you about a nickel's worth," Andy said with a smile. "What's the question?"

"Do you think Lafe Perrin is a truthful man?"

"Not very."

"That's what Pa says. Pa says Lafe likes to impress people. But he was awfully nice to me."

"Oh?"

Melinda unknotted the small white handkerchief she was carrying, took a pea-sized object out of its folds and placed it in Andy's hand. "Lafe gave me this. He said it was gold." She looked at him anxiously. "Is it?"

Andy held the piece of metal closer to the firelight, examined it, hefted it, tested its surface with a thumbnail. Nodding, he gave it back to her. "Seems to be. Worth twenty or thirty dollars, I'd say. Why did he give it to you?"

"Oh, just for luck, he said, and because I was from Missouri, like he was—"

"And because you're the prettiest girl he's seen in a coon's age?"

"Wherever did you hear that?" Melinda demanded, trying to look angry but not succeeding.

"People talk. Talk has it Lafe also drew you a map showing the gulch where he found it."

"He did! Oh, yes, he did!" Melinda flushed and lowered her head. "I know it's silly, Andy. Pa says the map is worthless. So does Mr. Kimball. But Lafe *did* have a sack of gold dust, didn't he? Where did he get it?"

"Trading with miners, likely."

"Where did *they* get it? What I mean is, *they* had to find it someplace and if they could find it . . . Anyhow, Will and I have been talking—"

"I know," Andy said sympathetically. "Well, let's have a look at your map."

Stirring up the fire, he put a couple of sticks of wood on it, took the map from her and squatted near the flickering light as the flames rose. Melinda knelt at his left elbow, a hand on his shoulder, her breasts rising and falling rapidly. Will Starr was on his heels at his right elbow, his face intent, his dark eyes fevered.

The story Lafe had told her, Melinda said, was that two years ago he and a friend had been traveling through the foothills of the Owyhee Mountains in the southwestern corner of what was now Idaho Territory when they camped one night in a certain gulch. Having seen signs of hostile Indians in the vicinity that day, they built no fire, and with dawn's first light they hastily rode on, but before doing so he had washed out one pan of gravel in the waters of the creek. And the nugget he'd given her had shown up.

"Lafe said he's sure there's lots more gold in the gulch," Melinda murmured, her fingers unconsciously tightening on Andy's shoulder. "He meant to go back some day but never did."

"Can you make anything of it, Andy?" Will Starr asked eagerly.

"Well, he's got his rivers and mountains in the right places. Likely there's a creek and a gulch somewhere near where he shows them to be. But that doesn't mean the gold is there."

"Could it be there?"

"It's possible."

"How possible?" Melinda persisted.

Andy started to answer her foolishly illogical question with a facetious remark, then, meeting her imploring gaze, he realized how deadly serious she was. She'd been poor all her life; so had Will Starr. To them, this was no joking matter.

"Well, it's the right kind of country for gold, if that's any help to you. So far as I know, none has ever been found there. All the strikes so far have been made in the Boise Basin, which is quite a ways to the north in another range of mountains. Still, the gold may be there, like Lafe says."

"If a man was to look for that gulch," Will Starr said doggedly, "how would he go at it? Where would he leave the train? What kind of equipment would he need and how long would it take him?"

"You considering it?"

"Why not?"

"That's bad Indian country down there."

Will Starr scowled across the fire at Levi, who was staring impassively at the ground. "Indians don't scare me."

"The chances would be a thousand to one against your making a strike."

"That's one chance more than I ever had before. Just tell me what to do."

The sensible way to go at it, Andy said, would be to wait until the wagon train struck the settlements along the lower Boise River in the far western part of Idaho Territory, outfit there, pack a few weeks' supplies on an extra horse, head south and west until striking the landmarks shown on Lafe's map, then follow them to the indicated creek and gulch. It would be best not to attempt the venture alone. To be safe from Indian attack, a man ought to have at least twenty well-armed men with him, and it would be a good idea if two or three of them were familiar with the country.

"No," Starr said, stubbornly shaking his head. "If I go, I'll go alone." He got to his feet. "Come on, Mellie, let's go talk to Mr. Kimball."

As the slim young woman and the huge young man walked away, talking excitedly, Levi eyed Will Starr sardonically. With a vehemence that surprised Andy, the Delaware grunted, "Damn fool!"

"Gold does that to a man."

"He's a fool over more things than gold."

Andy frowned. For some reason, invisible sparks of antagonism always flew between the two men, which puzzled him, for neither was a trouble-maker.

"What have you got against Will?"

Levi's eyes were veiled. "It's a sleeping dog. Let it lie." He was silent a while, poking idly at the fire, then he looked up and said, "You were talking about what we'd do after we got to the Willamette."

"If twenty thousand miners are going to winter in the Boise country," Andy mused aloud, "they'll have to eat. Last fall, cattle were dirt cheap in the Willamette Valley. I'll have five hundred dollars in wages coming when this job is done. Suppose I buy fifty steers in western Oregon and we drive them back to Idaho and sell them for a hundred dollars apiece. Now we've got five thousand dollars—"

"That's a big 'suppose.'"

"Wait, there's more. Now it's the middle of November, we're in Idaho and ain't got a thing to do. So we find ourselves a piece of grassland down in the low country, file on it, build a cabin, barn, and corral. When spring comes, we go back to the Willamette and buy more cattle—this time half the bunch she-stuff, with a few bulls—drive 'em back to Idaho, stock our ranch, and we're in business."

"Sounds all right."

"Sounds, hell—it *is* all right!"

"Gonna take us six weeks to drive them fifty steers east from the Willamette. Supposin' a big snow catches us up in the Blues?"

"Last fall we could have made it easy. There wasn't snow enough to cover the ground till the first of December."

"And two years ago half the cattle east of the Cascades froze to death."

Andy shrugged. "It's a gamble, sure. But all we're risking is five hundred dollars."

"So we're broke again," Levi said, his eyes twinkling. "Well, easy come, easy go."

"Damn it, Levi, be serious for a minute, will you? You know as well as I do this guiding business has played itself out. You don't like town life or farming and neither do I. Why not try our hand at ranching?"

A brooding look came into Levi's eyes. "Because it's your money, not mine. They'll be your cattle, not mine. It'll be your ranch—"

"We'll go partners."

"You don't want a dirty, ignorant Indian for a partner, Andy."

"No. I want you."

"How're your white neighbors gonna take to me? How's your wife gonna like me?"

"Whoa, now! I've got neither."

"You will have, once you settle down. They'll have no use for me." As Andy started to protest, Levi moved his hand in a sharp gesture, silencing him. "Sure, you're gonna say you and me have always got along fine. You can't see no reason why it can't go on that way. But I can. You're white. I'm not. That's all there is to say."

In Andy's opinion, there was a great deal more to say, but the bitterness in the Delaware's voice made him realize that now was not the time to say it. He shrugged. "Well, forget it. It was just a cockeyed notion I had. Come the end of this trip, we'll head back to Kansas and winter there. Next spring, maybe we can pick up another train—"

"Whoa, boy! You want to try ranching? Good—you try it. You want me to help you get started? Good—I will."

"But you just said—"

"I said we wouldn't go partners. But I'll stay with you till next spring." A ghost of a smile touched the Delaware's face. "Hell, Andy, a man can go back to Kansas any time."

Chapter Twelve

The morning after the train reached Fort Hall, where a two-day stop was planned for a general overhauling of the wagons, Melinda Belford helped her mother wash the breakfast dishes, air the bedding, scrub and hang out the clothes, and then was free to wander about and see what there was to see. That did not take long, for the post had been manned only intermittently the past few years, there was no civilian settlement outside its neglected, flood-damaged walls, and no Indian village other than half a dozen shabby Bannock tepees pitched in the scant shade of the willows along the course of the Portneuf.

A fine, powdery, yellowish-gray dust rose from underfoot as she walked; beyond the fort's ruins, bleak, summer-yellowed hills stood stark and ugly under the merciless late July sun. Idaho, she decided, was the most unpleasant, most inhospitable-looking country she had ever seen, and she found herself suddenly so homesick for Missouri's green, timbered hills that she felt like crying. Andy said it never rained during July and August out here. Who would want to live in such a dry, dusty country? And she had heard Andy say that ahead lay the Snake River desert, which he implied was much worse country (if that were possible!) than what they had seen of Idaho so far.

But beyond the desert's western edge rose the mountains where gold was to be found . . .

She fingered the nugget in the knotted handkerchief in the pocket of her gingham dress, as she had done countless times since Lafe Perrin had given it to her. Andy said it was worth from twenty to thirty dollars. She found that difficult to believe. Why, back home, skilled carpenters like her father were paid only two dollars a day; he would have had to work hard for two weeks to earn that nugget—a thought that intrigued her and brought strange fancies into her head.

"Pa," she could hear herself saying archly, "now that Will and I are rich, we've decided to build a big house. Bring your tools next Monday . . ."

It had been odd, she mused, that her father had made no objection to Lafe's giving her the nugget. Back home, if a strange man had tried to make her a present of that much money simply because he thought her the prettiest girl he'd seen in a coon's age, her father's reaction would have been immediate and violent. He would have considered it the worst kind of insult. And she herself would have been horrified. Why, for that much money a bad city girl who painted her face and made her living off men would be expected to . . .

Well, she wasn't sure just *what* a bad city girl would be expected to do for that much money, but certainly it would be a great deal more than smile and look pretty. Yet her father had not minded. He had merely been amused. And at first so had she, for it simply had not occurred to her that a man like Lafe Perrin would bestow a gift of any worth upon a pretty girl so casually.

She had been taught certain values. She had been taught to believe in God, in Virtue, in Heaven, in Hell, and in the Democratic Party. Her father had never bothered to teach her to believe in the value of gold, for it had not been a plentiful commodity in his household, and she had a suspicion now that despite all Lafe's talk, despite the evidence seen by his own eyes, he *still* doubted that there were mountains beyond the desert where even an ordinary man like—well, like Will Starr—could find gold and become rich.

But she was beginning to believe . . .

Her walk had taken her to a knoll overlooking the green, swift-flowing waters of the Snake, and as she paused to gaze at the river whose very name had long filled her with dread because of the tales she had heard about it, she suddenly noticed a strange man seated on a folding canvas stool a short distance away. A large red umbrella, whose long handle was thrust into the ground, shaded him from the sun; his back was to her and he was staring off into the distance in an odd manner, totally absorbed in whatever it was he was looking at, which—so far as she could see—was nothing but the slope leading down to the river, the river itself and the yellow hills beyond. She saw him lean forward suddenly toward a short-legged tripod before him, upon which rested an oblong object, and go to work with what looked to be a slender stick.

Curiosity impelled her toward him. He was tall and slim, she noted; he wore black riding boots, fawn-colored breeches that were well cut and expensive looking, a light brown shirt whose cuffs were turned up over his forearms, a blue silk scarf and a flat-crowned, broad-brimmed, pearl-gray hat, cocked at an angle, under which showed long, curly yellow hair. As one of her shoe soles scraped on a rock outcropping, he abruptly leaped to his feet, whirled around and stared at her.

"Where in the devil did you drop from?"

His angry outburst startled her. She felt her face turn crimson. "I—I'm sorry. I didn't mean to bother you."

"Don't you know any better than to sneak up behind a man without warning?" he snapped. "Only a stupid Indian would do that!"

"Well, I'm not an Indian and I wasn't sneaking," she said indignantly. "I was just walking like I always do. But never you mind. I won't pester you."

She turned away.

"No, wait!" he said.

She stopped. Pushing his hat to the back of his head, he smiled and came toward her. His eyes were gray, she saw, his face fine-boned and aristocratic looking, and, now that he was smiling, he struck her as very handsome. "Please accept my apologies. It was just that you surprised me."

"I didn't mean to."

"I know you didn't, my dear. The fault is all mine. I'm edgy when I'm working."

She frowned. "Working? At what?"

"Come here and I'll show you."

Taking her by the hand, he led her to the tripod. She found herself staring at a square of canvas upon which was painted the figure of an Indian, a horse, a greenish-blue streak that she took to be water and a series of vague, faint lines in the background whose meaning she could not begin to make out. She looked at him with amazement.

"Why, it's a painting, isn't it?"

"Yes, I'm an artist. Permit me to introduce myself. I'm James Randolph Warren—from Virginia, if that matters to you."

"I'm Melinda Belford."

He took off his hat, bowed and brushed the back of her hand with his lips. "Miss Belford, I'm enchanted to meet you."

No man had ever kissed her hand before, though she had read of such gallantries in books, and she was not at all sure what her proper response should be. He expected something from her, that was clear, for his smiling gray eyes were questioning as they studied her face. She stammered feebly, "I'm with the wagon train. We're from Missouri—that is, some of us are."

"Indeed?"

"Pa—that is, my father—is president."

"You don't say! Whatever became of that black Republican, Abe Lincoln?"

He was teasing her, she knew, but she felt more foolish than angry. "Of the wagon train council, I mean. You see, we had an election—"

"If you campaigned for him, Miss Belford," James Warren said, his manner suddenly quite sincere, "I'm sure he got every male vote in camp. Do you mind my saying that you're the most beautiful woman I've seen since I left Virginia? And I've been gone from there a long while."

Melinda dropped her eyes to the ground in confusion. "Mr. Warren, please . . ."

He laughed gaily. "I'm sorry if I embarrassed you, Miss Belford, but I'm in the habit of saying exactly what I think the instant I think it. A habit which gets me into all kinds of trouble, incidentally. Tell me, what do you think of my painting?"

Grateful to turn the conversation to less personal ground, Melinda studied the painting for a few moments before answering. Now that she could give it her full attention, her first reaction was one of shock. It was not merely a painting of a mounted Indian swimming a river; it was a graphic representation of a man and an animal caught in the act of dying. She could see the mortal terror in the horse's eyes as the weight on its back and the swirling force of the current pulled it down, its muzzle high, its mouth open, its lungs bursting for one last breath. She could see the Indian attempting to quit the horse's back, a dumb, savage desperation in his face as he sought and failed to find needed strength. His dark-skinned, naked back, she noted with sudden horror, was covered with blood, welling as from a fountain out of a spot up near the nape of his neck. In the next instant of time, she sensed, the horse would drown and a glaze of death would fill the Indian's eyes, then they would disappear beneath the surface of the water and be seen no more.

She shuddered and turned her gaze away. James Randolph Warren was smiling down at her.

"Well? "

"It—I just don't know what to say."

"Say exactly what you think."

"I don't think anything. But it makes me feel—"

"Even better! What does it make you feel?"

"A little sick. Like I'd just watched a man and a horse die horrible deaths."

James Warren's eyes sparkled with pleasure. "Wonderful! That's exactly the reaction you should have."

Melinda stared at him in amazement. "It is? But I always thought a painting should be—well, pretty."

"A common attitude, Miss Belford. But I am not a member of the pretty-painting school. I paint only what I see."

"You saw *that?*"

"Yes. That little incident happened a couple of weeks ago, as a matter of fact, when a Bannock Indian got drunk, stole a horse and attempted to swim the Snake River with it. One of the soldiers shot him as he took to the water and he and the horse disappeared from sight in the whirlpool yonder. You see the spot quite clearly from here." He pointed it out to her. "By a stroke of sheer luck, I was fortunate enough to witness the affair and I've been working ever since to get it down on canvas. When I've filled in the hill background and touched up a few details, it will be finished."

"What will you do with it then?"

"Add it to my collection, which I intend to exhibit in the East some day. I have some thirty major oils and water colors done, plus a whole trunkful of pencil sketches."

"Are they all like this one?"

"As brutal as this one, you mean? No. But they're not pretty, my dear. They're real—just as real as I can make them. Would you like to see them?"

"Well, we'll be here only a day or two," Melinda said hesitantly. "But if I have the time—"

"I'll insist that you make the time." He smiled. "Would you mind if I came to your camp this afternoon? I want to meet your father."

Melinda stared at him curiously. "Why?"

"You said he was in charge of the train. I'd like his permission to sketch some camp scenes. Do you think he'd object?"

"I don't know why he should."

"Good! Then I'll see you this afternoon."

Melinda did not quite know what to make of James Randolph Warren. Neither did her father. The artist spent the afternoon and evening in the emigrant camp, sketching in pencil, and, next morning, told Melinda's father that he would like to travel with the train as far as the Boise River.

"I'm fed up with soldiers and Indians," he said, "and I need a change of scene. I want to see what emigrant life is like. I want to live for a while in a gold-mining camp. If you'll let me travel with you, I'll be happy to pay my way. Would fifty dollars be satisfactory?"

Melinda's father said that it would be. When he tried, James Warren could be the most charming of men, Melinda learned, and she knew that he had made a favorable impression upon her father. Obviously he was a man of means. He let it be known that he was a Southern sympathizer and a Democrat. He owned a light wagon and six good draft horses, which he hired one of the Missourians to handle for him, while he himself rode one or the other of his two gaited saddle horses. He told Melinda's father that he had been knocking around the West for three years and planned to stay in the country until he'd seen all there was to see and caught it on canvas.

"When the war is over," he said, "I hope to exhibit my gallery in Philadelphia and New York. It's to be called *The Real West*. Perhaps it's immodest of me to say so, Mr. Belford, but it will be like no gallery ever seen by Easterners before."

At first the people of the train regarded James Warren with a suspicious reserve, resenting the free and easy way he prowled among them, sketching whatever struck his fancy, but as the wagons moved westward into the desert flanking the Snake they gradually got used to him, coming to regard him as a mild, harmless sort of lunatic. In many ways he was the most impractical of men. He never seemed to know or care where his wagon was, leaving its handling entirely up to the young man he had hired to drive it. He would ride miles ahead or linger miles behind the train, alone, totally indifferent to possible danger from Indians, setting up his umbrella, camp stool and tripod, and working for hours to record some feature of landscape that intrigued him. Though his wagon was stocked with an ample supply of food staples, he never thought of cooking a meal, cheerfully accepting the invitation to "have a bite" with whatever family he happened to be near when mealtime came, and then generously repaying their hospitality with gifts of food from his own supplies. More often than not as the days passed, it was the Belford family with which he took his meals.

He liked to talk about his work, Melinda discovered, and because he required of his listener no knowledge of art, but merely a sympathetic ear, she found him frequently talking to her. He would say, "It's high time some first-rate artist painted the West as it really is. It's never been done, you know."

"Hasn't it?"

"Look at the trash that's been reproduced in books and popular magazines. Why, it's atrocious, all of it! Either the artist's draughtsmanship is so stiff and artificial it can only be laughed at or the subject material is impossibly romanticized after the style of the old Italian masters. No artist yet has told the truth about the West. I intend to."

"How?"

It was a matter of light, he would say. And a matter of feeling. There was no softness in this western land—in light, in nature, or in man. The sun did not shine benignly down from a soft blue sky upon a soft green earth as it did in the Eastern states in summertime. Here the air was thin and light, with no moisture in it to filter out the harshness of the sun's rays; here the dry summer turned the grass yellow, reflecting the sunlight upward so piercingly that it hurt a person's eyes almost as much to look down at the earth as it did to gaze up at the sky.

He called her attention to what the light did to mountain ranges, making them draw deceptively close or recede into the heat-hazed distance when seen at different times of day under different angles of sunlight. Even when it was shining on water, sunlight could be blinding, he pointed out, proof of which was the fact that all the Snake River Indians who lived by fishing were afflicted with eye ailments caused by long hours of staring down at the mirrorlike surface of the water. And hadn't she noticed the flaming colors in the western sky at sunset?

"Violence is the artistic key to the West," he said. "And brutality. Take a close look at a clump of sagebrush. Does it grow straight and smooth, like a stalk of Missouri corn? Of course not! It's twisted and gnarled, as if every inch of growth it makes were fought for and suffered for against drought, wind, torturing heat and bitter cold. Even the rocks themselves show that the country was made in a time of violence. What can men who live in such a country be but violent and brutal?"

He expected no answers to his questions, even if she had been inclined to attempt answers, for already he had them worked out in his own mind. She had never known a man so self-assured. When he sketched a group of emigrants at some camp chore and then showed the sketch to her, he was not seeking her approval, but simply gauging the emotional effect the drawing had upon her. It did her no good to say, "But they don't look like *that* to me," for he would laugh and answer he had not been using her eyes, but his own, and *that* was the way they had looked to him.

"The whole point is, how do you feel when you look at the sketch?"

"Tired."

"Why?"

"Because the people you've drawn *look* tired. But they're not always like that. I think it's very unfair of you to show them looking their worst—"

"Ah, but, my dear, I don't sketch a vague time called 'not always.' I sketch a moment called 'now.' "

It did not surprise Melinda that Will Starr took an immediate, sullen dislike to James Warren. She supposed Will was jealous, for he could not begin to compete with the artist when it came to manners or small talk. Will was shy; James Warren was not. Will never talked about himself; James Warren went on for hours about places he had seen, things he had done and people he had known, bragging so immodestly yet brilliantly that he was forgiven much by his hearers. Will had difficulty expressing himself, even when his knowledge of his subject was sound; James Warren framed his opinions beautifully, even though he had not the slightest grasp of the topic he was discussing.

Will Starr's size, strength, and dogged devotion to the Belford family amused James Warren, though the artist was careful not to reveal his amusement except in Melinda's presence. One day he said to her, "Where on earth did you pick him up, Melinda?"

"Back in Missouri. He caught up with us on the trail one day and has been with us ever since."

"He reminds me of a pet bear. You've done a good job of taming him, I must say."

"You mustn't talk about Will that way," Melinda said indignantly. "He's been a great help to us."

"Are you going to marry him?"

"Don't be silly! He's just a family friend."

"Even family friends marry, Melinda," James Warren said, smiling. "Although that unhappy event does tend to spoil the friendship."

"Now you're teasing me."

"Not at all. Look what you'd be getting if you married him. Physically he's stronger than any two men you could find. You already have him trained to mind you. He's not long on brains, of course, but what matters in this country is a strong back. You could do much worse, you know."

She felt a sudden angry urge to defend Will Starr. Impulsively, she said, "You wouldn't look down on him if he were rich."

James Warren laughed. "No, I confess I wouldn't."

"Well, he just may *be* rich some day."

"Indeed?"

Even as she told the artist about Lafe Perrin's map and Will Starr's plan to go prospecting, she realized that she should not have done so. It would only amuse him. But, once started, she could not stop until she had told him the whole story. When she was done, James Warren said, "Is that the condition you've put on marrying him—that he must be rich?"

"Of course not!"

"But it would make a great difference, wouldn't it?"

"Well, it *would* be nice to have money."

"A very practical attitude, Melinda." He studied her face thoughtfully for a time, then said, "Do you really know how beautiful you are, my dear?"

"James, please . . ."

"And are you aware of the fact that a young, beautiful, unmarried girl is as rare in the gold camps as an egg-sized diamond? Why, I'll wager that in the Boise district alone you could find a hundred handsome, healthy, eligible young bachelors whose eyeballs would fall out at the sight of you. A few of them must have struck it rich. So if it's money you want, your only problem is to meet the young bachelor who has made the biggest strike—"

"James Warren! " she exclaimed, her face flaming. "How can you say such things! What do you think I am? "

He had a disconcerting habit of answering what was meant to be a purely rhetorical question with embarrassing frankness. Without hesitation, he said, "A *femme fatale.*"

She stared at him blankly. "A what? "He repeated the strange expression.

"Exactly what does *that* mean? " she demanded.

"A woman who makes things happen," he answered, and she could not tell whether the light in his eyes was mocking or serious. "A woman whose beauty creates havoc in male hearts wherever she goes, but who walks on serene and uncaring while blood flows ankle deep in the gutters, while men die, while empires crumble. That is what it means, Melinda. And that, in my humble judgment, is exactly what you are."

She laughed and told him he was being ridiculous. But later, studying the reflection of her face in her hand mirror, she recalled what he had told her . . . and she wondered. After all, James Randolph Warren was an artist. It was his business to see things in a person's face that other mortals could not see.

Wouldn't it be great fun if she really were what he said she was?

Chapter Thirteen

If Cornelius Belford had been inclined to wonder why Lafe Perrin preferred to remain in the middle of this hot, bleak, dusty Idaho desert rather than seek his fortune in the mining camps farther west, his wonderment ended the afternoon the emigrant train made camp on the south side of Snake River, a week's travel west of Fort Hall. At first glance, an uninformed person would call the flat-bottomed wooden barge, the ingenious system of pulleys and ropes and the heavy cable swung overhead between sturdy wooden towers on either bank a current-propelled ferry. But appearances were misleading.

The contraption was not just a ferry. It was also a gold mine. Zeke Pence, who had been bragging that "Cousin Lafe" had promised that the Missourians would be "treated right" when they reached the ferry, was the first to discover the bitter truth. And shirt-tail relation or not, he declared vehemently, he wished to hell he had shot Lafe for the thieving half-breed he'd taken him to be on first sight, as he'd been inclined to do.

"You know what it costs to cross a wagon on that ferry?" Zeke raged. "Seven dollars, paper money, or five dollars in gold! No wonder the son-of-a-bitch'es poke was full!"

In Lafe's absence, his partner in crime—a stooped, thin, gray-haired man named Dave Shoup—pointed out that it had cost a sight of money to build the ferry, seeing as how every board, bolt, nail, rope, and foot of cable had had to be fetched all the way from Salt Lake City by wagon, not to mention the time and effort that had gone into the building. Another thing you had to consider, he said, was that the Indians hereabouts could be mighty ornery when they put their minds to it, and it took a sight of tobacco, blankets, and trade goods to keep them on their good behavior. Sure, he knew the toll charges sounded steep, but he was a reasonable man; in lieu of cash, he'd accept old clothes, livestock, guns or 'most anything else the emigrants had to spare. 'Course, being *used* goods, he'd have to discount 'em some . . .

"An' they's no law says you got to cross the Snake here," he added helpfully. "You kin stick to the old trail, south of the river. Well, yes, it does miss Boise City. But it ain't more'n a hundred miles longer'n the new trail—an' the Injuns ain't kilt nobody along the old trail that I *know* of this year. They do say the grass along the old trail is fair in spots—that is, whar the Injuns ain't set it afire an' burnt it off, as they *will* do . . ."

Belford's efforts to bargain with Shoup met with no success. That was the fee, take it or leave it—seven dollars greenbacks or five dollars gold. Conferring with Daniel Lynn, Belford found that the Iowan had had no better luck in persuading Dave Shoup that for fifty wagons he should make some concession in rates.

"No question about it, it's the rankest kind of holdup," Lynn agreed angrily. "But what can we do about it?"

"There's the old trail along the south bank."

"It doesn't sound good to me. Matt advises against it. What does Andy say?"

"He agrees with Matt. But seven dollars—!" A blind, sullen rage stirred in Belford, making him suddenly blurt out, "Do you know what my people are saying, Mr. Lynn? That we should take over the ferry by force, cross our wagons, pay Dave Shoup two dollars apiece and let him howl at the moon for the rest."

"You know, I'm tempted to do just that," Lynn said, chuckling. "But I'm mighty surprised *you* are."

"The time comes when people's rights must be put above property's rights. Poor people can be pushed only so far."

"You're forgetting one thing," Lynn said, shaking his head. "The law is on Dave Shoup's side. He's got a charter to operate that ferry, or claims he has, which sets the legal rates he can charge. If we force him to ferry our wagons at our price, we'd be in a peck of trouble."

"Who granted him this charter? Lafe Perrin said Idaho hasn't elected a legislature yet."

"No, but it's got a governor, a U.S. marshal, and a set of federal judges. And there are soldiers stationed near Boise City, I'm told. You do as you please, Mr. Belford, but us, we ain't bucking the law."

In desperation, Cornelius Belford turned to Matt Miller, who had just strolled up, and said, "Is it possible to ford the Snake?"

"'Feared not," the old guide said, shaking his head. "This time of year, it's swimmin' depth most of the way acrost."

"What about floating our wagons, like we did across the Platte?"

"Might be done, but it'd be a risk. Why chance it when the ferry is there?"

Evening was nigh. Reluctantly, Belford agreed that the train should make camp on the south shore, ferrying the wagons and livestock across the next morning. Though they grumbled about it, the Iowans resigned themselves to paying the steep toll charges, but the temper of the Missourians became increasingly sullen and resentful. Joe Hatley, one of the younger married men, spent the remaining daylight hours prowling up and down the river bank, breaking dead sticks into short lengths, tossing them out into the water and then watching what the current did to them. When darkness fell, he returned to camp, walked over to where Belford and Armand Kimball stood talking by the fire, and harshly announced, "To hell with the ferry! Come mornin', I'm floatin' my wagon across."

Ever since leaving Independence, Belford had found Joe Hatley a difficult man to handle. Impulsive, quick-tempered, reckless, he could not be reasoned with once he had made up his mind to do a thing; the least opposition put him into a blind rage. But Belford felt he must make an effort to talk him out of this decision.

"It's too big a risk, Joe. Both Andy and Matt advise against it."

"To hell with 'em! They ain't tellin' me what to do!"

"They know the river."

"Reckon *I* know rivers, too. I'll show 'em!"

"If it's a question of being a bit short on cash, Joe," Armand Kimball said quietly, "I'll be happy to loan you the seven dollars."

There was a fevered, contemptuous light in Joe Hatley's eyes. "Keep your damned money, Armand. I may be short on cash but I sure as hell ain't short on guts, like the rest of you are. Come mornin', I'm floatin' my wagon across."

Turning on his heel, he walked away. Kimball said in concern, "Cornelius, that man is a little crazy."

"He well may be."

"What can we do to stop him?"

Belford shook his head.

In truth, short of disarming the man and tying him hand and foot like a raving lunatic, there was nothing that could be done to stop him, Belford told Joe Hatley's wife when she came to him and tearfully pleaded that he do something to dissuade her husband from his foolhardy notion.

"He's an adult, ma'am, and entitled to make his own decisions."

"But Joe ain't been himself lately, Mr. Belford. Lately he fights things so. He seems to think everybody's against him and he's got to keep fighting back at them. That gun he wears, for instance—he won't never take it off, not even after we've made camp of evenings. He says he might need it in a hurry to protect himself."

"From *us?*"

"He won't say, but he's suspicious of everybody. Even when he goes to bed, he puts that awful gun—all loaded and ready to shoot—under his pillow and sleeps on it. I'm scared to death it'll go off accidental and kill one of the children. Can't you do *something,* Mr. Belford?"

"I can't very well take a man's gun away from him, Mrs. Hatley."

"Well, at least ask some of the other men to talk to him and try to persuade him not to try floating our wagon across the river. I'm scared of the way Joe's acting. It's like—well, like he had to prove something. He says he'll float our wagon across or die. You've just got to find a way to stop him!"

All Belford could do was ask Will Starr and Andy Hale, whom he knew Joe Hatley respected as much as he did any men in the train, to go to him and attempt to talk him out of it. But their efforts proved fruitless. If anything, their arguments seemed to make him even more determined, for he appeared to enjoy having suddenly become the center of attention.

"Hell, I was raised on big rivers!" he boasted to Andy. "Why, I've swum cattle, horses, and wagons across the Mississippi, the Missouri, and the Platte. Do you think a piddling little river like the Snake scares me?"

"It's more river than it looks," Andy said. "Don't underestimate it."

"Watch me, come mornin'! Just watch me!"

Andy Hale quietly told Belford he intended to do just that.

When breakfast was done, next morning, every person in camp was on the river bank, watching Joe Hatley make his preparations. The Iowa members of the train were curious, doubting and skeptical; the Missourians, worried but hopeful. After all, Joe Hatley was one of their own; rash though his act might be, no one could question its bravery—and if he accomplished what no one else dared try, the Missourians would really have something to crow about.

Puzzled because the wagons were not moving toward the ferry, Dave Shoup came down to see why the crowd had gathered. The spot at which Hatley planned to make his crossing was two hundred yards downstream from the ferry towers. Here, a long, narrow island split the river into two channels, the near channel being some fifty yards in breadth, the far one three times that. Shoup stood squinting out across the glittering green-blue surface of the river, his eyes following it downstream to the point where it curved sharply to the left beyond the lower point of the island. He blinked sleepily at Hatley, who was on one knee tying a rope end to the base of a willow tree.

"What's the rope fer?"

"Fer hangin' bastards like you," Hatley answered, mimicking

Shoup's tone of voice so exactly that the Missourians gathered around whooped with laughter. "Wanta try the noose on fer size?"

Unperturbed, Shoup surveyed the thick coils of rope hanging from the horn of the heavy stock saddle set on the back of Hatley's big-barreled gray gelding. He nodded to himself, as if he now understood what the Missourian intended to do. He would cross first to the island, uncoiling line as he went, then swim the gray across the wider main channel to the far bank, where he would secure the other end of the line to a tree trunk. Returning to the south shore then, he would drive his wagon into the water and across the lesser channel to the island; there, he would tie the near rope end to the wagon, and, with his oxen swimming just enough to keep the wagon angled into the current, let the floating vehicle swing pendulum-like from the island across the main channel to the north bank of the river.

"Might work," Shoup said thoughtfully. Then he spat and shook his head. "But if you want my advice, this ain't the best spot fer it. Fact, you couldn't of picked a worse 'un."

"What's wrong with it?"

"Current is always mighty tricky above a bend. Kind of swirls around in all directions. Now, if you're jest bound to swim, you'd better pick out a straight stretch of river. Thar's a place a mile downstream—"

"You go to hell, you old fool! If I was takin' your advice, I'd be crossin' by ferry."

Joe Hatley swung into the saddle. His wife was standing nearby, her six-month-old baby in her arms, her three-year-old daughter clinging to her skirt on one side and her four-year-old son on the other. Her face was white and drawn, Cornelius Belford noted, her eyes red-rimmed from crying. Sitting atop a rock back a ways from the water's edge and above the crowd, James Warren held a sketch pad on his knees and was working furiously with a pencil, getting the scene down on paper. Sight of the man angered Belford. Confound him anyway! Did he have ice water in his veins?

As Hatley started to put the gray gelding into the river, Andy Hale stepped forward and took hold of the horse's bridle. Quietly, he said, "Shouldn't you tie the other end of the rope around yourself, Joe, instead of around the saddle horn?"

"It'd be in my way."

"Well, for God's sake, at least shed that gun and cartridge belt. Metal don't float, you know."

"What's a few pounds more or less? " Joe Hatley laughed recklessly. "Besides, I might want to shoot me a fish!"

"You crazy fool!"

"Get out of the way!"

Reluctantly, Andy moved back and the big gray horse walked into the water. A short distance from shore, the gelding began swimming, crossed the lesser channel without difficulty as Hatley paid out the rope coil by coil, and presently the beast was lunging up out of the water onto the island, where it paused. Joe Hatley turned and waved his hat triumphantly at the crowd, which cheered him lustily.

"Nothin' to it, folks! Get your wagons ready! I'll float 'em all across!"

"By God, I believe he can do it!" Zeke Pence exclaimed.

Belford saw the Delaware, Levi, ride up, leading a saddled horse, which Andy mounted. The two conferred with Will Starr, who was sitting his husky black; all three had ropes coiled on their saddle horns, Belford noted, whose unusual bulk indicated that several everyday lengths had been tied together. Nodding in agreement, Will Starr remained where he was, while Andy and Levi rode downstream toward the lower end of the island. Though the early morning sun already was warming the land, Belford felt suddenly chilled. Apparently Andy expected the worst to happen. Well, at least help would be handy.

His attention returned to Joe Hatley, who now was spurring the gray into the main channel. At once, it was evident that the current was much stronger here. Its force seemed to take the horse by surprise at first, for its head turned downstream and it momentarily went under. Mrs. Hatley screamed. Then the gray's head cleared water and Hatley was reining it around, forcing it to turn its head into the current, as it must do if it were not to be driven under. He succeeded. The gray's body was angled against the thrust of the current now in such a manner that it was being pushed across the channel as well as down it.

The point of equilibrium seemed to be a delicate one. If the horse faced the current too directly, it ceased to make any progress toward the far bank. If it turned its head too far to the left, the swift water, striking it broadside, tended to drive it under. But the gelding was a strong swimmer, did not panic easily and its rider had the good sense not to hinder it by too heavy a hand on the reins.

From Belford's vantage point, it was difficult to judge how far across the main channel the gray had swum when it got into serious trouble. Three-fourths of the way, possibly; possibly more. But suddenly, Belford observed with horror, the current seemed to reverse itself and run violently in the opposite direction.

Like a man walking sideways to a strong wind, leaning into it, then suddenly having the wind switch directions, the gray horse spun around, floundered and went under. Again Mrs. Hatley screamed in terror. After a moment, two shapes—separated by twenty feet—could be seen in the water. Zeke Pence lunged for the rope tied to the base of the willow tree, shouting, "Give me a hand, boys—we got to pull him out of there!"

A dozen men leaped to help him. Hand over hand, they hauled in the slack until the long line went taut.

"Got him!" Zeke cried triumphantly. "Now play him easy, boys! We don't want the line breaking when he hits the end of it!"

Him? *Oh, God,* Belford thought, suddenly recalling what everyone else seemed to have forgotten, *the other end of the rope isn't tied to Joe Hatley; it's tied to the gray's saddle horn!*

For a time, horse and man appeared to be moving upstream, as if caught in an eddy or whirlpool, then both were being swept toward the far bank. Will Starr spurred his black into the water of the near channel, heading for the island. The downstream thrust of the current had Joe Hatley and the gray in its grip now and was moving them rapidly along, still well apart, the gray in the lead. Zeke Pence yelled to his helpers to give slack on the line.

Animal and man were being swept toward the perpendicular face of a dark brown lava rock that jutted out into the river above the bend; Hatley could be seen struggling frantically to reach it. One arm lifted and a clawing hand sought for purchase, failed to find it, and he sank beneath the surface of the water.

Will Starr had reached the island, Belford saw. Shaking out a loop in his rope, he raced the black toward its lower end, paused there, set himself and made his throw at a target which Belford could not see. He reeled the loop in empty. Apparently still under the impression that he had both man and horse at the end of his line, Zeke Pence shouted a warning to his helpers, "Git ready, boys! Snub 'em off easy!"

The line slid through their hands, went taut, then parted like rotten twine.

Below the island, Andy and Levi had waded as far out into the river as they dared. The gray horse had vanished from sight now but against the silvery surface of the water Belford could see a man's figure struggling feebly. His lips framed a silent prayer. Levi threw, then Andy. Both casts missed. As the two men pulled in their slack ropes, a sound ran over the crowd, a releasing of held breaths, a mutual sighing. Sick to his very soul, Cornelius Belford went to Mrs. Hatley, put his arm around her shoulders and vainly tried to comfort her.

"God's will be done, my child. God's will be done."

Even though the emigrants remained camped on the south bank of the Snake all the rest of that day while parties searched the shallows and eddies for miles downriver, Joe Hatley's body was not found. A collection was taken up for the widow; it amounted to a little more than one hundred dollars, which Armand Kimball quietly doubled out of his own pocket.

Next morning, the train crossed the Snake on the ferry. The toll charges remained as posted: seven dollars greenbacks, five dollars gold for each wagon. But Dave Shoup did make one concession.

He let Mrs. Hatley's wagon cross free of charge.

Chapter Fourteen

Back at Fort Hall, James Warren had done a charcoal sketch of Melinda's father, titled it *The Leader,* signed it and made him a present of it. Melinda suspected that the artist had drawn the portrait in an attempt to flatter her father's vanity, and, if that were so, he had succeeded. Her father was pleased and said so. But later, after Warren had gone, she found her father studying the sketch with a disturbed frown on his face. He asked her what she thought of it.

"It looks just like you, Pa."

"He's made me look awfully grim."

"You were worried."

"But couldn't he have made me look more pleasant?"

Studying the portrait, she realized what Warren had done. He had caught her father's intolerance, his ambition, his passion to be recognized as an important man, and had set them down on paper unsoftened by any of his virtues. The resulting likeness was therefore ruthless and somewhat unfair. It was a true likeness as far as it went, but it was not the whole truth. And the title was a faintly mocking bit of irony that she knew her father never would see, though others would.

"Mr. Warren doesn't draw pleasant pictures, Pa. He draws real ones. He says you have a striking face. It was your strong features he wanted to bring out."

That satisfied her father. But it opened up an entirely new field of thought for Melinda. As the wagon train moved west along the Snake and she became better acquainted with James Warren, she came to understand that an artist did not necessarily draw what was actually there; he drew what he saw, filtering each scene through his own personal feelings toward it. She could not help but wonder how *she* looked through his eyes.

When the train halted for its nooning one day, she walked with James Warren to a bluff overlooking the river and sat beside him in silence for a time while he sketched details of scenery in pencil. By now, she had learned that landscape of itself did not interest him greatly.

"Water is water, sky is sky, mountains are mountains the world over," he would say. "Anyone's old maid aunt can paint pretty landscape scenes. I'm not looking for prettiness—I'm looking for meaning."

"Doesn't scenery have meaning?"

"How could it have? The world was created by a mindless violence."

"I thought God made the world."

He laughed. "Just who or what is God? An old man with gentle eyes and a long white beard who performed miracles in the Old Testament days and hasn't been heard from since? Perhaps. But I don't believe it."

"What do you believe?"

"I just told you—in a mindless violence. So that's what I paint."

"But you're always sketching bits and pieces of scenery like rocks, trees, rivers, and mountains," she protested. "If scenery doesn't interest you, why do you do that?"

"Because I want my paintings to give the illusion of reality. When I put a rock, a tree, a river, or a mountain into a painting, you can be sure it's one I've seen somewhere, some time."

"Why not use the ones that are there?"

"Where?"

"In the scene you're painting."

"They might not suit my purpose as well. Every painting I do has a point, tells a story, makes an emotional impact on its viewer. Man is the only thinking, feeling creature on the face of the earth; therefore, unless I show man in action, I accomplish nothing. But I can't show him acting in empty space. Form can evoke emotion. A rock can be ugly, a hill bleak, a river ominous, a mountain range forbidding. It's an artist's privilege to use form as he chooses to set the mood he wants to set. Who's to care if he moves his scenery around a bit?"

"Well," Melinda said, "it sounds dishonest to me."

Warren laughed. "I'm sure it does, my dear. But show me an artist that's not a scoundrel at heart and I'll show you a man lacking in genius."

"Are you a genius?" she teased.

"Yes."

"My, you're the modest one!"

"No, I'm completely arrogant where my artistic talents are concerned," he said, unruffled. "All artists are. It's an occupational trait."

"Would you like to paint me?"

"Not particularly."

She gave him a petulant look. "You drew Pa's picture. Why don't you want to draw mine?"

"Oh, if it's only a sketch you want," he said, casually flipping a page in the pad on his knee to a blank sheet, "I'd be happy to oblige. Turn your head away a little. Now lift your chin just a trifle. There! Don't move, now."

She heard the squeak of his pencil on the paper, a sound that always made her cringe, but she forced herself to sit still and unmoving. After what could have been no more than a minute or so, he said, "Here you are. Will this do?"

Gazing down at the sketch as he turned the pad toward her, she knew a momentary tingle of excitement. Though the sketch had been drawn with an amazing economy of line, it was her, all right, and he had drawn her pretty enough. But it was not at all that she wanted. She tossed her head indignantly.

"That isn't me."

His smile was mocking. "Isn't it?"

"It's just some lines on paper that look like me. I want a real painting of me in a pretty dress and a nice hat, with colors and everything."

"Why?"

She had no intention of telling him her real reasons, for she knew he would laugh and think her silly. But the truth was she had never met a man of his kind before and lately she had begun to imagine that she might be falling in love with him and he with her. Beyond her natural vanity to see a painting of herself done by an accomplished artist, she yearned to know how she looked through *his* eyes, for if he *were* falling in love with her that would be bound to show in the painting, wouldn't it? Furthermore, she still was not sure what a *femme fatale* was, despite his flippant definition of the term, and she was curious to see how he would picture such a woman. But she certainly was not going to tell him *that!*

"Oh, I guess you could say I'm just curious. After all, you're the first artist I've ever met. But if you don't want to paint me—"

"Portraits bore me. There's no challenge to them."

"You mean you'd rather paint ugly, violent things, like Indians drowning in rivers?"

"Not necessarily. But I like to make a point in my paintings. I like action and emotional impact. A portrait of you would be just another painting of a beautiful woman. It would be a static, wooden thing."

"You certainly pay nice compliments, Mr. Warren. What would you have me do, wrestle a buffalo?"

He threw back his head and laughed heartily. "Now there would be a scene I would love to paint! *The Europa of the Plains!* Where can we find a buffalo?"

"I'll bet you can't even paint women," Melinda said angrily. "Not well, anyhow."

"You'd be surprised, my dear, how well I do women."

"Have you ever painted them?"

"Many times when I was studying in Paris." His eyes began to twinkle. "However, I seriously doubt that you would consent to pose for me the way they did."

"How was that?"

"Nude."

Turning scarlet, Melinda leaped to her feet and turned away, as if to go back to the wagon. James Warren also rose. She hesitated, then turned to face him. "They didn't!"

"They did," he said solemnly. "Wasn't that awful?"

"The shameless hussies! What kind of woman would do a thing like that?"

"As a matter of fact, some of them were very nice girls. And very modest. To an artist, there's nothing indecent about the unclothed figure, you know. It's simply an animate object made up of lines, planes, curves, lights, and shadows."

"If Pa heard you talking like this to me, he'd—well, I don't know *what* he'd do!"

"And if your pet bear, Will Starr, heard me?" Warren said mockingly.

"You'd just better hope he doesn't!"

"You brought it on yourself, you know, when you questioned my ability to paint women."

"Well, I certainly don't want you to paint me now."

He laughed. "Of course you do! If you didn't, you wouldn't keep harping on the subject."

Melinda avoided his eyes. "All right, I do. But not *that* way."

"It would be a bit awkward to arrange, I'll admit." He studied her thoughtfully for a moment, then said, "Did I tell you I asked Will Starr to pose for me and he refused?"

"Why on earth would you want to paint him?"

"He intrigues me. All that power and grace packed into one immense, perfect body—"

"But he turned you down?"

"Flat."

"Why?"

"He didn't say. I have a feeling he dislikes me because he's jealous of anyone you show an interest in. But you've given me an idea. Suppose I agreed to paint you and Will posing together? Could you get him to do it?"

"Why together?"

"For contrast," Warren said, and Melinda could sense enthusiasm growing in him. "You're so small, so delicate, so lovely. He's so huge, so strong, so powerfully elemental. It's typical of the brutal contrasts of this country. It's—well, it's a sort of Beauty and the Beast thing."

"That's no way to talk about Will," Melinda scolded. "He wouldn't harm a fly."

"I'm not so sure. But the point is, the physical contrast is there. Painting the two of you together, I could compose a picture that would say something. Will you ask him?"

"Maybe I will and maybe I won't," Melinda said, tossing her head. "But I'll think about it. We'd better go back to camp now. They're hitching up."

After supper that evening, Melinda told Will Starr she would like to go for a walk; when they were out of earshot of the wagon circle, she said casually, "Why won't you let Mr. Warren paint you?"

"He makes everything he paints look ugly."

"He says he paints only what he sees."

"If that's so," Will said sullenly, "his eyes are bad. Look what he did to your pa. I ain't going to let him spit on me on canvas."

"Oh, Will!" Melinda said peevishly. "What do you know about art?"

"Nothing. But I know I don't like his pictures."

"What would you say if I told you Mr. Warren asked me to pose for him?"

He stopped walking, seized her by the shoulders and turned her to face him. She had never seen him so angry. "Don't you do it, Mellie!"

"Why shouldn't I?" she said defiantly. "Are you afraid he'll make me look ugly, too?"

"He'll do something nasty to you, you can bet on that. He's an evil man."

"That's a silly way to talk. You hardly know him."

"I got a feeling about him. A bad feeling. He's evil."

"But I want him to paint me, Will," Melinda said, putting a hand on his chest and smiling up at him appealingly. "I may never have another chance like this." She dropped her gaze and turned away. "Of course, if you don't want me to pose for him—"

"It's not my say-so what you do," Will said uncomfortably. "No, but I wouldn't want to displease you."

"Have you talked to your pa about it?"

"No, just to you. But Pa wouldn't care. *He* posed, didn't he?"

"Well," he said uncertainly, "if it really means so much to you—"

"Will, I've got an idea!" she exclaimed, turning to him with an eager smile. "Why don't we both pose for Mr. Warren— together! Wouldn't you like that, Will, a painting of the two of us?"

He scowled down at her, considering it, and as reluctant acceptance came into his eyes she knew she had been right in her approach. He said, "What if he don't want it that way?"

"I'll tell him it's that way or not at all. Will you do it, Will? Will you?"

"Well, if you're sure it's what you want . . ."

"Oh, Will, you're a dear!" Melinda exclaimed, raised herself on tiptoe and kissed him on the cheek.

Later that evening when she went to the artist's wagon and told him it had been arranged, he said, "Good! We'll start tomorrow."

"But you've got to promise me one thing," she cautioned him. "Will doesn't know that this is *your* idea. He thinks it's mine."

"How did he get that notion?" James Warren said, lifting his eyebrows in mock surprise.

"I can't begin to guess. But promise me you'll not say anything."

"My dear, I shall carry your little secret with me to my grave."

Quite unexpectedly, he took her by the elbows, pulled her to him and kissed her lightly on the lips. She recoiled, looked hastily around to make sure no one had seen, then murmured indignantly, "Why on earth did you do that?"

He chuckled. "What man can resist a *femme fatale?*"

Chapter Fifteen

For the next week or so, James Warren worked at the painting every moment the light lasted and his subjects could find time to pose for him. Always Will Starr posed in stony silence, showing no interest in the progress of the painting, refusing even to look at it. But Melinda found its gradual development fascinating.

Though her father had voiced no objections, she knew that his approval of the project was far from whole-hearted. Like the other Missourians, he had been taught that pictures of anything except Biblical scenes were frivolous vanities, almost sinful, in fact, like the heathen raising of false idols or the hated Papists' worship of symbols. Yet he respected Warren for his apparent wealth, talent, and gentlemanly manners, took a fatherly pride in the fact that his own flesh and blood was being immortalized on canvas, thus could not bring himself to deny Warren, despite whatever misgivings he may have had.

The single really pretty dress Melinda owned was a light, cream-colored satin, and when she showed it to the artist he said it was exactly right. She wanted to wear a hat with it, but he said, no, he wanted her head bare. However, she could hold the hat, as if she had been wearing it and had just taken it off to let the cool breezes of nearing evening play over her head.

He posed her in a half-reclining position on the flat surface of a dark-brown lava rock, as if, in party dress, she had just strolled away from a crowd celebrating some festive occasion and had sat down to watch the sunset and dream. She was gazing into the light, which had lost its daytime harshness and now was mellowing into orange and red tones; her head was slightly lifted and turned a bit to one side, as if her meditation had just been interrupted by a sound that had intrigued but not startled her. The expression he wanted, Warren said, was one of anticipation and virgin innocence. Her feet were folded under the circle of her skirt; she held her hat in her right hand and her left arm was raised, as if she had been in the act of smoothing down her hair when the sound had arrested her arm's movement.

Directly behind her, silently staring down at this typically feminine gesture, Warren posed Will Starr. The artist had kept his own point of view low to the ground, on a level with Melinda's eyes, so that the perspective was angled upward, and the man's figure towered immense, dark, and powerful against the purpling eastern sky. The top buttons of his gray flannel shirt were open, emphasizing the breadth of his chest and shoulders. He held a rifle in his left hand, gripped by its barrel, its butt resting on the ground, and by the way he handled it the viewer knew that its weight was nothing to his great strength. A pistol was holstered on his right hip, a sheathed knife was on his left. His right hand was reaching out toward the girl in such a manner that one could not be sure whether the gesture was kindly or menacing, but there was no mistaking the brooding hunger in his eyes.

The light reflecting from the girl's face was soft, warm, and revealed her as infinitely innocent and feminine. Yet by some trick of pigment or technique, the same light brought out the bronze and brown tones of the man's skin. Examining the painting one day after Will Starr had gone, Melinda commented on this.

"Why have you made his skin so dark and mine so light? "

"Because the contrast is there."

"That much?"

"In the light I'm using, yes. It's low-key but it's a rich light. Instead of washing out colors as noontime sunlight does, it mellows and deepens them. Of course the fact that you're wearing a cream-colored dress while he's in gray and brown is bound to point up your fairness and his darkness. But in any light, the contrast is there."

"You've made him look like a gypsy—or an Indian."

James Warren studied the painting thoughtfully. "So I have. But I paint only what I see." With the tip of a brush, he pointed out details of the man's face. "As a matter of fact, Will could pass for an Indian if he chose to. Note the high, slightly prominent cheekbones, the flaring nostrils, the shape of the eyes and the texture of the skin. Strip him to a breechclout, put moccasins on him and dress his hair in braids and he'd look as Indian as Levi does."

Melinda admitted that he did have some Indian features. "But that doesn't mean anything," she hastily added. "Lots of white people do. Take Pa—he's dark. So am I."

Warren laughed as he cleaned his brushes. "You probably have a redskin up your family tree."

"Oh, no! " Melinda said, horrified. "We couldn't have! '

"What would be so terrible about it if you did?"

"It's nothing to joke about. It's—well, it's the most awful thing a body could imagine." Her gaze went back to the painting. "James—"

"Yes?"

"Do you really think it's possible? About Will, I mean."
"What do you know of his background?"
"Nothing, really. He never talks about his family."
"Where is he from?"
"Texas, he said."
"That's right next door to the Indian Nations country. Why couldn't he have Indian blood in him? Cherokee, say, or Creek. Those tribes have been mixing with white people for generations back East." Seeing the look of distaste that came over her face, he peered again at the painting and found—or pretended to find—something he had previously overlooked. "Creek, in all probability. He has that sort of nose."
"You're teasing me!" Melinda said angrily.
"No, I'm not. And look here—this is very interesting. Do you see the faintest hint of a thickness of the lips?"
"What on earth do you mean?"
"The Creeks kept slaves. He may have a drop of Negro blood in his veins."
Melinda felt suddenly sick. "Oh, no!"
Warren was amused. "It's possible."
"It would be horrible!"
"Why? Are you in love with him?"
"Certainly not!"
"You said you might marry him if he struck it rich."
"I didn't! " Melinda said frantically. "I never said any such thing!"
"You like him, don't you?"
"I don't feel *anything* toward him. It's just that he's worked so hard to help us—"
"Oh, come now, where's your sense of loyalty?" Warren said chidingly. "It's obvious he worships you. You've been twisting him around your finger, using him, making him dance to your whims—"
"That isn't so!"
"It most certainly is. Are you going to turn against him now simply because I told you his blood may be slightly tainted?"
"You mean you're only guessing? You're not sure?"
"One can never be sure of anything in this world, Melinda. I recall an amusing incident that happened back home before the War when all the belles of the community set their caps for a rich, handsome, well-mannered gentleman who claimed to be of noble French and Spanish blood. In appearance he was rather dark but his manners were impeccable. And he *was* rich. A second cousin of mine—quite a snooty second cousin, I must say—won the competition and married him. And do you know what happened a year later?"

"I don't think I want to know," Melinda said, turning away.

"She had a baby—whose skin was coal black."

"Oh, no!"

"Oh, yes!" Warren put his brushes and paints away. "I never saw it, of course, but those things have a way of getting around. She killed the baby, killed herself, and her father killed the supposed nobleman."

"How terrible!"

"So, you see, there's no way of really knowing the truth until it's too late. It's possible that Will Starr's blood is perfectly pure, though I'm inclined to believe that there's at least a trace of Indian in him."

She shuddered. "That would be bad enough, even without the—the other."

"If you're not going to marry him, what difference does it make?"

She was too upset to answer. Glancing across the enclosure toward the Belford wagon, where Will Starr stood talking to her father, James Warren smiled and said, "Would it put your mind at rest if you knew the truth? I could ask him, you know."

She stared at him in horror. "Would you dare?"

Warren's eyes were mocking. "Or *you* could ask him. Just go up to him and say casually, 'Will, is it true you're part Indian and part nigger?'"

"James, please, it's nothing to tease about! Let's not talk about it any more! Let's not even think about it! Don't finish the painting—"

His smile faded, the mocking light left his eyes and his face went deadly serious. Taking her by the elbows, he said, "Listen to me, Melinda. Whatever his ancestry is, this is going to be the best painting I've ever done. I *must* finish it. Don't think about him, if that disturbs you. Think about the thousands of people who are going to look at the painting in years to come and wonder who the beautiful woman in it is. Just think about that."

It *was* a fine thought to cling to, Melinda told herself as she lay sleepless in the warm dark. But when she finally closed her eyes her dreams were filled with coal-black babies.

Chapter Sixteen

This would be their last camp on Snake River for a while, Melinda heard Andy Hale tell her father. Here the trail left the river and bore northwest across the sage-covered desert toward Boise City, which the train should reach in about five days, while the Snake itself flowed in a westerly direction. In reply to Will Starr's eager question, Andy said, yes, the low blue line breaking the regularity of the horizon far to the west and south was the beginning of the Owyhee Mountains, in whose foothills Lafe Perrin's gold mine was supposed to be located.

"You could save a little time by cutting directly across from here," Andy said. "But if I were you, I'd stay with the train to Boise City. No sense taking any more risks than you have to. If the gold is there, it'll wait for you."

The painting was almost done. These past few days Melinda had forced herself to treat Will Starr as she had always treated him, to smile at him, to be pleasant to him, to pretend to be enthusiastic when he talked about the gold mine which he was so sure he was going to find. But she walked no more alone with him and she found it difficult to meet his eyes for more than a fleeting moment. When he talked to her father, she watched him covertly, reading meanings in the timbre of his voice, the grace of his movements, the expression of his face that she had never bothered to notice before. When the curious Missourians came to watch James Warren paint and commented to one another about some feature in it that intrigued them, she listened, nerves tingling, wondering what would happen if somebody chanced to say the wrong thing.

She wondered if they saw what James Warren had seen. Was it merely her imagination or had Will Starr grown more sullen and hostile toward Warren these past few days? Had the crowd of onlookers grown larger? Was there something grimly disapproving in their faces now? Had the group of children that had run past last evening chanting a bit of doggerel in which the words "Injun" and "nigger" were constantly repeated heard their elders talking or had it been just another meaningless child's game?

She did not know. All she knew was it would be a great relief to her when the painting was done and put away in the artist's wagon.

The sun was down now. James Warren said, "All right, that'll do for today."

Will helped Melinda to her feet. The touch of his fingers on her elbow made her flesh crawl but she forced herself to smile at him. "Thank you, Will."

He stared down at her without speaking for a moment, something dark and brooding in his eyes. Then he turned away, crossed the enclosure to the Belford wagon, put away the rifle with which he had been posing and hunkered down on his heels beside her father, Armand Kimball, and Phil Duncan, who were talking by the fire. He had been on the verge of inviting her to go for a walk with him, Melinda suspected, as he had done last evening and the evening before, and she had had her plea of extreme weariness on the tip of her tongue. But he had changed his mind. Why? Had she somehow given herself away? Had he sensed her involuntary pulling away from his touch and been offended by it?

Indians *did* sense things like that, she had heard. Niggers, too. They were like domestic animals—dogs, say—that knew by the way a body spoke, looked, or acted whether you liked them or didn't like them, whether you feared them or didn't fear them. Maybe Will had heard that childish jingle, too, and was brooding about it. Maybe he'd decide to take a look at the painting presently. If he did . . .

"Like to stretch your legs, Melinda?" James Warren said pleasantly.

She hesitated. If they left camp and went for a walk together, Will Starr would see them. Not that he'd scold her for it; he wouldn't dare do that. But he would sulk. Perhaps the wise thing for her to do would be to go to him, talk to him, smile at him, tease him as she used to do, even invite him to go for a walk with her. But she could not bring herself to do it.

Not now.

"Yes, let's walk down to the river," she said nervously. "It's cooler there."

The grayness of dusk lay over the land as they crossed the enclosure, passed between two parked wagons and walked toward a low bluff overlooking the river. James Warren lighted a cigar and stood smoking, a reflective smile on his face as he gazed off into the distance. He looked tired but content; the intensity with which he had worked for the past few hours had drained away from him with the fading light. Moths and artists had much in common, he had once told Melinda jokingly. Light drove them to frenzy; darkness stilled their wings.

After a time, Melinda murmured, "What are you thinking about, James?"

"You."

"I don't believe it."

"I am."

"What are you thinking about me?"

"How old are you, Melinda?"

"Eighteen."

"What's the biggest city you've ever seen?"

"Independence, I guess."

"That's a mighty small place compared to New York or Paris. Wouldn't you like to see them?"

"Yes. But I never will."

"Why not? If you're clever enough to marry a rich miner, you can make him take you wherever you want to go."

"Where would I find a rich miner?"

"Idaho's full of them I'm told."

"But we're not going to live in Idaho," Melinda said impatiently. "We're going to live in Oregon. And maybe I don't want to marry a rich miner. Maybe I don't want to marry any man."

"Nonsense! You'll be married inside of six months."

"I won't!"

"You will. And you'll never see Oregon."

"How do you know?"

"I'm psychic."

"What does that mean?"

He laughed. "That I have the gift of prophecy. I can foretell the future."

"Oh, fiddlesticks!" Melinda said. "You can't do any such of a thing!"

"I can."

"Then tell me this. When will you marry?"

"Never."

"You don't like women, do you?"

"Of course I like women. My appetites are perfectly normal. When I lived in Paris, I had a veritable harem."

Melinda flushed. "That's not what I mean. I mean you don't like women enough to marry *one* and take care of her for the rest of your life, to raise a family and all that."

"Truthfully, no."

"You're selfish."

"Completely."

"And conceited."

"Self-assured is a kinder term."

"And the worst tease I've ever known."

"Not only that," James Warren said, tossing his cigar away and taking her hands, "I smoke, drink, use profanity, have no respect for religion, and possess a long list of other bad traits that would shock you out of your shoes if you knew about them. But all the same, you like me. And just for the hell of it, I'm going to kiss you right now."

"James!"

"Oh, stop squirming! You want me to kiss you—I know you do."

Angrily she tried to pull away from him. Laughing, he pulled her body hard against his, forced her chin up and kissed her fiercely. For an instant or two she stood stiff and unyielding, then she ceased fighting and clung to him, returning the kiss with a fiery abandon she had not known was in her. Presently he let her go. His voice sounded a little shaky. "There! That'll show you whether or not I like women."

She whirled away from him, intending to run back to camp, then stopped stock-still.

In the growing dusk, Will Starr stood staring at her.

"Oh!" she cried involuntarily.

He did not speak. He did not move. Save for the burning harshness in his eyes, his face was expressionless, but the rapid heaving of his chest betrayed the passion in him. After his initial start of surprise, James Warren had regained his composure, though his face was stiff and mask-like. He smiled.

"Caught in the act, weren't we? For a big man, Will, you certainly move quietly."

Starr still did not speak.

Indignantly, Melinda said, "You should be ashamed of yourself, Will, sneaking up on people that way. You don't own me. You don't mean a thing to me. And if you dare go and tell Pa—"

Without looking at her, without even appearing to hear what she was saying, Starr grunted, "I just looked at the painting, Mr. Warren."

"Oh?" Warren said. "And what inspired you to do that?"

"A feeling. I told Mellie you'd spit on me. I wanted to see if you had."

"Did I?"

"In the worst way."

"Come now, Will," James 'Warren said with a laugh. "It's not as bad as all that. An artist has a right to exaggerate, you know."

"Maybe. But not to lie. You lied about me, Mr. 'Warren. You made me out to be something I'm not."

"Rubbish!"

"Yes," Starr said. "That's what your painting is now. Rubbish. I cut it to pieces, Mr. 'Warren, and tossed it in the fire."

Melinda let out an anguished cry. Flinging herself at him, she slapped his face and aimed wild, futile, raking blows at him, so beside herself with rage that she was not aware of what she was saying. "You fool! You beast! You—you *nigger*"

"You misbegotten black bastard!" James Warren exclaimed, reaching under his coat. "I'll kill you for that!"

Starr thrust Melinda aside and stepped toward Warren. The artist moved backward, evading Starr's seeking hands, pulled out a small caliber pistol and fired point-blank into the big man's chest. Melinda screamed in sudden terror. Warren's heel caught and he stumbled. Starr jerked the pistol out of his grasp and threw it away. His huge hands closed on the artist's throat and squeezed down as he bent the man backward.

Shouting hysterically, Melinda tore at Starr's forearms, pounded at him with her fists, kicked at him with her feet, but her efforts had no more effect than raindrops falling on granite. She could see Warren's eyes bulging, see his face turning purple, see the implacable fury in Starr's face. Like a person caught in a nightmare from which the only escape is awakening, she turned and fled toward her father's wagon . . .

When he was sure that the artist was quite dead, Will Starr let the man's body sag to the ground. He turned, then, and gazed up the slope through the deepening dusk at the circle of parked wagons. He had not consciously planned to kill James Warren. Or had he? It struck him as odd now that instead of walking out from camp to where Warren and Melinda were he had saddled the black and led it here, tying it to a clump of sagebrush a short distance away. After destroying the painting it had been vaguely in his mind to get away from people for a time, he recalled having thought, and he meant to ride and meditate. But instead he had come here.

Face the truth. He had wanted revenge. He had placed his rifle and a full canteen of water on the saddle, acts which a man seeking only solitude for meditation would never have done. The caution of the blood. The door left open for escape. The old, instinctive Indian wisdom: *Never die futilely when by running away you can live to fight another day.*

Run, Indian, run. Run, Indian, run.

He walked to his horse, untied it and swung into the saddle. For some moments he remained motionless, his mind telling him one thing while his instinct told him another. His father, a white man, had married a woman who claimed that half the blood in her veins was white and the other half was Creek. So predominately he was a white man; he had thought it his right to live as one.

Why not act like a white man now? Why not remain quietly in this spot and tell the Missourians that James 'Warren had insulted him, threatened to kill him, and then had actually drawn a gun and shot him? A man had the right to kill in self-defense.

Yes. If he were white. All white.

But when the Missourians came, they would ask no questions, listen to no arguments. To expect otherwise was to be a fool.

He had crossed the line. Now he must run or die.

His choice made, he reined his horse about and gazed out over the dark surface of the river, aware of a dull burning in his chest but contemptuous of it. Immediate safety lay on the far side of the Snake, he knew, for the black could swim the river easily while few of the Missourians would dare try. Andy Hale might risk it. Or Levi. Well, there were ways to discourage them.

Once across the river, what then? Quickly through his mind flashed instinctively stored pictures of the country where Lafe Perrin's gold mine lay. Mountains meant water, grass, game, timber, places to hide. The Owyhees, visible faintly now in the distance to the southwest, were dangerous, Andy had said. So they might be—for white people. And if he lived, he would make them more dangerous still.

He put the black down the slope to the river. Men were running toward him now, shouting angrily, and in the twilight orange-white flames blossomed from rifle barrels, bullets whined past him, kicking up gouts of dust behind and splashes of water ahead. He ignored them. The black moved into the water, snorting distaste at its chill. As the animal reached swimming depth, Will Starr slid out of the saddle on the side away from the near shore, so that the horse's body was between him and the seeking leaden balls. In the failing light, the black could be no more than an indistinct blob to the men on the bank, he knew, and it was swimming easily, soundlessly, so that there were few splashes to give away its location.

Presently the horse struck shoal water. Will Starr led it up onto the bank, prudently moving it around behind a jumble of boulders as he took his gunbelt and six-shooter, which he had hung on the saddle horn to be out of the wet, and buckled the belt around his waist. For a time he stood listening. He could hear voices arguing heatedly on the far shore, some saying swim the river now, some saying no. He thought he could make out Andy's voice, urging caution.

A wise lad, Andy. He'll know I bear him no ill will. But he'd better know I'll kill him if he crowds me.

Drawing the six-shooter, Will Starr fired three shots at the group gathered on the far bank, and the wild howls of dismay that greeted them gave him a certain pleasure. That should do it. Only a fool would swim a river in the dark knowing an armed, wounded, desperate man might be lying in wait for him among the rocks along the far shore. They'll wait till daylight to cross. By then, I'll be miles away.

Mounting the black, he walked the horse silently up the slope through the soft sand, then, when he was sure its hoofbeats could not be heard, turned its head to the southwest and let it out to its best gait, an easy lope

The black was a big, strong horse, but Will Starr was a heavy man. By daybreak, the lope had slowed to a jog-trot. The growing light showed the mountains to be much nearer now. This was a wide, empty country, unmarked by wheel tracks or any sign that civilized man had ever crossed it. Sagebrush had given way to summer-yellowed bunchgrass and now and again the reddish-colored slopes of the increasingly broken terrain were dotted with the dusty green of stunted, gnarled cedar trees, indicating that the increase in elevation had been substantial. To the north, the land fell away in rolling folds toward the valley of the Snake.

The sun climbed higher. Early morning coolness gave way to pleasant warmth, then to ever-increasing heat that sapped the strength of both animal and man. The black slowed to a walk. Will Starr felt no pain, but the numbness in his chest, which through the night had been only a hand-sized spot, was spreading until now there was no feeling in him between his shoulders and waist. The outward bleeding had long since ceased, but something was happening inside his chest; strength slowly was draining out of him.

Feeling left his arms, his legs, his feet, his hands. He lost track of time. Vaguely he was aware that the day was growing very hot, that the black was beginning to stumble, that the country was becoming ever more broken. Now the sun was in his eyes instead of on his back. A mile or so ahead he made out a line of trees following the descending course of a ravine and knew that it marked a stream of live water. When he reached it, he decided, he would rest for a while.

The black stopped, shuddered, then fell with a gentle exhaling of breath no more complaining than a tired man's sigh as he sinks to rest in a chair by the fire after a long day's labor. As the horse went down, Starr threw himself clear of the saddle. He lay prone on the ground for long minutes, not wanting to rise but knowing he must, for the sun would soon kill him here. He struggled to his knees, came erect.

Without a glance at the black, without a thought of it, he staggered on afoot toward the line of trees.

No, Mellie, I don't need Lafe Perrin's map. It's in my head, plain, as plain can be. I've watched the landmarks all the way. The gulch is just ahead. I'll rest a while, then I'll get up and start digging. And we'll be rich, Mellie, rich—and nothing will matter then.

A dozen times he fell. A dozen times he forced himself up and moved on. And presently, when he fell again, there was shade around him and his groping hands were sinking into the cool wetness of water. He drank. He bathed his face. Then, crawling to the base of a tree, he raised himself to a sitting position, put his shoulders to its trunk so that he could watch his back-trail, drew his six-shooter and sat waiting calmly for whatever the fates had in store for him.

It was easy, Mellie. There was the gulch, right where Lafe's map said it would be, and in half a day I dug more pure gold than your pa's wagon can haul. So it's all right now. We're rich, and it's all right. But hurry, Mellie, hurry along with that wagon . . .

Numbness spread over his entire body. It enveloped his brain. The flame of consciousness that had driven him on was flickering ever more feebly, guttering out for lack of fuel. He fought the growing blackness. By sheer effort of will he kept his eyes open and the spark of consciousness alive until the last drop of fuel was spent.

Gold, Mellie. It was easy, so easy . . .

A curtain of darkness fell and his head sagged to his chest.

CHAPTER SEVENTEEN

It was midnight before the turmoil in the emigrant camp quieted down. Crossing to the Iowa side of the enclosure, Andy Hale found Daniel Lynn and Matt Miller having a last cup of coffee before turning in. As he hunkered down beside them, Lynn said, "Have you got the straight of what happened?"

Pouring himself a cup of coffee, Andy shook his head. "Nobody knows the whole truth except Melinda. Belford ain't letting her talk."

"People are saying Will Starr tried to rape her."

"I don't believe that. He wanted to marry her."

"They say he's got Indian and Negro blood in him. Do you believe that?"

"Levi is sure he's part Indian. But the other is only a wild guess. Warren's, maybe. Or Melinda's. But that's proof enough for the ridge-runners. They want his hide."

"Why should it matter to them *what* he is?" Lynn said in disgust. "Warren is dead, Starr is gone and it's still a long way to Oregon. Why waste time on a manhunt?"

"They ain't in a mood to listen to reason, Daniel. They want him caught."

"Do they figure on lynching him?"

"That's the talk."

"It'll take some doin' to ketch him, I'm thinkin'," Matt grunted skeptically. "How do they plan to go at it?"

"Oh, they're full of ideas," Andy said, taking a sip of coffee.

"Zeke Pence, Phil Duncan—"

"They both got diarrhea of the mouth!" Matt muttered. "But I'll bet they clawed fer cover when them bullets begun to whistle across the river. What are they fixin' to do?"

Their plan, Andy said, was to make up a party of fifty armed men, split it into two sections and cross the Snake, come morning, one group swimming the river well upstream from the rocks in which Starr was thought to be hiding, the other downstream. They then would close in on him from two directions, and, as Duncan put it, would "smoke him out." If he had left the rocks and fled into the desert south of the river, they would follow; they swore they intended to stay on his trail until they caught him, however long that might take.

Lynn gave a snort of derision. "Who's going to look after their stock and families while they're gone?"

"They figure you people will, I guess."

"This ain't our mess. Come daylight, we're moving on toward Boise City."

"Kind of thought that's what you'd want to do," Andy said with a smile. "In fact, I told them so. It made them awfully mad, hearing you'd desert their womenfolk that way."

"What do they expect us to do, twiddle our thumbs here while they ride off on a wild goose-chase?" Matt muttered angrily. "You know good and well fifty blundering green-horns got no more chance ketchin' Starr than a snowball's got in hell!"

"Yeah, Matt, I know that. But Belford is bound and determined to catch him and make him pay for what he did to Melinda." Andy toyed with his cup. "Seeing he felt that way, I made him a proposition."

"What?" Lynn asked.

"I told him two men could travel a sight faster than fifty. I told him, come morning, Levi and I would go after Starr."

"Did he agree to that?"

"Seemed glad to."

There was a silence. In the lantern light, Andy saw Matt regarding him suspiciously. "Jest how hard you goin' to try to ketch him, boy?"

"I told Belford I'd give it my best."

"Wal, I hope you lied."

"Why?"

"Goddam it, Andy," Matt said in exasperation, "don't tell me you're goin to risk yore neck trackin' down a man that ain't done nothin' really wrong jest so's a bunch of red-necked ridge-runners kin hang him. You ain't made that way."

"Starr killed Warren."

"Shore, he did. Kilt him with his bare hands after the fool cussed him, threatened him an' then shot him in the chest with a pistol. Where's the crime to that? An' he didn't even touch Melinda."

"That's not the way the Missourians are telling it."

"I know it ain't! But, damn it to hell, it jest happens I was over on the Missoury side of camp when that fool gal ran in screamin'. I didn't go down to the river bank like the rest of them ridge-runners done. I hung around Belford's wagon after they put her to bed an' I heard her tellin' her ma the whole sorry story."

"My, what big ears you've got!" Andy said, grinning at the old guide. "Why didn't you tell us this before?"

"'Cause you didn't ask me."

"Would you swear to that story in court?"

"Shore, if there *was* a court. But there ain't." Matt leaned forward and shook a warning finger at the younger man. "Now, you jest listen to me, boy. Go ahead an' pretend to Belford you're jest as anxious to ketch Starr as he is. But if that booger is hidin' in the rocks yon side of the river—which I doubt he is—don't crowd him. An' if he's rode off into the desert, you give him room—lots of room."

"Maybe I could talk him into coming back and facing the music."

"Belford's music? You know what tune *he'd* play!"

Finishing his coffee, Andy put down the cup and got to his feet. "Well, however it turns out, Levi and I are taking off, come morning. We'll catch up with the train somewhere west of here—in Boise City, likely. See you."

Trailing a pair of pack horses laden with a week's supply of food staples and several canteens of water, Andy and Levi crossed the Snake in the first flush of dawn, choosing a straight stretch of river a mile downstream from camp. They did not ride directly toward the cluster of rocks from which the bullets had come last evening; instead, they rode a wide, slow circle from river level up the slope and across the relatively open sagebrush plain to the west and south, carefully looking for sign. Presently they found it, the clear, fresh tracks of a horse leading off toward the distant mountains. Tracing the trail back to the river, they came to the spot in the rocks where Starr had hidden for a time and they saw the distinct stains of blood on the sand.

"How long did he stay here?" Andy said.

"Not long. Five, ten minutes."

"Think he's hit bad?"

"Maybe. But a man like him can go a long way with a bullet from a lady's pistol in him."

On the far bank Andy could see a crowd of Missourians milling around, all armed with rifles and eagerly hoping to get wing-shots when their wounded bird broke cover. Beyond them, the Iowans were already bringing in their stock and beginning to hitch up. Cupping his hands around his mouth, Zeke Pence shouted a question which the faintly stirring south wind muffled and made unintelligible; Andy guessed he was asking if they wanted help. Paying him no mind, Andy made hand-signs to Matt, indicating that Starr was gone, that the trail led southwest, and that he and Levi were off to follow it.

Matt indicated he understood. Mounting, Andy and Levi set their horses' heads toward the Owyhees.

The primary reason why Andy had promised Belford he would do his best to track Starr down was that he wanted to keep the Missourians from fruitlessly wasting time and energy. Whether they realized it or not, they had little to spare of either. It had been his experience that people bound for Oregon frequently lost all sense of proportion along this bleak stretch of trail and did things sane people would not ordinarily have done. Tired, irritable, half sick from dust and heat, they lost their mental balance.

If it were only the men that would suffer from the folly of letting the Iowans go on without them while they themselves wore out their horses on an aimless manhunt, that would have been different. A man had a right to make a fool of himself. But the women were bone-weary, Andy knew, and the children fretful and difficult to manage. A lot of tough miles still lay ahead, with two mountain ranges yet to be crossed and the early autumn rains to be endured at the tag end of the trip. Days lost now would be dearly paid for later on. And it would be the women and children that suffered the most.

The two men had been riding for an hour or so when Levi, who had been watching the ground for sign, suddenly said,

"No more blood."

"Good. Maybe he's not hurt too bad."

The Delaware brooded upon the wide reach of space before them. "What're you gonna do if we catch him?"

"Talk to him."

"What're you gonna say?"

"I'll try to persuade him to ride to Boise City with us and give himself up."

"To old Corny?"

Andy smiled, wondering what Cornelius Belford's reaction would be if he heard himself referred to in that way. "No, to the law."

"He won't listen to that kind of talk."

"What would *you* say to him?"

"Keep runnin'."

"How long can he live in this country, hurt and alone?"

Levi shrugged. "Longer'n he will if he rides to Boise City with us."

All day they followed the clear trail, which continued to head directly toward the mountains, making their camp in late afternoon in the depths of a steep-walled ravine which was filled with sandstone boulders. They built no fire and picketed the horses close by, sleeping and watching in turns through the night. When dawn came, they ate a cold breakfast and rode on.

They did not hurry. Levi agreed with Andy's notion that Starr had too big a start and was traveling too fast to be overtaken by hard riding. And they were getting so near to the mountains now that it was wise to raise no more dust than necessary, for dust-trails in the lower country could be seen a long way off by sharp-eyed watchers posted on the heights. As the day wore on, Andy's concern for their own safety grew. In open country, they had a fair chance of spotting hostile Indians and escaping them by turning tail and making a run for it. But in rough, brush-covered terrain, such as that lying ahead, they well might ride into a trap where they would have no choice but to stand and fight.

"That black is gettin' tired," Levi said.

"It's packing a lot of weight."

"He's pushin' it too hard. Gonna be afoot soon, he don't stop to rest."

They made an early camp that afternoon, for the wind had died and the dust from their horses' hoofs was beginning to rise straight upward on the still air, telltales that Andy knew would not long be missed by watchers in the foothills. As night came on, they sat with their rifles across their knees, alert for alien sounds, feeling the cool currents of air moving down from the mountain heights.

"How much longer we gonna trail him?" Levi asked.

"We'll let him go if he makes it to the timber."

"He'll hole up when that black peters out."

"I know."

"Supposin' we come on him and he shoots instead of talks. We gonna shoot back?"

"I've got no stomach for killing a man who's done no real wrong."

"Old Corny heard you say that he'd call you an Injun lover."

"Color has nothing to do with it. Will Starr is a man, just like you and me." Andy was silent a moment, lost in thought. "Why do you suppose he did it, Levi? Why did he pretend to be white when he wasn't?"

"Hell," Levi said, "every man wants to be white."

"Do you?"

"Sure. It's no fun being one of God's mistakes."

Unable to see the Delaware's face in the dark, Andy knew from the tone of his voice that he was not joking but was deadly serious. "I didn't know God made mistakes."

"Oh, sure, he makes 'em all the time."

"For instance?"

"Well, for instance, how else you gonna account for all the meanness in the world? How can you see the dirty things people do to one another without sayin' here Old Man God made another mistake and is trying to rub it out?"

"You think the Indian is a mistake?"

"That's what my grandma told me. She got it straight from Old Man God."

"Sounds like she was on close terms with him."

"She was. She talked to him every day."

"And he told her that?"

"Yeah. He said when he finally finished makin' the world and got around to makin' people, the first man he made was black. That one wasn't so good so he made another. The second one turned out red. That one was better, but still not right. So he tried a third time and made a white man. That one satisfied him. So then he quit."

"Sure he wasn't disgusted rather than satisfied? Maybe he gave up on man of *all* colors as an impossible chore."

"Well, it was my grandma's story and that's the way she told it to me."

"She had quite an imagination, I'd say."

"Call it that if you want. But she was usually right. She used to say a man had to be what he was born to be. She said it was God's business, not man's, to correct his mistakes and you had to let him do it in his own way. That's where Will Starr went wrong. Now he's gotta pay for it."

Andy was not inclined to argue that.

The two squaws were wrinkled, thin and old. Their children were long since grown, their husbands were long since dead and now they themselves were of little worth to the roving band of Snake Indians to which they belonged because their waning strength was sufficient only for gathering berries in season, fetching in small dead sticks for the fires and doing other inconsequential chores. Being of such little use, they were always the last to be fed when food was ample and the first to go without when food ran short.

When the band moved, as it must constantly do now that the whites had driven it away from the big rivers in which the salmon ran, the grassy valleys where the buffalo grazed, and the high mountain meadows where the rich camas roots grew, the two old squaws were left to straggle along behind afoot as best they could; horses were only for the strong and young.

On some not distant day, they would straggle behind too far, these two worthless old women; when that happened, they would quietly sit down where weariness stopped them, cover their heads and wait for death to take them. Next snow, perhaps, this would happen. But summer lay on the land now; its heat had warmed their stiff old joints and brightened their eyes; this was the moon when the purple berries ripened on the low bushes along the streams of the mountain foothills— and life was good.

The two old squaws pushed through the screening bushes beside the pool formed by the shallow creek, thinking to slake their thirst and cool their feet in its waters. Both women saw the man at the same instant. Their toothless mouths opened wide in astonishment but they made no sound, for instinctively each had raised a veined, bony hand to her lips in a gesture of surprise.

For a moment, they stared at the apparition—which had dropped from the sky for all they knew—then, like rheumatic snakes, they wriggled back through the bushes, got to their feet and fled in terror.

They did not run far. Exhaustion stopped them within a hundred yards and they sat down on a fallen log, gasping for breath, trembling. When they had recovered their wind, they began to argue—as women will. One said that the man was white; the other said he was not. One said he was dead; the other swore she had seen his chest move. One was sure she had seen a shiny metal firestick that shot many times lying on the ground beside him; the other claimed he had no arms other than the knife in his belt. One, who was afraid, said they must hurry back to camp and tell the men of their find; the other, who was curious, said, no, let us first go back for another look.

As happens with women, curiosity won.

Approaching the pool cautiously this time, the two old squaws soon learned that they both had been partly right. The man was not dead, but he looked to be dying. In appearance, he was as dark as an Indian and had some Indian features, but he was wearing white man's clothes. A firestick lay on the ground beside him, but there was a knife in his belt, too.

One of the old squaws gingerly picked up the firestick and the other lifted the knife out of its sheath. In whispers, then, never taking their beady eyes off the man for so much as an instant, they debated what to do. In years past it had been their privilege to entertain themselves with the still-live bodies of their people's enemies by inflicting all manner of painful tortures upon them; this would be rare pleasure to the two old women now. But custom and superstition stayed their hands. In the first place, no woman dared touch an enemy's body until her menfolk were finished with it. In the second place, this stranger— whether white or red—might not be hurt as badly as he appeared to be. In the third place, he might not be a man at all, but a monster, a spirit-devil whose very breath would turn them to ashes if they touched him.

So, as women will, they argued—and did nothing.

Suddenly the man's head moved to one side, twisted, lifted. Terror-stricken, the squaw with the firestick tried to raise it and shoot, but its weight was too great and her hands too shaky. The squaw with the knife pulled it back to strike, then, gazing at the immense chest through which the blade must be thrust to reach a vital spot, her courage failed her and her arm dropped to her side.

The man's eyelids fluttered open. His eyes were dark and deep and the light in them was as faint as the last flicker of a dying fire. But there was a brief instant of recognition in that flickering, as if the mind behind the eyes had looked, had seen and now was trying to communicate a message.

A huge hand came up to shoulder level; thumb and fingers shaped themselves into what the two old squaws suddenly realized was meant to be a sign. Then the hand dropped, the eyes closed and the head sank back to the chest. But the question had been settled.

Whatever it was and wherever it came from, the monster wanted it known that he was an Indian.

Taking the knife and gun with them, the two old squaws got to their feet and stumbled stiffly toward camp, excitedly gabbling about the brief moment of glory that would be theirs when they told the menfolk what they had found . . .

CHAPTER EIGHTEEN

The morning was two hours old when Andy and Levi found what was left of Will Starr's horse. That was not much, for the animal had been skinned and butchered and its saddle, bridle, hide, and meat carried away, leaving only the inedible offal and skeleton behind, upon which a swarm of immense black ants and a number of slim-waisted, vicious-looking wasps were vying for what shreds of flesh remained. The black had been a beautiful horse once; now it was only a pile of bones. The hideous sight made Andy's stomach churn and he turned his gaze away. Numerous moccasin prints and the tracks of unshod horses in the vicinity of the skeleton left no doubt as to the identity of the butchers.

Levi was prowling in widening semicircles, his eyes intent on the ground. Andy said, "What happened to Starr?"

"His tracks lead yonder."

Andy's eyes followed the pointing hand up the slope toward the beginnings of the timber a mile or so away. A prickling feeling ran over his skin, as if it were covered with the same insects that were cleansing the bones of the dead black. Starr had killed Warren Monday evening. Likely he had reached this spot Tuesday afternoon. This was Thursday morning, which meant that two nights and parts of two days had passed since Starr had been set afoot. Andy shook his head.

"The poor bastard!"

"We gonna follow?" Levi said.

"No, it's too risky. But I can't help wondering . . ."

Levi drew a finger across his throat in a slashing motion. Andy nodded. Death must have been Starr's fate; wounded, weak and afoot as he was, he could not have eluded the Snakes for long. Yet he continued to stare at the nearby fringe of timber.

Reading his doubts, Levi said, "You ain't sure he's dead?"

"He must be. But it's hard to imagine. A man as big and strong as he was—"

"That black horse was big and strong, too. Look what's left of it."

Impatiently, Andy mounted. "Alive or dead, there's nothing we can do for him now. Let's get out of here before those damn Snakes decide to make meat of us, too."

They rode in a general northerly direction toward Snake River, which Andy guessed lay some twenty or thirty miles away. Boise City would be another thirty or thirty-five miles beyond the river and slightly to the east, he judged, though he was not familiar enough with this part of the country to be sure of their exact whereabouts. By the time they reached Boise City, they would have covered roughly twice the distance that the wagon train must traverse, for they were riding two legs of an approximately equal-sided triangle while the train made only one, which meant that the emigrants likely would reach town a day or so ahead of them.

"What're you gonna tell old Corny?" Levi said.

"All there is to tell. That the Snakes got him."

"He won't like it. He had his mouth set for a hanging."

Andy's breakfast had turned into a leaden ball in his stomach. The fatigue and tension of the long ride, the brutal reality of the stripped skeleton, his knowledge of the tortures Starr must have suffered at the hands of the Indians and still might be suffering now, all had combined to turn his digestive juices sour within him. Levi's mention of Belford gave him a sudden mind-image of Will Starr staked out naked on the ground while human-sized ants and wasps stripped the living flesh from his bones.

"Well, if Belford is disappointed," he said harshly, "you can cheer him up by describing in detail what the Snakes likely did to the poor devil."

The ravine they were following had been carved by a stream which at this time of year was only a few inches deep and a yard wide. The slopes were strewn with reddish colored boulders, some no larger than a man's head, some as big as houses. Though he had never been within miles of this spot before, the odd feeling grew in Andy that it was familiar to him. He frowned, puzzling over that, then suddenly it came to him. Lafe Perrin's gold-filled gulch was supposed to lie a day's ride west of the Bruneau River, which they had crossed early yesterday morning. Lafe had described the gulch as being filled with red boulders. Doubtless there were other boulder-strewn gulches in this foothill country; still, this could be the very one in which Lafe had found his nugget.

The pressing need to put this rough, broken, dangerous country behind as quickly as possible stifled Andy's urge to pause and dig and see if the gold were really here, but as they rode on he studied the creek's banks and shallows with more observant eyes. In the space of the next few miles he was surprised to discover unmistakable evidence that a number of other white men had recently passed this way. Here in the dried mud were week-old prints of shod hoofs. Here in the lee of a boulder were discarded food tins and the blackened remains of a fire. Here where the gulch widened the grass had been eaten down, tree limbs had been hacked off, bottles had been broken and a quantity of earth had been gouged out, leaving a lateral, trench-like scar running from the creek's sands up the slope.

Levi's sharp eyes saw the sign, too. "What're prospectors doing here? I thought the gold was yonder."

Faint in the haze to the north a line of mountains could be seen, the beginnings of the range at whose southern foot Boise City lay. To the best of Andy's knowledge what Levi had said was true. But men eager for gold were a restless breed, willing to travel any distance and dare any danger to test virgin earth.

"They must think it's here, too."

"Suppose they found any?"

"God knows."

By the time they stopped to eat and rest the horses at noon the gulch had spread out into rolling benchland covered with a good stand of bunchgrass. Not a mile had passed without their having seen signs of prospecting parties, some small, some large, some weeks old, some more recent. Yet they had seen no human being, white or red.

Andy let his eyes roam over the gently undulating country. As always in this land, an increase in elevation meant an increase in moisture, and the changes in types of vegetation from river level to mountain height were striking. In the middle distance lay the Snake, glinting like a ribbon of silver under the hot sun. Line of sight, it would be at least ten miles away, he judged, and a thousand feet below them. Down there, the summer-parched land supported nothing but scraggling sagebrush, but as the terrain sloped upward a broad belt of grassland appeared, and it was this that caught his eye now.

Knee-high, yellow as ripe wheat, rippling in the wind like an endless yellow sea, the bunchgrass covered the benchland eastward and westward as far as the eye could reach. Invariably, he knew, stockmen from the States turned up their noses in disbelief when told the nourishment that was in that grass. To them grass must be green to be of any worth. But Andy had long since learned that stock grazed on bunchgrass put on pounds as quickly as when fed the best sun-cured meadow hay.

And the beauty of bunchgrass rangeland was it took care of itself. Set fire to it in late summer, as the Indians sometimes did, and it came back from the roots next spring stronger than ever. Summer's heat and drought merely turned it yellow without affecting its value as stock food; winter's cold and snow merely turned it brown. Spring's heavy rains, which gullied the higher mountain slopes and the lower sagebrush plains, seldom loosened its tenacious grip on the soil where it grew—and summer, autumn, winter, and spring, yellow, brown, or green, stock thrived on it.

Hardly aware that he was voicing his thoughts aloud, Andy murmured, "This might be it."

Levi, who had been dozing, opened his eyes. "What're you mumblin' about?"

"It just hit me. This might be the spot for our ranch."

"What're we gonna do, raise beef for them renegade Snakes?"

"They'll be cleaned out sooner or later."

"Good! Let's wait."

Levi had spoken in jest, Andy knew; still, there was wisdom in what he said. Ranching in this part of the country would be a dangerous business until the hostile Indians scattered through the nearby mountains were starved out or killed off. But it might be years before the government got around to that chore. There was a war on back East. What few troops were stationed out here were too busy patrolling the emigrant trails, stagecoach roads, and freighting routes to concern themselves protecting lone ranchers foolish enough to turn their cattle loose on grass far removed from the settlements.

But there lay the grass. And yonder, north of the river, were thousands of meat-hungry men whose pokes were lined with gold. Ranchers would come, Indians or no, and they would be a different breed of men from any this country had ever seen before. They would not be fur trappers interested only in getting their beaver pelts and moving on. They would not be emigrants hastening through to Oregon nor prospectors whose only thoughts were of gold. They would not be soldiers hampered in their dealings with the Indians by Army rules and regulations.

These would be men of property—property on the hoof— come to take and hold the land; hard-eyed, hard-fibered men with no compunctions against tracking down and killing all predators that preyed on their herds, whether they be wild animals or wild men. In his travels about the West, Andy had met a few of these pioneer cattlemen and he knew how hardy and self-sufficient they could be. Whether theirs was a special kind of courage or a special kind of foolhardiness, he could not say. But wherever the grass grew, they went, building their cabins and corrals, grazing their cattle, making peace with their Indian neighbors when they could, fighting without quarter to protect their own when they could not. Now and again they paid for their venturesomeness with their lives; but as sure as one was killed, two more moved in to take his place.

Until twenty-five years ago, Andy knew, there had not been a beef-strain cow in the Pacific Northwest, save for those in the small herds owned and jealously hoarded by the Hudson's Bay Company posts on the Columbia and Puget Sound. Then the Americans came and saw the grass. Unable to buy cattle from the Britishers, too impatient or too short of cash to wait for beef cattle to be driven overland from the States or shipped around the Horn by boat, they had gone down to California and bought scrawny, light, longhorned stock from the Mexicans at dirt-cheap prices and driven the beasts northward into the Willamette Valley.

There had been no trails through that rugged country then. No matter. The Americans made their trails as they went. Used to roaming freely over the wide valleys of central California, the Mexican cattle were wild as deer. The Americans tamed them as they traveled. In the forests of northern California, in the Siskiyou Mountains along the border, in the Rogue River country of southern Oregon, meat-hungry Indians attacked time and again. The Americans tamed them, too.

Since that day, Andy knew, the quality and number of beef cattle in Oregon and Washington Territory had grown tremendously. And the men who owned the herds had lost none of their daring. Once they realized that the grass and the market were here, they would come—despite this country's dangers. And the first-comers would take the best of the range, while the late-comers must be content with the leavings.

Levi was still eying him quizzically. As they mounted, Andy laughed and said, "Wait, Levi? That's what broke the wagon down."

Under Matt's guidance, the wagon train reached Boise City late Friday afternoon and made camp on the north bank of the Boise River, west of the town. There was little grass and few trees here; dust lay thick on the ground and the once clear, sparkling stream was yellow with washings from mining operations upriver. Daniel Lynn eyed the campsite with disgust.

"Can't we do better than this?"

"'Feard not."

Lynn gazed to the east, where a pall of dust hung in the air, limiting vision. All that could be seen of the Boise Valley were seared yellow foothills rising to the north, a lower rim of sage-covered highlands to the south, and the ugly river winding between bordering lines of sickly looking willows and cottonwoods. The newly completed military post called Fort Boise sprawled across the elevated benchland to the north, while a conglomeration of tents, shacks, frame buildings, log buildings, and every conceivable combination thereof covered the lower ground along the river. Lynn eyed Matt dubiously.

"This is the garden spot you've been bragging about?"

"It was a purty valley once," Matt said sadly.

"That must have been a long time ago."

"Only a year."

"What's happened to it?"

"People. Seems they're bound to spile things. They're swarmin' in like flies."

"Is there that much gold here?"

"Ain't no gold down here in the low country. But they're makin' new strikes every week in the mountains to the north, they say. I hear tell there's been some big strikes in the Owyhee country, too, which is down south a ways."

"If the gold is in the mountains to the north and south," Lynn said, looking puzzled, "why are all these people pouring into Boise City?"

"Miners got to buy grub and supplies. This is a handy place to outfit. All the trails meet here. It's kind of a passing-through place."

"Well, from what I've seen of it," Lynn grunted, "that's exactly what we're going to do—pass through. And the sooner, the better."

Something besides dust in the air. Strolling about the enclosure, Armand Kimball could sense that, though he could put no name to what the something was. Usually after camp had been made, the slow fading of day into night made the world of the emigrants grow smaller, more compact, until it shrank to the dimensions of the wagon enclosure itself. The flickering of firelight against canvas, the glow of lanterns, the murmuring of voices as people talked, all inclined a person to give no thought to what lay beyond the circle of parked wagons, for he knew that there was nothing out there except space—dreary space with no seeming end to it—and he had seen enough space during the long, weary, traveling hours to be heartily sick of it.

But now the space outside the circle no longer was empty. There was a town nearby—no, by God, it called itself a city, and its inhabitants already were bragging that it was going to be a big one. And there was traffic on the nearby trail, ceaseless traffic. Strings of heavily laden mules and horses heading upriver to the mines. Men walking or riding by, some giving the emigrant camp no more than a curious glance, others turning off the trail to come near and call out cheerfully, "Howdy, folks! Where you bound?"

"Oregon City!"

"Hell, I just come from there! Where do you hail from?"

"Iowa!"

"Missoury!"

"Hey, mister, how'd you leave things over in the Willamette Valley?"

"Knee-deep in mud, by God! Rainin'est place I ever did see!

"Say, any of you from Pike County? My wife's back there . . ."

Soon the camp was full of strangers, eager to trade news of the West for news of the East. Distracted emigrant women called vainly to children who had quit their firewood-fetching chores to watch more intriguing sights. Angry women, supper ready, wondered aloud where on earth Pa had got to when he'd been here just a minute ago. Likely as not, Pa would be found sharing a bottle with some dusty, bearded stranger.

"He knows the Gradys back home, Ma! Imagine that! He just come up from Californy and I've asked him to stay for supper. Lay out an extra plate, Ma . . ."

Less than an hour after camp had been made, two handsome young Army lieutenants from Fort Boise rode up. Scrupulously polite, they said they wished to convey the respects of the post's commandant, Major Lugenbeel, to the emigrants, to welcome them to the valley, and to invite all the young ladies in the train to a ball to be given at the fort tomorrow evening. Oh, yes, indeed, they assured the mothers, the ball would be well chaperoned. In fact, the major had suggested that as many of the girls' mothers as wished to attend do so as his personal guests. No, ma'am, no intoxicating beverages will be served—the major is quite strict about such things— and none of the town roughs will be permitted in the hall.

Five minutes after the two officers had ridden away, a sergeant and three corporals came hurrying into camp. They appeared to be somewhat out of breath, for they had come afoot, but their sunburned faces were freshly shaven, their uniforms clean and neat, and their manners just as respectful as the officers' had been, though not quite as polished. On behalf of the noncoms and enlisted men, the sergeant said, he wished to welcome the emigrants to Boise City, and if the young ladies were going to be free tomorrow evening . . .

No? Well, then, how about a picnic Sunday afternoon? After church services, of course. Yes, ma'am, most all the enlisted men attend church services whenever they get the chance. You say there'll be preaching in your camp Sunday morning? Well, now, that will be fine, just fine! A lot of the boys will want to come. And afterward—well, ma'am, there's a real pretty spot for a picnic up the river a ways . . ."

Something besides dust in the air, Kimball thought with a smile. Indeed there was! Although he was tired and had planned to go to bed early, he continued to stroll about the enclosure as dusk fell, an odd sense of excitement and anticipation in him. As he walked, he caught snatches of conversation.

"Oh, Ma, I don't care if he *is* a Yankee soldier! It's been so long since I've gone to a dress-up dance . . ."

Young Isaac Shelby, who'd been keeping company lately with a pretty, black-eyed Iowa girl named Beulah Baker, was saying sullenly, "All right, go ahead and *go* to that stupid ball. I won't miss you."

"What will you be doing?" Beulah asked suspiciously.

"Oh, some of us fellows got plans."

"Like what?"

"Like going into town and stirring up some fun."

"What kind of fun?"

"Who knows? Maybe we'll have ourselves a few drinks—"

"Isaac, you wouldn't!"

"—and pick up some town girls—"

"Isaac! You're horrid, just plain horrid! There aren't any nice girls in Boise City!"

"Who wants nice girls? A fellow can have more fun with the other kind."

Something in the air. Daniel Lynn was having a cup of coffee with a compactly built stranger who, by his dress, was a farmer. Kimball heard Lynn say, "You're located in the Payette Valley? Where would that be from here?"

"Thirty miles northwest."

"How long have you been there?"

"Since March."

"What do you raise?"

"Potatoes, cabbage, beans, melons—anything a man sticks in the ground does well there if you irrigate. Why, compared to the Willamette Valley—"

"Have you tried corn?"

"Tried corn? Mister, I've got the prettiest patch of sweet corn you ever saw in your life. Just last week I took a wagon-load of roasting ears up to Placerville and sold the whole works for a dollar a dozen in gold. Come over to my place tomorrow and I'll show you . . ."

On the Missouri side of the enclosure, Cornelius Belford was listening attentively to a red-headed man with a Southern accent, who was saying, "But we Democrats have the votes, Mr. Belford! When the Territorial elections are held this fall, we're bound to take over the Legislature, I tell you! And I'll tell you something else. The capital's not going to be in Lewiston— not for long, anyway. It's going to be right here in Boise City. If you'll come to our meeting tomorrow night . . ."

Something in the air. Passing by Melinda and her mother, who were arguing heatedly, Kimball heard Melinda say, "But he won't know, Ma! He'll be going to that meeting and you know how he is when he gets to talking politics—he stays up till all hours. Please, Ma, please let me go to the ball!"

"But, child, you don't even know how to dance."

"I do so—enough to get by, anyhow. Please, Ma!"

"If your pa finds out—"

"He won't. I'll be in bed long before he gets back."

"Well . . ."

Something in the air. A tall, rawboned man, whose face bore a striking resemblance to Abraham Lincoln's, was standing on an upended barrel making an impassioned speech to a crowd of Missouri and Iowa men. Kimball paused to listen. The speaker was asking the emigrants why they had come West? And why were their minds set on Oregon? What did they expect to find in the Willamette Valley? Farms, jobs, peace, better opportunities for themselves and their children? Well, if so, all those things were here. Right here.

Listen . . .

And the people were listening, Kimball observed as he let his eyes roam over the crowd. The tall man was a good speaker with a compelling voice and an instinct for sensing unasked questions and answering them in a way that made one feel he knew what he was talking about. Are you a young, single man eager to try your luck in the gold diggings? Then take a ride up the Boise River and have a look at Bannock City, Placerville, Pioneerville, and Rocky Bar. Or ride south, down into the Owyhee Mountains to the newer diggings along Jordan Creek, for there's gold there, too. And there have been rumors of silver . . ."

You're a family man and a farmer, you say? Fine! Linger a while and look carefully at the empty acres of fertile, rock-free valley land along the lower Boise, Payette, and Weiser rivers, and pay no mind to how deep the dust lies. Why, there was a man came up from Oregon this spring—an Englishman, mind you—and dug a ditch and put water on a few acres of bottom land . . ."

You've got some milk cows with you, you say? They're worth their weight in gold! You're a carpenter? A blacksmith? A skilled worker at any trade? Keep it quiet, then, else you'll be waylaid when you go into town, where they're so desperate for men who know how to drive a nail or bend a piece of hot iron that they're apt to rope you and put you to work at a dollar an hour for as many hours a day as you can stay on your feet.

You've still got your mind set on having a look at the Willamette Valley? Well, I wish you luck. But it'll be slow going for wagons on the trail across the Blues because that trail is choked solid with eastbound traffic. And there'll be fog and rain in the Willamette Valley by the time you get there, for you'll miss the dry season, which lasts only a few months. But you'll get your look eventually—next Fourth of July, say. And you may even find a small piece of rain-leached, sour farmland you can buy from some disgusted Webfoot anxious to sell out and come to Idaho . . .

Something in the air . . .

Listening to the speaker, watching the crowd, Kimball now could put a name to what that something was. Like himself, all these people had brooded a long while before making the big decision to pull up their roots and head West. Once that decision had been made, once they had joined the other movers, they had become part of a river seeking the western sea; they were like water moving inexorably downgrade along a well-defined channel toward an ocean-level bay which they vaguely knew lay in the distant West and was called Oregon.

But water had been running down that channel for thirty years. Now the bay was filling up. Now the direction of the current was reversing itself; and here in this dust-hazed valley they had reached its first lapping backwash. The emigrants were surprised, bewildered, confused. They could go on, true. But it would be upstream work now; they would be exerting themselves to travel against the current, where before they had been moving with it. They were weary. They had expected their journey to last two more months; but if it could end here, if the promised land they were seeking were not all milk and honey, as they had thought it to be, if the people living in that promised land were deserting it to come here, why go on?

An Iowan, Cal Weaver, called out, "You got a mighty slick tongue, mister. But why are you so all-fired anxious to git us to settle here?"

"Because I think Idaho will be good for you and you will be good for Idaho."

"You don't know nothin' about us."

"I know you're family people. That's enough."

"Ain't prospectors family people?"

"Very few of them. All they're after is gold. Get rich and get out—that's their philosophy. One family of your kind of people is worth ten of their breed when it comes to building a state."

"What's your trade?" Zeke Pence demanded.

"I'm a newspaperman."

"Which cause do you hold to—North or South?"

"Neither, my friend," the tall man answered with a faint smile. "I believe in a bigger cause—that of the West."

"You sound like a fence-straddler to me. Speak plain. Are you a dirty Republican or a good Democrat?"

"Sir, I refuse to answer that question. If I did, at least half of you would immediately dislike me and I want to be friendly with you all. But let me say this. The columns of my paper— once I start publishing it—will be open to dirty Republicans, clean Republicans, good Democrats, bad Democrats, and supporters of all other political parties on a free and equal basis. There's nothing I like better than a lively fight. And, believe me, gentlemen, if I am any judge there are going to be some beautiful fights in Idaho before this Territory decides which political road it intends to travel. Why don't you stick around and take part in the fun?"

There was general, good-humored laughter from the crowd as the man stepped down from the barrel. Making his way to him, Kimball said, "I'm Armand Kimball."

"Hiram Jackson."

"You're a convincing talker, Mr. Jackson."

"Did I convince you?"

"Partially."

Taking him by the arm, Jackson said, "I'm so dry I'm spitting cotton. Come to town with me, join me in a drink and I'll endeavor to make your conviction complete."

Full dark had fallen by now. The pace set by Hiram Jackson as they left the wagon enclosure behind and strode through the warm night was an energetic one. Dry though he claimed to be, his vocal cords still were well enough lubricated to permit him to talk emphatically and illuminatingly.

He had been in Boise City only a few weeks, he said. Though he had not yet started his newspaper here, he intended to do so just as soon as he could rent a building and bring in printing equipment. He had lived and published papers in a number of gold boom towns in California, Oregon, and northern Idaho. His personal fortunes, Kimball gathered, had waxed and waned many times, but he appeared to be the kind of man financial reverses did not daunt for long.

"I've made mistakes, Kimball, but I've learned from them. For instance, I'll never again publish a paper in a mountain mining town. When the gold is gone, there's nothing left. I've seen it happen time and again. While the boom is on, business property sells for fifty dollars a street-front foot. When it fades, you can buy the whole town for a song. Get rich and get out—that's the prospector's dream. There's always a new strike over the next hill, he thinks. Finally he runs out of hills—then the whole region dies. But here's a curious thing about these gold booms, Kimball. Always when they're done, somewhere nearby, down in the fertile valleys of the low country, a prosperous, permanent city is left. Like Sacramento. Or Denver. Or Walla Walla. No gold was there when those towns began. But when the boom ends, there are the towns— alive, healthy, and growing."

"What do they live on?"

"Permanent, solid things. In all likelihood, they began as outfitting centers, transportation centers, drinking, wenching, and hell-raising centers, whose chief occupation was the separation of fools from their gold. But when the gold and the fools are gone, the towns discover that they have become farming centers, trade centers, and political centers that are going to stay reasonably prosperous as long as babies are born and crops and livestock grow."

"You think Boise City is such a place?"

"I do. It's going to be the hub around which the entire Territory of Idaho spins."

Kimball was inclined to discount that prediction. For one thing, he suspected that Hiram Jackson was prejudiced in his judgment. For another, he had recently been told that Idaho Territory's eastern boundary included Fort Laramie, two months travel by wagon away, and it seemed utterly ridiculous to assume that a town as far removed from the geographical center of the Territory as Boise City was could ever become its hub. And yet, he admitted, the more he saw of this country the more he realized that in it utterly ridiculous things happened with surprising frequency.

"What's your trade, Kimball?" Jackson asked.

"I'm an attorney."

"Oh, hell!"

The disgust in Jackson's voice was so evident that Kimball bridled. "What's wrong with that?"

"It's been my personal experience, sir, that the law profession is full of unscrupulous scoundrels who live on humanity's troubles as vampire bats live on blood."

"The same could be said of doctors."

"True. But my health is excellent."

"I take it your financial affairs are not?"

Hiram Jackson sighed. "You take it correctly. If you had gone through as many financial fiascos as I have, if you had married the fiendish-minded woman I married . . . Well, never mind. I said I'd buy you a drink and I will. Here, this is as good a place to start as any . . ."

When Andy and Levi rode into the emigrant camp Saturday noon, they found it virtually deserted. As Sally Lynn fixed them a bite to eat, she told Andy that her father and several other Iowa men had gone off that morning to have a look at the Payette Valley. Likely they'd be gone several days. Zeke Pence and a group of Missourians had ridden upriver to Bannock City to see what the Boise Basin was like. Most of the women were in town shopping. She hadn't seen Matt since yesterday evening nor Henry since early this morning.

"The officers are giving a ball at the fort tonight," she said.

"And tomorrow afternoon the enlisted men are having a picnic. All the girls are invited."

"Are you going?"

"No."

"Why not? Don't you like to dance and eat?"

"Not with strangers."

"They wouldn't be strangers long if you'd give them a chance to get acquainted."

Sally flushed as she filled their plates. "Well, you can bet I won't." She stood silently watching them eat for a time, then said hesitantly, "Did you find Will Starr?"

"No. From the sign we saw, the Snake Indians got him."

"Oh, that poor man!"

Through the long, hot afternoon Andy lay around camp, resting, rousing himself from time to time to chat with men returning from town. None of them showed more than a casual interest in Will Starr's fate. All Cornelius Belford said was, "Well, it's good riddance," then left Andy to eat a hasty supper and hurry back to town. Obviously he and the other men had more important matters on their minds.

Dusk brought four covered Army ambulances from Fort Boise to pick up the girls and their chaperones and take them to the ball. Soon after the ladies departed, a dozen of the single young men, led by a grim-faced Isaac Shelby, set out afoot for town. Matt drifted into camp, quite drunk, carrying a half-empty whisky bottle. Seeking Andy out, he put an affectionate arm around his shoulders.

"Shore glad to see you, boy. Did you git the booger?"

"No. The Snakes did."

"Jest as well. Here, let's drink to the poor devil, God rest his soul."

They drank, but when offered the bottle Levi shook his head. His dark eyes held a faintly mocking light. "Andy don't think he's dead."

Matt scowled. "What would them Snakes want to keep him alive for?"

"I didn't say that, Levi," Andy said sharply. "What I said was it was hard to imagine him dead. A man as full of life as he was . . ." He shrugged impatiently. "Forget it." He grinned at Matt, who was eying him owlishly. "What have you been up to—besides drinking?"

"Thinkin'."

"Now there's a chore."

"An' talkin'." A vague, evasive look came into the old guide's eyes. "Run into a fella I used to trap with. Charley Davis. He runs a livery stable in Boise City now. Wants me to go in business with him."

"Doing what?"

"Herdin' a saddle train."

"A pack train, you mean?"

"No, goddamit, a saddle train. Fer people. Ain't you never heard of such a thing?"

Andy said he hadn't. Well, Matt said, it seemed there wa'n't no stagecoaches running into Boise City yet, but Charley Davis owned a string of riding horses and his notion was there ought to be a lively business transporting passengers back and forth across the Blues between Boise City and Umatilla Landing on the Columbia River. Say they charged fifty dollars a head and made the pilgrims furnish their own grub and do their own cooking. There wouldn't be the work to running a saddle train that there would be to packing. Old and stove-up though he was, Matt could handle the job easy.

"Who's going to take the wagon train on to Oregon?"

"You an' Levi. Hell, boy, you don't need me."

"What does Lynn say about your quitting him?"

"Ain't told him yet. Truth is, he's got half a notion to settle here himself."

"Any of the others thinking that way?"

"Lot of 'em. Kimball, Cal Weaver, Zeke Pence, Phil Duncan. An' I seen Belford talkin' to a fella in town today . . ."

The meeting was held at ten o'clock on Wednesday morning, and for the first time since the Iowans and the Missourians had met back at Fort Laramie perfect harmony prevailed. The proposition to be voted upon was quite simple. Cornelius Belford read it to the assembled crowd.

"Whereas, a number of people in this wagon train have expressed a desire to go no farther than the Boise Valley at the present time, and

"Whereas, the jointly employed guides, Matt Miller and Andrew Hale, agree that our obligations to them shall be fully satisfied if they are now paid off at the daily rate agreed to when first employed, from the date of said employment to and including this date, August 12, 1863,

"Be it therefore resolved that said guides be paid off and said wagon train be disbanded." Belford paused and raised his head from the paper which he had been reading. "Are there any questions before the vote is called?"

"I got a question," a disgruntled voice called from the back of the crowd. "What if the majority votes to disband and pay off the guides but some of the rest of us still want to go on to Oregon? Who's gonna see us through?"

"Andy, do you want to answer that?"

Andy hesitated. Now that the decision had been made, now that the possibility offered itself that he and Levi might be free to ride on to the Willamette Valley unhampered by slow-moving wagons, he was all a-fever to be on his way. But he said, "If you want to go on, I'll take you through."

"Any other questions?" Belford asked, his gaze roving over the crowd.

"Call the vote!"

"Yeah, let's get it over with—we know what we want to do!"

Belford raised a hand for silence. "All in favor of the proposition will say 'Aye.'"

Oddly, then, there was a moment of utter silence. It was as if all present had suddenly realized that the time for idle talk was done, that the word spoken now meant an old dream abandoned and a new dream embraced, a turning aside from a worn road to follow a strange road, a forsaking of the vaguely known certainties of a reasonably well-settled, four-year-old state called Oregon in favor of the unrealized, unknown opportunities of a five-month-old territory called Idaho.

Watching the faces in that moment of silence, Andy thought he saw hesitation, thought he saw doubt. Then an uneven, rumbling, swelling chorus of "Ayes!" came from the crowd and he knew he'd been wrong.

The hesitaters, the doubters, had long ago been left behind in Iowa and Missouri.

He heard Daniel Lynn's voice, strong and sure of itself, like the man himself, and he knew why Lynn was voting "Aye!" He had seen the soil, the water, and the crops growing over in the Payette Valley, and already he knew the piece of land he intended to settle upon. Phil Duncan was voting "Aye!" too; he'd been offered a job tending bar in town. Armand Kimball, smiling quietly, had his hand raised and the look of a man already making plans. Belford had plans, too; carpenters were making a dollar an hour in town, and, by Heaven, this country could be whatever the Democrats chose to make it.

And the Shelbys were voting "Aye!" Obidiah, looking grim and stern—as if he'd just lost a son, which he had—was voting "Aye!" And Benjamin (what a wallop young Isaac must pack to have moused his older brother's eye that way!) was voting "Aye!" too. What else could they do? They had to stay now and hope Isaac would come back to the family. Sure, the boy had done wrong, getting drunk with those other young hellions, picking up those two old whores and trying to bust in on the officers' ball at Fort Boise, but Obidiah should have known better than to try to punish the youngster with a razor strop, and, when he refused to hold still for the blistering, Benjamin should have had better sense than to try to force him to submit to the indignity. Lord knows where Isaac was now; gone up to the Boise Basin mines, likely, with horse and gun, on the make for trouble. So the Shelbys would have to settle down here and wait for him to come to his senses—if ever he did. And so would the Bakers, for Beulah had tearfully declared she'd *die* before she'd go on to Oregon and leave Isaac behind.

Cornelius Belford asked for the "Nays." As expected, Adam Schramm voted a belligerent negative, for it was a matter of principle with him always to oppose the crowd. Four others joined him—two Missouri family heads and two Iowans. Andy heard a woman's anguished cry, "Oh, no, Sadie—you're all the kin I've got!" There were sudden tears, sudden argument, then a man's tired voice saying, "All right, woman, *all right!* You always do get your way. Aye! We're changin' our vote to 'Aye!'"

"Wal, damned if we're a-goin' to travel alone with damn Yankees!" shouted a man's voice in a harsh hill twang. "We'll stay hyar till spring, anyhow. Change my vote to 'Aye!'"

Who would want to travel with a crazed old coot like Adam Schramm? As one man, the two Iowa household heads hastily allowed that they could stand Boise City for a few months, dry, dusty, and hot though it was, and changed their votes to "Aye!" And even as Andy was contemplating the unsavory prospect of being alone in Adam Schramm's company, the old bachelor shook his fist at the crowd and yelled in a cracked, high-pitched voice, "To hell with everybody! I don't need no guide! I kin find my way to Oregon by myself!"

Thus, matters were settled.

Half an hour sufficed for Andy to collect his pay and say his goodbyes while Levi saddled the horses and lashed light packs on a pair of spares. His goodbyes were brief and casual, for already he'd told his friends that he would be coming back. And each man's mind was turning to the immediate problems facing him. The wagons had been circled together for the last time. One by one now they would pull out and go their separate ways, and never again would this group of people be gathered in the same place at the same time.

Daniel Lynn shook Andy's hand. "You'll look us up as soon as you get back?"

"Sure."

"Any idea when that will be?"

"Before snow-fly, I hope."

"Ain't you and Levi going to have trouble handling all them cattle?" Henry said eagerly. "Won't you need some help?"

"Henry, for goodness sake!" Sally said in exasperation.

"Well, it don't hurt to ask, does it? I'd like to see the Willamette Valley."

"It's not what you said I'm criticizing but the way you said it. Won't you ever learn grammar?"

"Andy understands me. Don't you, Andy?"

"Sure, boy, sure." Andy started to give the boy a friendly pat on the shoulder, then changed his mind and gave him a man-style handshake instead. "You'd be welcome, Henry, but your pa needs you worse than we do. Be good to your sister, now. She'll need looking after with all these single men around."

"Aw, who'd want to marry her?"

"Can't never tell. Some fat Indian buck, maybe."

Sally walked with Andy to the spot outside the wagon enclosure where Levi was waiting with the horses. Unconsciously she put her hand on his arm as he paused to say goodbye.

"You *will* come back?"

"God willing."

"Is it a bad trail?"

"No worse than those we've been following." Suddenly he realized that she was crying; strangely touched, he put his hand under her chin and lifted her face. "Why the tears, Sally?"

"No reason. No reason at all."

"Girls don't cry over nothing."

"Well, maybe it isn't nothing. I just feel sad, realizing it's all over. We traveled so long together—all of us—and came such a long way. And now it's finished."

"We couldn't keep traveling forever."

"No. But endings are sad, just the same. They always make me cry."

He wanted to kiss her goodbye, but, because it was broad daylight, because Levi was watching, because at this moment she seemed so young and childlike, he did not. Patting her hand, he turned away, mounted his horse and rode off, not looking back for some moments.

And then, when he did look back, she was waving to him, her tears gone, a calm smile on her face, no longer a child but a woman. Soon, he guessed, she'd forget her sadness over the ending of one thing and lose herself in the excitement of beginning another.

Part II
The Valley

The Star of Empire Westward takes its way . . .
When Bishop Berkeley wrote, was very true;
But were the Bishop living now, he'd say:
That brilliant star seems fixed to human view.

From Eastern hives are filled Pacific shores—
No more inviting sunset lands are near;
The restless throng now backward pours—
From East to West they meet, and stop right here.

Away our published maps we'll have to throw—
The books of yesterday, today are lame;
So swiftly, rapidly ahead we go,
Ere map or book is made, we're not the same.

The stranger wishing for a pocket guide,
Must learn that here we fairly fly around;
And towns and roads are made on every side
In shorter time than books and maps are bound.

—Author Unknown
Owyhee Avalanche
Silver City, Idaho Territory
February 10, 1866

Chapter One

Maybe remorse would come later, Isaac Shelby brooded as he rode up the Boise River trail that warm Sunday morning, but right at the moment he felt damned proud of himself. In a vague way, he had realized for some time now that there were certain things a young fellow had to do before he could call himself a man. And, by God, he'd done them all in little more than twelve hours.

First, he'd told his steady girl to go to hell and showed her she couldn't boss *him* around. Second, he'd gone on his first honest-to-God drunk. Third, he'd picked up a painted woman and treated her the way a *real* man was supposed to treat such creatures. Fourth, he'd gotten involved in a rip-snorting brawl, in which he had more than held his own, and, afterward, had defied his own father and blacked his older brother's eye. Last, and most important, he had told them flatly that from now on he intended to be his own man, responsible to nobody but himself, and had ridden out into the world to make his own way.

Mentally he took stock of his assets. He possessed a horse, a saddle and bridle, a pair of blankets, a skillet, tin cup and eating utensils, a shotgun, a rifle, a Navy Colt, holster and cartridge belt, a hatchet, a knife, the clothes on his back and fifty dollars in cash. Benjamin had objected strenuously to his father's giving him the money, but Obidiah had said grimly, "He's entitled to it, Ben. Let him prove he's the man he thinks he is by using it wisely."

"Likely he'll spend it the first day on whores and whisky."

The hell I will, Isaac thought angrily. One spree don't mean I intend to waste my life tom-catting around. All it means is I'm fed up to my eyeballs with being treated like a wet-nosed pup, being told to do this and do that, being little-brothered by Ben and mothered by Ruth and given Pa-knows-best talk by my old man. Sure, all of you mean well, but enough is enough.

The trail climbed steadily. The gold-mining country was located in the mountains a day's ride northeast of Boise City, he'd been told, and the heart of it was a place called Boise Basin. The diggings (that was a miner's word he'd already learned to use) extended along Moore's Creek, Grimes' Creek, and numerous other streams he'd heard mentioned but couldn't remember now; and towns such as Bannock City,

Placerville, Centerville, and Pioneerville (every settlement in Idaho, apparently, had either "City" or "ville" tacked onto its first name) boasted populations of five to fifteen thousand souls, according to who was doing the estimating.

Such a country must be mighty lively and exciting, he decided. And if a fellow used proper judgment, it shouldn't be any trick at all to make himself a pile of money in a hurry. That was the key—be smart. Wander about through the diggings for a week or two, keeping your eyes open and your mouth shut, working at odd jobs for your keep (there's lots of work for those who want it, he'd heard), save your hoard of cash till you know the ropes, find a likely looking spot to start digging, buy the necessary tools and go at it. Then, when you've made your pile—next spring, say—sell out for a fat price to some newcomer (that was the smart thing, he gathered; unload your claim while it was still showing good color), and pay your family and your girlfriend a visit—wherever they happen to be by then.

That last thought gave him a momentary twinge of conscience. Where *would* they be, come spring? There had been some talk among the emigrants, he knew, about stopping over in Idaho for the winter rather than journeying on to the Willamette Valley. But, good Lord, where would they live and how? They would have to start from scratch. Ruth had been ailing ever since the baby had come; Pa wasn't the man he used to be, so far as physical labor was concerned; and the long months on the trail had honed Ben down to where he was as thin as a razorback hog. Beulah's pa, who'd been a storekeeper back in Iowa, didn't know how to drive a nail. Both families could use some help . . .

Oh, the hell with 'em! To get ahead in the world, a man's got to think first of himself. And, by God, I'm going to get ahead.

By noon, the rocky, lava-strewn canyon of the Boise River and the yellowed, parched slopes of the lower country were well behind him. Around him now were pine woods and steep hills; the air had a sweet mountain taste to it, the sky was a sharper blue, and the creeks which he followed or crossed tumbled swiftly along their courses, brownish-yellow with placer washings, much lower at this time of year than they had been earlier in the summer, uglier than the clear streams back home, but real mountain streams just the same.

Back home, hunting and fishing had been his favorite spare-time sports; a goodly share of the meat served at the family table had been supplied by his skill with gun, hook and line. Carefully wrapped in oilskins and secured inside his blanket roll, broken down, were his treasured hunting rifle and double-barreled shotgun, along with plenty of ammunition and fishing tackle. He had had little opportunity to use the guns on the trip west, for game was scarce along the well-traveled wagon trails, but he had caught enough fat trout in the high meadow pools around South Pass and in the waters of Bear River to know that the streams of this western land were alive with fish. He had looked forward to wandering at will through this well-watered, well-timbered mountain country northeast of Boise City, for he had been sure that in it a man with his skills need never go hungry. But now ...

Good God, no fish could live in *this* polluted water! Well, there must be streams higher up, above the diggings, that still ran clean and pure. Lakes, too. Of course deer, bear, squirrel, quail, grouse—few of these game animals and birds likely would be found near the trail along which he was riding, for it was too well traveled. But back in the mountains, away from people ...

Well, maybe quite a way. He was passing now through the beginnings of the gold-digging country, and visual evidence of hasty, ruthless prospecting was constantly in sight. Trees had been hacked down for firewood, shelter materials, sluice boxes, animal corrals, and troughs in which to bring water to hillside claims. Fire-blackened snags stood stark and lonely on slopes burned either by accident or design. The scars of test-holes, ditches, trenches, and tailings showed new and ugly along both sides of the creek which he now was following, as well as in the gulches running laterally in either direction. Human litter was everywhere.

Pa would hate this. In Pa's opinion, a man content to live in the midst of his own litter was of less worth than a cat— which at least licked itself clean and buried its excrement— and was fit to live only with the hogs, which didn't care how filthy their surroundings got. But here, obviously, nobody had cared about appearances. Dig and move on. Litter and leave. Burn and burrow, hack and destroy, and then when the gold is gone pack up and travel and find a new gulch over the next hill to treat the same way. Get the gold and then get out.

Kind of a shame, in a way, ruining what must have been a pretty country, Isaac mused. But what the hell? This isn't Missouri, this is Idaho. Who'd want to live *here* after the gold is gone?

Rounding a bend in the trail, he suddenly was roused from his musings by the sight of half a dozen horses grazing in a meadow beside the creek. Nearby, a man lounged against a stump, eating. As Isaac drew nearer, he saw the man shift to a more erect position, transfer the sandwich he was munching on from his right hand to his left, move his right hand into close proximity of the six-shooter holstered on his hip and eye him alertly. Isaac reined in.

"Howdy."

"Howdy, yourself."

"Am I headed right for Bannock City?"

"Yeah."

The man had cold blue eyes, sandy hair, a week's beard stubble on his dust-grimed face and appeared to be in his early twenties. He took his time looking Isaac over, inspecting his person, his horse, his saddle, and his blanket roll with an appraising insolence that made Isaac feel uncomfortable and very young. Presently the man grunted, "First trip up this way?"

"Yes."

"*You* look familiar to me. Didn't I see you hellin' around Boise City last night?"

"Could be. I was there."

"You weren't by any chance with that bunch of wagon train ridge-runners that picked up Booby Blanche and Oregon Kate and tried to bust into the officers' ball at the fort, were you?"

"Happens I was," Isaac admitted modestly.

"The hell you say!" The man threw back his head and laughed heartily. "That must have been a real brawl, boy, from the talk I heard in town!"

"It got right lively for a spell," Isaac said, permitting a faint, rueful smile to touch his lips. "But we were outnumbered."

"Wish I'd been there to see it, truly I do!" Impatiently the man motioned Isaac to dismount. "Light and sit, friend. I ain't got much in the way of food and drink, but you're welcome to share what's here."

What was here, it turned out, was bread, cheese, cold beef, two fresh tomatoes, and a couple of bottles of lukewarm beer. Isaac, whose stomach was still queasy from last night's drunk, protested that plain creek water would do him fine, but the man insisted that a beer was just what he needed to quiet his belly's butterflies. He was dead right, Isaac admitted, for, though the first two swallows gave him trouble, he shortly felt relaxed and hungry.

They exchanged names, handshakes, and sketchy backgrounds. The man said his name was Gilbert Gillis, but most everybody called him plain old Gil; he came from Arkansas; he had wandered out to California five years ago, knocked around Oregon, Nevada, Washington Territory, and the mining country of northern Idaho, and finally had drifted down this way late last fall. Sure, he'd tried his hand at prospecting here and there. Any luck? Why, sure, lots of luck—all bad. But one way or another he'd managed to make a living.

"Right now, I'm runnin' a horse ranch," he said, "over in the upper Payette country."

"Is there money in horses?"

"Sure, if a man's smart. Grass and water don't cost nothin' and there's lots of both handy. Fellas comin' to the diggings or leavin' 'em got to have transportation. But a horse is just a damn nuisance to 'em while they're here. That's where I come in."

"Buying and selling?"

"Some. But mostly I just take their horses off their hands for a spell, chargin' 'em three bucks a head per month for keep. I got stations in Boise City, Bannock City, and all the mining camps. Every week or two I make the rounds, pick up the horses, take 'em over to the ranch and turn 'em loose."

"What happens if one strays or gets stolen?"

Gillis shrugged. "That's the owner's worry, not mine. But it don't happen often."

"Sounds like a good business to be in."

"Well, it beats diggin' for gold by a damn sight. That's a game for fools with strong backs and weak minds. If a fella's smart, he can make his pile in this country by usin' his brains 'stead of his hands."

"Reckon you're right there."

Gills eyed him thoughtfully. "What are you of a mind to do, Ike?"

"Figured I'd look around for a spell. You know, kind of get the lay of the land."

"Got any money?"

"Not a whole lot," Isaac answered cautiously. "But I guess I can get by for a week or two without starving."

"Hell, you don't have to be cagey with me!" Gillis said, laughing genially. "I ain't about to hit you up for a loan. But from what you've told me, I know things in this neck of the woods are new to you. It's goin' to take you a while to learn your way around."

"I can look out for myself."

"Sure you can. But I was just thinkin' maybe you'd want to give me a hand for a few days."

"Doing what?"

"Lookin' after these horses I've got here, makin' the rounds of my stations in Bannock City, Placerville, and the other mining towns with me, then takin' the horses we pick up over to my ranch on the Payette. Be a week's work, more or less. Can't pay you any cash money, but I'd take care of your bed and board." Gillis winked at him. "Could be I might even get you a free drink here and there and introduce you to some lively gals I know. A man in my business gets acquainted with a lot of people."

The beer, the food, the fresh mountain air, the pleasure of being his own man, and meeting a kindred soul on the trail, all combined to give Isaac a sense of well-being. *This* was the way to live, by God! Every day an adventure. Every night something new and exciting to look forward to. He returned Gil's grin.

"Why not?" he said. "I got nothing better to do."

It had been a wild, fantastic, impossible sort of dream. Wakening from a deep, drug-like sleep, Isaac Shelby stared dazedly up at the dimly visible poles supporting the slanting roof above him, not moving a muscle other than those controlling his eyelids and lungs, not wanting to move them, not daring to move them, vaguely aware that his blankets were spread on a dirt floor, that other men lay sleeping around him, that the room smelled of sweat, whisky, tobacco, leather, horses, grease, and woodsmoke, aware that time had passed and a great number of things had happened, aware that soon he would have to return to the life of full consciousness but not wanting to just yet, preferring just now to lie quietly, remembering his wild, fantastic dreams, thinking about them, making sure they were just dreams and not reality . . .

Be logical. Where else but in a dream would one see a fat, jolly Irishman carrying a fiddle in his hand and packing a small, black-eyed Indian boy dressed in a Confederate uniform upon his shoulder, waddling the length of a room jam-packed with drunken, cheering men—all respectfully stepping aside to make way for him—climbing a ladder to a raised platform suspended by iron rods from the roof joists, pulling the ladder up after him, then standing waiting as imperially as a king for silence, getting it, getting a silence so hushed and expectant that even a cough drew scowls, then inclining his head to the crowd and saying, "First, gentlemen, I should like to play *That Darling Old Mother of Mine.*"

No, music like that could not be made by an earthly fiddle. And in real life, rough, lusty, brawling men who, moments ago, had been stomping around the sawdust-covered floor with hefty dollar-a-dance German hurdy-gurdy girls, doing what could only be described as a buffalo mating dance—such men did not go soft-eyed and cry unashamedly like little boys. Nor would such men in real life push and shove and fight to flood the floor of the high platform with coins, schooners of beer, and glasses of whisky to show their deep gratitude to the fat Irish fiddler when his tune was done.

"More, John, more! Give us *My Mother's Grave!*"
"Give us a lively tune, John! Give us a jig!"
"Shut up, goddam you, 'fore I bust you one! I want *My Mother's Grave!*"
"Let the boy show us his stuff, John! Give us the boy!"

Now the dream got really wild. Imagine this shy, black-eyed little Indian boy dressed in his miniature Confederate uniform standing on the high platform facing the crowd, bending his head slowly backward, backward, backward, while the crowd shouted in unison, "Down! Down! Down!" until his tiny, skinny little body was bent double—the wrong way—and the top of his cap brushed the floor directly behind his heels—then the chant changing to, "More! More! More!" and the head moving forward, then, between the legs, farther, farther, until at last the olive face and the black eyes were peering directly out at the crowd from a position impossible to achieve by any human being whose spine was not made of rubber.

Isaac shuddered. My God, what a horribly obscene dream *that* one had been! But had he dreamed Gil Gillis' standing at his elbow, nudging him and shouting over the crowd's approving roar, "Bet you never seen nothin' like that before, did you, Ike? Say, I tell you, old Fiddlin' John Kelly can fiddle the spots off a speckled dog! An' he taught that Injun kid them contortion stunts all by himself! Picked the little booger up when a bunch of the boys cleaned out a nest of the red bastards down along the Snake last spring. Been trainin' him ever since."

Isaac broke into a cold sweat. All right, so that part had been real. Let's see, we stopped at a couple of places along the road and had beers; we met some friends of Gil's and they had a jug of whisky; we camped somewhere; we took a bath in some hot springs that smelled of sulphur; we came on to Bannock City, did the town, and it was in a saloon there we saw Fiddlin' John Kelly and, his little Indian boy. After that . . .

Well, what came after that *had* to be a dream. Broad daylight in a town built around a central square. A crowd of men breaking up as they rode in, two of them carelessly dragging what appeared to be a limp bundle of old clothes over to an alley between two frame buildings, dumping it, leaving it there, and a newcomer saying, "What happened?"

"Oh, nothin' much. Usual man fer breakfast."
"Killed dead?"
"Busted his head open like a squashed canteloupe."
"Who was he?"
"God knows. Seems he got likkered up, chose ole Snappin' Andy to

bully, an' Andy taken an ax handle to his skull. *Squish!*" That's all there were to it.

In real life, you buried a dead man or at least covered the remains with a blanket until a grave could be dug and the corpse be decently interred. You did not callously drag it over to an alleyway barely clear of the boardwalk and let it lie there all day to be seen by every passer-by on the boardwalk, sightless eyes staring up at the clean blue sky, head broken open and brains oozing out, flies gathering . . .

Isaac felt his belly churn. Placerville. Yes, that was the name of the town where he'd seen the dead man. Then he'd had some more drinks—taken fast to blot out the memory—and they'd spent another night making the rounds of the saloons, then had moved on. And he'd dreamed—yes, he was sure he'd dreamed this—he'd dreamed he'd seen a man killed in cold blood, killed as a practical joke, killed just to stir up a little excitement. Now how did *that* dream go?

A knot of men lazing around on benches in front of a general store. A packer with a string of mules coming down the street, pausing at the town well to draw water for himself and his beasts; one of the men rising, winking at his companions and saying, "Watch this—it'll be good."

The man walking to the well, taking the bucket of water from the packer, then deliberately flinging its contents into the packer's face. The packer, blinded, staggering back, reaching for the red bandanna handkerchief sticking out of his right hip pocket to wipe the water out of his eyes. The other man drawing his Navy Colt, cocking it, and shooting the packer full in the breast. The packer falling, dead. The man walking back to his friends, his face solemn, and saying, "Boys, you seen that, didn't you? Bastard called me a name and drew on me. Ain't that right, Ike?"

No, Isaac thought frantically, *that* didn't really happen. It was a dream. Well, maybe not. Maybe it did happen. But I wasn't one of the men lazing in front of that general store, half drunk, and it wasn't me who joined the other witnesses in nodding and solemnly swearing to the lawman, when he finally came, that there had been an argument at the well, an epithet thrown, a gun reached for, a shot fired in self-defense. I dreamed it or imagined it or heard Gil and his friends telling about it. But it wasn't me. Not me.

Suddenly wide awake and violently sick, he lurched to his feet, staggered through the sleeping figures, stepped on a leg, an arm, was roundly cursed, found his way out the open side of the shed, fell to his hands and knees and retched. Nothing came up. But the spasms continued for some moments before they finally subsided, and when at last they were done he felt so spent and weak that he collapsed on his back and lay for a time sightlessly staring up at the sky.

The time was early morning, he realized. How blue and clean the sky was! How sweet and fresh the air! My God, he thought, what have I done? Just what Ben said I'd do. Now I'm broke, sick, dying . . .

"Hey, Ike!" Gil said, leaning down, shaking him. "Come out of it, boy! Sick as you was 'fore you went to bed last night, you're just throwin' up from memory now."

"Leave me be!" Isaac groaned.

"Fellas, come out here!" Gil shouted at the shack. "Got a mighty sick Injun on our hands. Guess we'll have to give him the treatment. All right, Duke, you grab his ankles whilst I get him under the shoulders. We'll tote him over and dump him in the crick . . ."

Hands laid hold of him. He fought, squirmed, twisted, cursed, but could not get free. He was lifted, carried, dropped. Icy water closed over him. He gasped, snorted, lunged up, fell. Rage seethed in him, making him forget his weakness, his sickness, and he came stumbling blindly up out of the gravelly creek bed into a knot of jeering, hoorawing men, swinging his fists wildly. Then he subsided and sat down, meekly accepting the tin cup of hot coffee thrust into his hand.

"Drink this, Ike," Gil said cheerfully. "It'll put new life into you. Then we'll cook us some breakfast."

Sheepishly Isaac drank the strong coffee, which had been liberally laced with whisky. He looked around at the half dozen unshaven, bleary-eyed men who had made their way out of the lean-to and now were washing their faces in creek water and pouring themselves eye-openers like his own. A rough-looking lot, sure. But he guessed he would take no beauty prizes at the moment himself.

In the meadow beyond the shack, he could see some forty or fifty horses grazing, and, farther to the east and north, pine-timbered hills rising in green folds. A pretty spot, this. Real pretty.

"Well, Ike?" Gil said. "What do you think of my horse ranch?"

"Looks all right."

"Beats a gold mine, boy. No diggin' to do. No fences to build or mend. No herdin' to speak of. We git paid to tend horses we don't have to be responsible for and there's a good market handy for 'em when we take a notion to sell." He winked broadly. "Yes sir, Ike, runnin' a horse ranch beats workin' a damn sight. Stick with me for a while, you'll see what I mean."

Chapter Two

"Faith, an' me wife's a jewel," said Pat. "She always strikes me with the soft end of the mop."

—Boise News
Bannock City, I.T.
December 12, 1863

Back East, there was a war on and the Union needed Idaho's gold. That, at least, was the only sensible motive Armand Kimball could discern underlying the Organic Act passed by Congress and signed into law by President Lincoln last March proclaiming Idaho a legally constituted Territory of the United States. Possessed of an orderly mind, well-grounded in law, history, and politics, acutely aware of the sprawling expanse and relative emptiness of the Territory after having recently crossed it, he found himself both appalled and intrigued by the legal and political chaos he encountered everywhere he traveled and the average citizen's utter indifference to it.

A governor, a secretary, three judges and a U.S. marshal had been appointed by Lincoln as Territorial officials a week after the Act had been signed, Kimball learned, but as yet none of them had set foot in Idaho. Where were they? Nobody knew. When would they put in an appearance? Nobody knew that, either, or particularly cared. Was it true that Lewiston would be the captial? Yes, that was the talk. And where was Lewiston?

"Up north."

"How far is it from Boise City?"

"Oh, the way a crow'd fly it'd be two or three hundred miles," his informant answered vaguely. "'Course there ain't no road north across the mountains, so most folks take the long way 'round."

"How far is it that way?"

Well, that depended on the time of year you took a notion to travel. You had to cross the Blue Mountains over the Oregon Trail first to the Columbia River, which you could hit at either Umatilla or Wallula Landing. If the water wasn't too high, too low, or froze over, you could take a steamer up the Columbia and the Snake to Lewiston. Otherwise, your best bet was to catch a stage at Wallula and go overland by way of Walla Walla. Either way, a week to ten days would be good time—in good weather. In bad, it took a sight longer. Come a heavy snowfall, you'd best stay at home.

When Kimball expressed the opinion that Lewiston appeared to be an out-of-the-way place in which to establish the Territorial capital, his informant shrugged indifferently. "They can put it in an outhouse in Hell, for all I care. What does Idaho need a government for? All politicians know how to do is pass tax laws and spend money. I'd as soon things stayed the way they are."

The way things were, Kimball was not long in discovering, attorneys-at-law found few clients in need of their services. The miner was king and all property rights were secondary to his desires. Each mining district made its own rules, and invariably those rules favored first-discoverers. A member of a prospecting party finding pay dirt in a new region could file a creek claim, a bar claim, a hill claim, a gulch claim, and, in some cases, another of each for a non-present friend. If a town developed adjacent to a gold-mining district, the prospector could dig test-holes big enough to engulf a mule in the center of its main street or undermine its buildings with tunnels to the point of collapse without being liable for damages or responsible for filling up his burrowings when he was done.

Few of the miners took any interest in politics, law enforcement, or government. A fellow attorney whom Kimball met and fell into conversation with in a Boise City saloon—a San Francisco man named Arthur Creed—made the surprising statement that, in his opinion, since the third day of March that year the Territory of Idaho had been without a code of laws of any kind.

"Impossible!" Kimball protested. "Congress passed an Act organizing the Territory."

"Have you read it, Mr. Kimball?"

"I have. There's a tremendous hole in its middle that I'm sure you'd see in a moment if you took the trouble to examine it."

"What sort of hole?"

"Point one," Arthur Creed said, holding up a finger. "Prior to March third the region now designated as Idaho was a part of Washington Territory, thus subject to that Territory's laws. Point two. The Organic Act separated Idaho Territory from Washington Territory, set its boundaries and listed the executive and judicial offices to be filled by presidential appointment. It further specified that at a time to be designated by the Territorial Governor, Idaho would elect a delegate to Congress and a Territorial Legislature, which then would meet and draw up a Constitution and a code of laws. That has not yet happened.

Point three. The Act severing Idaho from Washington Territory, in my opinion, ended the jurisdiction of the previously existing laws—and nothing has been done to replace them."

"Surely there was an interim provision," Kimball protested, "extending those laws until Idaho could draw up its own code."

"There was not," Creed said, shaking his head. "That's the hole."

"In other words, we're living in a state of anarchy."

"Precisely."

"Has this lack of law been questioned in court?"

"Not yet. The local courts go merrily on trying civil and criminal cases under Washington Territorial statutes that are no longer in force, passing judgments in blissful ignorance of the fact that they have no legal validity whatsoever. But mark my word—the day of reckoning will come."

"Isn't it logical to assume that when a Legislature is elected and meets," Kimball said, "it will write into whatever code of laws it adopts an affirmation of the courts' right to assume that Washington Territorial statutes were valid during the interim period?"

"If the subject is brought up, yes. And so far as civil cases go, it might stick. After all, it's the usual practice, where property rights are concerned, for a Territorial government to recognize local custom prior to formal organization. But in criminal cases—ah, that's a horse of a different color. Take murder, for instance."

"Surely *that's* illegal!"

"How can *any* crime be illegal when there is no governing code of laws to be violated? An indictment must state the true facts, must it not? If I kill you five minutes from now, the indictment must state that the act took place in Boise City, Idaho Territory. That being the case, how in God's name could my trial and conviction under the statutes of the Territory of Washington—which no longer apply—be affirmed by a court of appeal?"

"If you're right," Kimball said with a wry smile, "this would be an excellent time for one to dispose of his enemies."

"I should advise discretion on that score," Creed answered. "A lot of these miners coming into Idaho are Californians. They've learned that a rope, a knot, and a stout tree limb save a lot of fuss and bother. From that kind of justice, there is no appeal."

Back in St. Louis, Kimball's law practice had been in the commercial rather than the criminal field; he had done work for and owned stock in companies engaged in river and rail traffic; he had acquired considerable valuable real estate; he had been a partner in a brokerage firm that bought cotton in the South and sold it in the North; and he had been Western representative for a number of New England manufacturers whose finished products were marketed in the deep South and the Border States commercially tributary to St. Louis. Financially, he had prospered, and, though the war had dried up some of his sources of income, he had been clever enough to find in the booming city two new financial opportunities to replace each one he lost.

But he had had a shrew of a wife . . .

Well, hardly that. Say that from the very beginning their marriage had been a mistake. Say that she was cold in one fashion, he in another. Say that she set values on things he thought frivolous—society, for example—while he respected things she treated with utmost contempt—money, for instance, which was to him a thing to be acquired, to her a thing to be spent. God, how Martha could run through money! And how little she gave a man in return.

Love was a word ten years of marriage had emptied of all meaning for him. If there had been children, Martha might have transferred some of her selfish interest in clothes, possessions, social affairs, and Church (she was a devout Catholic) to them, he supposed, and he in turn might have devoted less time to money-making (Hell, a man *had* to make money the way Martha spent it!), and in their mutual interest in the children they might have found some measure of affection for each other, or, at the very least, respect. But children there had not been. And now, there was nothing.

Divorce was out of the question. Martha would never consider it. Even if she should do so, the scandal of it would ruin him professionally in highly Catholic St. Louis, and Martha's myriad relatives (Martha not only came from a St. Louis first-family, but her brothers, uncles, and cousins were prominent men in politics, banking, the law, and trade in cities all over the North and East) would see to it that the name Armand Kimball was quietly blacklisted in places and ways that would hurt him the most.

After long and serious thought, Kimball had decided that there was only one feasible way out. Go West. Gradually, during the course of the previous year, he had prepared Martha for his departure from St. Louis on what he pretended was to be a business trip of only a few months' duration, while at the same time he discreetly converted his business interests and property holdings into readily transferable assets which he could get at, when the proper moment came, and his wife could not.

He set no time limit on the transition period between having and supporting in high style a wife he had long since ceased to care for, and not having and not supporting her. Two years, three, five—a great deal depended on circumstances. First, he must arrange his financial affairs. Second, get away. Third, find the place and opportunity that appealed to him in the West. Fourth, transfer his funds. Fifth, divorce her (Territorial or State Legislatures in the West, he had been delighted to learn before leaving St. Louis, often possessed this power and used it freely for their friends). Sixth and finally (what a pleasure this would be!), let her know that she was no longer his wife.

But there was no hurry . . .

Armand Kimball spent the first six weeks following the arrival of the wagon train in Boise City looking around, talking to the northeast and the even newer towns in the Owyhees to the southwest. Each region was a day's ride or more from Boise City; each was in high, rugged, timbered country slashed by small streams whose flow dwindled drastically in late summer; each was praised by its boosters as being the biggest strike yet.

The trails leading up to both districts from the Snake River lowlands were fit only for pack animals and horseback travel, though already there was talk of improving them so that they could be negotiated by stagecoaches and freight wagons. As there were no public funds available with which to cut down trees, grade hills, build bridges and ferries, these improvements must be undertaken by private individuals or companies, in return for which it might reasonably be assumed that exclusive franchises would be granted to charge toll. Recalling the ferry operated by Lafe Perrin and Dave Shoup, Kimball mentally made note that here might lie one profitable field for investment; however, beyond becoming acquainted with and listening sympathetically to several men whose ambitions to be road- and ferry-builders exceeded their means to realize those desires, he did not commit himself for the time being.

He did risk a mercantile venture. In trying to sell his wagon and ox teams, which he felt he would have no further use for, he discovered that no one would offer what he considered to be a fair price. The other emigrants were in the same position. Thus, when Beulah Baker's father casually remarked to him that he would give his eyeteeth to possess a stock of goods and a building in Boise City in which to open a store, Kimball said, "Do the prospects look favorable to you?"

"Lord, yes! Why, if I had a place for my family to stay and could rent a store building and stock it, I'd like nothing better than to go into business right here in Boise City."

"What's the closest point of supply?"

"Salt Lake, I suppose. Or Portland—though they do say the freight rates from there are highway robbery. But if a man were to take a couple of wagons down to Salt Lake City on his own and load them up with flour—" Baker shrugged. "Oh, hell, I'm just talking. The first thing I've got to do is get a roof over my family. But maybe next spring—"

Next spring was six months away, Kimball said; let's see what can be done now. A great deal could be done, he presently decided after making some discreet inquiries. Twenty wagons, the oxen or horses to pull them, the young men to drive and guard them, all could be purchased, leased, or hired at reasonable terms. Ninety days of decent traveling weather could be anticipated before winter came and the round trip to Salt Lake should not take much over sixty.

Arthur Creed, who was planning to open a law office in Boise City, needed quarters; so did Baker—both for the store and his family; so did Kimball himself. Cornelius Belford possessed the required skills to supervise the work; lots near the growing town's center could be purchased cheaply enough; and Kimball had the cash necessary to swing the deal.

No, he told Baker, he was not interested in a partnership. Let Baker invest what he could; Kimball would take his note for the balance at a reasonable interest rate. Shall we say two percent per month? Fine! And I'll rent you the building and quarters for your family. Don't worry about a thing, Mr. Baker; just run along to Salt Lake, buy your stock, and when you get back your new store building will be ready.

Arthur Creed suggested a law partnership, and to this Kimball readily consented, for he liked Creed, respected his intelligence and felt that the man's knowledge of the West—particularly in the field of mining—might prove to be extremely useful. For example, it was Arthur Creed who explained to him the vast difference between placer and quartz mining, both of which he knew well from his years spent in California and western Nevada.

"All a man needs for placer mining is a grubstake, a strong back, water, and a few simple tools," Creed said. "But when a gold or silver vein runs into hard rock, you've got an entirely different proposition. Say you find a hill with a vein containing a million dollars' worth of gold. By the time you tunnel several hundred feet through the hardest kind of rock to get out that ore—which means labor, explosives, timbering, hoisting—then crush it, separate it and so on, it may cost you a quarter of a million dollars. A lot of that money has to be paid out in cash before any returns start coming in."

"Which means capital investment. Where does it come from?"

"San Francisco or New York."

"Has quartz mining developed much locally?"

"No. But there are indications it's the coming thing. I was talking to a man yesterday—Waddingham, his name is—who's forming a company to do some hardrock mining on some promising leads up at Rocky Bar. He claims to have unlimited Eastern capital behind him. It's a development worth watching."

Indeed it was, Kimball mused, for corporate organization was a subject whose intracacies he understood. But for the present there were other developments on the local and Territorial scene to be observed with interest.

Word came in late September that Governor William H. Wallace had at last arrived in Lewiston; his first official act was to decree that on October 31 an election would be held to select a Legislature and a Territorial Delegate to the National Congress; his second was to declare himself a candidate for the Territorial Delegate position, which caused a rash of jokes to the effect that even the Governor of Idaho, after one quick look at the place, figured the best thing to do was mine whatever political gold he could and then get the hell out.

Democratic and Union party nominating conventions were hastily convened in the various districts; slates of candidates were selected; torchlight parades, speeches, and saloon debates stirred up brief, mild flurries of excitement. But, for the most part, the citizenry showed little interest in the campaign or in appearing at the polls when voting day came. Arthur Creed, who ran as a Union candidate for Council Representative from the Boise City district, was elected by a comfortable majority. Cornelius Belford, who ran as a Democratic candidate for a House seat, was rewarded with the first political victory of his life. For a time it appeared that William Wallace had barely slipped in or perhaps even lost in his race for Territorial Delegate, then, weeks after the polls had closed, official returns arriving from distant Fort Laramie—which showed him winning by six hundred votes there—made his majority decisive.

The Democrats howled "Fraud!" Good God, they pointed out, there weren't *that* many white men living in the far eastern part of Idaho Territory, even if you counted soldiers, which of course you shouldn't, for soldiers weren't residents and therefore could not vote. But the election stood, just the same. Back East, there was a war on and nobody in the Federal government cared what happened politically in Idaho, so long as it went Union. And in establishing the residence requirements for voter eligibility prior to the election the unique theory had been proposed and accepted that residence need not mean actually living on Idaho soil for a specified period; if a man left Ohio in March, say, *intending* to go to Idaho to live, that made him eligible to vote there, even though he did not arrive until a week before election day.

To Armand Kimball, the curious thing about the election results was that the final tally showed that less than ten thousand people had bothered to register their desires one way or another.

"Either the population of Idaho has been vastly overestimated," he observed to Arthur Creed, "or our fine citizenry just doesn't care. Which would you say it is?"

"Both, probably."

"I'm not sure whether I should offer you my congratulations or condolences on being elected, Arthur. It appears to me you've stepped into an awful mess."

"Well, someone has to clean it up."

"From your campaign speeches, I gather you're for the Union and against taxing the mines. Is that all you stand for?"

"When a man runs for office," Creed said, "he doesn't bare his soul. Two planks, well braced, supported and nailed, are platform enough. Now that I've been elected, I'll let the people tell me what *they* want done."

Immediately following his election as Delegate to Congress, William H. Wallace resigned as Governor and left the Territory. Secretary Daniels, as Acting Governor, issued a call for the First Legislature to convene in Lewiston in early December, the session to last forty days. Aware of the fact that Arthur Creed's financial resources were limited and that his pay as Councilman was to be only four dollars a day—in greenbacks, which were generally accepted at no more than half their face value—Kimball offered to loan his new partner whatever money he needed to keep him going. Creed politely declined.

"I'll get by. But to show you how much I appreciate your thoughtfulness, Armand, I'll give you a valuable piece of advice"

"Such as . . . ?"

"Buy land in and around Boise City. Buy all you can get. Because when I come back from Lewiston, I'll be bringing the capital site with me."

Kimball understood then why Arthur Creed was not overly concerned about finances. Businessmen, real estate speculators, men interested in obtaining Legislature-granted franchises for toll roads and ferries, all lately had been eager to wine, dine, and entertain

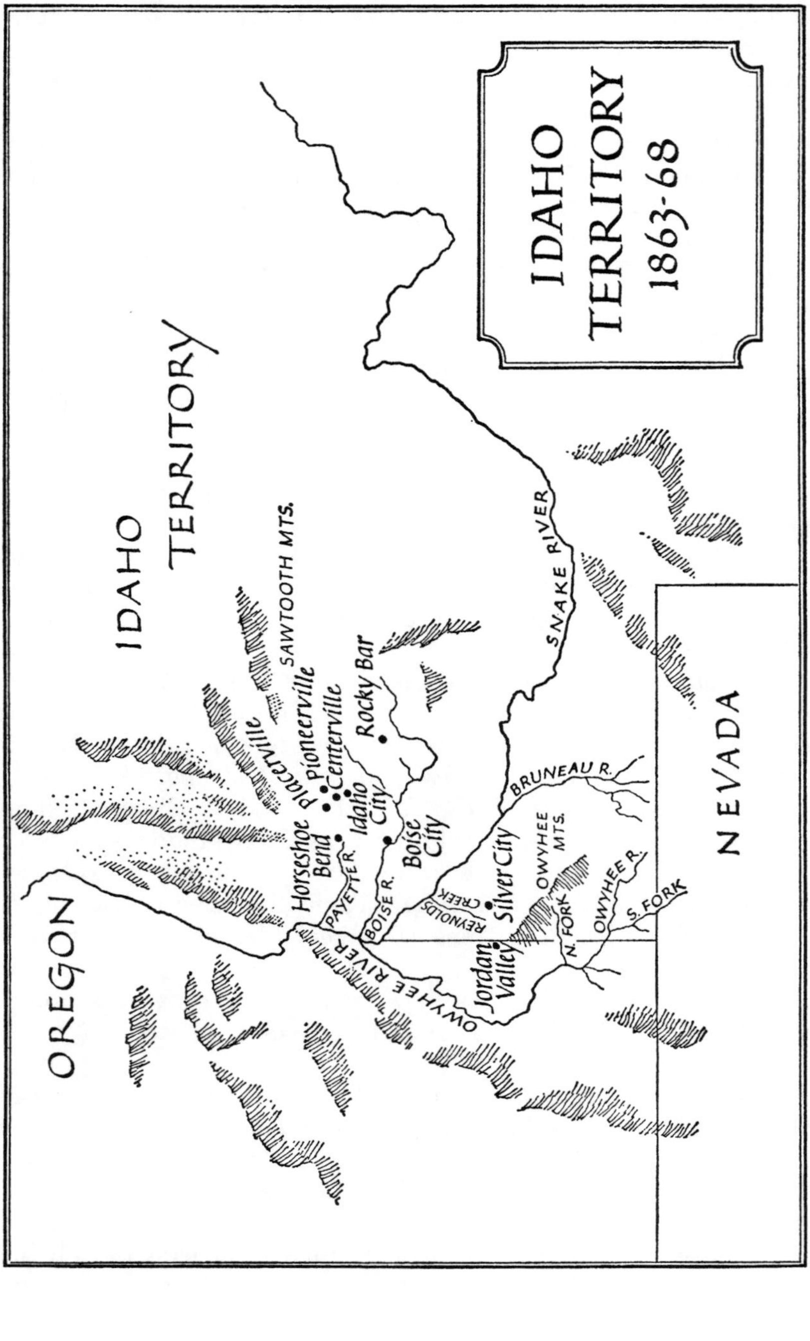
IDAHO TERRITORY 1863-68
IDAHO TERRITORY
OREGON
NEVADA
SAWTOOTH MTS.
SNAKE RIVER
Placerville
Pioneerville
Centerville
Rocky Bar
Horseshoe Bend
Idaho City
Boise City
PAYETTE R.
BOISE R.
BRUNEAU R.
OWYHEE MTS.
Silver City
REYNOLDS CREEK
Jordan Valley
OWYHEE RIVER
N. FORK
OWYHEE R.
S. FORK

Councilman Creed; if they chose this belated hour to make contributions to help defray his campaign expenses, who could criticize that?

Quietly Kimball extended his holdings in real estate.

The weather remained relatively mild through late fall and early winter, with only an occasional snowfall in the low country, which soon melted; so little snow accumulated in the mountains to the north and south that the miners became concerned lest the stream flow next spring and summer fall far short of their needs. Water literally was gold to them.

With the store building completed and a successful round trip to Salt Lake City accomplished, the Baker store opened to a brisk and continuing business early in November. Shortly thereafter, the *Boise News* in Bannock City published the first reports of a sensational multiple murder in the northern part of the Territory that furnished fuel for saloon conversation for months to come. Arthur Creed, who arrived in Lewiston a few days after the story first broke, kept Kimball posted on developments with an occasional letter.

A merchant named Magruder had left Lewiston in late August with sixty laden pack mules, crossed the Bitter Root Mountains to the mining camp of Virginia City, sold his goods there for $30,000 in gold dust and headed home in early fall. His party totaled nine men, three of whom apparently decided to murder him and make off with his gold. Magruder's closest friend in Lewiston was a hotel-keeper named Hill Beachey; it was this man who brought the grisly, fantastic tale to the attention of the public.

"Beachey had a premonition, a vision or a dream," Creed wrote, "which told him that something terrible was going to happen to Magruder. He loaned Magruder a gun and warned him to be careful. Included in the party starting back from Virginia City were three men of somewhat shady reputation, D. C. Lowry, David Howard, and James Romain; also along was one Billy Page, a witless, weak-spined fellow, not necessarily evil but too lacking in character to oppose his companions' dastardly plans . . ."

As the time came and passed when Magruder should have returned to Lewiston, Creed continued, Hill Beachey grew increasingly worried about the safety of his friend. Learning presently that four suspicious-acting men had left some mules and saddles at a ranch near Lewiston and then had taken an early stage for Walla Walla, he examined the animals and saddles and recognized them as having belonged to his missing friend. Now he was positive that there had been foul play.

"Beachey got descriptions of the four men, went to the Governor and insisted that he be given requisitions on the governors of Oregon, Washington Territory, and California," Creed wrote, "then he and a man named Tom Pike set out in pursuit of the fugitives. The trail led overland to Walla Walla and Wallula Landing, then downriver by boat to Portland. There, Beachey learned, the four men he wanted had boarded a ship bound for San Francisco.

"The nearest point from Portland at which telegraphic communication with San Francisco could be had was Yreka, in northern California. Leaving Tom Pike in Portland to take the next steamer, Beachey rode the stagecoach three days and and nights over the worst kinds of roads to Yreka, wired a full description of the suspects to the chief of police in San Francisco, and, when their ship made port, they were immediately arrested . . ."

A writ of *habeas corpus* had briefly delayed the return of the four suspects to Lewiston for trial, but the San Francisco court—apparently caring no more for legal nit-picking than Idaho did—denied the writ, and on December 7, the same day the First Legislature convened in Lewiston, Hill Beachey and Tom Pike arrived home with their prisoners.

"As an attorney, you no doubt will be interested in the legal niceties of the situation," Creed wrote. "In the first place, there were no bodies with which to prove that murder had been done. This was neatly solved by a confession from Billy Page (Hill Beachey is a most persuasive man) relating in horrible detail how Magruder and four other men had been murdered and their bodies dumped into a canyon deep in the mountains, where they no doubt now lie buried under many feet of snow.

"Secondly (as I pointed out to you a few weeks ago), Idaho Territory had no code of laws. This the Legislature remedied by enacting a Civil and Criminal Code patterned roughly after the Common Law of England. It took effect January 4, 1864. District Court convened in Lewiston January 5, Judge Samuel C. Parks presiding; Howard, Lowry, and Romain were indicted for murder in the first degree, were duly tried and convicted. On January 25, Judge Parks sentenced them to be hanged; and on March 4 the sentence was carried out.

"Billy Page, who had turned state's evidence, was permitted to depart following the trial," Arthur Creed concluded, "but rumor has it that he has since been killed—in what manner or by whom no one knows or inquires into. This, then, is Idaho justice. Simple, direct, effective—and not subject to appeal."

Upon the recommendation of Judge Parks, Kimball noted later, the Legislature passed an appropriation of $6244 to reimburse Hill

Beachey for expenses incurred in the pursuit and return of the murderers of his friend. And, when spring at last melted the snows in the high country to the east, Beachey and a party of men journeyed to the deep canyon into which Billy Page had said the five bodies had been dumped, found the remains exactly where he had said they would be, and gave them a decent burial.

Some months afterward, Arthur Creed, appealing the conviction of a client accused of highway robbery in September 1863, won a reversal from the Idaho Supreme Court, which ruled that no Code of Criminal Law had existed at that time. When Kimball reminded him of the fate of the Magruder murderers, Creed shrugged fatalistically.

"As Pat said to Mike's widow when he found out the posse had hung the wrong man: 'Sure, 'twas but an honest mistake we made, ma'am—the joke's on us."

Chapter Three

A rural bachelor advertised in a newspaper for a wife. He received replies from 18 husbands saying he could have theirs.
—*Idaho Statesman*
Boise City, I.T.
November 3, 1864

It had been Andy Hale's judgment that the longer he let the cattle he and Levi had driven in from western Oregon graze on the good bunchgrass covering the benchland south of Snake River, the more pounds they would put on and the better price they would bring as meat grew scarce in the settlements. He had set Christmas as the date beyond which it would not be safe to risk keeping the fifty steers any longer; but the December weather remained so mild, the grass so good and the cattle in such fine condition, he decided to hold onto them for another month.

"Come a blizzard," Levi warned him, "you may be sorry."

"Last winter was mild, they tell me, with hardly any snow or cold weather."

"Yeah. But the winter before, snow piled up six feet deep, the thermometer hit thirty below, and half the cattle in the Walla Walla country froze to death. You're taking a gamble."

Maybe he was, Andy admitted, but if he were to go into ranching permanently in this country he would have to find out sooner or later whether stock could be carried through the winter without feed. The one-room cabin built of undressed pine logs, which he and Levi had hastily thrown up as a shelter, set on a rise of ground a hundred feet from a creek winding down out of the mountains to the south. The pine woods covering the higher elevations began a couple of miles upstream; here, the creek valley widened and flattened out; low ridges a mile to the east and west defined the grazing land over which the cattle habitually wandered, while to the north the benchland sloped gently down to the sagebrush flats flanking the Snake.

The main-traveled trail to the Owyhee mining settlements ran past the cabin, and traffic on it had become increasingly heavy these past two months. As yet, neither Andy nor Levi had visited Ruby City, the nearest of the mining towns, for, though it was somewhat closer in terms of miles than Boise City, the trail to it was steep, twisting, narrow, and abominably bad, while that to Boise City was relatively easy once the Snake River had been crossed, and a ferry recently established made swimming one's horse unnecessary.

Since bringing the cattle here, Andy and Levi had made it a rule that one or the other stay close to home at all times. Unfriendly Indians were seldom seen hereabouts, but hardly a day passed without news from travelers going to or from the mines that Indian mischief had been done. Remotely situated as they were, the Owyhee Mountains offered ideal shelter for the fragmented remnants of half a dozen Idaho, Oregon, and Nevada tribes—Snakes, Paiutes, Bruneaus, Bannocks, Winnemuccas—which had resisted all efforts of the government to pacify them and place them on reservations. Attempts by both the military and Citizen Volunteer groups to bring them to bay and exterminate them also had failed, for the country was so broken and the desert expanse surrounding it so vast that no campaign conducted on terms of civilized warfare had any chance of success.

Rumor had spread among the whites that all the hostile Indians in this part of the country had recently become united into a well-organized, well-armed band numbering into the hundreds under a cunning, murderously inclined chief, whose ambition was nothing less than the complete extermination of every white man in the land. Rumor even gave him a name—*Oulux, We-na-wa-ha, Nam-puh* (the name varied according to the teller)—credited him with being of giant size, and mounted him on a giant horse. Andy discounted such tales. Western Indians as he knew them were not easily organized nor had he ever known any giants among them. Will Starr at once came to mind, of course; but Starr had been as much white as Indian. And Starr was dead . . .

Following a raid on a pack train on the trail just three miles upstream from the cabin, in which two white men were killed and three others seriously wounded, the residents of Ruby City raised such an outcry that the commandant at Fort Boise sent a company of mounted infantry down into the Owyhee country to pursue, catch, and punish the offending Indians. With their supply wagons, their cannon and their long-barreled Harpers Ferry rifles they made quite an impressive show of force as they rode uptrail past the cabin four days after the attack on the pack train (it had taken two days for the news to reach Fort Boise, a third to get organized, and a fourth to come this far), but Levi, watching them pass, grunted skeptically, "That's like huntin' ducks with a brass band. Do they think them Indians gonna bunch up to get shot at with that cannon?"

Two weeks later, supplies exhausted, cannon lost, and bearing one casualty (a private had accidentally shot a comrade in the leg while hunting jackrabbits), the Fort Boise company repassed the cabin, homeward bound. No, the soldiers had encountered no Indians. But the expedition had been a success, the Army claimed. Had not the hostile band been scattered to the four winds?

Indeed it had. But it would regroup when it so chose.

One morning a steer was found with an arrow in its flank. On another occasion, hearing a suspicious noise in the night, Levi slipped outside, saw a blob of shadow on the far side of the creek and shouted a challenge. His answer was a shot, which missed him, then a hurrying scurry of hoofbeats as a shot from his own rifle lanced out in the shadow's direction. Reading the sign in daylight, next morning, he told Andy that he could not be sure whether the visitor had been white or red; all he knew was that the horse had been steel-shod.

"Lot of trash around, these days," he said. "Fella told me yesterday they run some white roughs out of Ruby after they got drunk and started a brawl. Could of been one of them."

What Levi was thinking but not saying, Andy knew, was that to a certain type of man killing an Indian—any Indian—was a sport on the same level with hunting wolves or mountain lions. These were the men who proposed, whenever an Indian outrage had been committed in the community, that a bounty be placed on "Injun" scalps, regardless of tribe, sex, or age, because, as they put it, "An Injun's an animal that can't be tamed— and nits grow up to be lice."

Such men were a minority, but they made a lot of noise. Even sensible, fair-minded white men could be driven into blind, unreasoning prejudice by the horror of their first sight of victims of Indian killings, for an Indian—given sufficient time—could dismember and desecrate corpses in unspeakably obscene ways. If a white woman happened to be among the victims, sight of the remains was a thing a man remembered for the rest of his days, and his hatred toward the persons responsible for it was apt to be a racial rather than an individual feeling.

Well aware of this, Levi kept his hair trimmed short, wore white man's clothing, abstained from drink and minded his manners in public far better than most white men did. He did not cringe or slink; he was far too proud for that. But he was comfortable only when alone or with Andy; on other occasions, he remained alert, on guard, willing to go many steps out of his way to avoid trouble, but holding deep in his secret soul some final point, some dead-line, some standard of dignity, which, if pushed to and beyond, would force him to react as the lethally dangerous man Andy knew he could be.

They never discussed the matter, though a few times Andy quietly made it clear to unthinking white men that they would answer to him in a way they would not soon forget if they abused his friend by word or deed. It was the bitterest kind of irony, Andy realized, that merely by being white he could protect a man far more skilled than himself in the vital art of self-preservation. But such was the case; there was no altering it.

In early February, with the weather still holding mild, the Army Quartermaster at Fort Boise issued a call for beef bids, and Andy, after discussing it with Levi, offered the entire herd of fifty steers at eleven and a quarter cents a pound, live weight. He could have gotten considerably more, he felt sure, by selling in Ruby City or Silver City, but a recent snowfall in the high country had made the trail to those towns difficult to negotiate; no single buyer could handle such a quantity of beef; and losses by accident or Indian raid en route seemed too likely to make the gamble a profitable one.

A few days after the bids had been opened, a representative from the Quartermaster's office rode down, inspected the herd and accepted the bid, contingent upon delivery and weighing at Fort Boise. Andy and Levi took a leisurely week to drive the cattle to town, ferrying the steers across the Snake and paying toll charges rather than risk loss of animals or tallow by swimming them across the cold river. When the sale had been completed, the warrants—payable in "legal tender," which meant greenbacks rather than gold—totaled a shade over four thousand dollars.

There was no reason to hurry back to the ranch now, for there were no cattle left to look after, so they spent a couple of days in town. Boise City had grown amazingly during the past few months; it now boasted a hotel, several stores, livery stables, barber and bath shops, dozens of saloons and residences, and its streets were crowded with people, who, Levi said, must make their living doing one another's laundry. The Delaware was never at ease in a crowd. He did consent to sleep with Andy in a rented hotel room, but, except for a couple of hours spent laying in a stock of supplies at the Baker Mercantile Co. store, he spent most of his time at the Charley Davis Livery Stable, talking horses, hunting, and the pilgrim-transporting business with Charley and Matt Miller, both of whom were old-timers enough to look deeper into a man than the color of his skin.

Stacked on a table in the hotel lobby was a tattered, well-thumbed supply of Western newspapers, some of them months old, and Andy indulged himself in the dubious pleasure of bringing himself up to date with what was happening in the world. Some of the papers had a strong Union bias, others a distinctly Copperhead taint, and the news invariably reflected editorial prejudices. The war was still going on. The South was crumbling; the South was planning a big spring offensive; the North was crumbling; the North was mounting a gigantic spring campaign that would bring the South to its knees. Lincoln, the country's beloved leader, would run again for President and win by a landslide; Lincoln, the most hated man in the country, would not run but McClellan would, and "Little Mac," when elected, would negotiate an honorable peace.

Northern Idaho was "played out," a southern Idaho paper said, and it was inevitable that the Territorial capital be moved to Boise City. The Owyhee silver strike was "bigger than Washoe," another Idaho paper boasted, and, in retaliation, Nevada and California papers sneered that Owyhee was "strictly humbug." The Bannock City Sliding Team had challenged all comers to a downhill sled race; Pioneerville had accepted; two skulls, an arm, and three legs had been cracked in a collision at the foot of a sliding hill, and it was editorially deplored that "grown men should engage in such boyish foolishness, particularly when judgment is befuddled by alcohol."

A rough by the name of Hugh Donahue had killed a man in a brawl in Placerville and escaped before charges could be brought against him. One Joseph O'Brien, brought before a justice of peace in Lewiston on charges of promiscuous use of firearms and brawling in a public place, had been fined:

"For shooting off pistol in bar, $1.00;
"For " " mouth " court, $5.00."

On a dare, an enlisted man from Fort Boise had gone to a ball dressed as a woman. Before the evening ended, he had been "found out"; how or by whom not specified.

Reliable rumor had it that the Acting Governor, Secretary Daniels, was planning to leave Idaho Territory presently, which would drop the mantle of Governership onto the dubious shoulders of Clerk Silas D. Cochrane. Lewiston was prepared to use armed force, if necessary, to retain the capital site. A newly arrived Federal Judge was lauded in one paper as being "an excellent man, possessed of as fine a judicial mind as there is in the West"; while another paper called him "a stupid old drunk—God help Idaho if he's ever sober enough to write out an opinon . . ."

Irish jokes made good filler material:

"Sure, an' I drink to the Gallant 69th!" said Pat to Mike, raising his glass. "Last in the field and first to leave it!"

"No, no, me friend, you've got it all wrong!" Mike replied. "To the Gallant 69th! Superior to none!"

"Why are the Irish like ocean waves?"
"Because they never cease lavin' the shores of the Old Country."

"Who's dead?" asked Pat, as the funeral procession passed by.
"Faith, an' it must be the poor man they're burying," Mike replied.

Between stints of improving his mind with such uplifting material from the civilized press, Andy visited with old friends from the wagon train, a number of whom he ran into during his ramblings about town. Cornelius Belford, recently returned from the first session of the Legislature at Lewiston, was so busy supervising half a dozen workmen erecting a new building to house a saloon and billiard emporium that he could take only ten minutes off from his labors to give Andy a lecture on the faults of the Territorial government and what he proposed to do to correct them during the coming spring and summer. Melinda Belford, looking as beautiful as ever and a bit more mature, chattered gaily about social events at the fort and introduced him to Sergeant O'Neil, a handsome, husky, redheaded soldier in whose company she was doing the family shopping, and who glowered suspiciously at Andy as if suspecting him of being a rival for the young lady's favors.

Phil Duncan, working as a bartender in a town saloon, magnanimously treated Andy to a drink, boasted about how well he was doing, and confided that he just might be taken in as a full partner in the saloon ere long. Armand Kimball, genuinely glad to see Andy, took him to dinner, asked sympathetic questions about his cattle venture, seemed pleased that it had gone well, and volunteered nothing whatsoever regarding his own doings.

Loading their supplies on a pack horse, Andy and Levi were preparing to head back to the ranch the morning of the third day when a stocky, familiar figure came hurrying along the muddy street to the livery stable.

"Andy!" Daniel Lynn called out. "I heard you were in town! How are you, boy? Levi, good to see you!"

They shook hands and exchanged news. Lynn said he had just driven over from the Payette Valley to stock up on groceries and other needs; when he learned that there was no urgent requirement that the two men return to their ranch immediately, he insisted that they go home with him.

"We haven't seen you since August, Andy—and you did promise to pay us a call, you know. You've got to see our place. If Henry and Sally found out I'd run into you and hadn't brought you home, they'd make life miserable for me."

By noon, Lynn had made his purchases, loaded them into his wagon and they were on their way, Levi riding along behind leading Andy's horse and the pack animal, Andy on the wagon seat beside Lynn. His farm was located near Horseshoe Bend on the Payette, Lynn said, roughly thirty miles north and slightly west of Boise City. The direct route climbed an intervening mountain spur over a road impassable to a wagon at this time of year; thus, it was best to take the road that stayed in the lower country, even though it was twenty miles longer. This meant a two-day trip but they could put up for the night at a place called Halfway House.

"It's a thieves' den if ever I saw one," Lynn grunted angrily. "The old biddy that runs it puts out food that'd turn a hog's stomach, but it's a roof and a fire. A man can stand it for one night when he knows there's better waiting for him at home."

"You're comfortable, I take it?"

"Well, our place ain't yet up to what we had back in Iowa. But give us time and it will be."

"Do you have neighbors nearby?"

"There's a dozen or so families scattered up and down the valley. The Robertsons, the Baileys, the Shelbys—"

In town, Andy had heard that young Isaac Shelby had quarreled with his father and brother and was running with a wild crowd. He asked Lynn if these tales were true. Lynn nodded grimly.

"His folks are worried sick about that boy. Horses, guns, whisky, loose women, and easy living—that's all the gang of hellions he runs with cares about. If he doesn't shake loose from them soon, he's headed for bad trouble."

The food and grudging hospitality of the Halfway House, Andy discovered, were every bit as bad as Lynn had said they would be; after a night of battling bedbugs and being kept awake by the boisterous talk and laughter of half a dozen drinking, card-playing men who stayed up to a late hour in the adjoining main room, he envied Levi, who had chosen to sleep in the wagon parked outside, despite the night's cold. Though he knew Daniel Lynn had small tolerance for ne'er-do-wells who wasted their time with drinking, card-playing, and foul-mouthed talk, he was surprised as they drove on, next morning, at the vehemence with which Lynn spoke.

"Scum, Andy! Human lice! This whole valley is infested with them. And the worst of it is they seem to be organized. You noticed, didn't you, the way they gave us the eye?"

"Yes."

"Chances are the word has already been passed to them that you're carrying several thousand dollars in government warrants. Watch yourself. If they get the chance, they'll knock you on the head and make off with everything you own."

"Is this the gang Isaac Shelby runs with?"

"Lord knows. But we hear some ugly rumors. The main trail from the Boise Basin mines west to Oregon runs through this valley and every now and then a man known to be carrying gold dust is robbed or killed. If you're riding a good horse and traveling alone, you're just asking for trouble. So far, they haven't pestered us farmers much, but if things keep up the way they're going I'm afraid our turn will come."

"Isn't the law any help to you?"

"Very little. All the officers are Democrats and as big a set of crooks as the roughs are. Not that I'm saying *all* Democrats are roughs, mind you. But what I do say is all the roughs vote the Democratic ticket—and the men they put in office protect them."

"We've had considerable Indian trouble down our way. Are they much of a nuisance around here?"

Lynn shook his head. "No. The white roughs are so ornery there's no meanness left for Indians to do. We're getting mighty sick of it. The law is no help. But if worst comes to worst, there's always the rope . . ."

Before returning to the ranch, Andy and Levi spent three days visiting the Lynns and the other emigrant families that had settled in this part of the Territory. Of all the districts Andy had seen in Idaho so far, this fertile, peaceful-appearing farming community seemed the one least likely to spawn violence, despite Lynn's talk of vigilante action. For some twenty or thirty miles along the Payette the soil lay deep and rich, the hills on either side of the river at times pinching it into steep-walled canyons, then falling away to enclose flat, easily tilled expanses of land seven to eight miles across. The climate was mild; a young farmer named McConnell, who had been here since last spring, claimed that the soil would grow anything—even watermelons—and had been most helpful in getting the newcomers established.

Already acquainted with one another from having traveled together in the wagon train, the people settling in the valley formed a closely knit community; by pooling their labors and skills they had built good houses, had broken ground and planted late summer vegetables in extensive garden patches that had produced bountifully, and already were planning to import and set out fruit trees and lay out the network of irrigation canals and ditches that would be required to bring water to their fields during the coming summer's long rainless months, which McConnell said usually lasted from late June to early October.

An informal school for the children of the community met in the Lynn home during the winter months, with Sally Lynn acting as an unpaid teacher. For a time, Andy learned, a lively overnight lodging and meal business had been done at the Lynn farmhouse to accommodate travelers passing to and from the mines, but several unpleasant incidents involving men who drank too much and talked too roughly had forced him to call a halt to that, even though the cash income had been welcome. Now when a traveler stopped at the Lynn home for a meal or a night's rest, it was as a non-paying guest—or not at all.

One evening after supper, Daniel Lynn said casually, "Levi and Henry and I are going to run over and chew the rag with Billy McConnell for a while. Can you and Sally entertain each other, Andy?"

"We'll try," Andy answered.

Save for the dishwashing sounds coming from the kitchen and the crackle of burning wood in the living room fireplace, the house was silent after they had gone—uncomfortably silent. Andy smiled ruefully into the fire. There was nothing subtle about Daniel Lynn. The notion had struck him that Sally and Andy might like a couple of hours alone together; he had made no bones about arranging it. Getting up, Andy went into the kitchen. In the lamplight, Sally's face appeared flushed.

"Wasn't that silly of Pa? You *all* could have gone over to see Mr. McConnell. But Pa doesn't like to leave me home at night alone. He could have made Henry stay, though, instead of you—"

"Would Henry dry the dishes for you?" Andy asked, picking up a dish towel.

"If I threatened him with a club, yes."

"Well, I'll do it for a smile."

"Oh, Andy, you're such a tease! Do you tease Levi this way?"

"No. He's not as pretty as you are when you blush."

"Who does the dishes at your place?"

"Oh, we just set 'em outside the door and let the coyotes lick 'em clean. Saves a lot of fuss and bother."

"Is your place comfortable?"

"It breaks the weather—that's about all you can say for it. But Levi and me don't need fancy quarters. You know how bachelors are."

Sally glanced at him, then away. "No, I don't. But I can imagine. I'll bet your place is a mess."

"It needs a woman's touch. I keep telling Levi he ought to get himself a squaw to keep house for us."

"What does he tell you?"

"Same thing. Maybe we'll flip a coin someday to see who gets stuck."

Sally abruptly changed the subject. "Now that you've sold your cattle, do you plan to stay on in Idaho?"

"That depends."

"On what?"

"Whether we can bring in another batch and build up a herd. Whether we can pull a calf crop through a hard winter. Whether the Indians will let us alone. Whether there'll be a market for beef, if we do manage to raise some."

"You don't sound very happy, Andy. Don't you like Idaho?"

He shrugged. "I've seen worse country. But the way things are right now, how can a man make any plans to stay or not to stay?"

"We're going to stay. I'm sure of that."

"How can you be sure?"

"Because I feel it inside me. There's something inside me that says: 'We're here, we're going to stay.' Once you get that feeling, you'll stay, too. And you'll be happy."

He scowled. "What's being happy got to do with it?"

"Everything." With a laugh, she dried her hands, took off her apron, and seized him by the hand. "Thank you, sir, for your help. Come into the living room. I want to show you a project I've been working on to keep myself out of mischief these long winter evenings."

The feel of her hand in his was warm, vibrant, and exciting. As he walked into the living room with her, a vagrant, wicked thought flashed across his mind: Lord, oh, Lord, she's a grown up woman now! Wouldn't I love to think up ways to keep her out of mischief these long winter evenings, if only I had something better to offer her than a boar's nest in a lonely, dangerous piece of wilderness! He checked the thought sharply. Someday, perhaps. But not now . . .

Turning up the wick of the lamp resting in the center of the table at which the family ate its meals, she sat him down beside her and opened a large notebook.

"Do you remember what I said to you last summer, when our wagon train broke up in Boise City?"

"Something about endings being sad."

"Yes. We had traveled so long together, I said, and had come such a long way. I cried because it was finished. But it *wasn't* finished. Our traveling together was finished, true, but something even more exciting was just beginning. That's my project. Keeping track of what's happening to the people in our wagon train."

"All of them?"

"Of course! See, I've written down the names of every single family. I've drawn a map of southwestern Idaho Territory, with Boise City as its center, and I've placed each family where they settled down."

"Lord love you, Sally! You've taken on quite a chore."

"It's fun, sort of," she said wistfully. "And it gives me something to do evenings."

"How on earth do you keep track of all those people?"

Sally smiled. "Oh, I read every Idaho newspaper I can get my hands on, no matter how old. I write a lot of letters. Whenever neighbors like the Shelbys and Mr. McConnell come home from trips to Placerville, Centerville, Pioneerville, or Idaho City, I pump them for any bits of news they may have picked up about our old friends. And when Pa takes me to Boise City, I visit around a lot."

She picked up a pencil. "Show me exactly where your ranch is, Andy. I'll put it on my map."

Strangely touched, Andy stared at her in amazement. Who but Sally Lynn would conceive such a project! Call it female curiosity. Call it a warm-natured interest in her fellow human beings. Call it a yearning to re-establish the roots torn up back home in Iowa when the war took her two brothers and her mother away from her and forced her father to seek a new life in the West. Call it loneliness—a special kind of loneliness that only a husband, a home, and children of her own could cure.

Call it what you liked, a man ought to do something . . . Damn it all, if only he had a safe home to offer her . . .

"Well, the first thing we've got to do is fix your fool map," he said brusquely. "You've got my part of the Territory drawn cock-eyed. Look, here's Snake River. Here's the trail to the Owyhee mines. Here's Reynolds Creek. Here's my ranch . . ."

During Andy and Levi's stay with the Lynns, the neighbor, Billy McConnell, stopped by on several occasions. He was a slim, quiet-spoken, polite young man whom Andy judged to be not more than twenty-five; yet it was surprising how intently Daniel Lynn listened to whatever he had to say and the respect which the older man seemed to have for his judgment. And to Henry Lynn, McConnell was quite a hero.

"Billy may not look it, but he's tough as a boot," Henry bragged. "He don't take nothing off nobody."

"Is that so?" Andy said with a smile.

"Just try him out, if you don't believe me! He's got all the roughs buffaloed."

Andy said he would take the boy's word for that. Eying McConnell more closely on their next meeting, he conceded that the young man did have a certain firmness of mind and body, a certain alertness, a certain quickness of eye and hand, that made him stand out in a crowd. Even so, it was difficult to believe that it had been he who had suggested recourse to vigilante action, if all other means of controlling the roughs failed, and had implied that he stood ready to lead the movement.

But the day came . . .

Chapter Four

"I can catch any thief that ever walked these prairies. The next man who steals a horse from me is my Injun. There will be no law-suit about it."

—William J. McConnell Boise City, I.T.
October 1864

In July, while taking a pack-string load of garden produce to the Boise Basin mining towns, Billy McConnell lost a bay horse with a white blaze on its forehead, worth, at the most, fifty dollars. In October, he found it in the Charley Davis Livery Stable in Boise City, claimed it, proved that it was his, and, after a bit of legal red tape, led it home to his farm a few miles above Horseshoe Bend in the Payette Valley. Shortly thereafter, he paid a call on Daniel Lynn, who, with his son, Henry, had just come in from the fields for the noonday meal.

"Well, Daniel," he said quietly, "I found that bay horse I lost three months ago over near Centerville."

"Who had it?"

"A restaurant keeper named Gilke."

"Where did he get it?"

"John Kelly gave it to him."

"How did Kelly come by it?"

"A friend gave it to him, he said. He wouldn't tell me his name at first. So I said, 'John, your friend is a horse thief.'"

"And then?"

"John said I didn't have the guts to call his friend a horse thief to his face. I told him to try me. So he told me the man's name—and I did it."

"'What did he do?"

"Nothing, I'm sorry to say. But before I could get my horse back, I was forced to go into court and bring suit for it."

McConnell paused, his eyes cold, his face calm, but his voice harsh with an inner rage. "The court costs came to seventy dollars."

"The rascals!" Lynn exclaimed. "I'll bet those Boise City roughs hoorawed you to a fare-thee-well!"

McConnell nodded. "They did, Daniel. There were a dozen or so of them—including the man I'd called a horse thief to his face—loafing outside a saloon as I passed headed for home. They made some remarks. So I stopped and told them I wanted to make a little speech."

"What did you say?"

"That some of them may think they're mighty big men in their tribe, but I recognize no chiefs. That the next man who steals a horse from me is my Injun."

"Good for you, Billy!" Lynn grunted, nodding approvingly.

A worried look crossed his face. "You know what you asked for, don't you?"

"Yes. That's why I dropped by, Daniel. They think they've got the law and the courts in their hip pockets. They'll try to put me in my place. When they do, the fireworks will begin."

"We're all behind you, you know that. Just whistle if you need us."

A few nights later, four good mules and five horses—worth at least two thousand dollars, Henry's father estimated—disappeared from Billy McConnell's farm and the farms of two of his neighbors. The sign indicated that the theft had been accomplished by four men, that the animals had been driven west along what was known as the Brownlee Ferry trail, and that, in all likelihood, it was planned to drive the horses and mules across the Blue Mountains to the Columbia River Valley, where they could be sold without any need to prove ownership. Caught up in the excitement of the event, aware of the meetings being held by the men of the community, making a guess at what the nature of the fireworks was going to be, Henry Lynn would have given his right arm to be selected as a member of the pursuing party. After all, he was almost a man now; he could ride, he could shoot, he could tie a hangman's noose in a rope . . .

He was not chosen, of course. Nor was his father. Two men in addition to himself would suffice, Billy McConnell said, for they must travel light, fast, and perhaps far.

"It comes down to this, Daniel," Henry heard McConnell say to his father, "either we teach these devils a lesson or we give up and move out. It's as simple as that."

McConnell and the two men who had ridden off with him were gone two weeks; when they returned, the four stolen mules and the five horses were in their care and were turned over to their rightful owners. One of the men had a bandaged arm; he said he had taken a fall upon sharp rocks. No questions were asked, no explanations made, no tales told—at least not in Henry's presence, which disappointed him mightily. When pressed for an account of what had *really* happened, Henry's father shook his head and said grimly, "Justice was done, Henry—that's all anyone needs to know."

"Well, there's one thing sure," Henry boasted. "This'll put an end to the roughs trying to push people in *this* valley around, won't it?"

"An end? Maybe. But it could be a beginning, Henry—a beginning of something mighty ugly."

Chapter Five

To start a balky horse, fill his mouth with gravel. It gives him something else to think about.

—*Idaho World*
Idaho City, I.T.
May 13, 1865

The main reason why he had been unable to effect the removal of the capital site from Lewiston to Boise City during the First Session of the Legislature, Arthur Creed told Kimball, was that Idaho's Governor took no interest in the matter. The word "Governor," he hastened to add, was one which he used advisedly, for it was a moot question as to whether Idaho Territory even *had* a Chief Executive on any given day, and, if so, who he might be.

Immediately after his election as Territorial Delegate to Congress, William H. Wallace had resigned and gone East. Secretary Daniels, who had become Acting Governor, had lingered just long enough to preside over the First Session of the Legislature, had certified the laws passed by it, then had departed for San Francisco—ostensibly to have those laws printed—and had not been heard from since. Clerk Silas D. Cochrane, elevated by the rules of succession to the Chief Executive position, was rumored (in Boise City, at least, though Lewiston residents hotly denied the slander) to be a man who spent more time diminishing the Territory's supply of bad whisky than he did in running its political affairs. And, to further complicate things, Caleb Lyon of Lyonsdale, New York, had been appointed the new Governor of Idaho Territory in late February 1864, but was taking his own sweet time packing his valise and making the journey west.

In September, with the new governor still truant from his domain, Creed said to Kimball, "Surely he'll show up in time for the Second Session, which is due to convene two months from now. We've laid the groundwork to transfer the capital site; we've got the votes to swing it. If Lyon proves to be an even halfway reasonable man, he'll be bound to go along with us."

"What do you know about him?"

"Only that he's said to be a prominent New York state politician, a scholar, a gentleman, and well thought of by the administration. It's rumored that he bathes frequently, changes his linen once a week whether it needs it or not, and has a fetish for wearing a swallow-tailed coat on formal occasions—all of which idiosyncrasies will guarantee him the hostility of the unwashed Democratic Party. But being a Republican, he could expect that anyway."

Early in October, Caleb Lyon of Lyonsdale did indeed show up, arriving in Boise City with a flourish, and great was the rejoicing of the local citizenry. At Fort Boise, cannon salutes were fired in greeting, a huge banquet honoring the new governor was held, speeches of welcome were made, and Caleb Lyon —freshly bathed and resplendently dignified in a swallow-tailed coat—responded with a most scholarly oration of thanks.

For the next five weeks, Governor Lyon toured southwestern Idaho, accompanied by an escort of officers from Fort Boise, and was royally wined, dined, and entertained by the populace of the mining towns, each of which tried to outdo all the others. Between social events, the governor found time to parley with Chief Tam Tomeco and two hundred and fifty Indians of the Bruneau, Boise, and Shoshone tribes (the settlers usually called them all "Snakes"), and tentatively reached an agreement on the boundaries of a reservation within which they would presently be confined.

Down in the Owyhee district, the citizens of Ruby City and Silver City were so favorably impressed by their new governor that it was proposed that a brick of solid silver be made up and given to him as a token of esteem; a collection of freewill offerings from the miners and businessmen was instigated to that end. Not to be outdone, the residents of Rocky Bar, Placerville, and Idaho City (there was another Bannock City farther east, it had been learned, so the name had been changed) started a campaign to raise funds for *their* presentation brick, this one to be made of solid gold.

Even Jim Reynolds, saturnine editor of the Boise City *Idaho Statesman* and a man not given to flowery compliments, was sufficiently impressed to say in print: "The people are indebted to the prompt and energetic action of Governor Lyon, who goes to work with a will."

Armand Kimball himself, having done no more than shake hands, exchange brief greetings and endure a lengthy evening of dining and speech-making with the new governor, preferred to reserve judgment. Certainly it must be said that Caleb Lyon of Lyonsdale (he always signed his name thus) had a way with words. For example, one of his first official acts was to issue a Thanksgiving Proclamation, which began:

Thanksgiving let us give to the King of Kings, and the Lord of Lords, for the foundation, preservation and perpetuation of the Government of the United States against the manifold schemes of wicked men, the attacks of open enemies, and the machinations of secret foes . . .

But this gem, Kimball observed, paled into syntactical insignificance when compared to the magnificently sonorous opening sentence of Governor Lyon's address to the Second Session of the Idaho Legislature, which convened in Lewiston, November 16, 1864:

Amid this hour, when clouds of civil war darken the atmosphere lighted only by the sunbursts of glory that surround the achievements of our heroic army and devoted navy; when a wicked rebellion lies like a writhing serpent;—death-wounded in the last hours of its venomous existence, and over its gory form the shining waters of peace sparkle temptingly, just beyond our lips;—in this hour, when our hearts are still bleeding for the loved ones who have fallen nobly in this great strife for the Union and the Constitution of our fathers, when the tears are undried in the eyes of the widow, and the death-damp still pales the cheek of the husband;—when the resources and blood and treasure have all gone forth as precious sacrifice upon freedom's holiest altar;— when the rights of self-government are imperiled by this contest, and Emporers and Kings stand ready to cast lots for the parted robe of departing Liberty;—thus you meet, the servants of confiding constituencies, to aid Idaho's advancement toward Statehood, by the patriotism of your purposes, the soundness of your judgment, and the wisdom of your deliberations . . .

The somewhat stunned servants of confiding constituencies, Arthur Creed wrote his law partner, had been congratulated by the new governor on the general health, prosperity, laws, justice, soil, harvest, mineral wealth, energy, and high moral purpose of the people who had elected them. Caleb Lyon had then submitted for consideration by the legislative bodies the items which he considered to be Idaho's most pressing needs:

Schools (*. . . the blessings of free schools, like the dews of heaven, fall on the rich and poor alike. . .*); law revision and codification (the First Session had enacted a Code of Laws, but as it had not yet been printed no one knew for sure what the Code was, though rumor had it the laws were so full of errors and contradictions that they were completely unworkable); economy in government; more pay for government officials; roads, ferries, militia; legislation designed to invite outside capital to develop mining resources (. . . *the gold and silver bearing quartz ledges, unrivaled by those of Mexico or Peru, a glorious climate, with Syrian summers and Italian winters. . .*); removal of obstructions to navigation in the Snake; new military posts; a Mint and Assay office; mail routes; and, lastly, a railroad to connect Idaho with the great population centers of the East and West coasts. The more ambitious and costly of these projects, Governor Lyon hastened to point out, should be carried out not by an onerous taxing of the Territory's citizens but by the Federal government.

The Second Session lasted some sixty days. Other than generously granting divorces and toll road and ferry franchises to any and all confiding constituents that had asked for them (and had secretly paid a fair price), the Council and House passed only one major piece of legislation—to transfer the capital site from Lewiston to Boise City. As was to be expected, Lewiston objected strenuously.

"The citizens here are up in arms—literally and actually," Councilman Creed wrote. "They have placed the Territorial Seal and Archives under armed guard and are defying their removal. A court test has been scheduled—not in Superior Court, mind you, which would seem to be called for, but in the local Probate Court. A restraining order against removing the capital has been issued; the legality of all the laws passed by the Second Legislature has been questioned; and the issue has even been raised that Lyon is not really Idaho's Governor. In a word, complete chaos reigns. However, those of us in favor of the capital removal do have plans. Your friend, Cornelius Belford— even though a Democrat—has been most cooperative, by the way . . ."

In Boise City, Jim Reynolds filled the editorial columns of his paper with bitingly sarcastic comments on the goings-on in "lewiston" (he was so contemptuous of the northern Idaho town that he invariably spelled its name with an initial lowercase "l," using the smallest type in the shop), castigated Alonzo Leland, editor of the Lewiston *Radiator,* as ". . . the 'lewiston lelander,' flea-brained king of the fleapatch . . ." and accused Federal Judge Alex Smith—whose First District Court was loftily attempting to ignore the whole matter—of drunkenness, illiteracy, and of being chief judicial officer not of a Superior Court but of a court ". . . than which none is inferior . . ."

Accustomed as he was to the more discreet writings of Eastern presses, Armand Kimball was both shocked and amused by the vituperative rantings of the Territorial newspaper editors. Acid-dipped though Jim Reynolds' pen was, opposition papers such as the Idaho

City *World* and the Lewiston *Radiator* gave back as good as they got, for H. C. Street, *World* editor, and Alonzo Leland, *Radiator* editor, both doubled as elected Legislators, and were far from being tongue-tied.

"I see where Jim Reynolds said he stole an hour yesterday to stroll around town," Street wrote. "What did you steal today, Jim?"

"The trouble with Jim Reynolds is he's a sour-tempered old bachelor," Leland pointed out. "But that's understandable. What woman would have him?"

"It is reliably reported that a fat Dutch hurdy-gurdy refused to dance with Jim Reynolds the other evening, even though he had managed to steal the dollar fee from a sleeping blind man. When asked why she refused, she replied that she had danced for pay with drunken miners, unwashed cowboys, sheepherders, Chinamen, and even Digger Indians, but, she concluded, 'A girl *has* to draw the line somewhere.'"

The impasse over holding the governor prisoner and keeping the Territorial seal and archives locked up in Lewiston was at least partially resolved in mid-January, 1865. "Caleb Lyon pretended that he was going duck-hunting on the Idaho side of the Snake," Creed wrote. "We arranged to have a rowboat handy, and, as dusk fell, we transported him across the river to the Washington side, where he hastily took a stagecoach to Walla Walla. In all likelihood, he'll be in Boise City by the time you get this. For the time being, we'll let Lewiston keep the Seal and Archives. After all, *we* have the governor—and that's the important thing."

Sad to say, Kimball soon learned, Boise City did *not* have the governor. As the days passed, bits of news filtering east to Boise City from Oregon indicated that Caleb Lyon—if he did indeed intend returning to the new capital—was taking a very roundabout route. On February 7, he was reported to be in The Dalles; a week later he was in Portland; in another week he was said to be on his way to San Francisco, where he had pressing business—perhaps he intended to look for Secretary Daniels and the missing Code of Laws. However, he was quoted as saying, he had made all the necessary arrangements for the Idaho Seal and Archives to be transferred to Boise City at an early date.

From San Francisco, word eventually drifted back to Idaho that Governor Caleb Lyon of Lyonsdale had told a reporter he had such a great quantity of important matters to be communicated to the National Capital at Washington City it seemed more economical to make the trip East himself, rather than go to the great expense of telegraphing. Still later, a brief item picked up from the New York *Tribune* relayed the information that Governor Lyon, lately of Idaho, had been so exhausted by his journey East that he had retired to his Lyonsdale home for a rest.

When that news was received, Jim Reynolds wrote with unaccustomed kindness and a trace of sadness: "It was expected of Governor Lyon that he would proceed to execute the law according to the intent of the Legislature. But we have found that the peacefully natured fine old country gentleman was not made of stuff stern enough to deal with the brow-beating and ruffianism of lewiston; that he yielded to the pressure of the villainy that opposed him, and has long ere this sought quiet among the hills of Lyonsdale . . . It is hoped that President Lincoln will see fit to appoint a new governor soon . . ."

But back East, there was a war on, though now that April had come the end appeared to be in sight, and there were more important matters than Idaho on President Lincoln's mind. Acting Governor of Idaho now was Secretary DeWitt C. Smith, a moody, ill, recluse of a man, who, Clerk Silas Cochrane claimed, was drunk much of the time . . .

"A lie and a villainous slander!" Jim Reynolds raged in the columns of the *Statesman*. "As for Silas Cochrane, it is common knowledge that he himself is *generally* drunk!"

Whether Clerk Cochrane, Secretary Smith, or both drank to excess soon turned out to be a purely academic question, so far as the affairs of the Territory were concerned. Arriving in Lewiston in early March, Acting Governor Smith demanded the seal and archives from Clerk Cochrane, got the major portion of them and brought them to Boise City, where the jubilant citizenry gave him a triumphal welcome to which he responded unenthusiastically.

"Gentleman, I thank you," he said wearily, "but my trip has tired me. I must have some rest . . ."

During the spring and summer, he made a feeble gesture at playing the part of Chief Executive, touring the mining towns in the Owyhees to the south, visiting Idaho City, Placerville, Yuba, Rocky Bar, and the other mining towns in the mountains to the north. But he made few speeches, few friends, and spent much of his time secluded in his room.

And on August 24, he died. Of habitual drunkenness, unkind men said. Of an incurable ailment, kinder men claimed.

It really didn't matter.

"Now who's Governor of Idaho?" Armand Kimball asked his law partner.

"God knows!" Creed answered with a shrug. "But I doubt if He cares."

That was an unfair thing to say, for the Lord in His Infinite Wisdom even at that moment was looking out for the Territory's welfare, though inscrutable indeed were His ways. In faroff Lyonsdale, New York, Caleb had at last stirred from his peaceful hill. First word of that stirring reached Armand Kimball in early October, when Councilman Creed hurried into the law office waving a copy of the *Statesman* and exclaimed: "He's coming back, Armand! That pompous old fool is coming back!"

"Who are you talking about?"

"Caleb Lyon! Old Kale! He's still Governor, it seems, and he's on his way back to Idaho with a satchel full of money!"

"Whose money?"

"The Federal government's money! The Governor of Idaho, as you should know, doubles as Indian agent for the Territory. Caleb went down to Washington City and convinced Andrew Johnson that the only way to settle Idaho's Indian problem is to rub it with a soothing poultice of greenbacks. There's no definite confirmation of the amount of money he's been given, but it's rumored to be in the neighborhood of one hundred thousand dollars!"

"All that for a few hundred Indians?" Kimball said incredulously. "How much of it do you suppose will get into their hands?"

That, said Councilman Creed, was a mighty interesting question.

Down in the Owyhee mining district, the businessmen reactivated their long-suspended project of taking up a freewill offering and presenting their esteemed governor with a solid silver brick. In no time at all the fund reached one thousand dollars.

CHAPTER SIX

Ferdinand J. Patterson, a professional gambler charged with attempting to scalp his mistress, has been released from jail on $500 bail. Patterson is the rabid Secessionist who achieved local notoriety some months ago by killing Captain Lew Staples in a gunfight—a crime of which he was acquitted, we regret to say, in a sad miscarriage of justice.

He is reported heading upriver to the Idaho mines.

—*Oregonian*
Portland, Oregon
December 10, 1864

By odd coincidence, the horse ranch on which Isaac Shelby now spent most of his time and the farm on which his family had settled were both located in the upper Payette Valley, separated by only a few miles of trail. Only once had he ridden downriver to visit the family, only once had Benjamin ridden upriver to see him, and on both occasions their exchanges of conversation had been stiff and strained.

If his father and brother had said, "Look, Isaac, we acted like damn fools," it might have been possible to effect some sort of reconciliation, Isaac reflected in quiet, brooding moments when alone, for then he could have admitted that he himself wasn't any too proud of the rash things he had done in anger. But instead they had acted like nothing had happened, like they'd done nothing wrong, like it was he rather than they who should apologize and ask forgiveness. What did they expect him to say? Sorry I wouldn't let you whip me, Pa; get your razor strop and I'll bend over now and let you blister my backside good. Sorry, Ben, I blacked your eye; take a swing at me—I won't hit back.

So he was stubborn. So he figured he was too old to be tanned by his pa or bossed around by his older brother or mothered by Ruth . . . No, she wouldn't try that any more, for he'd seen understanding in her eyes, seen respect for him as a grown man, seen sorrow. And she, at least, hadn't been so all-fired proud—like Ben and Pa were—that she wouldn't humble herself to him.

"Please, Isaac, come back to us. We need you so."

"That ain't what Ben says. He says you're getting along just fine."

"And you told him *you* were doing fine, didn't you?"

"Well, I am."

"I'm sure you are. But even if you weren't, you'd be too proud to tell him so, just as he's too proud to tell you how badly we need you. Stay here. We'll make room for you."

"I've got a mighty comfortable place where I am now," Isaac said, shaking his head. "And it's one I made for myself."

That was true, for though Gil Gillis, Duke, Vinegar, Portugee Pete, and the half dozen other rootless men who casually came, went and in bad weather stayed in the carelessly thrown-together shack at the horse ranch headquarters, living in a boar's nest—as he called it—had soon palled on Isaac. With no help from any of them, he had built himself a small, tight, weatherproof room adjacent to the one good wall of the shack, a room which could be entered only by an outside door, and, though it had caused him a quarrel or two, he had made it clear to all of them that this was *his* room, to be entered by his invitation only, and when they did come in, by God, they would abide by his rules of cleanliness.

"Hell, Ike," Vinegar protested, "you're as fussy as an old maid schoolteacher. What's a room for if a man can't spit on the floor and pee out the doorway? You're puttin' on mighty fancy airs, it seems to me."

"I wasn't raised in a pigpen," Isaac snapped. "If you don't like how I keep my room, stay the hell out of it."

By degrees, an arrangement had been worked out between Isaac and Gil Gillis that suited them both fine, with Gil spending much of his time gone from the ranch and Isaac spending most of his staying close to home. Every week or so Gil would bring in a dozen or so thin, trail-weary horses to be turned out to graze; every now and then he would select a few sleek, rested animals and take them away with him—presumably back to their owners or to buyers. He seldom volunteered information as to where the horses had come from or where they were going, nor did Isaac bother to ask him.

They had agreed that in exchange for looking after the animals Isaac was to receive one dollar out of the three-dollar monthly fee charged the owners, but Isaac soon learned that Gil had no taste for bookkeeping and no head for figures. If he happened to have a bit of money on him and was mellow with drink, as he often was, he divvied up generously enough; if broke and hungover, as he more frequently was, he was surly and best left alone.

The truth was, Isaac admitted to himself, Gil, Duke, Vinegar, Portugee Pete, and the others were lazy, ignorant, unambitious men whose only aim in life was to avoid work and have fun—and fun to them meant whisky, women, horseplay, yarn-spinning, and doing just as they pleased.

At first, Isaac had been awed by their rough talk of the fist-fights, knife-fights, and gun-fights they had engaged in and won; if their accounts were to be believed, each one of them had a man for breakfast every morning of the week. But presently, observing firsthand some of the brawls they got into and then listening to them describe the events afterward, he came to realize that the further away the escapade was in space and time the more glorified it became in the telling.

For example, Vinegar's favorite story these days was how he had avenged an insult to the honor of his beautiful lady love, Lydia, by stripping the clothes off the man who had given affront and then horse-whipping him, jaybird naked, the whole length of Idaho City's Main Street. It made a good yarn, but the plain truth had been that the beauteous Lydia was a fat, red-headed whore well past her prime, who had drunkenly appealed to Vinegar—who was even drunker—to hold a non-paying customer down while she beat him to death with a boot. The attempted feat had been a dismal failure, though it was true that the gentleman had run the length of Main Street jaybird naked. The seamy facts had been revealed next day in a justice of peace court when the customer had pressed assault charges against Lydia and Vinegar and had been awarded a ten-dollar judgment to assuage his wounded dignity. But Vinegar never let facts spoil a good story.

Younger than the others and a newcomer, Isaac had taken quite a hazing at first and had been made the butt of many raw, rough practical jokes. For a while he took it all in good spirit. But upon discovering one noonday that the spongy, oval object in the bottom of the bowl of stew he had just eaten was a ball of horse manure, he decided enough was enough. Setting the bowl down, he got to his feet, gazed around the circle of studiously averted faces and said quietly, "I can whip the bastard that did that."

Nobody spoke. But as it was quite evident to Isaac that all present were in on the prank and were prepared to share equally in its enjoyment, establishing individual guilt seemed immaterial. He fixed his angry eyes on Duke.

"You're the biggest, Duke. I'll fight you."

"Aw, come off it, Ike. It was just for fun."

"You're a dirty bastard, Duke."

"Now, Ike—"

"You're a son-of-a-bitch, Duke."

"Watch your tongue, Ike—my mother was a good woman."

"She was a whore. And she gave birth to a yellow bastard—" Duke lunged to his feet with a roar of rage and charged him. Beginning in the lean-to side of the shack, the fight surged outside, where there was more room to maneuver, and for a while Isaac feared he'd bitten off a bigger hunk of trouble than he could chew. Duke outweighed him by fifty pounds, was strong as a bull and knew every trick of barroom brawling in the book. But at least half of his weight advantage was whisky fat, his very strength made him muscle-bound and slow, and Isaac was ten years younger.

Twice Duke's sledge-hammer blows caught Isaac on the side of the head and put him down; cat-like he rolled over, avoided Duke's clumsy attempt to stomp him, bounced to his feet and resumed his slashing attack. Stinging blows to Duke's face opened a cut over one eye and split a lip, but, realizing that his own knuckles were suffering more damage from an attack to the head than his adversary was, Isaac feinted a left to the face, brought Duke's guard up, then sank a good right into the older man's midsection.

"*Augh!*" Duke wheezed.

"Good boy, Ike!" Vinegar whooped. "That got him where he lives!"

"Grab hold of him, Duke!" Portugee Pete yelled encouragingly. "Bear-hug him!"

Duke tried. Side-stepping the charge, Isaac stuck out a foot, tripped Duke and sent him sprawling. The watchers cheered lustily, some for him, some for Duke. Ignoring the advice of one of his well-wishers that he jump on the fallen man and grind his face into the dirt, Isaac stayed clear and let him get up. This was his fight and he would fight it his own way.

Even though he had found the bigger man's soft spot, Duke retained cunning enough to make him pay dearly to reach it. Twice more Duke's blows sent him sprawling; twice more Isaac sank his fist deep into the bigger man's middle and doubled him over, blue-faced for lack of breath. Isaac's ears were ringing now; his vision was beginning to blur. But at last he became aware of the fact that he and Duke were facing each other, blood streaming down their faces, arms dropped, panting like winded hound dogs. Gil stepped between them.

"Had enough, boys?"

Duke nodded.

"You, Ike?"

Isaac could see that Duke's eyes were glazed and his knees were rubbery; he appeared possessed of neither the power nor the will to defend himself any further. One more blow, which Isaac knew he still had the strength to deliver, would send him down to stay. But he made no attempt to give it; instead, he nodded mutely.

"I declare this here fight a draw!" Gil shouted, seizing an arm of each and raising them high. "Shake hands, gents, and let bygones be bygones!"

Grinning sheepishly, Duke mumbled, "Suits me. You're a bearcat, Ike."

"Likewise. You're a buzz saw, Duke."

Portugee Pete had fetched a bottle from the shack, which he uncorked with a whoop of delight and handed to Isaac. "Have a drink, boy! That's the best damn fight I've seen in a coon's age!"

Isaac drank, then passed the bottle over to Duke, who lifted it and drank, too. By the time the bottle had passed around the circle twice, it was empty. The sad discovery was made that there was no more whisky in the shack, and Vinegar cried, "Let's saddle up an' head fer town! This calls fer a celebration! All in favor say 'Aye!'"

The proposal carried unanimously.

The events of the rest of that day, that night, and the day and night that followed were forever afterward unclear in Isaac's mind. He vaguely remembered going from town to town and saloon to saloon surrounded by laughing, happy friends, buoyed up by a wonderful feeling of belonging, of having made a place for himself in the world. Whooee! I'm a great man! I can outfight, outsing, outdance, and outbrag any peckerwood in this whole peckerwood world! And Duke's my friend! The best old friend a man ever had. We've got the keys to the door of the world, Duke and me have! We've oiled the hinges, we let in or let out just our own special crowd, and ain't it just fine! Whooee!

On the morning of the third day, sick as a poisoned pup, he woke up in a cell in the Idaho City jail. And the keys to the door of the world were missing.

"Well, boys," Sheriff Pinkham said with an unsympathetic smile as he unlocked the cell, "it's time to pay for your fun. Rise and shine. The judge is waiting."

What the judge was waiting with, Isaac learned as he sat on the sinner's bench with Gil, Duke, Portugee Pete, Vinegar, and the rest of the most wonderful fellows in the world, was charges of drunkenness in a public place, disorderly conduct, malicious mischief, resisting arrest, and committing various and sundry nuisances. Gil sent for a lawyer friend, a personable young man named Ed Holbrook, who did his best to persuade the court to reduce the charges. Sick as he was, Isaac thought this a waste of time; he was perfectly willing to plead guilty to anything, for he knew good and well he was going to die within the hour anyway.

"Thirty dollars or thirty days apiece," he heard the judge say. "Next case."

Ed Holbrook, whose eloquent plea that these were only high-spirited young fellows out for a bit of fun had fallen upon stone-deaf ears, held a low-voiced conference with Gil, with the court clerk, and finally with Sheriff Pinkham, who nodded, then herded them all out of the courtroom and into the clerk's office, where he ordered them to sit down and wait.

"You see," Gil whispered to Duke. "I told you Ed would fix it for us."

"Where'll he raise the money?"

"Don't worry—Ed's got a lot of friends."

As Isaac started to seat himself beside the others, Sheriff Pinkham tapped him on the shoulder and grunted, "Come outside, son. I want a word with you."

Isaac let the officer escort him out of the building and motion him to a seat on a wooden bench facing the street. The bright morning sunlight stabbed knife-like into his eyes, making him wince and let out an involuntary groan. The sheriff chuckled.

"You'll learn, boy—you'll learn."

Sheriff Sumner Pinkham was a big man, standing well over six feet, with a barrel chest, an ample paunch, prematurely white hair that aged his appearance beyond his years, a ruddy-complexioned face and a solid jaw. Republican in his politics and a fervent Unionist, he had made himself many enemies in predominately Democratic Boise County, but even they were as quick to admit as the most loyal of his friends that he was a man not to be trifled with when he undertook to enforce the law. In the election to be held next fall, he undoubtedly would be defeated by the Democratic candidate for the sheriff's office; but, meantime, he still ran Boise County with an iron hand.

Sitting down on the bench beside Isaac, Pinkham said, "I know your family, Ike."

"Oh?"

"I hear you had a falling out with Obe and Ben."

"That's our business."

"Sure, Ike. A young man your age ought to strike out on his own." He paused. "But he ought to know where he's headed."

"I do."

"You picked a poor crowd to run with."

"That's your idea."

"My ideas are generally right."

"So—?"

"I like your pa and brother. They're fine men. And Billy McConnell, their neighbor over Payette way, is a mighty good friend of mine."

"Since when does the sheriff of Boise County admit he's a good friend to a Strangler? McConnell is bossing the Payette Vigilante Committee—that's common talk."

"If you take my advice, you'll listen to common sense, not common talk. The way things are going in Idaho right now, a man's more apt to get away with murder than horse-stealing. The crowd you're running with—"

"You accusing us of being horse-thieves?"

"People are beginning to talk."

"And *you're* listening."

Sheriff Pinkham shook his head. "Just a word to the wise, Ike. There's going to be a lot of rats' nests cleaned out before long, one way or another. Just make sure you ain't in one when it happens."

As they rode back to the horse ranch, Gil asked curiously, "What did Old Pink say to you?"

"Nothing important," Isaac answered sullenly.

"Oh, bull! What did he say?"

"He knows Pa and Ben and Billy McConnell. They put him up to telling me I'm running in bad company."

"The meddling old fool! He'd better keep his big red nose out of our business."

"Yeah," Duke grunted. "Hell, come Election Day he's going to be out on his fat ass anyway. Without a badge, he'll get himself run clean out of Idaho."

"Or killed," Vinegar grunted. "If you ask me, the Unionist son-of-a-bitch has just been beggin' fer a bullet in the belly. One of these days the man'll come along with guts enough to give it to him."

Maybe, Isaac brooded skeptically. But to kill Sumner Pinkham, he'd better be quite a man.

True to local predictions, the Democratic candidate for sheriff, O. A. Bowen, defeated Pinkham by a comfortable majority, riding the general wave that swept Republicans out and Democrats into elective offices throughout Idaho Territory in the autumn of '64. Edward Dexter Holbrook, the handsome, energetic, well-liked Idaho City attorney who ran as Democratic candidate for the Territorial Delegate to Congress post, won easily, replacing former Governor William H. Wallace, who had apparently sensed which direction Idaho's political winds were blowing and had not entered the race.

Now it was the Republicans' turn to cry "Fraud!" But their charges got nowhere, for, although the federally appointed judges, U.S. marshal, and governor were at least outwardly loyal Republicans, there was a war on back East, governor and marshal were absent from the Territory most of the time, and the voice of the majority was the final law of the land.

Duke, Vinegar, Portugee Pete, Gil, and the others openly bragged that each of them had voted from three to six times for their pet candidates. "When *I* believe in a man," Vinegar boasted, "*I* support him, by God!"

Though urged to vote early and often like the others, Isaac had not bothered to vote at all. Hell, what did he care who ran Idaho? And the truth was, he admitted to himself, the bitter memories of what his family had suffered because of their Unionist beliefs back in Missouri were still too vivid to permit him to vote for any man sympathetic to the Secessionist Cause, which most all Idaho Democrats were; if he had gone to the polls, his conscience would have compelled him to vote the Union ticket right down the line, and, though the way a man voted was supposed to be a secret known only to himself and his Maker, such secrets hereabouts were ill-kept and he would have lost friends. So on Election Day he had stayed home.

According to the newspapers which Gil now and then brought back to the horse ranch, Sumner Pinkham had left Idaho shortly after turning his badge of office over to Sheriff Bowen. Because he feared his many enemies, one editor hinted; because he wanted to pay a visit to his aging mother back East, another said. At any rate, he was gone, and, though he insisted that he would return to Idaho eventually, Portugee Pete claimed to have it on good authority that Old Pink had left for good because he knew he would soon be a dead man if he stayed.

Immediately following the general Republican defeat at the polls, Isaac began to notice a new confidence, a new arrogance, in the crowd of men that came and went from the horse ranch headquarters. When sober, they talked guardedly in his presence, for though Gil and Duke repeatedly assured them that "Ike's one of us," they were aware of the fact that his father and brother were on friendly terms with Billy McConnell, a man whom they all hated and feared; when drunk, their tongues loosened, and though Isaac deliberately tried to ignore what they were saying, he could not help but hear, absorb, and be concerned by their talk.

McConnell and two of his neighbors had recently pursued four men into Oregon, they said, had caught them with horses and mules claimed to be stolen, and had hanged them without benefit of jury trial. Encouraged by the ease with which those murders had been accomplished, the settlers of the lower Payette Valley had sent for McConnell, enlisted his aid and organized a Stranglers' Committee of night-riders, which declared itself to be the Final Law. On the least provocation, the committee could horsewhip, banish, or hang any man that offended them, and was using its power to terrorize the entire lower valley.

"Remember Dave Conklin? No harm to the fella. The worst anybody could accuse him of was havin' a poor eye fer tellin' bad dust from good. Well, seems like somebody passed off some bogus dust on him an' them damn Stranglers caught him with it. You know what they done to the poor bastard? Give him twenty-four hours to git out of the country, that's what!"

"Did he go?"

"Shore. What else could he do?"

Isaac remembered Dave Conklin, who on several occasions had spent the night at the horse ranch and once had lingered several days. Seeing smoke rising out of a secluded gulch several miles from the shack while checking the horse herd one morning, Isaac had investigated and found Dave Conklin nursing a fire over which an odd-smelling concoction was brewing in a kettle. When Isaac asked him what he was doing, he was told with a self-conscious laugh, "Jest brewin' me up some drinkin' whisky, boy. Jest brewin' me up some moon.

If he were doing that, Isaac mused, it was the oddest moonshine still *he* had ever seen, and he'd seen more than one in the Missouri hills back home. But he let the man be and said nothing about it to Gil and the others. His guess was that Conklin had been engaged in a bit of alchemy. Bogus gold dust was getting to be a problem in the mining country, he knew, for the merchants and businessmen were beginning to complain bitterly about it. With paper money greatly discounted and minted silver and gold coins scarce, raw gold dust had to be used as the common medium of exchange. Even when well cleaned, which it frequently was not, dust coming from the different camps varied widely in real value; it might be worth $16 per ounce, $14, $12, $10, $8, or be, as one newspaper editor sarcastically pointed out, "completely worthless until people start plastering their cabin walls."

There were a hundred and one different ways to cheat when passing or accepting gold dust. An altered scale, a hollowed-out weight, a long thumbnail, a too-vigorous breath to "blow away the trash"—by any of these means and dozens more could the merchant cheat the miner. On the other hand, lead shavings galvanized with a coating of gold, bad dust deposited for credit where it was known that it would be mixed in with good which could eventually be withdrawn—these were but two of the many ways by which the crooked passer could beat the businessman.

Knowing these things, Isaac suspected that if Dave Conklin had been caught with bogus dust on him he likely knew he possessed it; considering the ugly mood the local merchants were in, he could count himself lucky that his sentence had been merely banishment. These days, bogus dust passing was beginning to be regarded as serious a crime as horse-stealing—and the usual sentence for that was the rope.

"You heard how them Payette Stranglers jumped the Stewart boys down at Washoe Ferry? Sneaked up on their house at night, pretendin' they was pilgrims from Oregon wantin' to be ferried acrost the Snake, then the minute they got inside they throwed down guns on 'em and said they was under arrest. Give 'em a trial, sentenced the Stewart boys to hang and told their friends to git out of the country."

"Did they hang 'em?"

"Naw. The Stewart boys got away an' headed downriver. Ed Holbrook run into Alex Stewart over in Walla Walla, found out what had happened an' got madder'n a singed hornet. Ed says, 'Alex, they got no right to treat you that way. You go back to Idaho. We'll take Billy McConnell and his crowd into court and sue the pants off them.'"

Alex Stewart had come back and instigated a lawsuit, Isaac knew, for he himself had happened to be in the Boise City Saloon in whose backroom Stewart was staying when Billy McConnell stalked in looking for him. McConnell was armed and looked to be in an ugly mood; he marched the length of the saloon's main room, went into the backroom where Alex was sleeping and roughly shook him awake. The light was poor. Groggy with sleep, Alex mumbled, "What the hell—"

"It's me—Billy McConnell."

"What do you want?"

"You know good and well what I want, Alex. When the committee sentenced you and your brother to be hanged as horse-thieves, who let you escape?"

"You did, Billy."

"Who gave you a hundred and fifty dollars for your guns so that you'd have money to travel on?"

"You did, Billy. And I was mighty grateful to you."

"But you forgot my terms. Which were that you were to leave Idaho and never come back; that if you did come back and tried to make trouble for me and my friends, I'd move heaven and earth to see that the sentence passed on you was carried out. Didn't you believe me?"

"Well, it seemed a hard thing to lose all we owned, Billy, and to be run out of the country that way. Ed Holbrook, he said—"

"I don't care what *anybody* said. You made me a promise; I made you one; and, by Heaven, if you won't keep yours I'll keep mine. I want that lawsuit withdrawn and I want you to leave Idaho. You've got just twenty-four hours."

The sheer audacity of McConnell's action and the blunt directness of his threat had so stunned Alex Stewart's friends that not a man in the saloon had raised a finger to stop the young farmer as he came out of the backroom, walked the length of the main room and went out the street door. And the angry discussion that followed, the promises of moral support, the bold assurances to the white-faced, badly shaken Alex Stewart that "McConnell can't do this to you!" influenced him not one whit. Firmly convinced that Billy McConnell not only could but *would* do exactly as he had promised, Alex Stewart wasted no time in leaving Boise City—and was seen in Idaho Territory no more.

Later that winter, Isaac heard, there had been a showdown between the Payette Vigilantes and the element opposed to them; it had involved fifty or more men on each side, and, for a time, had appeared certain to erupt into wholesale bloodshed.

Backed by court-issued warrants for the arrest of McConnell and other suspected vigilante leaders, Constable Short had rallied a crowd of well-armed deputies from among his Democratic friends in Boise City and had ridden toward Horseshoe Bend on the Payette, taking the long way round because of the deep snowdrifts covering the intervening hills. Learning of the expedition, one of McConnell's friends in Boise breasted the drifts, crossed the ridges by the shorter route and warned the Payette Valley "Vegetable Peddler" (as his enemies contemptuously called him) that a posse was coming to get him.

"Well," McConnell said quietly, "if it's trouble they want, let's meet them halfway."

Rounding up his neighbors, McConnell soon raised a force of fifty or so men, took to the trail, surprised the posse as its members rested at a roadhouse and challenged Constable Short to show his hand. In the bitter, confused, angry confrontation that followed, violence was averted by only the slimmest of margins.

"My God, Billy," Constable Short pleaded, "let's not have any shooting over this!"

"There won't be any shooting unless your crowd starts it,"

McConnell answered grimly. "You've got a warrant for my arrest, I'm told."

"That's right."

"What made you think you'd need a mob of roughs backing you when you served it?"

"Well, talk was you'd make trouble—"

"So you rounded up a gang of drunken, gun-packing roughs that have been bragging all over Boise City that they were going to rub out Billy McConnell and his farmer friends—"

"Now, Billy, these men are legally appointed deputies. I warn you against any attempt to resist arrest. I call on you all to give up your guns—"

"Serve your warrants, Constable. My friends and I respect the law. We'll appear in the Boise City court at any hour and day we're requested to do so; we'll answer all charges brought against us; but we will not surrender our guns."

Eventually, both groups dispersed and returned home. A few days later, McConnell and the alleged vigilante leaders rode into Boise City, employed legal counsel, went to court and succeeded in getting the charges against them dismissed. Some months afterward, the final word to the fiasco was written when a bill introduced in the Territorial Legislature for the payment of expenses entailed in arresting and bringing the Payette Vigilance Committee to trial went down to a thumping defeat.

"Some day," Vinegar muttered prophetically, "Billy McConnell's goin' to get what's comin' to him, wait an' see."

The wait, Isaac suspected, was apt to be a long one.

Unlike the extremely moderate weather of Isaac's first winter at the horse ranch, the December to March months of '64—'65 proved to be bitterly cold and marked by frequent heavy falls of snow. For weeks at a time, deep drifts blocked the trails in all directions and work in the mountain mining towns came to a standstill. The horses in Isaac's charge kept alive only by stripping low-hanging limbs of willow, cottonwood, and alder off the trees along the stream courses and by pawing away the thick-crusted drifts to reach scant mouthfuls of frozen grass, while range cattle down in the lower, more open country—less well-equipped than horses to survive in such weather because of their cloven hoofs—died of starvation by the hundreds. By mid-January, Isaac heard, Andy Hale and his Delaware Indian partner, Levi, had lost at least sixty percent of their she-stuff, almost all of their calves, and, unless a thaw came or they could buy some hay, stood a good chance of being wiped out completely.

With the first snowfall, Gil, Duke, Vinegar, Portugee Pete, and the others had decided to head for Idaho City, where, they announced, they intended to sit out the winter in more comfortable surroundings. Gil urged Isaac to come along. "Hell, Ike, there ain't nothin' you can do here."

"What's there to do in town?"

"Why, there's cards, whisky, women, talk, fun—"

"And not a damn thing left to show for your wasted time, come spring, but a mess of unpaid bills, a muddled head, and a sore gut from too much bad whisky. No thanks, Gil, I got other plans."

"You'll get cabin fever, stayin' here all alone."

"I'll risk that."

"You're a queer one, Ike. But suit yourself. How're you fixed for supplies?"

"Fine. But I'd be obliged if you'd send me out some newspapers when you can. I like to read in the evenings."

To his friends, he *was* a queer one, Isaac knew, for they could not understand why any man would rather sit out a long winter in a snow-bound valley with no other company than a herd of horses, a bit of reading material and his own thoughts when he could be comfortably loafing away the time in a warm saloon. But in the year that had passed since he had broken with his family and struck out on his own, Isaac had developed a mind and a will of his own. He meant to prove himself a man capable of standing on his own two feet. He meant to show Pa, Ben, Ruth—yes, Beulah Baker, too—that he could start from scratch and with no help or advice from any of them do just as well in this country as any other full grown man could. The fact that they all looked down on the crowd he'd taken up with and were convinced he would come to no good end, made proving himself doubly important.

Because he'd been raised to believe that idleness bred mischief, he kept busy. Last spring, he had fenced off a two-acre plot of ground, planted a garden, weeded, watered, and nurtured it—grimly ignoring the wisecracks of his friends, to whom any sort of physical labor that could not be accomplished on horseback was an abomination—and the garden patch not only had kept him supplied with fresh vegetables during the summer and given him produce to sell for cash in the mining towns, but also had filled a carefully prepared root cellar with more than enough potatoes, carrots, parsnips, turnips, and other storable vegetables to carry him through the winter. Before heavy snowfall made hunting difficult, he spent long days in the woods of the higher slopes, killing deer; enough quarters of venison hung now in the bearproof meathouse he had built adjacent to the shack to assure him of a winter's supply of meat.

From a farmer living a few miles down the valley he bought a hog, six hens and a goose, brought them home, fattened them for a few weeks on cull vegetables, then, following the first hard freeze, butchered them and hung their carcasses up in the meathouse against the day when he might want a change from wild meat. Several sacks of flour, beans, ten pounds of coffee, ten more of sugar, two of salt, and a single quart bottle of whisky—all purchased in Placerville—exhausted his funds, but he was not at all unhappy with his prospects. If he couldn't make out quite nicely on what he had laid by for the winter, he damn sure deserved to starve.

As the snowdrifts deepened and the cold became more intense, he worried about the horses. True, most of them were not *his* horses and it was the custom in this country to let livestock winter as best they could. Certainly the three dollars per month that the owners were paying for their care didn't mean that the horses were entitled to a weather-tight stable, ice-free drinking water, and a feed of hay and grain once a day. Hay, Isaac had heard, now was priced at $200 a ton in the valley towns, with almost none available; grain of any sort was being boiled and eaten by hungry people and was not to be wasted on livestock. All the same, it struck him as a crime of the worst sort that a man should expect a horse to work for him without complaint nine months out of the year and then shift for itself when the weather turned bad—particularly when that man, by showing a little foresight, could have provided his animal with the shelter and feed needed to see it through.

Why, by working a few weeks in late summer, a man with a mowing machine and a hayrake could put up enough wild hay to carry a large herd of horses or cattle through the winter. Even if he owned no livestock, the Army post at Fort Boise and the stagecoach companies which were now establishing regular runs in all directions offered a good cash market not only for hay but also for grain. Oats and rye should do well in this country. If he bought a plow, next spring, and broke some land . . .

As the snowdrifts deepened, he found it increasingly difficult to travel far from the cabin afoot. Getting around in deep snow was a new experience for him but he had read newspaper descriptions of "Norwegian runners," which he gathered were long, narrow slats turned up at one end, on which a man could skim over the surface of the snow like a bird. He made himself a pair, tried them out but found them impossible to manage in thick timber or to steer any direction but down on steep slopes; after almost breaking his neck a number of times, he decided that though a Norwegian might be able to skim over the surface of the snow like a bird, he was not. Having also read about snowshoes, he turned his attention to fabricating a pair of these. Here, he had better luck. Though clumsy and tiring to use, the snowshoes proved to be a slow but sure way to get around. Now, except for days when bitter cold or driving blizzards kept him close to the fire, he spent most of the daylight hours doing what he could for the horses, chopping firewood to be hauled home on a light toboggan he had made, splitting rails for the fences he intended to build in the spring, hunting, and exploring the countryside.

By the time the first thaw came in early March, he had made up his mind to file a homestead claim in the upper valley of the Payette and a timber claim in the adjoining foothills; as he understood the law, a single man was entitled to 160 acres of land on each type of claim. At the first opportunity, he would ask Gil if he had filed a claim on the land where the cabin set; if he had not, Isaac would settle here; if he had, Isaac would move farther up the valley. But this much he knew beyond any doubt: to make anything of himself, he must begin soon and he must begin here.

Warm winds and bright sunshine in late March and early April turned the snowdrifts to soggy melting masses, sent the streams over their banks, and transformed the bottomlands into bogs of mud. Deciduous trees budded and leafed out, evergreens sprouted new growth, grass and wildflowers carpeted the slopes above the receding waters, birds reappeared and winter became only a bad memory.

Checking the horse herd, Isaac found that of the hundred animals left in his charge last fall some seventy-five had pulled through, which was better than he had expected. One balmy mid-April day, Gil, Duke, Vinegar, and Portugee Pete— bloated, soft, and jaundiced-looking from long months of idleness indoors—rode out from Idaho City, bringing him newspapers, a couple of bottles of whisky, and half tipsy assurances that they were delighted to see him looking so well. Irritated because they had not bothered to communicate with him since last fall, despite their solemn promises to do so, Isaac was not overly friendly in his greetings.

"Fat lot you cared how I was doing. What happened to those papers you promised to send me?"

"Got 'em right here," Gil said. "A whole mess of 'em."

"Hell, they're months old now."

"Aw, don't be sore, Ike. We've had a tough winter."

"I'll bet you have! And not sober a single day."

"Have a drink, Ike. Ain't nothin' like a couple of snorts of whisky to make a man remember old friends."

"No thanks—I've got my dinner to tend to."

"Hey, Ike!" Duke chortled, putting a comradely arm around his shoulders. "You got enough in the pot to feed us, too?"

"I can rustle up enough to go around, I guess."

"Good old Ike! Best damn cook in the world! Dish up, boy, dish up! We ain't ate a square meal in a coon's age!"

From the ravenous way they all gobbled down the food Isaac presently set before them, he guessed that their statement that they had been living on a straight whisky diet for weeks was not too much of an exaggeration. With deep snowdrifts blocking all trails to the outside, the supply of food staples in Idaho City had run short long before winter was done. Flour, rice, beans, and the like had become so scarce that the merchants had jacked prices up to astronomical proportions, eventually causing riots among the hungry wintering miners that had done considerable damage and caused a great deal of bad feeling. Twice, attempts had been made by a person or persons unknown to burn down the town, a feat not hard to accomplish once a fire got started among the frame buildings of the settlement. Robberies, murders, sporting house and saloon brawls had reached a new high. All in all, Idaho City did not sound like a pleasant place in which to winter. Isaac felt grateful that his own winter had been passed in a quieter, more productive manner, despite its many hours of loneliness.

Catching Gil in a mellow mood that evening, Isaac invited him into his own room, got the still half-full quart of whisky he had bought in Placerville last fall down off the shelf, poured them both drinks, then said, "Gil, I've been doing some thinking."

"Small wonder, with no women around all winter!" Gil chuckled. "Bet you'll give the gals hell when you go to town!"

"What I've been thinking about, Gil, is this place."

"Well, what about it?"

"Have you filed a claim on it?"

"Hell, why would I do a fool thing like that? There ain't no gold here."

"I mean a homestead claim. Do you want to own this particular piece of land?"

"God, no! All I care about is the grass."

"What do you intend to do with the horses?"

"Why, I reckon I'll collect what fees I can from their owners—when and if I can run them down. A lot of the damn fools have pulled up stakes and left the country. A lot more are broke and can't pay, which means I'll get title to their horses. Soon as they've put on some flesh, I'll sell what I can—"

"Even though some of them may be stolen?"

"Look, Ike, a horse is a horse to me. When a man asks me to take care of it for him, I can't make him prove he's got clear title to it. If somebody claims it and proves his claim in court, fine—I'll turn it over to him soon as he pays me for its keep. Otherwise, I'll sell it to the first buyer that wants it."

"Sheriff Pinkham said last summer—"

"I know what Old Pink said, Ike. And I know what them damn Payette Stranglers are saying. But they ain't runnin' things in Idaho now. I got friends where it counts—Bowen, Holbrook, men like that. They won't stand for seeing me and my friends hung for horse-thieves. If that's what's eatin' you—"

"What's eating me is I want a place of my own," Isaac answered, shaking his head. "You gave me a start. I want to stay friends with you, Gil. But I want out of the horse ranch business. I want a settling of accounts between us. And, if you've got no use for this place, I want to file a claim on it."

Gil stared at him, a puzzled look in his eyes. Pouring himself another drink, he said, "Who you been talkin' to, Ike?"

"Nobody."

"That's a lie! You been talkin' to your pa and your brother, ain't you? You been talkin' to Billy McConnell. You say you ain't but you're lyin' in your teeth."

"No. I'm not lying, I've talked to nobody and I won't argue with you about it, Gil. All I'm saying is I intend to strike out for myself. Here, if you'll clear out. Somewhere else, if you won't. Think it over, Gil."

Gil was silent a long while, staring at him with veiled, suspicious eyes, then he nodded and grunted, "Well, Ike, give me a few days . . ."

The unusual series of events that occurred during the next few days so occupied their attention that neither Isaac nor Gil had time to discuss the matter again for a while. Back East, the war ended; President Lincoln was assassinated; all saloons and business establishments in the mining towns closed for a day in mourning; turmoil ensued as Union men screamed for vengeance upon all Southern sympathizers and took out their fury upon any Copperhead or Democrat indiscreet enough to express approval of the deed.

Just as the atmosphere was growing a bit calmer, Idaho City, after four unsuccessful attempts by arsonists to put it to the torch in a single week, caught fire one warm, windy night in late May and, by the next morning, had become only an ugly heap of smoldering ashes.

During the fire there had been wholesale looting, Isaac heard, which Sheriff Bowen had been powerless to control. Rumor had it that the fire had been set in a hurdy-gurdy hall by a drunken Democrat with Secessionist sympathies. Not so! Democrats cried. They had solid evidence that the arsonist had been a rabid Republican, who had fired the town in hopes that his act would give his friends an excuse to loot and pillage the mercantile establishments owned by members of the Democratic party.

A thousand Unionists had formed a secret committee of Stranglers, still another rumor went, which was rallying to its aid vigilantes from communities all over southwestern Idaho for a wholesale hanging party. Untrue! Republicans shouted. It was the Copperheads that were organizing. Now, by God, was the time for all good Union men to come to the aid of their government, else rebellion would surely triumph!

It was not cold reason that soothed inflamed passions and set men back to rebuilding the town; it was the completeness of the catastrophe. Blame-passing cleared away no ashes. Accusations raised no buildings. There was work to do.

Under the warm spring sun, melting snows in the high country had filled the streams with water, not a running inch of which the miners working the placer claims dared waste. Now that the trails to the outside had been opened, laden strings of pack animals were arriving daily with stocks of food, hardware, and soft goods, all of which must be gotten under cover. Lumber was needed, labor needed, credit needed, everything by which men lived needed—except the wasting of precious hours in pointless bickering.

So Idaho City went back to work rebuilding. But deep in the memories of the laboring men lay unhealed wounds .

It was in June, Isaac later recalled, that he first heard someone mention the fact that Sumner Pinkham, ex-sheriff of Boise County, had written to a friend saying he was planning to return to Idaho City after a long stay in the East. And it was about that same time that Gil told him of a newcomer to the Boise Basin whom he had recently met—a man named Ferdinand J. Patterson.

"He's quite a hunk of man, Ferd is," Gil said. "A 'chief,' if ever there was one."

Chapter Seven

Oh, we'll hang Jeff Davis to a sour apple tree!
Yes, we'll hang Jeff Davis to a sour apple tree!
Oh, we'll hang Jeff Davis to a sour apple tree!
As we go marching on . . .
                —Vocal by Sumner S. Pinkham
                              Idaho City, I.T.
                              July 4, 1865

In his habit of dress, Ferd Patterson was something of a dandy. He normally wore a pair of custom-made, high-heeled boots which fitted his shapely feet to perfection, a pair of plaid trousers foxed with buckskin, a cassimere shirt, and a fancy silk vest, across the front of which dangled a heavy gold chain fashioned of California nuggets; topping all this finery, except on extremely warm days, was a long frock coat made of heavy pilot-beaver cloth, tastefully trimmed with sea-otter fur. His age was forty or so; his hands were the soft, white, supple hands of the professional gambler; his sharp, restless eyes were blue. Whatever the occasion, he always wore a gun.

The fact that he went armed and was reputed to be quick-tempered may have been why no one ever accused him of being a dandy—at least not to his face. In height, he stood an inch or more above six feet, weighed over two hundred pounds, had sandy-red hair and carried himself like a man in top physical condition; these attributes may also have contributed toward making him immune to criticism regarding his fondness for fine apparel.

He made no secret of the fact that he was a Southerner born and bred, that he mourned the South's Lost Cause, and that he would never stop grieving over the South's defeat or cease despising the people who had brought it about. Exactly what section of the South he came from and why he had chosen to dwell in the Far West were subjects he never chose to discuss; and, being the kind of man he was, it was he—not others—who generally channeled conversations.

Exciting things invariably happened, one gathered, wherever Ferd Patterson chanced to travel. Though it was said that he had engaged in a number of gunfights in California and in western Oregon, not once had he been bested by any man; even when haled into court to answer to the law for his deeds, he had always emerged victorious.

When in a good humor from drink, he was not averse to giving vague, amiable confirmation to some of the fantastic tales being told about him. Well, yes, it was true after a fashion, he would admit modestly, that he, his lady companion of the moment and a group of his friends had taken over an ocean steamer on the high seas between San Francisco and Portland and made its captain, its crew, and all its passengers dance to the tune that the Patterson crowd wanted to play. But it had all been in fun, boys; just good, clean fun. Hell, boys, sea voyages can be dull as dishwater unless the bar serves free whisky at all hours, the orchestra keeps playing, there's food available whenever you want it and no silly restrictions as to dancing, gambling, drinking, and bed partners. All in fun, boys; all in fun. And fun was what we had.

The gunfight with Captain Staples? Yes, there are a lot of conflicting stories about that and there's no use in my trying to straighten them out at this late date. Say he insulted me in a way no gentleman could permit. Say he waved the wrong flag at me. Say it was my honor and the South's honor at stake, plus a trivial personal item or two not worth mentioning; guns were drawn, shots exchanged, he's dead, I'm not— and the court called the killing justified.

The woman I was accused of scalping? Now that was a real laugh! I have an odd philosophy about women, boys, which I've developed over a long spell of years and a varied assortment of females. To state it briefly: when a woman's mine, she's mine—and she'd better not blink her eyelashes at anything else in pants. This one—well, never mind her name—did a bit of blinking. I warned her once, I warned her twice, and when that did no good, I decided to throw a scare into her. Little lady, I said, I've got Indian blood in me. When a squaw is unfaithful, I scalp her. Well, I took out my knife, grabbed her by the hair, threw her down in a chair and made a pass at her— just to scare her, mind. You know what the little fool did? Squirmed, that's what! And first thing I knew, my knife whacked off a wee flake of skin.

No, no, it isn't true that she came into court wearing a wig over her peeled head and testified in my behalf. Not true at all! But she did raise the bail money for me and begged me to forgive her for bringing charges. She writes me every week or so from Portland, wanting me to come back to her or let her come to Idaho, but I don't answer. After all the trouble she caused me, why should I do her favors?

Sumner Pinkham? Yes, I had a run-in with the Abolitionist son-of-a-bitch a couple of nights ago. He was drunk, celebrating a Union party get-together with some of his Republican friends. No point in picking a fight with him then and there, I felt, though he did say a thing or two that got under my skin. Yes, it's true I warned him; I said, Mr. Pinkham, I won't take that kind of talk off anybody—not even the ex-sheriff of Boise County. Next time we cross paths, keep a civil tongue in your head, sir, or I'll have to teach you a lesson in manners.

He's a tough customer, you say? Well, the breed isn't new to me. Not new at all . . ."

It was a damnable shame, Sumner Pinkham announced to all present in the saloon that evening, that with the Union saved, the martyred President newly laid in his grave, and Jeff Davis, the traitorous leader of the Confederacy in chains (he was captured while wearing his wife's clothes, by God, which just shows what kind of man *he* is!) with all these great events having so recently transpired, it was a shame, a crime, a shabby show of patriotism that the loyal citizens of Idaho City had not made arrangements for a parade, a cannon, a brass band in full uniform, and a royal Fourth of July celebration next week, with fireworks, orations, and a huge mass picnic.

"But, Pink," a loyal citizen protested, "Idaho City ain't *got* no brass band! We got no instruments, no uniforms, no leader—"

"Well, get 'em, I say!"

"Where?"

"Don't pester me with damn fool questions! I'll take care of the details myself. Just spread the word that at noon, come Fourth of July next week, Sumner Pinkham expects every loyal Union man, woman, and child in Boise County to fall in behind the brass band, which Mr. Pinkham will supply and lead himself, at the upper end of Main Street. We'll march through town in regular military formation, then go to a picnic spot where we'll have food and beer waiting—"

"Hey, what about Warm Springs? That ain't too far out."

"Good! The very place! Let's see now—I'll take care of getting the band and the cannon, but we'll need committees on arrangements, speakers, beer, food . . ."

It had been Pinkham's notion that the commandant at Fort Boise would be happy to send up the Army's brass band, a cannon, flags, and all the other paraphernalia necessary to a full dress parade. But because the patriotic citizens of Boise City already had arranged to stage a Fourth of July celebration of their own, all the commandant sent was his regrets. Pinkham raged, pleaded, pulled strings—but to no avail.

"I can spare you a fifer," the colonel said, "a drummer and a flag—no more."

"Well, send 'em, then! But can't we have a cannon, too?"

"Sorry, Mr. Pinkham. It's against regulations to loan heavy ordnance to civilians."

Muttering dire threats that his political friends in high places would hear about *this,* Sumner Pinkham grudgingly accepted the fifer, the drummer, and the flag, saying that what was lacking in military pomp and splendor would be made up for by civilian ingenuity and enthusiasm or, by God, he'd know the reason why.

As was usual on the single holiday of the year judged important enough to suspend all mining work and close all business establishments except saloons, the drinking started early. After all, loyal Unionists had a great deal to celebrate. Because of the recent conflagration in Idaho City, the supply of fireworks was small, but in the constant bark of rifles, crack of pistols, boom of shotguns, and roar of blasting powder set off inside used tins, this lack was scarcely noticed. By noon, roughly half of Idaho City's population—plus sizable contingents of patriotic citizens come into town for the day from the outlying mountain mining districts—had assembled at the upper end of Main Street on the outskirts of town. The other half of the populace, Democrats most of them, milled about on the board-walks—between quick trips into convenient saloons for thirst-quenchers—prepared to boo, heckle, disrupt, confuse, and otherwise demonstrate that this was indeed a free country by turning what Union men bragged was to be the grandest parade ever into a complete fiasco.

Some minutes later than scheduled, Sumner Pinkham, who was to lead the march, conduct the band, and carry Old Glory, raised and dropped his right hand, which was the signal to fire the improvised cannon. This piece of ordnance—guaranteed by its inventors to make fully as big a boom as the biggest cannon in the Fort Boise arsenal— most certainly did make a satisfactory amount of noise. Constructed of a length of rusty iron pipe, aimed in the general direction of the town's business district and amply stuffed with blasting powder, it had not been loaded with a projectile (though more than one man had suggested it would be great fun to drop a big ball of lead through the roof of a certain saloon notorious for the rabid Secessionists that patronized it, just to give the bastards a taste of what they had missed by not supporting Jeff Davis with deeds as well as words); but unfortunately, in seeking a maximum boom, the strength of the iron pipe had been overestimated. Thus, when the cannon went off, it went off in all directions.

"It is a deplorable situation," wrote H. C. Street, editor of the Idaho *World,* in a later issue of the paper, "when supposedly grown men of mature judgment get so carried away by patriotic fervor (or was it whisky, boys?) as to construct a noise-making instrument whose disintegration causes a rain of jagged metal to fly out in all directions at a high velocity. At least a dozen persons were wounded—fortunately none of them seriously—hundreds more were frightened out of their wits, a great number of windows were shattered, and a valuable milk cow belonging to Jake Hennessey (which was grazing a good three hundred yards away from the blast site) was killed outright, as a result of the explosion of the Union Party Fourth of July Parade cannon. Ironically, the inventors and firers of the cannon received not so much as a scratch. Please, gentlemen, let's be more careful."

Off to this somewhat disturbing start, the marchers never did quite catch the rhythm of the drumbeat and fall into orderly ranks or step, but what they lacked in these departments was more than made up for by the volume of their singing. Caustic-tongued observers commented that no two people appeared to be singing in the same key, nor, for that matter, were they singing the same song. Even the uniformed fifer and drummer were out of step with each other, it was noted; as for Sumner Pinkham, he appeared to waddle rather than march, and even his waddle was wobbly, for he was far too patriotic a man to refuse any toast offered to the Union on such a Great Day, and he had many friends.

The best the watchers could make out, the drummer was beating time to "Battle Hymn of the Republic," the fifer was tootling "Yankee Doodle," and the crowd behind was just making noise—but there was no doubt in anybody's mind as to the song Old Pink was lustily singing:

> *Oh, we'll hang Jeff Davis to a sour apple tree!*
> *Yes, we'll hang Jeff Davis . . .*

As the parade reached the center of town, where the crowds lining the boardwalks on either side were denser, the booing, the heckling, the tripping, the shoving, became more active and intense. Here and there a scuffle broke out; now and again blows severe enough to bloody noses and puff up lips were landed; an empty whisky bottle tossed into the marchers' midst in a high, relatively harmless arc, came whizzing back with no visible hump in its line of flight, narrowly missed the head of a quietly smiling, perfectly innocent, politically neutral observer, struck the front window of a barber-and-bath shop run by a Negro named Jack Johnson and shattered it utterly.

"Lawdy, Lawdy!" he was heard to exclaim in dismay. "Look what comes from bein' free!"

Exactly what triggered the fuss between Ferd Patterson and Sumner Pinkham up at the head of the parade was never afterward firmly established. It may have been that the bully-boy crew of roughs that had been making a game of forming a human wedge and thrusting their way from one side of the street to the other through the marchers by brute force, thus destroying unity, tired of that sport, persuaded Ferd Patterson to join their group, and he—with his customary brilliant thinking—suggested that the marchers now be split lengthwise, beginning with Old Pink himself, with Patterson leading the charge. It may have been that sight of the yellow cur dog which some Democratic prankster had painted with red, white, and blue stripes, then tin-canned and tossed at Pinkham's feet, so offended the fervent Unionist that he swerved from his line of march and bumped into Patterson, thus instigating the scuffle himself. Or it may simply have been, as was later claimed by many, that Ferd Patterson yelled out to Pinkham—who was still lustily singing—that if he didn't shut his mouth he'd shut it for him, Pinkham invited him to try and he did.

In any event, there was a brief scuffle between the two men, the result of which was that Old Glory fell into the dust of the street. Some witnesses later swore they saw Ferd Patterson spit on it; others swore he simply laughed and turned away. Some witnesses claimed they heard Pinkham (who was unarmed at the moment) swear he would kill Patterson for that; others claimed that the falling of the flag to the ground so shocked him that he said nothing, simply stooped, picked it up and then looked around for Patterson. But by then a swarm of indignant men of both political parties—unwilling to see the flag of their country deified—had separated the two men and warned the heckling roughs to let the patriotic parade proceed.

On one point, however, everyone agreed. Sooner or later a showdown must come between Old Pink and Ferd Patterson. And when it did, blood would flow.

It happened one hot Sunday afternoon in late July . . .

The Warm Springs resort a mile or so down Moore's Creek from Idaho City was a fine place to picnic, swim, drink, or steam out one's body poisons with a relaxed soaking in one of the number of private, zinc-lined, wooden tubs on either side of the long hall of the bathhouse. Strongly impregnated with sulphur and other health-restoring minerals, water heated far down in the bowels of the earth to a never-varying ninety degrees gushed out of a steep hillside to the west, filled a huge, wooden-lined, recently completed swimming pool in which properly attired gentlemen or ladies could paddle, play and float away all their aches, and was conveniently available on tap in the individual bathrooms for those who preferred a private soaking in the raw.

Built on a slope, the front part of the resort had a long veranda bordered by a railing; to enter, a person had to climb several steps leading up from ground level to the veranda, walk its length, pass into the main room—Which contained a bar—cross it, then go down the hall that led into the bathhouse section.

Sundays always were busy days; the resort-owned hack which plied between Warm Springs and Idaho City brought a new load of red-eyed, long-faced, unhappy-looking men every hour or so, who, as they got out of the conveyance and climbed the steps to the veranda appeared to be breathing their last. That the builder of the health spa had both an eye for profit and a keen knowledge of human frailty was evidenced by the fact that the room through which one must pass to reach the baths—or, in busy times, must sit and wait—was amply stocked with the very poisons which most of the customers had come here to sweat out of their systems.

Badly hungover men preferred quiet, solitude and rest to crowds, activity, and noise; thus, the suggestion when the private bathrooms were occupied that the customer might like to get into bathing dress, climb the hill—which was steep—and take a swim in the outdoor pool until a private room became available, usually was greeted with a baleful stare and a profane suggestion as to what the host could do with his so-and-so swimming pool.

A drink, then, while you're waiting, Joe? Ha-Ha! Nothing like a bit of hair off the dog that bit you, Joe! No, thanks. No, really. No—well, a small beer, maybe. And a jigger of whisky to give it some flavor. Did that help, Joe? Yeah, considerable. Sure, I'll have another. But skip the beer, this time; 'tain't good for a man to get too much liquid in his system . . .

Hey, boys, tell you what let's do—let's go for a swim! Last one up the hill's a monkey's uncle!

Both Ferd Patterson and Sumner Pinkham came to Warm Springs, that Sunday, both were armed, both had friends with them, both took the waters in one manner or other, and each of them knew the other was there. Beyond these simple facts, later testimony of the many witnesses present finds no common ground of agreement.

Pinkham's friends say that he tried to avoid a showdown. They say he was cold sober, did little if any drinking, and that he politely brushed Patterson aside as he was challenged crossing the barroom on his way to a quiet private bath, saying, "That's all right, Patterson. We won't quarrel about it here." Pinkham's friends further state that they are morally certain Ferd Patterson's sole purpose in coming down to Warm Springs that day was to murder Pinkham, whom he secretly feared; that his boasting had placed him so far out on a limb he must kill Pinkham or become the laughingstock of his crowd; that, fearful of the results of a fair fight, he had planned murder and brought his friends along so that they might witness the foul deed, then protect his life afterward by falsely swearing he had killed in self-defense.

The Ferd Patterson partisans tell it otherwise. They claim that Pinkham was the aggressor, that he called Patterson a name, that he drew first, that he fired first.

Ferd Patterson, it was testified, had just come out of the barroom onto the veranda. Pinkham was standing at the far end of the veranda, awaiting the hack. Both friendly and hostile witnesses agree that Patterson called out these words:

"Will you draw, you Abolitionist son-of-a-bitch!"

or

"Oh, you *will* draw, will you, you Abolitionist son-of-a-bitch!"

or

"Draw on *me,* will you, you Abolitionist son-of-a-bitch!"

... but opinions differ as to the order and inflexion of the words.

A pistol shot sounded. Sumner Pinkham staggered. A second shot sounded, a third—and, some witnesses swear—a fourth, though a later examination of the weapons of the two antagonists make this appear doubtful. At least one of the shots came from Pinkham's pistol, at least two from Patterson's.

Then Sumner Pinkham, ex-sheriff of Boise County, fervent Unionist, band leader, patriot, and prominent citizen, slumped to the floor of the veranda, dead . . .

Men being the fallible creatures they are, courts of law have long since learned to expect only a small portion of the full truth from even the most reliable of eyewitnesses. A murder in cold blood or the eruption of passions into sudden action by both parties are totally different in the eyes of the law; but both acts happen the same way. Without warning. Without prologue. Without a referee's calling: "Come to time!"

A rider about to mount a horse hears a pistol shot ten paces away on a peaceful Sunday afternoon; and for minutes thereafter is too busy fighting his spooked mount to watch two men trying to kill each other. A purified bather sleepily gazing into the distance as he leans on a veranda railing is too interested in preserving his own life as bullets singe his coat-tail to recall afterward whether he ran down the steps and sought shelter behind a stump as any prudent man would do or blindly dove over the railing and cravenly crawled under the porch. Later, of course, he puts the best face possible on his reactions and swears *his* account is the *true* account.

But these things are known beyond doubt:

While Pinkham's stunned friends milled about uncertainly, Ferd Patterson's cronies hustled him away, mounted him on a saddle horse that may or may not have been brought along for exactly that purpose, and sent him galloping off—not toward Idaho City, but downvalley, toward Boise City. Word of the killing soon reached Sheriff Bowen, who set out in pursuit of the fleeing man. Minutes ahead of the sheriff and riding hard was Orlando Robbins, familiarly known as "Rube," a close personal friend of Sumner Pinkham, a former deputy under him, and a tough-minded, hard-fibered man. Some twenty miles down the trail, Robbins overtook Patterson, ordered him to halt and give up his firearms. To Robbins' great disappointment (as he later confided to a friend), Ferd Patterson obeyed the order and surrendered "as meek as a lamb."

Minutes after the former deputy had disarmed the prisoner, Sheriff Bowen showed up and took him into custody. It well may be (as many Idaho City residents later claimed) that Sheriff Bowen was a .22-caliber man trying to hold down a .45-caliber job; but this much must be said for him—he got his prisoner back to Idaho City without a hand being laid on him, which, considering the fact that a lynch mob of a thousand or so angry Unionists was determined to take him and hang him to the nearest tree despite anything the law and a large crowd of his friends might do to protect him, was no small feat.

Then, with Ferd Patterson secured behind bars, Sheriff Bowen quietly turned in his badge.

Deputy Sheriff Crutcher, unexpectedly elevated to the top law enforcement job, proved to be a man made of sterner stuff. "The prisoner is mine," he declared. "I'm going to use every means at my disposal to preserve his life. If necessary, I'll throw a screen of riflemen around the jail and give them orders to shoot to kill. I'm deputizing every honorable man in Idaho City—"

"*'Honorable men,'* he says!" howled a Unionist in the crowd gathered in the street near the beleagured jail. "You know what he means, don't you, boys? Roughs! Scum! Secesh Democrats! Come on, fellas, what are we waiting for?"

Well, what *are* we waiting for? A leader. A brave, strong man who'll tell us what to do. No, not *what*. On that, we're agreed; we simply want to take Ferd Patterson out of the jail and hang him. But *how* to accomplish this little chore without starting a second Civil War is the burning question.

Say the word, Rube Robbins. You ain't afraid of the devil himself; you were Old Pink's deputy; you were Old Pink's friend; you know the ways of violence. Ah, there's the rub! You're not a fool; you know if we charge the jail some of us will die. And just because you yourself wore a badge once under the ablest peace officer the Territory has ever known, you've got a sneaking, grudging, reluctant smidgen of admiration for Jim Crutcher's guts in doing his duty as he sees it . . .

"Now, boys," Rube Robbins said, "let's not go off half-cocked. Now, boys, let's do some figuring . . ."

All right, goddamit, let's figure. Figure away the night, figure away the next day, figure, figure, and figure through the days and nights that follow. And all the figures add up to are a passel of damnfool suggestions.

"What we need is a cannon!"

"Sure, Louie and Karl can make us one, like they done for Fourth of July—"

"Oh, Lord, no! We don't want *that* kind of cannon!"

"Well, Paul and Johnny served in the Union Navy. They say they know how to make hand grenades. We'll get 'em to make us a batch, then we'll sneak up close to the jail and heave 'em—"

"Count me out on *that* idea, bully-boy! A rifle can throw lead a damn sight further'n a man can heave a grenade!"

"Hey, I got an idea! We'll ride down to Fort Boise and borrow a cannon—"

"The colonel won't loan us no cannon, you know that."

"We'll steal one, by God! We'll get some of them soldiers drunk—"

Well, now, *there* was an idea that just *might* work. Appoint a committee to ride to Boise City. Take up a collection to buy enough whisky. Dig deep, boys, it goes toward a worthy cause.

More meetings. More figuring. More procrastinating by the Democrat-dominated justice machine to keep the fires of indignation burning in the breasts of Old Pink's friends.

Ferd Patterson was being treated like no ordinary prisoner, it was said; instead, he was being wined, dined, and feted like a royal guest. The grand jury, which happened to be in session the day after the killing, refused to bring an indictment against him. Judge Milton Kelly congratulated Sheriff Crutcher and the hundreds of Democratic roughs he had deputized to guard the jail for their outstanding work in upholding law and order. The only reason that Patterson did not walk out of the jail a free man, it was rumored, was that at the moment he felt safer inside its walls than out.

"He's damn sure right there!" an outraged Unionist declared.

"Once he walks out of that jail, he's a dead man!"

The only cause for rejoicing that Pinkham's friends had during the next few days was the ruling by Federal Judge John McBride, who arrived in Idaho City two weeks after the killing, that a new grand jury must be impaneled. Nudged by his stern urgings, this one did indict Patterson for murder in the first degree and the court set a date for his trial.

"Which doesn't mean he'll be convicted," a former Republican official pointed out. "Hell, we all know that the county sheriff picks the jury panel. He can pick a jury to acquit or convict, just as he likes. We know what Crutcher will do, don't we, boys?"

"Sure, we know! He's a Democrat, ain't he?"

"Here's something else to think about, boys. In the past three years, there have been sixty murders in the Boise Basin. *Sixty,* mind you! And how many murderers have been convicted and sentenced to hang? Not one! *Not one single solitary killer has ever paid the supreme penalty!* You can mark my word, boys, if we expect justice to be done, we've got to do it ourselves!"

By now, the delegation sent to Boise City to borrow or steal a cannon from the fort had returned with the sad report that their mission had been a failure. Hearing of what had happened, the Fort Boise commandant was being very careful with his cannons, these days. Furthermore, he had seen fit to issue a stern warning that, in view of the fact the Idaho City jail contained Territorial as well as County prisoners, any mob attempt to take it by force very well might bring Federal troops to its defense.

"If that don't frost the cake!" an angry Unionist cried in disgust. "Threatenin' us with United States government troops when all we want to do is hang a goddam Secessionist!"

Despite the growing pressure on him, Rube Robbins still urged forbearance. But Sumner Pinkham had had many friends. His funeral had been the largest, most impressive ever seen in this part of the world; and sight of the immense numbers of fellow mourners attending it had given men formerly reluctant to take the law into their own hands a knowledge of their strength. In spite of Democratic rumors to the contrary, no Vigilante Committee had as yet existed in the Boise Basin; now, responsible men were openly suggesting that an organization of the righteous was the only way to clean up the country.

"Count me in," said John Gilkey, an amiable, normally placid-natured blacksmith from Buena Vista Bar. "Over in Virginia City, I hear, the roughs had things all their way till decent men hung Sheriff Plummer and twenty-five of his cronies. Things have been peaceful there ever since. If that's the answer, let's get on with it."

Elder Kingsley, a highly respected Methodist minister, was asked his opinion. He made more converts for his church from one brief statement than he had ever made in a two-hour sermon, by saying, "Gentlemen, I'm prepared to fight or pray, as required."

It was then that Rube Robbins decided to act. "Boys, we seem agreed as to what must be done," he said quietly. "The question is how to do it. Sit tight till you hear from me. I'm going on a little trip."

"Where to, Rube?"

"Over to Horseshoe Bend. Billy McConnell was Pink's friend, too. He'll know what to do."

Chapter Eight

"You may give Patterson his trial without hindrance. Since the evidence has been arranged to secure his acquittal, he can go forth into the world. But the world is not big enough to hide him."
—William J. McConnell
Idaho City, I.T.
September 1865

Benjamin Shelby had just gotten up from the breakfast table, that late summer morning, when Rube Robbins and Billy McConnell came riding into the yard. Going out to greet them, he knew from the grim set of their mouths that they were on no casual errand.

"Morning, Rube. Morning, Billy. Had your breakfast?"

Both men nodded. "Ben, I'm riding over to Idaho City with Rube," McConnell said. "I may be gone several days. I'd be obliged if you and Obe would keep an eye on my place while I'm gone."

"Be glad to, Billy."

"Henry Lynn will tend to the chores. But I wanted you to know I'd be gone, just in case anybody comes snooping around. You know what I mean."

Ben nodded; he knew exactly what Billy McConnell meant. Since the Payette Valley Safety Committee had been formed, the farmers, innkeepers, and businessmen living along the well-traveled trail from the upper valley down to the Snake had taught the local roughs to leave them alone, for the Safety Committee's lines of communication were efficient, its retribution swift. But now and then a drifter passed through the community who must be given a lesson in the sanctity of private property.

"We'll look after things, Billy."

Ruth and Obidiah came out of the house and said their good mornings to the two riders. David, past two now, lively as a cricket and as fearless of animals as his older sister, Naomi, had been when his age, slithered past his mother and ran gleefully out to make friends with the horses. Ben caught the boy and held him at his side.

"Are you mixed up in this Patterson thing, Billy?" Ben's father asked.

"Rube tells me there's talk of forming a Vigilante Committee in Idaho City. They want my advice."

"Which will be—?"

"That I can't tell you, Obe, for I don't yet know myself."

"Are they planning to take Patterson out of the jail and hang him?"

"There's talk along that line, yes."

"Well, I'm all for it. Sumner Pinkham was a mighty fine man."

Worry cast a sudden shadow over Ben's mind. Local conditions had long since forced him to accept the necessity for concerted action against the roughs by the settlers of this valley; he had participated in it along with Lynn, McConnell, and the rest of his neighbors, and, like them, was prepared to answer for whatever wrong he may have done. But here it had been a question of cleaning out bands of lawless men who were preying upon the substantial citizens of the community; neither politics nor sectional loyalties had been involved. Even more important, the accused criminals had not been in custody of legally elected officials whose sworn duty was to protect them, as was now the case in the Boise Basin.

"If they do form a committee in Idaho City," he asked, "will they want help from us?"

McConnell shook his head. "Rube understands I have no authority to commit our people to anything. I'm to give advice only on the matter of organization."

As the riders started to wheel their horses around, Ben called anxiously, "Oh, Rube!"

"Yes?"

"Did you pass by Isaac's place on your way over here?" "Yes—'long about the middle of the afternoon yesterday."

"Did you see him or talk to him?"

"No. He didn't appear to be around."

"Well, earlier—in the last week or two, say—have you seen him in Idaho City? What I mean is, is he mixed up in this thing, too?"

Obviously impatient to be on his way, Rube shook his head and said curtly, "I haven't seen him, talked to him, or heard a word about him, Ben, for at least a month. All I know is when I rode past the horse ranch yesterday he didn't appear to be around—in fact, nobody was."

"Do you mind if I saddle up and ride along with you as far as his place? I want to talk to him."

"Sure, but shake a leg."

Ben's father followed him out to the barn, watching him narrowly as he saddled the sorrel mare. As he led her out of the barn and started to mount, Obe said, "What's eating you, Ben?"

"You know how Isaac is—if trouble starts, he's got to be right in the middle of it."

"And you want to make sure he's guarding horses instead of jailbirds?"

"Pa, all hell is going to bust loose in Idaho City if a bunch of Pink's friends storm that jail. You've read the papers. Sheriff Crutcher swears he'll deputize a thousand armed men, if he has to, to protect Patterson. If a mob tries to take him, somebody's bound to get hurt."

"Well, if Isaac is fool enough to line up with the wrong side, I don't see there's much you can do about it. He's been drifting in that direction for over a year now. He's a man growed—or thinks he is."

"I ain't arguing that, Pa. But I wouldn't feel right if I didn't make one last try to save him." Ben swung into the saddle. "If he isn't at the horse ranch, I'll ride on over to Idaho City with Billy and Rube. Explain to Ruth, will you, if I don't come back tonight. And remember to keep an eye on Billy's place."

"Sure, son, sure. Take care of yourself."

The horse ranch shack was deserted, Ben found, and, from the looks of the garden patch adjacent to it—which badly needed watering—nobody had been working hereabouts for several days. Not a single horse was in sight along the expanse of grass-covered valley floor visible from here. Not having passed this way for some months, Ben was surprised to see a ten acre, newly fenced field above the shack producing a good stand of rye and oats. He gave McConnell a puzzled look.

"Who planted that?"

"Ike did. He figures there'll be a good market for feed, come winter. That's his garden, too."

"What happened to the horse herd?"

"Why, he told me he and Gillis called it quits. He made Gil get the horses off the place. You see, it's Ike's place now."

"He bought this land?"

"Yeah. He gave Gil a hundred dollars for his squatter's rights. Then he filed a homestead claim on the land."

"When did he tell you all this?"

"A month or so ago. I ran into him down in Boise City one day. He was trying to locate a mowing machine and a hayrake. Seems he's got the notion he can put up wild hay and sell it to the Army and the stagecoach companies, come winter." McConnell smiled. "He's a worker, that boy is."

"Then why isn't he home tending to things," Ben said angrily, "instead of chasing around with his no-good friends?"

"Now, Ben, don't you go borrowing trouble. If you're worried about him, come on along with us to Idaho City. If he's there, you can find him and talk some sense into him."

Talking sense to anybody in Idaho City, Ben judged as he circulated about the crowded settlement that evening, was apt to be uphill work, for if ever a town resembled an open powder keg awaiting a dropped match, this one did. The jail was being guarded by a large group of armed men, which would permit nobody except known friends to come near. Seeing Gil, Duke, Vinegar, and Portugee Pete among the jail guards, Ben was convinced that Isaac must be there, too; but, though he twice approached as close as he dared and called out his brother's name, hoots, catcalls, and shouted obscenities from men who sounded half-drunk drove him away before he could make his mission clear.

Determined groups of Pinkham friends were holding meetings in various places around the town. Driven by a curiosity he did not attempt to deny, he went with Billy McConnell and Rube Robbins to one of these meetings, this one held in the fireproof cellar of a newly rebuilt store. In the eerie gloom of the long, barrel-lined room dimly lighted by lanterns which faintly outlined the faces of the forty or fifty men present, he listened as Billy McConnell quietly told the crowd how the Committee must be organized if it were to work efficiently.

No, McConnell said in answer to a question, he did not wish to hold any office in the group. Yes, the Payette Committee would be informed of what was decided upon and, if they so chose, individual members could participate in whatever action was taken. But he was not authorized to commit any man. He was here only to advise and to do his bit as a man who had been Sumner Pinkham's close friend.

The organization was quickly effected, an executive board elected and a captain chosen. Immediately following these actions, Ben and Billy McConnell left the cellar and parted company, Ben making a third futile attempt to locate Isaac and talk to him, McConnell transacting some private business of his own.

Secret though the nature of the action decided upon by the newly formed Committee was to have been, Ben, like every other man in town, knew by mid-afternoon next day that the showdown was to come shortly after dawn the following morning. Meeting place for the mass of men which was to storm the jail was to be the cemetery, which was located on a pine-covered rise of ground just outside town, half a mile or so from the jail. By twos and threes the Committee members were to go there during the hours of darkness, quietly wait, then, when all had assembled, the swift, sudden, surprise attack would be mounted in the still hours of early dawn. A demand would be made on Sheriff Crutcher to turn over his prisoner. If not met, Vigilante Captain Gilkey—the blacksmith from nearby Buena Vista Bar—would give the signal, hand grenades would be lighted and thrown, then the jail would be stormed.

From several friends, Ben by now had gotten positive confirmation of the fact that Isaac was among the constantly increasing group of armed deputies guarding the jail; apparently his station was within the walls. Seeing Gil Gillis come out of a saloon on the far side of the street and turn down the boardwalk toward the jail, Ben recklessly crossed the dead-line beyond which no Union man was supposed to go and shouted, "Gil! Oh, Gil!"

The man stopped and stared at him suspiciously. "Yeah?"

"I'm Ben Shelby—Isaac's brother."

"Hell, I know that. What do you want?"

"Is Isaac inside the jail?"

"What if he is?"

"I've got to talk to him. Will you take me to him?"

"No," Gil grunted. "But I'll tell him you're out here."

As he waited in the center of the street, a watching Unionist called angrily, "Watch your tongue, mister!"

"Isaac is my brother."

"I don't care if he's Jesus Christ's brother—he's on the wrong side."

After a time, Ben saw Isaac come through the line of guards ringing the jail and walk up the boardwalk toward him. He had a holstered Navy Colt strapped around his waist and was carrying a rifle. Ben himself was unarmed, his own rifle and revolver left behind in a nearby store. Having seen his younger brother only twice during the past year or so, he was amazed at the change in his appearance. Isaac looked taller, harder, more muscular, more mature; with an odd sense of shock, Ben thought: *Why, he favors Pa more than I do; Ruth's always said that but I never saw it till now.*

Isaac stopped a few paces away and stared at his brother, unsmiling. "Well, Ben?"

"What in God's name are you doing here, Isaac?"

"A job for Sheriff Crutcher. I'm a legally appointed deputy hired by the day to help keep the law."

"Since when did the crowd you run with start caring about keeping the law?"

"Since the crowd *you* run with decided to break it."

"We're only protecting our property, Isaac."

"Is Ferd Patterson your property? Did he steal anything from you?"

"Pinkham was our friend."

"Well, so far as that goes, I had nothing against Old Pink. But he's dead now and Jim Crutcher says if there's going to be a hanging he'll do the honors. Jim Crutcher's the man I'm working for."

"You've turned against your own people! You've hired yourself out as a paid gunman to protect a killer—"

"Well, the wages are good and I can use the money," Isaac said. "You'd be surprised how fast money runs through a man s hands when he spends as much on whores and whisky as I do."

From the crowd of guards behind him came a cheer. "You tell him, Ike!" From the group of men behind Ben came angry mutterings. "Damn Secesh bastard! We'll take care of *him,* when the time comes!"

Sweat moistened Ben's palms as he stared helplessly at his brother. This wasn't the way to do it; this wasn't the way at all. Not standing here in the center of the street between two hostile groups of men where every word he and Isaac said could be heard and judged by all. To say, look, Isaac, we're brothers, let's not stay on opposite sides of the fence, let's just walk away from this mess and let these damn fools stew in their own juice, would be to brand himself a traitor to his friends and Isaac a turncoat to his.

"What shall I tell Pa and Ruth?"

"Whatever you please."

"They don't want to see you hurt, Isaac. Neither do I."

"If you and your friends stay away from the jail and let Patterson have his trial, nobody's going to *get* hurt, Ben—not me, not you, not anybody. Tell your friends that."

There was nothing more to say. Blindly turning away, Ben went into the store where he had left his firearms, picked up his gunbelt and buckled it around his waist with unfeeling fingers. A hand dropped on his shoulder and a voice said, "Go home, Ben. If worst comes to worst, we'll try not to hurt him."

Ben shook his head. "No, Rube, I can't leave now. I've got to see this through."

By Ben's estimate, more than nine hundred heavily armed men had assembled in the cemetery between the hours of midnight and dawn. Rumor had it that at least that many, perhaps more, were waiting within and around the walls of the Idaho City jail. All chance of a surprise attack had long since vanished, for even if the Committee ranks had not become thoroughly infiltrated by spies and informers—as was evident it had been—assembling such a large body of men so close to town could not possibly be accomplished unnoticed.

In the gray light of dawn, Captain Gilkey appeared ill at ease as he conferred with Rube Robbins, Elder Kingsley, and the other members of the executive board. The chill of the mountain night, the headboards of the nearby graves, the deep stillness under the tall pines cast a sepulcher-like gloom over the spirits of the waiting men, making them talk in whispers if they talked at all. Now as the light grew, an uneasy stir ran over the crowd, for Captain Gilkey had walked over to the knee-high stump of a downed tree and mounted it.

"Well, boys . . ." he said, then paused. The pause lengthened. Ben saw him swallow hard, straighten his shoulders, take a deep breath, and nerve himself to try again. "Well, boys, I guess the time has come—"

"Captain Gilkey! May I say a word?"

Captain Gilkey peered into the shadows on the fringe of the crowd, attempting to make out the identity of the man who had called out to him, then, giving an audible sigh of relief, he stepped down off the stump and said, "You sure can, Billy! I didn't know what to say next anyhow."

Coming through the crowd, Billy McConnell stepped atop the stump, gazed out over the assemblage for a moment, then said quietly, "Gentlemen, I told you I would go along with any action you decided upon. But you should know what you're in for. Ten determined men might have managed to meet secretly and take the jail in a surprise attack. A thousand cannot. Sheriff Crutcher and the roughs know we're here. They're ready for us. If we storm that jail, a lot of good men are going to get hurt."

"That's sensible talk!" Ben cried.

"Suppose we attacked the jail and took Patterson at the cost of fifty lives among us. Is that a bargain?"

"Not to me, it ain't!" a man called out toward the back of the crowd. "Particularly if it's me gets his ass filled with lead!"

Laughter ran over the crowd; even McConnell smiled. "Well put, my friend. We all feel the same way, I'm sure."

"But what are we going to do, Billy?" another voice cried.

"Are we going to let Ferd Patterson get off scot-free?"

"It's not my place to give orders, gentlemen. Captain Gilkey is a fine man—"

"A fine blacksmith, you mean!" Gilkey interrupted without the least trace of ill will. "But when it comes to leading a Vigilante Committee, I don't know which end of the horse gets the oats!"

"Now, Captain, you're a good, sensible—"

Whatever compliment McConnell tried to pay the amiable blacksmith from Buena Vista Bar was lost to Ben Shelby in the spontaneous cheer that went up from the crowd. A chant began: "We want Billy! We want Billy! We want Billy!" Vainly McConnell tried to still it by raising his hands in protest, but it was not until John Gilkey himself leaped atop the stump and put an arm around the younger man's shoulders that quiet came.

"Gents, I hereby resign as Captain of the Vigilante Committee, nominate Billy McConnell for the job, and make a motion he be elected by acclamation! All in favor say 'Aye!'"

The thunder of voices that replied made requesting a "Nay" vote unnecessary. As Gilkey shook hands and stepped down off the stump, Ben saw a faint smile touch Billy McConnell's lips.

"Very well, gentlemen, if that is your wish. As your new captain, I now issue my first order." He paused. "You are dismissed and requested to return to your homes. We'll skin our cat some other way. That's all, gentlemen."

The cheers this time were even louder and more enthusiastic than before, Ben noted. Nobody's was more heartfelt than his own.

If the defenders of the Idaho City jail had repressed their desire to gloat over their "victory" and Sheriff Jim Crutcher had had the good sense not to show off his "authority," the matter might have ended there, Ben later reflected. But with passions roused to their present height, it was asking too much of human nature to expect "victors" not to gloat or "authority" to refrain from showing off. The direct result of these errors was what came to be known locally as the Battle of Buena Vista Bar.

With a number of other men who had been members of the Committee, Ben, Billy McConnell, and John Gilkey were quietly discussing events of the past few days when a group of Unionists galloped up to the blacksmith shop. Seeing McConnell, one of them shouted excitedly, "All hell's busted loose in town, Billy! We got to do something quick!"

"Oh, what's happened?"

"Rube Robbins and Elder Kingsley have been arrested and throwed in jail, that's what! We got to get them out!"

"Whoa, now, not so fast. What are they charged with?"

"Disturbing the peace, inciting to riot—stuff like that. Our boys are spreading the word around. What you'd want us to do, we figured, was all meet here, lay out our plans, then make a march on the jail—"

"No," McConnell cut in. "That won't do at all."

"But, damn it, Billy, don't you see what they're up to? They think they've got us whipped. They're picking off our leaders one by one—"

"All I see is that Rube Robbins and Elder Kingsley have been arrested on petty charges," McConnell answered. "Judge McBride is in town. He's not the type of man to lose his sense of proportion. He'll insist that Rube and Elder Kingsley be brought before him and formally charged. He'll set a reasonable bail, they'll meet it, and he'll release them."

"Do you really think so?"

"Yes."

"Seems to me it's mighty risky, letting them roughs get their hands on two of our boys."

"I know Judge McBride, Joe. Let's just sit tight. By this time tomorrow, I'll bet, both of our boys will be free men."

True to McConnell's prediction, both Committee leaders were released on bail, next morning. Whether in celebration of this small victory or moved by a natural desire to gather and talk things over, a crowd of Unionists began to gather at Gilkey's blacksmith shop early in the day. Adding to their numbers were twenty members of the Payette Valley Safety Committee, led by Daniel Lynn, who had ridden over to see what was going on. Most of the men were armed, for these days nobody went far from home without his gun.

Presently word drifted down from town that an unusual amount of activity had been noted among the jail guards; they had been seen forming up in military-looking groups near a sawdust pile close by the jail; each group seemed to have its set of officers; pistols, rifles, and shotguns were being cleaned, checked, and inspected. The alarming rumor spread that Ed Holbrook, the Territorial Delegate to Congress, had persuaded Sheriff Crutcher that he must take the offensive and put down the "insurrection."

"Gonna put us all under arrest, they say!"

"Gonna make us give up our guns or go to jail!"

"Well, let 'em try, I say—just let 'em try!"

By noon, most of the nine hundred-odd men that had assembled in the cemetery a couple of nights ago had joined the mass milling about the blacksmith shop, the creek banks, the ditches, ridges, and flats surrounding it. Whether any order had been given to fortify and prepare for battle, Ben never found out; it very well could have been that these independent-minded miners, long used to acting on their own when it came to defending their property and their lives, simply decided as individuals that if a fight were coming, they would make sure of their own shelter. But whatever the case, activity became frantic as cordwood was piled, sacks of sand were stacked, prospect holes were deepened, and ditch sides were burrowed into—until the entire area looked like a defensive battlefield.

"Here the bastards come!" a man shouted.

They were coming, Ben saw, both afoot and mounted—coming by the hundreds—breaking up into irregular columns, one on the left bank of the creek, another on the right, still another moving up into the timbered foothills, its aim apparently being to flank the defensive works and take them from the rear. Billy McConnell watched the nearing masses of men for a time, then deployed his own forces.

"Rube, I want you to take fifty men and fall back on the bend of the creek. Al, you take fifty more and keep your eye on the flats yonder side of the ditch. Rube, you watch the timber."

"That was Ed Holbrook leading the bunch that took to the hills," Rube said. "I'd know his strut anywhere."

"Have you got any scruples against shooting a politician?"

"Not if he's a Democrat."

"Good! Now remember, boys, we'll let them start it—then we'll finish it."

Finding himself among the fifty men under Rube Robbins' command, Ben moved like a person in a dream. He checked his rifle, he checked his pistol, he took his place in the deep, well-protected ditch close by the pine-covered foothills as directed to do, and he felt utterly calm. Nothing would happen. This was a game, no more. Two thousand sane, reasonable men did not meet in a deadly test of arms under such a lovely blue sky on such a warm late summer day for so little cause. Nothing would happen—unless a horse stumbled, a gun went off accidentally, a half-drunk man got trigger-happy . . .

"Keep your eyes open, boys," Rube said quietly. "Don't pay any mind to what's happening down along the creek—it's the timber we're here to watch."

Yes, Ben thought, I must watch the timber. A grouse, a deer, a bear might break cover at any moment, and I'd feel like the worst kind of fool if I missed an easy shot. Ruth always teases me when I come home from a hunt empty-handed. Of course, Isaac seldom gets skunked. Why, from the day he got big enough to tote a rifle Isaac has been able to shoot the eye out of squirrel at fifty paces. By God, little brother, I wish you were lying beside me here in this ditch right now! Then what that grouse, that deer, that bear flushed .

"That's far enough, gentlemen!" he heard Billy McConnell cry. "Stop right where you are!"

"Who's in charge here?"

"I am."

"Might I be havin' a word with ye, Mr. McConnell?"

"Who are you?"

"Faith, an' I'm Under-Sheriff Gorman, sir. I call on ye, Mr. McConnell, to order these rioters, these disturbers of the peace, these vigilantes or whatever ye call 'em, to give up their firearms and disperse—or else."

"Or else what?"

"Or else the last divil of ye will be kilt, that's what else!"

McConnell's laugh rang out, and Ben marveled that he could keep his sense of humor at such a time. "Now there's a voice from the Emerald Isle, if ever I heard one! But I'm not bandying words with under-sheriffs, Mr. Gorman. Is Sheriff Crutcher in your crowd?"

"He is that."

"Send him out, then. I'll talk to him and nobody else."

In the silence that followed, Ben stared up the slope, watching the trees, watching the bushes, hearing the light breeze faintly stirring the pine needles overhead, hearing or imagining he was hearing other rustlings below. Suddenly he stiffened. He was sure he had heard a twig crack.

"Rube!" he whispered hoarsely. "Up yonder!"

"I heard it, Ben. Crawl up and take a look, will you?"

As Ben climbed out of the ditch and began to snake his way on hands and knees through the undergrowth, he heard a worried voice cry out on the flats below, "In the name of God, Billy, can't this be stopped?"

"It is stopped, Sheriff Crutcher. It's stopped right here. Don't you admire the way my men have dug themselves in?"

"We don't want a battle, Billy!"

"No? Then tell your bully-boys not to come a step further."

"Let's talk sense, Billy."

"All right, let's do. What's your idea of sense, Jim?"

"That you order your men to give up their firearms and return peaceably to their homes."

"Will your men do the same thing?"

"Of course not! They're legally appointed deputies, sworn to uphold the law. But I give you my word, if you order your men to surrender their firearms not a one of them will be harmed. And their arms will be returned to them within thirty days."

Howls of derision came from the entrenched men. Pausing a moment to look and listen before crawling into a particularly dense thicket, beyond which he was sure he had heard something moving, Ben heard McConnell laugh again.

"Sheriff, this is a mighty pretty gun I have here. It was given to me by a friend over in Centerville. He'd be hurt no end if he found out I thought so little of his present as to give it away. So, if it's all the same to you, I'll keep it. In fact, all my boys are mighty fond of their guns."

"Billy, I'm warning you—"

"No, Jim, *I'm* warning *you*. We didn't attack your jail the other night and we're not planning to attack it now. Patterson can have his trial. If he's acquitted—as he will be, for you've rigged it that way—we'll deal with him at another time and place. But if you and your bully-boys want to fight here and now, let's get on with it."

"We have you surrounded—"

"You just think you have, Sheriff. We've got every one of your forces spotted and covered. Yes, even that cute little fox, Ed Holbrook, who thought he could flank us by sneaking around through the timber. Rube Robbins has got him lined up at this very moment in the sights of his rifle. If you start a fight, Idaho Territory is going to be minus a mighty clever politician. We'd have to elect another Delegate to Congress. Wouldn't that be a shame, Sheriff?"

Ben was sure now; just beyond the thicket a bear or a man was moving. He edged forward, gently parting the bushes with his left hand while his right hand grasped the stock of the rifle close to its trigger guard. He moved two yards, three, then paused, listening intently. He heard a metallic click, as if a rifle hammer were being cocked. Unless bears carry rifles these days, he thought, that settles it; it must be a man. As silently as possibly, he cocked his own rifle. The click sounded ungodly loud. He reached out with his left hand to part the leafy bush directly ahead. But before his hand could touch the limb, another hand on the far side grasped that same limb and pushed it aside. From a distance of three feet, he found himself staring directly into the face of the enemy.

"Isaac!"

"Ben!"

For a moment they stared at each other in surprise, Ben feeling more ridiculous than he had ever felt in his life, and the sheepish grin beginning to spread now over Isaac's face indicating that he was feeling a bit ridiculous himself. At last, Isaac grunted, "As a fellow said to me the other evening, what in God's name are you doing here, Ben?"

"I'm on a scout for Captain Robbins. And you?"

"Well, I'm sort of a scout for Lieutenant Colonel Holbrook. My orders were to feel out the enemy strength and look for soft spots."

"My soft spot," Ben said, "is my head. If it held the brains God put into a goose, I wouldn't be in this mess."

"You know, I'm beginning to feel the same way. All I seem to be doing here is making a damn fool of myself."

"Well, you've got a lot of company."

Carefully they eased down the hammers of their rifles, squirmed out of the thicket, got to their feet and walked along the hillside to a clearing where a fallen tree lay; there, they sat down. Ben said, "Your garden's looking mighty dry."

"Well, what happened was I just came to town for the day. Jim Crutcher needed men and I need money—"

"For a mowing machine and a hayrake?"

Isaac grinned. "Yeah. The damn things cost a fortune."

"Lynn's got a mowing machine and we've got a hayrake. We've been trading work around. If you're interested, we could make some sort of a deal."

"What's a strong back worth?"

"Considerable—if it's got some ambition behind it."

"I bought Gil out, you know, and filed a homestead claim. My place is still kind of a boar's nest but I'd like for Pa to see it. Ruth, too. Maybe you could bring them over . . . ?"

"Sure. And I'll stop by on my way home and give your garden a good watering. Be a shame to lose those nice tomatoes and melons."

"You're heading home now?"

"Just as straight and quick as I can go. I'm a lousy soldier, I've decided."

"Well, look, Ben," Isaac said, "suppose you take me along. We'll pretend you captured me. That'll make you a hero and me a prisoner entitled to draw full pay for the duration of the war. When it's over, we can both apply for pensions."

Ben laughed and said that suited him fine. Arm in arm they strolled down the hill, as chummy as brothers.

CHAPTER NINE

Orlando R. ("Rube") Robbins and William J. ("Billy") McConnell have been appointed Deputy United States Marshals for their respective districts of the Boise Basin and the Payette Valley, we are informed by Judge Milton Kelly, who recently swore them in. Both, in our opinion, are good men.

—*Idaho Statesman*
Boise City, I.T.
September 23, 1865

THE PATTERSON TRIAL—The public interest felt in the trial of Mr. Patterson entitles the evidence to the prominence we have given it in our columns, to the exclusion of much other matter. A panel of over one hundred persons was exhausted before a jury was obtained. The prosecution was conducted by Acting District Attorney May, assisted by Mr. J. C. Henley. Messers. Douthitt, Merrit, and Ganahl conducted the defense. Both sides were managed with great ability—creditable to all the attorneys. Probably it will be many years before another criminal case will come before the courts of this Territory in which as much talent, industry and learning will be combined among the counsel.

The peculiarities of style of each advocate appeared vividly on his argument. Henley went to work with a zealous activity strengthening the weak points of his ranks with quotations from the statutes and common law authorities with a quick perception and ready mind: Douthitt patiently explored every recess of the conflicting testimony, held up its inconsistencies, and with steady, ponderous blows broke the way through his adversary's evidence and shivered it into fragments: Merritt marched direct upon the enemy with a straightforward, resistless tread, and with a manly vigor poured a steady continuous volley of argument, law, logic and eloquence into the broken ranks of the opposition: Ganahl rode upon the field for the final charge, in the chariot of war. Opening his case with a peroration of remarkable beauty, he turned with a burning sarcasm upon the recoiling enemy—surrounding them by groups—and with the merciless composure of retributive, avenging power "lashed them naked through the world."

The cowardly, malicious press which has poured its stream of falsehoods into the public ear, the hounds of an ignorant and excited population "with halters in their hands, murder in their hearts, and a prayer on their lips," the tergiversations of squirming witnesses confounded by their own folly—were one after another scorched and extinguished in the course of that fiery circle.

Mr. May's prosecuting forces were in a very disorganized condition when he rallied them on Saturday morning for the last charge. But he brought them up to the fight with a skill and effect that surprised his most intimate friends. All the resources of a great advocate—familiarity with the testimony, profound knowledge of criminal law, ready tact, and an unconquerable persistence—were brought to bear through a speech of three and a half hours. It was a masterly effort and if it did not succeed in convincing the jury, it was only because there was not evidence enough to sustain it. Both friends and foes concede it to have been one of the greatest forensic efforts ever heard in the Territory.

The charge of Judge McBride was too lengthy to publish this week. It will appear in our next issue. It was able and impartial. Judge McBride we believe has conducted the trial in a manner which neither side of the case can object to. Whatever may be the result, at this time of writing unknown to us, Mr. Patterson has had a fair and impartial trial.
—*Idaho World*
Idaho City, I.T.
November 4, 1865

NOT GUILTY—We have delayed publication till evening to obtain the verdict in the Patterson case. The jury, after two hours absence, came into court and rendered a verdict of "Not guilty." The Judge congratulated the prisoner, and ordered his immediate discharge.
—*Idaho World*
Idaho City, I.T.
November 4, 1865

Ferd Patterson has been acquitted, as expected. Idaho juries do not inquire whether a crime has been committed. All they ask is: "Was it a fair fight?" If so, they cry: "Not guilty! Bully for the boy with the glass eye!"

Apparently anticipating that the Idaho climate will not be salubrious to his health this winter, Ferd Patterson is said to be departing presently for Portland or San Francisco.
—*Idaho Statesman*
Boise City, I.T.
November 7, 1865

Ferd Patterson has left Idaho City for an extended visit to his old home in the East. His name will long be remembered in Idaho.
—*Idaho World*
Idaho City, I.T.
November 18, 1865

Ferd Patterson, the professional gambler recently in the news for the killing of ex-sheriff Pinkham in Idaho, is now in this city plying his trade in the saloons. His plans for the future, he says, are indefinite.
—*Walla Walla Statesman*
Walla Walla, W.T.
December 15, 1865

WALLA WALLA STATESMAN
"THE CONSTITUTION AND THE UNION"

Walla Walla, Washington Territory,
Friday Evening, February 6, 1866

At an early hour on Thursday morning, our town was thrown into a fever of excitement by the announcement that Ferd Patterson, who had been spending the winter at Walla Walla, had been shot and instantly killed. Immediately on hearing the report we proceeded to Dan Welch's saloon, and there found Patterson stretched on the floor, with the life blood oozing from four or five wounds, either of them sufficient to produce death. The circumstances attending the shooting, as near as we can gather them, are as follows: About half-past eight o'clock that morning, Patterson had gone into Richard Bogle's barber shop to get shaved. A few moments later, Donahue, the man who killed him, entered the shop from the rear, and seated himself in the back room, from which he had a good view of Patterson being shaved. Not a word passed between the two men, and the barber had finished shaving Patterson, and was dressing his hair, when Mr. Wood, the daguerrean artist, who happened to be present, noticed Donahue advance toward Patterson, holding at the same time his hand behind his back, and grasping a revolver. Donahue being a policeman, Wood supposed that the intention was to arrest Patterson, and that he (Donahue) thus held the pistol in order to be prepared for resistance. After advancing to within a few feet of the deceased, Donahue paused for perhaps thirty seconds, and then hastily rushing on Patterson with his pistol, said, "Patterson, you must kill me, or I'll kill you!" Before Patterson had time either to speak or move, Donahue discharged his pistol, the ball from which entered the right side of his face nearly on a line with the mouth. On being shot, Patterson exclaimed, "Oh, my God!" and sprang toward the door. Whilst thus endeavoring to escape, Donahue discharged two more balls, one of which took effect, the other passing through a front window, at an elevation considerably higher than a man's head.

Patterson succeeded in getting out of the barber shop, and reached Welch's saloon, which is next door. The moment he got inside the door of the saloon, he sunk down helpless, and whilst in this position Donahue, apparently determined to make sure work, again advanced on the prostrate man, and discharged two more balls both of which took effect. After completing his bloody work, Donahue went and delivered himself up, and was forthwith committed to the county jail.

As the news spread, it created the wildest excitement, and forthwith a thousand and one rumors were current as to the origin of what everybody pronounced a cold-blooded murder. —One of the reports was that Donahue and Patterson had a difficulty in Portland a year or two since, and that the killing was the result of an old grudge. Another version was that Patterson had been noisy the night previous, and on being remonstrated with by Donahue, replied, "The next time I see you, I'll kill you!" None of these reports could be traced to a reliable source, and at this writing the whole murder remains a mystery. The friends of the deceased even say that Patterson was an entire stranger to Donahue, and the assassination was part of a deliberate plan to get him out of the way. The examination, which will possibly be held today or tomorrow, will most likely throw some light upon a deed that for the present is shrouded in mystery.

THE PROVOCATION.

In justification of his deed, Donahue states that his life had been threatened by the deceased. It appears that about a year since Patterson got into a difficulty about a woman in Portland, and that Donahue, who was then a policeman, was very active in endeavoring to effect his arrest. Patterson it seemed harbored malice on this account, and meeting Donahue some two weeks since, told him that "he had his (Donahue's) name down in his book and that he would settle with him shortly." On Wednesday night the parties again met, when the threat was repeated. On this second warning, Donahue armed himself, and determined to shoot Patterson on sight. They met in the barber shop on Thursday morning, and the result is known.

THE EXAMINATION.

At ten o'clock this (Friday) morning, the case was called for examination before Judge Horton. The prisoner was brought into Court in custody of Sheriff Seitel. As he appeared in Court he was very pale and gave evidence of great nervous excitement. F. P. Dugan, Esq. appeared for the defense, and after consultation the examination was continued until Monday morning, at ten o'clock. The prisoner was then remanded to the custody of the Sheriff, by whom he was returned to his quarters in the county jail.

ANTECEDENTS OF THE PRISONER.

On inquiry, we learn that Donahue lived for a number of years in Portland, where he acted in the capacity of policeman and private watch. Those who know him state that he maintained an excellent character, and was regarded as an efficient officer. On the recommendation of his Portland friends, a number of our merchants employed him as a private watchman, in which capacity he gave satisfaction. We give these statements as coming from a reliable source, but cannot vouch for their correctness.

THE FUNERAL.

Patterson was buried on this (Friday) afternoon at one o'clock. The funeral cortege was very large, and everything passed off quietly and creditably. Thus ends the last chapter in the history of a man who certainly led a stormy life.

The jury came into Court, having been out from four o'clock P.M. yesterday, and informed his Honor that they could not agree, (standing seven for acquittal and five for conviction), when they were discharged, and the prisoner returned to the charge of the Sheriff. He will probably not be tried again this term.

—*Walla Walla Statesman*
Walla Walla, W.T.
April 27, 1866

Thomas H. Donahue, who foully murdered Ferd Patterson in Walla Walla a few months ago and was awaiting a second trial, recently escaped from the county jail of that city. His jailers, it appears, by accident or design, left the cell door unlocked and he was permitted to walk away unhindered. It is reliably reported that he was well paid for the killing.

—*Idaho World*
Idaho City, IT.
July 7, 1866

Thomas H. Donahue, charged with but never convicted of the killing of Ferd Patterson, is reported to have boarded a ship in San Francisco bound for China.

—Idaho Statesman
Boise City, I.T.
February 9, 1867

Chapter Ten

Now I lay me down to sleep;
I pray the ledge its width may keep.
— Quartz Miner's Prayer

"Wilson P. Waddingham has the fat, ruddy cheek and laughing eye," wrote a favorably impressed newspaper correspondent, "which is the unvarying accompaniment of a splendid digestion, glorious sleep, and a clear conscience."

That description of the Rocky Bar district mine manager was an accurate one as far as it went, Armand Kimball conceded, but if he himself had written it he would have added that Wilson P. Waddingham also appeared to be a monumental gambler, a phenomenal salesman, and perhaps even a gigantic fraud. When Kimball privately voiced his assessment of the man to his law partner one day, Arthur Creed laughed and said he could be right.

"But he's successful," Creed added. "And who ever argues with success?"

"Not I, certainly. But I've never met anyone like him, Art. Why, the way he throws money around literally takes my breath away."

"It's not *his* money, Armand. It's the stockholders'."

"He intimated to me the other day that he owns one-fourth of the shares in the Ada Elmore. That mine is capitalized at $600,000."

"True. But I have reason to believe Waddingham has exchanged a number of his shares in it for an interest in the Confederate Star and several other gold mines."

"Why did he do that?" Kimball asked in sudden concern.

"Does he think the Ada Elmore is a fizzle?"

"Lord knows—and even He is usually two jumps behind Wilson Waddingham's thinking." Creed eyed Kimball quizzically. "Speaking of the Ada Elmore, I hear you bought some stock in it yourself."

"Well, yes," Kimball admitted. "I happened to mention to Waddingham that I owned some property in St. Louis. He offered me one hundred shares in the Ada Elmore for ten city lots, sight unseen."

"What were the lots worth?"

"Oh, a thousand dollars, I suppose."

"Then you've turned a neat paper profit, Armand. Right now, a hundred shares of Ada Elmore would fetch ten thousand dollars on the San Francisco Exchange."

"As a matter of fact, I sold fifty of my Ada Elmore shares last week for five thousand," Kimball answered. "Then I reinvested that money in a silver mine down in the Owyhee district."

"Shades of Wilson P. Waddingham!" Creed exclaimed, throwing back his head and laughing heartily. "You're as much of a gambler as he is!"

"Not at all! It's one thing to play around with a thousand dollars' worth of property, as I've done. But it's quite something else to recklessly spend hundreds of thousands of dollars of stockholders' funds, as he appears to be doing. Mining, it seems to me, should be conducted on a sound, conservative, businesslike basis."

"Maybe so. But most men go at it like rolling dice or fighting a tiger. Waddingham isn't most men, however. He thinks big, talks big, acts big—and gets big results."

That seemed to be true, Kimball admitted. Wilson P. Waddingham was in a class by himself. When the first gold-bearing veins were discovered in the Rocky Bar district sixty miles east of Boise City a year or so ago most of the locaters tried to work them as one-man or two-men operations. But drilling into the tough quartz rock by hand, breaking it up, opening extensive tunnels and shafts, using mule-powered arrastras to pulverize it, then separating the gold by tedious placer mining methods proved to be a painfully slow business. Modern expensive machinery was obviously needed, which meant an investment of capital far beyond the means of most individuals. In order to raise that capital, individual miners formed paper companies, chipped out a few samples of rich ore, then attempted to sell stock in Idaho, Washington Territory, and Oregon—a usually not too successful project, for the kind of money required simply was not there.

Wilson P. Waddingham acted more dramatically and effectively. As a newcomer to the district with a background as a real estate speculator in Walla Walla and other growing Western towns, he may not have known too much about hardrock mining in the beginning but he learned fast. More important, he knew how to raise capital. Securing an interest in a promising mine called the South Boise Comstock, he hired laborers to hack out not a mere sackful of samples but fifteen hundred pounds of rich, carefully selected ore, shipped the ore down to San Francisco and had it assayed by reputable experts. Learning that the discoverer of the famed Nevada Washoe Lode, Henry Comstock, was currently in the Rocky Bar district seeking yet another bonanza, Waddingham made friends with him and then saw to it that Comstock's statement that prospects here "exceed anything seen in my life . . ." received appropriate publicity. Still not content, Waddingham loaded sixty-five mules with twenty thousand pounds of the richest ore he could find, sent them overland to San Francisco, had the ore refined there, then made sure that the resulting $800 to a $1000 per ton yield was announced in newspapers from coast to coast.

With his groundwork thus laid, he then journeyed east to New York City and exercised his not inconsiderable charms as a salesman in convincing capitalists there that Rocky Bar was bound to be "bigger than Washoe." Now that the Civil War was being brought to a successful close, he reasoned, new opportunities for investment would be welcomed in the war-rich North. He had not reasoned wrong. While less visionary Idaho hardrock miners were still limping along with inadequate capital, attempting to work their prospects with slow, old-fashioned arrastras, small, inadequate stamp mills and outdated, inefficient amalgamators and recovery equipment, he returned to Rocky Bar as agent and resident manager of an Eastern-financed company backed by seemingly unlimited capital which he used to buy every likely looking mine prospect in sight, regardless of price, and to purchase huge-capacity ore-crushing and refining machinery.

Ignorant though Armand Kimball admitted to be of hardrock mining, long experience in the business world had taught him caution. "It seems to me Waddingham is investing a great deal of money in Rocky Bar," he told Creed. "What I want to know is do the prospects justify it? How much gold is he getting out?"

"He has a five-stamp and a twelve-stamp mill running full time, I understand. According to the *Statesman,* he recently made a $9400 cleanup from a thirteen-day run."

"What were his costs?"

"Search me. Cartee and Gates are crushing some ore for him at their custom mill, too, he says, at a flat twenty-five dollars a ton. Of course, at that price he can't afford to work quartz that goes less than eighty dollars a ton—"

"Wait a minute, Art," Kimball interrupted. "What happened to all that eight hundred to a thousand dollars a ton ore he's supposed to have?"

"That was hand-sorted."

"Meaning higher labor costs, I assume?"

"Right. But he has a forty-stamp mill on its way up from San Francisco. When he gets it to running, he'll be able to crush seventy-five tons of ore a day just as it comes out of his mines. Say it goes eighty dollars to the ton. That's six thousand dollars a day, Armand."

Creed did some hasty arithmetic with a stub of pencil and a scrap of paper. "At that rate, a year's production would come to two million, one hundred and ninety thousand dollars. Which is not to be sneezed at."

Kimball laughed. "You figure like a farmer I knew back home, Arthur. He owned a thousand hens whose eggs he sold in St. Louis at a net loss of a penny a dozen. When this was pointed out to him, he tried to solve his problem by buying a thousand more hens and doubling production. But he did nothing to alter his basic cost per dozen, so the only thing the increased production did for him was to run him twice as deep in the red. Producing two million dollars' worth of gold a year isn't going to help Waddingham's stockholders one bit if it costs him three million to get it out."

Creed sighed. "Have you ever seen a quartz mine, Armand?"

"No."

"Then it's high time you did. I'll give you a tour. Tomorrow morning we'll rent a couple of saddle horses and a pack mule and take a trip up to Rocky Bar. It's about a three-day ride. We'll take along a tent, some camping gear and our fishing tackle. We'd better pack some whisky, too, in case of snake-bite. Are you game?"

"It sounds like a pleasant holiday."

"Well, at least it will give you an opportunity to look over some hardrock workings. I'll let Wilson P. Waddingham himself explain the difference between a quartz mine and an egg farm."

In the two years that had passed since the wagon train had disbanded in Boise City, Matt Miller had aged considerably, Kimball noted with a feeling of sadness. No, Matt said as he helped saddle the horses and load the pack mule, he and Charley Davis weren't in the pilgrim-transporting business no more. Improved roads and the new stagecoach companies had put an end to that. Yes, he'd heard Daniel Lynn was doing well farming over in the Payette Valley. But Andy Hale and Levi, he gathered, were having a rough time of it trying to raise cattle down Reynolds Creek way.

"What critters didn't git froze to death last winter are bein' stole by the damn Snake Injuns, Andy says. What's the Army doin' about it? Nothin'! Hell, Armand, them Fort Boise tin soldiers don't know beans about fightin' Injuns. The enlisted men are all foreigners—Germans, Irishmen, Danes—an' don't even know how to shoot n'r ride. The officers are all Eastern dandies. Takes 'em a week to git ready to go out on a scout, they spend two weeks lookin' fer the varmints, then they run out of supplies and have to come back to the fort."

"I heard the Army was establishing summer camps in the worst parts of the Snake country," Kimball said. "Won't that help?"

"Summer ain't no time to hunt Injuns. They're too fat an' sassy then an' their horses are too well fed. No, Armand, what a man's got to do is go after 'em an' keep after 'em when they hole up fer the winter. I told Andy that. What he'd ought to do, I told him, is round up a couple dozen of his neighbors, come fall, an' go Injun-huntin'. Do like General Connor did with them Californy Volunteers of his'n on Bear River a few years ago. Ketch the red bastards holed up an' then pour it to 'em. If I was jest a few years younger . . ."

No, he hadn't gone over to see the Lynns or down to visit with Andy and Levi, he admitted; he saw them in town when they came in; he'd intended to pay them a call, but lately his old bones ached so it seemed like all he had strength to do was sit in a chair outside the livery stable on sunny days and shoot the breeze with old friends that chanced by. You're headed up to Rocky Bar, you say? Yeah, I know that country; trapped all through it years ago. In '40, I believe it was. Or maybe '42. Let's see, there was me an' Joe Meek an' Doc Newell; we had a fuss with some Injuns, one day . . . Must be ruined now, that country, what with the beaver gone and miners all over the place . . .

With the horses saddled and the pack mule loaded, Armand Kimball was about to mount when a feminine voice exclaimed in delight, "Why, Mr. Kimball! Where in the world are you off to?"

"Good morning, Miss Belford. How have you been?"

"Fine—as if *you* cared! You haven't been around to see me for ages."

"Business is a cruel master, Miss Belford." He gave her a faintly mocking smile. "As I recall, the last time I paid you and your family a visit you were so preoccupied with your handsome red-headed sergeant you hardly knew I was there."

"Oh, pooh, I was only trying to make you jealous!" she laughed, seizing his arm and squeezing it teasingly. "But do you know what happened? It was Sergeant O'Neil who saw green. He wanted to know all about you."

"You told him, I trust, that I was merely an old friend of the family?"

"I did no such thing! I told him you were wildly in love with me, that I had spurned your advances, and that you were threatening to shoot yourself out of sheer grief." She giggled. "Do you know what he said?"

"I can't begin to guess."

"He said if you botched the job he'd be glad to give you instructions in the use of the pistol! Wasn't that *awful* of him?"

At Kimball's elbow, Arthur Creed cleared his throat meaningfully. Kimball introduced him, and, after a brief exchange of pleasantries, Melinda Belford said goodbye and moved on down the boardwalk. The two men mounted and rode for a few moments in silence, then Councilman Creed gave Kimball a sidelong glance and said, "How many shares do you own in *that* ledge, Armand?"

"None, I'm happy to say."

"Oh, come now! You can't be so old or so blind as to ignore a young lady as pretty and friendly as *she* is!"

"There are complications, Art. Charming as she may appear to be to you, she's a brainless little vixen and a trouble-maker."

"Is Cornelius Belford her father?"

"He is. That's one of the complications."

"So it would be," Creed said, nodding. "He would insist, I suppose, that the intentions of any man that came calling on her be honorable. And who could endure that pompous little blow-hard as a father-in-law?"

"Exactly."

"What a pity!" Creed sighed. "She's really a beautiful creature. Why, if her father didn't keep such a close eye on her, she'd have every bachelor in town fighting for her favors."

"He doesn't watch her *that* close, Art. She's a vain little bitch and well aware of her powers. Men *have* fought over her. Someday I'll tell you about two poor devils in our wagon train who died because of her . . ."

Because the Rocky Bar district lay in a high, mountainous, extremely rough country, a road capable of carrying wagon traffic had been a vital first necessity, Creed told Kimball. Backed by assurances from his friends in the Territorial Legislature that he would be granted a toll-road franchise, a man named Julius Newburg organized the South Boise Wagon Road Company, raised the necessary $16,000 and completed the road so that it was passable in good weather, running it not in a direct line due west to Boise City, which would have been prohibitively expensive because of the rough terrain, but south to connect with the emigrant trail down on the sagebrush plains.

"He claims it cost him eight thousand dollars for the last eight miles alone," Creed said. "Maybe it did. All I know is, I'd rather own his so-called road than one of Waddingham's gold mines."

For a horse and rider or a laden pack animal, the fee charged at the toll-gate was one dollar in gold; for a wagon, five. Nobody but the surly gatekeeper and his firm-jawed, solid-looking wife knew how many animals and wagons passed through the gates during a day's time at the height of the season, Creed said, but he would not be in the least surprised if the cash take approached one thousand dollars for a twenty-four hour period. There had been some slight difference of opinion between Julius Newburg and the gate-tending couple, he gathered, as to the accuracy of the cash turned into the company's coffers, but so far no audit had been made.

"It's not that Newburg is afraid of the gatekeeper," he told Kimball. "It's the wife that gives him pause. Every time he questions the cash take, she picks up a butcher knife and starts sharpening it. He says he's not sure which she's about to carve—the supper roast or him."

As he greeted his visitors, Wilson P. Waddingham appeared to be as ruddy of cheek, as laughing of eye, as clear of conscience, and as genial as ever. Yes, things were going splendidly. Splendidly! No, gentlemen, you will *not* pitch your tent and rough it; you will stay in the boardinghouse with my engineers, mechanics, and workmen; it's not a luxury hotel, I must admit, but the beds are clean, the food is good, and, by God, gentlemen, it's high time we had a drink!

For four exhausting but exhilarating days Armand Kimball explored tunnels and shafts, hefted specimens, watched sweating laborers drill, set charges, blast, load ore, and haul it away to the noisily pounding stamp mills. He saw the gold-streaked chunks of rock pulverized into a grayish colored dust, turned into a thick mud paste as water was added, flushed into the amalgamators, then out, until finally only raw gold combined with the mercury used to collect it was left in the separators. He saw the mercury heated in retorts until it released its precious burden, saw its fumes condensed and saved for re-use, saw the final product—bars of pure gold bullion—carefully weighed, stamped, and put away for future shipment to the mint.

But what he did not see—although time and again he hinted strongly to Wilson P. Waddingham that he would like to see them—were the company's account books containing an accurate record of expenditures and receipts. When questioned about specific items such as wage scales, freighting charges, food costs, machinery costs, digging costs, or the past week's production of any one mine, Waddingham plucked figures out of the air with the greatest of ease—and invariably, Kimball found, they were accurate. But he appeared to have no idea as to whether his constantly expanding mining operations were showing a respectable profit or a substantial loss.

"You must realize, Armand, that at this stage we can't draw up a balance sheet. It costs money to make money, you know that. For example, down in Nevada mine laborers are paid three dollars and fifty cents a day. In the Owyhee district, they're paid six. But in this district living costs are so high labor comes much more dearly. The handsome new mill of my friend, Dr. Farnham, you'll note, hasn't worked a pound of ore all week. Why not? Because seven dollars a day is all he will pay his workmen—and he's slow pay, at that. I pay eight to my newer men, ten to my more experienced workmen, and I pay on time in gold. I've never lacked for laborers. Do you judge my policy an extravagance?"

"Under the circumstances, no."

"Then there's the matter of lumber and timbering materials, Armand. When I first came here, there were all kinds of trees growing near at hand but no sawmill. Cartee and Gates told me and a number of other mine managers that they would build a sawmill if we would assure them of a steady cash market for their output. This we did. But I'm the only manager that has kept his word. Dr. Farnham is so deeply in debt for the lumber he got from them to build his beautiful big building to house his ridiculous little ten-stamp mill, they won't sell him another board. The other managers are almost as bad, when it comes to paying their justly contracted debts. But when I say to Cartee and Gates, 'I want a hundred thousand feet of lumber and timbers of such-and-such dimensions,' they know I'll pay on delivery and pay in gold. They deliver on time and I never lose a minute's work. Is *that* policy one of extravagance?"

"Certainly not. It's simply good business."

"Pay as you go, Armand, pay as you go—that's always been my philosophy."

"I'm not questioning that at all," Kimball protested. "What I'm trying to find out is how your capital investments in machinery and your labor costs in getting out the ore compare with the amount of gold bullion you're producing."

"Well, there are many factors to consider, Armand. Let's say we have a ledge that assays an average eighty dollars to the ton. That means roughly five ounces of gold in every two thousand pounds of rock. The first thing we must do is break that rock up into pieces we can handle. Then we must move it to the crushers, pulverize it, get rid of the worthless waste and recover the precious metal. Do you follow me, Armand?"

"Yes, I've seen all that demonstrated clearly enough."

"Gold-bearing ledges never run in straight lines and they constantly vary in width and richness, In the Rocky Bar district, I'm firmly convinced, the deeper the ledge goes the richer it becomes, but of course we can't be sure of that until the shaft is actually sunk. Let's say we have a ledge twelve inches wide at the surface of the hillside where we find it. It may run horizontally, vertically, or at an angle into the earth; three hundred feet into the hill, it may pinch down to two inches in width; at six hundred feet, it may expand to twenty inches. But the laborers working that ledge, Armand, come in irreducible sizes; they must have tunnels, shafts, and drifts big enough to swing a pick or sledge in; to guard against collapse, those tunnels, shafts, and drifts must be timbered. All of which means a great deal of relatively unproductive labor."

"I understand."

"Now, a stamp mill capable of pulverizing seventy-five tons of ore-bearing rock a day sounds like an efficient, time-saving, cost-saving piece of equipment," Waddingham went on. "But unless we can keep it working at full capacity on rich ore, it becomes a profit-eating monster. Do you realize, Armand, that in the forty-stamp mill due here shortly from San Francisco my company will have invested over one hundred thousand dollars?"

"I've heard that, yes. But apparently you feel such an investment is justified?"

"I most certainly do. Here's an item that may interest you, Armand. Down in the Owyhee district recently an assay of the tailing dump from a single stamp mill indicated that fifty thousand dollars in gold has passed through the amalgamators with-out being recovered. Why? Because the ore-bearing rock was not being crushed finely enough. From fifty to seventy-five percent of the gold, engineers estimated, was being lost due to faulty processing equipment. The mills we are currently using here, I suspect, are doing no better."

"But you hope that the new mill from San Francisco will?"

"Unless it improves our recovery rate by at least twenty percent, I shall be sadly disappointed. After all, it's costing my company twenty-five thousand dollars in freighting charges alone to bring it across the Blues from Wallula Landing."

"What does it cost you to get out the ore?"

"My engineers estimate that every foot of horizontal tunnel sets us back eighteen dollars, every foot of shaft, twenty-five. Of course, if we have water seepage problems—as we have had in the east branch of the Ada Elmore—the pumping expense adds to our costs."

"And yet you keep on buying more mines."

Waddingham laughed heartily. "Why not, Armand? In my opinion, the potential of this district has barely been scratched." He took Kimball by the arm. "Talking is a dry business. Let's go up to my office and have a drink." As they walked, he went on cheerfully. "One of the company's New York directors is due here in a week or two, Armand,

and if I'm any judge he's going to ask me a lot of mighty shrewd questions, just as you've been doing. But do you know what I'm going to spring on him? A proposal to raise two hundred thousand dollars in new capital! First, of course, I'll suggest that the company declare a dividend. Then I'll take enough gold bullion back to New York to pay it off. After that, I'll try to convince the board that we should install a new type of amalgamator that's being used with great success down in Colorado. I'm going to suggest, too, that it would be a great economy to hire and import a truly skilled English or German hardrock mining expert, no matter what salary he demands. Compared to England and Germany, we here in America are mere beginners in this business, you know . . ."

Heading back to Boise City with his law partner after a final evening of good food, good whisky, and good talk, Armand Kimball felt slightly hungover in mind as well as in body. In the world of business that he knew, men simply did not commit such huge sums to risky distant enterprises so casually. And yet, he mused, change was a vital fact of life in the world of finance. Twenty years ago, who had dreamed that gold discovered in the Far West would spawn a financial colossus like San Francisco? Who had dreamed that steam power would turn the transportation and manufacturing worlds topsy-turvy? Who had imagined that slavery would be abolished and the formidable Southern cotton economy that it supported would topple into the dust?

Was it possible that Wilson P. Waddingham was the forerunner of a new type of financier that would break all the old molds? If so, what business interests would be hurt as the molds shattered? What business interests would profit?

"Well, now you know all about quartz-mining," Creed said, interrupting his reverie. "What do you think of it?"

"To tell the truth, I'm puzzled," Kimball confessed. "I can't decide whether Waddingham is a scoundrel or a genius."

"He could be both, you know."

"A valid point, Art. Certainly his ideas appear to be sound. But it's going to take a tremendous amount of rich ore to pay for all that expensive machinery he's bringing in. What if the gold isn't there?"

"Roll the dice, fight the tiger," Creed said with a shrug.

Both the San Francisco forty-stamp mill and the New York representative of the board of directors arrived in Rocky Bar in mid-October, Kimball learned; while the one was being set up on the firm foundation of a six-thousand-pound iron bed-plate Wilson P. Waddingham apparently was able to convince the other that the company's finances were on equally solid footing. A cent and a quarter dividend, payable as of December 1, 1865, was declared on the company's $600,000 capital stock. An elaborate dinner in celebration of Wilson P. Waddingham's imminent departure for the East was given him at Rocky Bar, during which, according to the papers, he was gratefully toasted for having done more to advance Idaho quartz-mining than any other single individual. Up in the high country, the first snowfall had come; soon the Newburg Road would be closed to all but snowshoe travel and the only mining done would be deep work in tunnels and drifts unaffected by subzero cold. But next year, everybody agreed, would be a tremendous year in Rocky Bar . . .

Well, not quite everybody. Dr. Farnham, the mine manager whose activities had run Wilson P. Waddingham a close second for flamboyance and extensiveness, appeared to be in a bit of trouble. Since completing the magnificent new building to house his amalgamators and separating equipment early last August, he had been able to get out only enough ore to keep his tenstamp mill running at infrequent intervals. Now his creditors were filing lawsuits for unpaid bills. Angry teamsters had taken Dr. Farnham prisoner in his office, wrote the Rocky Bar correspondent to the *Idaho Statesman,* and were saying they would have their back pay or the mine manager's hide. Engineers, carpenters, mechanics, and underground hardrock miners had surrounded the other buildings on the property and were making like demands, which, if not met, they implied might be partially satisfied by the joy of setting a torch to the entire works. The sheriff, wrote the correspondent, was urging forbearance—with no visible results.

Julius Newburg had at last nerved himself into calling the gate-keeping couple to an accounting of funds. Heated words had passed between Julius Newburg and Mr. P. (which was as far as the correspondent would go toward identifying the gentleman), the net result of which had been a stern order from Newburg that Mr. P. get off the property of the South Boise Wagon Road Company forthwith. Mr. P. fled like a craven. But the enraged Mrs. P. attacked Julius Newburg with a well-sharpened butcher knife

"Assault charges have been filed against her," wrote the correspondent. "However, the sheriff as yet has made no arrest and Mrs. P. continues to occupy the toll-gate house. She pleads illness, claiming she is in too delicate a physical condition to endure imprisonment in our new jail. The sheriff has not disclosed what future course of action he intends to take . . ."

With Waddingham off for New York and mining operations in the high country at a virtual standstill, a disease which Jim Reynolds sarcastically called "quartz fever" ran its epidemic course through the miners wintering in the low country. While it was perfectly true that the Rocky Bar and Owyhee districts had already demonstrated themselves to be fabulously rich in gold and silver deposits, the acid-tongued editor wrote, the sale of wildcat feet to Eastern capitalists on a purely speculative basis could do Idaho great harm. No one paid the editor's warning the slightest heed. Every outbound stagecoach carried its contingent of men headed for San Francisco or New York, each one equipped with rich ore samples, assay reports, claim papers, affidavits attesting to the fact that their claim did indeed adjoin the Ada Elmore, the Confederate Star, the Atlanta, or some other fabulously rich mine, and, most essential of all, a plausible manner and a glib tongue.

Whether Armand Kimball's earlier mild case of the fever had given him an immunity to the more virulent form of the disease or whether he had instinctively weighed Wilson P. Waddingham's arithmetic and found it faulty, he could not say. It may even have been that the mine manager's willingness to trade shares in mines known to be rich for sight-unseen property in distant St. Louis had reminded Kimball that in the long run real estate was apt to be a much sounder investment than quartz-locked gold far underground. Whatever the cause, Kimball took advantage of the epidemic while it was at its height to do some swapping. When it was concluded, his mining stock holdings had been reduced to twenty-five shares of Ada Elmore, fifty of Confederate Star, and fifty more of Poorman, which was a silver mine down in the Owyhee district that in time past had produced quite well although now tied in a complicated legal knot for whose unravelling he and Arthur Creed had recently been employed by the management.

In return, he had acquired title to a dozen lots suitable for business buildings if Boise City's growth continued at its present rate, a quarter interest in a fast-freight company that proposed to give the local merchants quicker service on goods ordered from Portland, an eighth interest in a stagecoach company that was establishing a new route south to Owyhee, Chico, and Sacramento, ten acres of farm land a few miles west of town, and two thousand pounds of butter which an enterprising young man had just brought in by pack mule from Portland.

"What in God's name do you intend to do with two thousand pounds of butter?" Creed asked in amazement. "Eat it?"

"No, sell it."

"You're a lawyer, not a grocer. Where will you store it? How will you make sure it doesn't spoil?"

"Those were exactly the young man's problems, Art. He had some spare cash to invest, he put it in butter, he brought the butter here—and his total costs came to fifty cents a pound. The best offer the storekeepers made him was seventy-five. On a whim, I offered him a dollar, got the whole lot and paid him off."

"Tell you what I'll do, Armand, just as a special favor. I'll buy two pounds at a dollar-ten. And I'll mention you favorably to my friends—"

"Sorry—you're too late. The Baker Grocery and Mercantile Company has already agreed to take the entire two thousand pounds. The price I quoted them was a dollar and a quarter. They'll retail it, I imagine, at a dollar and a half."

"Wait a minute!" Creed exclaimed. "Why would a storekeeper pay you a dollar and a quarter when all they would offer your young friend was seventy-five cents?"

"My terms were better, Art. He wanted cash. I offered Baker credit for sixty days—or longer if he needs it." Kimball smiled. "At two percent interest per month." He spread his hands wide, palms up, mimicking a local German clothing merchant they both knew well. "Everybody makes money, everybody's happy, everybody's got butter on his bread. Dot's vot makes de vorld go round, mine goot fran'."

Up in the Rocky Bar district as the snowdrifts deepened and the cold intensified, the chief product now seemed to be lawsuits against mine managers by unpaid workmen and merchants. Except for the Confederate Star, which continued to be a steady producer, most of the mines were closed. Rumor had it that workmen at one mine had struck an incredibly rich ledge and immediately been laid off by the management, which had chosen to play the "freeze-out" game. The way that cozy little game went, Kimball gathered, was to cover up the pay ore with tons of country rock blasted down from the tunnel roof and walls by well placed charges, make the announcement that the tunnel had collapsed and a great deal of money must be expended to clear away the debris, sit back and wait until the grumbling shareholders lost all faith in the mine and were willing to sell out for a song, then gobble up the cheap shares and reopen the lead.

Another mine prospect had been blatantly salted, a second rumor went, its unscrupulous owners cleverly filling it with rich ore samples stolen from producing mines, selling it to a group of Eastern capitalists who failed to detect the fraud, then gleefully fleeing the country with their loot.

Poor judgment was not monopolized by the gullible and foolish,

Kimball observed; even shrewd financial giants in the East made blunders. The prime example of that was the costly error made by the Astor & Vanderbilt Company.

In the Rocky Bar district last spring the miners and merchants had been stimulated by the news that this company, backed by unlimited resources, had acquired substantial holdings and had placed orders for such a vast amount of the latest type of mining machinery that seventy-five wagons, each one drawn by six yoke of oxen, would be required to freight the equipment across the country from Council Bluffs. That such an enterprise might fail, that the expensive machinery might never even reach its destination—let alone work a pound of ore—were thoughts that entered no one's mind. Yet that was exactly what happened.

Where the miscalculations regarding time and space had been made, no one could say. In Pittsburgh, in Chicago, in the iron mines that furnished the raw materials, in the fallible human beings who designed, fabricated, and packed the new machinery for shipment, in the transfer from freight wagon to rail car and then back to freight wagon again, in the gathering of so many oxen in a railhead region depleted of work stock by a long, just-ended war, in labor troubles, in threats of Indian raids which forced detours from anticipated routes, in breakdowns on the trail, in inadequate bridges, ferries, and fords, and, finally, in a failure to realize that of all the thousands of miles that lay between Pittsburgh, Chicago, Council Bluffs, and Rocky Bar, the last twenty were more difficult to traverse than any of the others—in any one or all of these things lay ample opportunity for losing precious, irrecoverable time.

The forty-five wagons carrying Waddingham's forty-stamp mill turned north from the emigrant road in mid-October and won the race against the early mountain winter by the merest whisker. Arriving at approximately the same point a few weeks later, the seventy-five laden wagons of the Astor & Vanderbilt Company lost.

For weeks, the tiring oxen and their weary drivers struggled against deepening snows, increasing cold, and steepening grades to transport the heavy mining equipment up into the mile-high country which it must reach this fall if it were going to get there before next summer. The effort failed. Charley Barnes, the veteran mail-carrier, expressman, and stagecoach driver who had traveled every trail in southwestern Idaho in every season of the year by every means known to man, calmly predicted that it would.

"Hell's fire, Armand, come the first snowfall on that Newburg Road, ain't nothin' kin travel it 'cept a man on snowshoes. Why, I've seen winters carryin' the mail when two miles a day with a forty-pound pack on my back was makin' mighty good time."

"There's over 500,000 pounds of machinery in that wagon train, I'm told," Kimball said with a smile. "Why don't you tell the Astor & Vanderbilt manager to break it up into forty-pound packages and let you carry it in for him on snowshoes?"

"Fer a dollar an ounce, I'd take the contract, Armand. But it'd be hard-earned money, even at that."

By mid-January, the effort had been written off as hopeless, the mining machinery had been dumped and abandoned along the roadside, and, though there was some talk of trying again when the snows melted and the ground dried out, next summer was long months away.

From New York, news drifted out to Idaho that salesmen of perfectly good stock in Rocky Bar and Owyhee district mines were being discredited by lies told by wildcat feet salesmen from Colorado and Nevada. It was common knowledge among mining experts, Jim Reynolds pointed out, that the Nevada mines were almost "played out," that the Colorado boom was waning rapidly, and that the majority of the West's underground treasure lay in the quartz districts of southwestern Idaho. Proof would be forthcoming next summer, wait and see. But the lies hurt, nevertheless.

In late February, Wilson Waddingham wrote Kimball that the prospects for raising new capital looked excellent. In March, be wrote that he would be happy to trade $25,000 worth of personal mining stock for any St. Louis property Kimball might wish to dispose of, intimating that he could more readily raise cash by mortgaging real estate than mine shares (he did not say why he needed immediate cash, but Kimball gathered he was in a bit of a hurry for it). Tempted by past successes and the opportunity to transfer a good-sized chunk of his unmoveable assets from St. Louis to Idaho, Kimball regarded the proposal favorably at first and was about to write an affirmative reply when he noted a brief item reprinted in the *Statesman* from the New York *Tribune* regarding the recent steep drop in price of Colorado mine shares on the Eastern Exchange. Cause of the drop was not determined; nevertheless, he decided to postpone writing the letter for another week.

By then, he noted, the district court convening in Rocky Bar had forty-three lawsuits against local mine managers on its docket. Although it was anticipated that the mines managed by Wilson P. Waddingham would settle their legal difficulties within a week or two and re-open, wrote the Rocky Bar correspondent, he had to admit that at the present moment things were quite dull. However, he had it on good authority that new capital had been raised in the East and that Waddingham would be heading back to Idaho before long . . .

Kimball decided not to write the letter.

In May, an Idaho resident who had wintered in New York wrote Jim Reynolds that the market for Idaho quartz was very slow. Blame for this should be placed squarely on the shoulders of stupid, extravagant managers, he said, who spent more money buying expensive machinery than they did in developing their mines. They had promised too much too soon; the shareholders had been too impatient and too greedy. Mining should be conducted on a sound, conservative, business-like basis . . .

"Shrewd businessmen have long since foreseen and foretold the present very flat state of mining affairs both here and in Eastern cities," Jim Reynolds wrote in the *Statesman,* late in September. "Idle mills and disgusted capitalists are just the results that were sure to follow the insane plan of operations that has been in almost every instance adopted by individuals or companies. There are probably more than two thousand idle stamps in Colorado today . . . There are too many idle stamps in Idaho, but it is the fault of the owners and not our mines

Wilson P. Waddingham did not come back to Rocky Bar. Sometime early in the summer, Kimball heard, Waddingham mortgaged his interests in the Ada Elmore, the Confederate Star, and his other holdings for $50,000. He spent some time in St. Louis; later he was reported to be in Santa Fe, where, it was said, he was obtaining title to old Spanish land grants and cheerfully predicting that within ten years time he would have made his first million dollars and be working on his second.

"Would you bet against that?" Creed asked.

"No," Kimball answered. "But I wonder how long it will stick to his fingers?"

After taking a two weeks trip through the Rocky Bar district the following summer, a correspondent wrote:

"This is a desolate looking place. About half the houses were broken down by the snow last winter, and not more than half of those left standing are now occupied. This was once a lively place. Only one mill is running now. It is the poorest in the place. There are twelve stamps, nothing more; no pans, settlers, amalgamators, nor any of the improved facilities for saving the precious metals. How, then, do they succeed? I inquired for their bookkeeper. Mr. Green, the superintendent, kept the books. The office was closed. Mr. Green was not in a saloon, but at the mine. Thither I repaired, and found Mr. Green running a wheel-barrow from the tunnel to the dump-pile. In the course of a short conversation, he said: "We hire no hands. All that are employed are members of the company."

"There was the secret of their success. These men needed no lazy superintendent to watch them. They worked in company for a common interest. I wish their strong arms and willing hearts success; and they will achieve it."

Perhaps they would, Armand Kimball mused ruefully. He, too, wished them well. If the day ever came when Mr. Green and his fellow workers exhausted the gold ore in their mine, maybe they could be persuaded to take their picks, their shovels, and their wheel-barrow over to the Ada Elmore and work its untapped millions . . .

Chapter Eleven

It was with a great deal of satisfaction that the citizens of Boise City heard the news, on Tuesday morning, of the arrival of Governor Lyon. We are now too well pleased at his return to remember he has been gone . . .

—*Idaho Statesman*
Boise City, I.T.
November 9, 1865

When invited to contribute to the fund being raised to purchase a silver brick for Caleb Lyon, Andy Hale had politely declined. Yes, he admitted, it *was* a friendly, gracious gesture on the part of the citizens of Owyhee County toward the Territory's Chief Executive. But right now he was not in a particularly friendly, gracious mood. He would be glad to give Governor Lyon the charred remnants of a haystack which the Indians had recently burned. Or a rifle ball that had parted his hair and embedded itself in the cabin wall one morning last week. Or the arrow-pierced hide of a steer slaughtered two days ago. But until it was proven to him that Governor Lyon intended to take firm measures to end the Indian outrages in this corner of Idaho once and for all, whatever cash money *he* had was going to be spent on ammunition for his rifle and six-shooter.

Levi was more charitable. "Maybe I should chip in a couple of bucks to buy old Caleb that silver brick," he observed thoughtfully after reading a copy of the *Avalanche* one evening. "He's got a big pile of government money to give away. I'd ought to put in for my share."

"What makes you think you'd get any of it?"

"Well, it says here he's got a hundred thousand dollars to treat Indians with. I'm an Indian. If I talked nice to him, maybe he'd treat me."

"You're reading it wrong, Levi. He's not supposed to treat Indians—he's supposed to treat *with* them."

"Oh? What's the difference? Ain't we gonna get paid for being good?"

"You're not a wild Indian, you're civilized," Andy said with a smile. "You're supposed to be good for nothing."

"Well, I'll say this for old Caleb," Levi grunted as he put the paper aside. "If words were bullets, he'd kill every wild Indian in Idaho with one speech. Did you read the one he made up at Ruby City the other day?"

Caleb Lyon had been in fine form, Andy observed as he picked up the paper and scanned a synopsis of the governor's recent remarks. Among many other things, Lyon had said:

In the vast future that awaits Idaho, you are to have no second place. What the Pactolus was to the Greeks—what the Ophir was to the Jews—what the Arno was to the Romans, the Choco to the Peruvians, and the Coast of Guinea to the English—the Jordan Creek is to you—with this difference: the Old World's gold-bearing streams are nearly worked out, and the fruition of yours has just begun . . .

On the point of tossing the paper aside in disgust, Andy refrained as his eyes caught a paragraph set off between column-wide rows of asterisks:

* * * * * * * * * * * *

"There is no greater source of keen regret to me than the frequent occurrence of Indian outrages—their running off stock and their atrocious murder of peaceful citizens. As far as in me lies, this state of things must cease. You must and shall have protection in your peaceful pursuits *(cheers);* with sleepless vigilance I shall watch over your safety and guard your thoroughfares. Within the next year I hope all these offences against law and order will be among the things that were." *(Cheers.)*

* * * * * * * * * * * *

Cheers indeed! Andy mused sardonically. *Three hip-hoorays and a big loud tiger!*

Though the road from the Owyhee mining towns to Boise City passed close by the cabin, stagecoaches normally did not stop there. But at noon, next day, while Andy and Levi were eating their dinner, the northbound stage ground to a halt with a squealing of brakes, a snorting of horses, and a well-rounded volley of oaths by the driver, Pete O'Leary. Getting up from the table and going outside, Andy got a fleeting glimpse of a well-dressed elderly man making a beeline between the open door of the coach and the outhouse behind the cabin, a man in too much of a hurry to offer a greeting or pause for introductions. From the high seat, Pete O'Leary spat a stream of tobacco juice, grinned down at Andy and Levi, who had followed him outside, and said, "He wants to use your privy. I told him you wouldn't mind."

"Not if he makes it in time, no."

"You should feel honored, Andy. It ain't every settler that kin say the Governor of Idaho set in his privy."

Andy laughed. "We'll gild the glory hole, Pete. We'll put a bronze plaque on the door. But one thing worries me. Does he have the silver brick in his pants pocket?"

"Naw, it ain't been presented to him yet. They're plannin' a big doin's down at Boise City next month, with a dinner, speeches an' all. A committee from Owyhee is goin' to give him the brick then."

"He looked like he was in mortal pain. Is he sick?"

"Naw, jest got the trots. Too many oysters an' too much champagne, he says, an' he ain't the man he used to be." Casting a hasty glance in the direction of the outhouse, O'Leary lowered his voice, winked and said, "Between you an' me, Andy, some people are sayin' he never *was* long on anything but talk. I'll say this fer him, though—he's the only man I ever met that could talk two solid hours, never repeat himself, an' end up with me still wonderin' what in the hell he said."

"According to the papers, he made a speech down in San Francisco last spring saying the government ought to take over Idaho's mines, work them with Negroes and use the gold and silver they produced to pay off the war debt. What do the boys in Owyhee think of that notion?"

"Oh, they jumped him about it, don't think they didn't. But he claims he said no such thing. 'What he *really* said, he claims, was that the niggers ought to be put in uniform and sent West to clean out the Injuns . . . Look out, here he comes now."

A shade paler than before but more composed and in less of a hurry, Governor Lyon paused at the washstand at the south end of the cabin, hung his hat and long frock coat on the wooden pegs driven into the wall, poured water into the basin from the bucket, meticulously washed and dried his hands and face, donned hat and coat again, then turned and strode toward Andy with a smile on his face and his right hand outstretched.

"Good day, sir. I am Caleb Lyon of Lyonsdale, Governor of Idaho. Whom do I have the pleasure of addressing?"

"Andy Hale."

"A pleasure, Mr. Hale! A genuine pleasure, I assure you!" "Glad to meet you, Governor Lyon."

"And you, sir?" Caleb Lyon said, turning to smile at Levi.

"Folks call me 'Levi.'"

"Don't you have a last name?"

"Sure, but nobody can pronounce it."

"Ah, you're not a native American, then! Now I mean no offense by that, sir—some of this country's finest citizens have come to these shores from distant lands. I have traveled widely abroad myself. May I take the liberty of guessing the country of your birth?"

"Sure, guess away."

"There are certain Latin features to your face. Yet the texture of your hair suggests a less sunny clime. Your eyes, however, have something of the Middle East in them. Arabia? No! India? Hardly! All right, I'll take a shot in the dark—you are an Armenian by birth!"

"Shoot again, Governor, that one missed."

Knowing Levi's ironic sense of humor as he did, Andy was well aware of the fact that the Delaware would let the farce go on until his questioner had made a much greater fool of himself than he already had, so he ended it himself by saying curtly, "Levi is pulling your leg, Governor. He's more of a native American than either you or I are. He's a full-blood Delaware Indian."

Caleb Lyon, who had been grasping Levi's hand, released it. "Oh? Well, it's a pleasure to meet you, sir, whatever kind of American you may be. Some of our finest citizens have Indian blood in their veins." Turning away, he gazed out across the autumn-yellowed expanse of bunchgrass covered benchland for a moment, then said, "A splendid ranch you have here, Mr. Hale. Do you raise many cattle?"

"A few."

"How do you get along with the Indians?"

"Poorly, Governor. They're stealing us blind."

"So I hear, so I hear! Well, Mr. Hale, I intend to put an end to that. As soon as I possibly can, I intend to set up reservations for the Bruneaus, the Boises, and all the other recalcitrant tribes—"

"Begging your pardon, Governor," Andy interrupted, "but it's not the Bruneaus and Boises that are raising hell hereabouts. So far as we've been able to tell, they're Winnemuccas, Paiutes, and renegade scum from half a dozen Nevada, Oregon, and Idaho tribes. But they're certainly not Bruneaus or Boises."

"Of course, of course!" Lyon said absently. "As I explained to Major Marshall, we'll lay out a reservation for the Boises northeast of Boise City and another for the Bruneaus south of Snake River. We will offer them blankets, food, and farming tools. We will say in effect: 'We will feed you or fight you— the choice is yours.' Later, of course, I plan to go up to northern Idaho for another conference with the Nez Perces."

"*That* will be a big help to the ranchers around here."

"Yes, I'm sure it will be," Lyon said, nodding, his pleased look telling Andy that the sarcasm had gone completely over his head. "If you have any constructive suggestions to make, Mr. Hale, I trust you will come to Boise City and lay them before me. I'm always happy to talk to people."

"I'll keep that in mind, Governor."

Until the Governor of Idaho honored his privy with a personal visit, Andy had taken it for granted that the prime duty of the Chief Executive was to maintain law and order within his domain and provide, as far as he was able, for the needs of the people residing therein. He had assumed, furthermore, that the men elected to serve in the Territorial Legislature, coming as they did from districts whose urgent requirements they knew well, would spend the major portion of their time while the Legislature was in session drawing up laws that would substantially contribute to the growth, peace, and well-being of the farmers, ranchers, miners, and businessmen whom they represented. Government meant stability, did it not?

Well, eventually perhaps. Jim Reynolds acidly commented that Idaho *must* have a stable government, judging from the number of jackasses the voters had elected to serve in the Legislature. Joe Wasson slyly pointed out: "In the beginning was the Word . . ."; and Caleb Lyon of Lyonsdale greeted the Gentlemen of the Council and House on their third assembly early in December with a veritable vintage selection of well-chosen words:

The temple of war is closed! No more shall its iron mouthed and brazen throated cannon peal forth dread miserere's over half a thousand battle fields, where sleep their last sleep the victor and the vanquished. No more shall the ear of night be pierced with the echoes of fierce assault and stubborn defense from encompassed and beleagured cities. The conflict is over, and with it expired the cause . . .

Following this belated reminder that the Civil War had ended six months ago, Governor Lyon proceeded to set forth a comprehensive, ambitious program of things needed to be done to promote Idaho's welfare. The assembled Legislators listened intently, applauded heartily, and then, retiring to their respective meeting places, ignored the program utterly.

As a requirement for holding public office, the National Congress had passed a law that every elected person must take the Oath of Allegiance. To a substantial number of Idaho Democrats, like Cornelius Belford, swearing allegiance to the Federal government was as distasteful as vowing undying loyalty to the Republican party; so, for several angry, bickering sessions the furtherance of Idaho's welfare was postponed while an attempt was made to introduce and pass a bill repealing the hated Oath. By a narrow margin, the bill failed on its first trial, though whether the fact that a Territorial Legislature had no power to repeal a Federal law influenced a single vote was highly dubious.

The next order of business taking precedence over Idaho's welfare was the pressing need to abolish the offices of Territorial Treasurer and Auditor, both of which were now occupied by Republicans, and create the new offices of Territorial Controller and Receiver, which, if the Legislature had its way, would be held by Democrats. It also struck the Legislators as urgent to pass a bill relieving Boise County from paying into the Territorial coffers the sum of $8500 (tax money with which a Democratic county official had absconded) and reimbursing Sheriff Crutcher (also a Democrat) the sum of $11,000, which he claimed he had expended upholding law and order during the recent Patterson-Pinkham affair.

It seemed equally important to the Legislators to pass bills cutting the salaries of all appointed Republican officials (though maintaining their own), postponing payment of the debts now accumulating in most Idaho counties by "funding" them on a "preferred creditor" basis (which meant arranging matters so that loyal Democratic creditors would get paid now while less fortunate Republican creditors must accept paper "IOUs" to be paid on some indefinite future date when the Territorial Treasury possessed a surplus), and awarding the printing contract for the revised statutes to Pat Malone, who, oddly enough, just happened to be as firmly Democratic in his politics as Jim Reynolds was solidly Republican in his.

Governor Lyon vetoed the printing award bill, to which action the Legislature promptly responded by overriding the veto with a two-thirds vote. Cheered by this victory, the confident Legislators re-introduced the bill repealing the Oath of Allegiance requirement, passed it, and then happily pitched into the backlog of requests from confiding constituents for toll-road franchises and divorces.

Following these great events in the newspapers dropped off at his cabin door, Andy waited in vain for some sign that Governor Lyon and the Legislature had at last agreed on some firm course of action to be taken against the hostile Indians, whose raids against ranchers, travelers, ferrymen, and stage-station keepers throughout southwestern Idaho and along the Nevada and Oregon roads to California were becoming intolerable. But beyond some fine-sounding speeches made by Lyon, the Legislators and Major Marshall, who was currently in command of the Federal troops stationed at Fort Boise, nothing happened.

What the Territory needed, Caleb Lyon declared, was a well-armed, well-trained, alert Citizens' Militia; he recommended that the Legislature frame and pass a measure to that effect. In view of the fact that such a Citizens' Militia must be paid, armed, and supplied, the Legislature replied, a memorial to the Federal government for funds seemed more in order; however, if the Fort Boise quartermaster would issue a few hundred rifles to a Volunteer group, which would act as auxiliaries to the Regular Army, a start might be made. Sorry, Major Marshall answered, but I have no authority to issue rifles or employ auxiliaries. However, if the residents of the affected areas would take it upon themselves to organize committees whose duties it would be to note the place, time, date, and nature of any and all outrages committed and to communicate them at once to this post, I can promise a swift, thorough investigation of each offense . . .

"For God's sake, Joe, what kind of government have we got in Idaho?" Andy complained bitterly to Joe Wasson, editor of the *Owyhee Avalanche,* who had stopped over for the night on his way home from Boise City. "Can't it do *anything* for us?"

"Oh, but it has done something for us, Andy."

"Name one constructive thing. Just one."

"Well, last week the Legislature declared Snake River navigable from Olds Ferry to Salmon Falls. That's a marvelous thing to know, my friend, in case, somebody brings a steamboat across the Blues and starts looking around for a place to sail it."

"Oh, hell! Name something constructive, I said."

"Well, Caleb Lyon donated five hundred dollars to the fund being raised in Boise City to outfit a group of Volunteers that proposes to go wild-Indian hunting through this part of the country. The money came, he said, out of his own pocket."

"Which is not the same pocket he put the Federal government's hundred thousand dollars in?"

"Oh, Heavens, no!" Wasson exclaimed in mock horror. "*That* money was to be used to settle the Indian problem peacefully. He wouldn't dare use it otherwise."

"Damn it, Joe, it just doesn't make sense to me. The only Indians he bothers to talk with are tame, friendly Indians like the Nez Perces, the Bruneaus, and the Boises."

"They're the only ones that *will* talk with him."

"But what good does talking with friendly Indians do us? Every day in this corner of the Territory cattle are being stolen, travelers are being attacked, stage stations are being burned, and white people are being killed. Yet Caleb Lyon and Major Marshall sit around gabbing with the Bruneaus for weeks, guarded by a hundred soldiers. Why don't they send those soldiers after the red bastards that are doing the mischief?"

"Because *those* red bastards won't stand still, Andy. How can you talk with an Indian that won't stand still?"

"Captain Walker managed to make a few of them stand still down in the Malheur country a while back," Andy muttered sourly. "In fact, he made them *lie* still—under a foot of dirt. If he were in charge at Fort Boise instead of that old fool Major Marshall, we'd get something constructive done."

"True," Joe Wasson agreed, nodding. "But in my humble opinion, it wouldn't be what Caleb Lyon *wants* done."

"What does he want done?"

"You've got to realize, Andy, that Caleb Lyon is a politician through and through," Joe Wasson answered, getting up and pouring himself another drink without waiting for an invitation to do so. "He's ambitious to improve his station in the political world. To such a man, pacifying Indians is an end devoutly to be sought; killing them a thing to be avoided at all costs."

"Indians don't vote."

"No, my friend, but Indian-lovers do."

"Well, if it's votes he's after," Andy said disgustedly, "he damn sure won't find many Indian-lovers in Idaho."

Levi, who customarily listened without comment to discussions such as this one, took his pipe out of his mouth and grunted, "Me, I'm one. I love me."

"It's wild Indians we're talking about."

"Them I got no use for. Not when they steal my cows and shoot at me. What do they think I am, a white man?"

"In his usual subtle, oblique way Levi reinforces the point I'm trying to make," Joe Wasson said with an approving smile. "The throne of political power is in the East, and, to an Easterner, an Idaho Indian is a poor, ignorant savage that should be taken gently by the hand and tenderly led along the road to Salvation and Knowledge. He is Massasoit bringing corn to the starving Pilgrims; he is Hiawatha communing with nature in a birchbark canoe; he is Pocahontas saving John Smith's head from the executioner's ax—"

"Look here, Joe," Andy interrupted angrily. "Over on Burnt River a while back, the Indians killed a settler and his wife, stripped off their clothes, hacked them up and did such nasty things to the corpses that you didn't dare print the details in your paper. Caleb Lyon 'deplored the tragedy' and Major Marshall promised 'swift retribution if the offenders can be found.' That was all. Now suppose that this same thing happened not out here but in the East—on the road, say, between Baltimore and Washington City? Suppose some of Levi's Delaware relatives, who still live in that part of the country, got drunk and reverted to the kind of savages they used to be? What would happen?"

"Well, first, Horace Greeley would write an editorial in the New York *Tribune* demanding that three regiments of Federal troops under a brigadier general be furnished at once to guard all roads. Second, every person with Indian blood in his veins would be jailed. Third, a few dozen people that *looked* like Indians would be lynched. But it hasn't happened there, Andy; therefore, Easterners are positive it can't be happening here. Lyon is an Easterner. Though he does his best to conceal his true feelings, in his secret soul he thinks all white residents of Idaho are crude, uncultured roughs, and he believes nothing they tell him—unless it happens to concern diamonds. He does not even believe what he sees with his own eyes. He reads *Leslie's, Harpers,* and the New York *Tribune* and takes their word as Gospel. He reads Jim Reynolds' paper and my paper and shrugs off everything we say as lies. Why? Because he doesn't give a tinker's dam about Idaho and its people; all this Territory is to him is a steppingstone to bigger things."

"What bigger things?"

"Well, my suspicion is he's pulling every string he can back East to get Idaho admitted to the Union as a state. If that happens, he'll take sole credit for it and get himself elected United States Senator—he thinks—which would put him in Washington City, where he's dying to be. If it doesn't happen—and it seems to me unlikely it will—he'll try to use his record as Idaho's finest Governor to date—he thinks—to wangle some more lucrative appointive post out of President Johnson. Note carefully, my friend, how closely his public statements on Reconstruction parallel those coming from the White House. Note further, my boy, that now that Democrats outnumber Republicans in Idaho he no longer seeks approval of Idaho's Republican editors like Jim Reynolds but fawns over Democratic editors like H. C. Street and Pat Malone."

"Jim Reynolds is starting to criticize him, I see."

"I know. And Jim tells me we ain't seen nothing yet."

"What do you plan to do?"

Joe Wasson sighed as he refilled his glass. "I've come to realize, Andy, that the only thing a newspaper editor gets from straddling the fence and being fair, as I've tried to do, is a sore crotch and brickbats from both sides. I don't like politics but I do like Idaho. In my opinion, what Idaho needs is a governor that's a man, not an old imbecile like Caleb Lyon. Which is exactly what I'm going to say in print—and soon."

THE GOVERNOR AT MASONIC HALL.—On Saturday evening last the Assembly Room was crowded at an early hour, to welcome Gov. Caleb Lyon of Lyonsdale, who delivered to a delighted audience of the wealth and intelligence of Idaho City, an enthusiastic and *extempore* address . . .

With his infinite affable nature, anecdotes, and kind mention of the ladies, Gov. Caleb Lyon of Lyonsdale made himself immensely popular with his audience . . .

At the close the Governor was saluted with three rousing cheers . . .
—*Idaho World*
Idaho City, I.T.
December 9, 1865

Our Governor has made a grand mistake in supposing that he was carrying out the policy of the President when he approved so many unrighteous measures of the Legislature, measures which he himself condemned but refused to veto for the sake of "policy." That was a mistaken policy . . .

The fact is there is a vast difference between the whipped and repentant returning rebels of the South, who frankly confess the errors of the past and take the oath of allegiance, and the unrepentant, defiant Democratic legislature of Idaho that repealed the oath of allegiance with so much gusto, while they still vociferously denounced the government as "tyrannical and odious . . ."

To yield to these demands will prove to be a ruinous "policy" to whomsoever adopts it.

—*Idaho Statesman*
Boise City, I.T.
January 27, 1866

STILL FURTHER.
. . . the following letter is from New York, December 28th, which, after speaking of mining statistics, says of Lyon: "He has not the least influence here . . . last summer when Lyon came home, the President, Secretary of State and Secretary of Interior were determined to turn

him out, and Wallace's commission was made out and signed. But Weed, through Morgan's influence, stopped Wallace's commission in the State Department. Now these men, Weed and Morgan, think nothing of Lyon only as a tool . . ."

We have slowly and regretfully begun to expose the shallow trickery of this old demagogue sent out here for a Governor because we were at first disposed to give him credit for some honesty of purpose and attribute his short-comings more to imbecility, if not actual craziness, than downright villainy. But we have given him up entirely. The proof is overwhelming that his duplicity and meanness are only limited by his ability . . .

We are not half through with Caleb yet . . .

—*Idaho Statesman*
Boise City, I.T.
February 6, 1866

NO HELP.—Mr. Bohannon went back to Owyhee empty handed and alone, so far as any assistance in putting down the Indians is concerned. Governor Lyon informed him that he could furnish and expend large sums of money to feed and "treat" with Lo! but not a dollar to fight him . . .

—*Idaho Statesman*
Boise City, I.T.
February 20, 1866

THE "VENAL PRESS".—Governor Lyon is reported 'to have devoted considerable of his speech, the other night, to the *Statesman*—denominating it a "venal and lying press," and applying to it other choice and select terms. It is quite natural that he should. We have never known a man to fail to denounce a press that he could not buy . . .

—*Idaho Statesman*
Boise City, I.T.
February 27, 1866

Governor Lyon has been commissioned by the Idaho Legislature to draw the design for the Territorial Seal. The Gov. claims to be the originator of the California State Seal, which is a curious compound of Grecian mythological figures, grizzly bears, honest miners and modern ships, with a perspective filled up by zoological specimens native to the Golden State. To be consistent, the Seal ought to be made of soft-solder.

—*Idaho Statesman*
Boise City, I.T.
February 27, 1866

WANTED IN IDAHO.—A Governor that is a man, not an old imbecile as we have now . . . We don't want any importations, but men of I.T.—not of any New York or Eastern dale. We want *something* or a simon-pure vacuum or nonentity, not a living nothing.
—*Owyhee Avalanche*
Ruby City, I.T.
March 10, 1866

A CARD
TO HIS EXCELLENCY, THE GOVERNOR OF IDAHO.

Reynolds Creek, Feb. 27, 1866.
My dear, very dear Sir: This evening, I feel constrained by a power beyond control, an irresistible impulse, to write to you—you dear old compound of all the sins of all the political parties living or dead . . .

You may not be aware—you dear old conglomerate of the French dancing-master, American demagogue and East Indian monkey, especially the latter—that I am the fortunate individual who was temporarily taking care of Hill Beachey's stage horses, at Cold Spring Station, when it was attacked on the morning of Feb. 18, '66. Well, Gov., I am the man that was shot at and not hit by one of your lamblike pets, and it is partly to tell you this that I write you now—you sweet old amalgam of French manners and Turkish voluptuousness . . .You may have done right, dear old Gov., to refuse to aid those naughty Volunteers who threatened to shoot the males, murder the squaws and scalp the babes of poor Lo, the innocent and forbearing red man of the desert and plain, who has seldom been known to do worse than steal our stock, burn our houses, murder our people and torture to death those unfortunate beings who may have fallen into their hands while life lasted . . . your future political prospects in Idaho cannot be damaged, for, like hen fruit with dead chickens therein, they are incapable of further injury . . .

Dear old Gov., dear old womans' rights convention in a very small concentrated dose—you and I differ as essentially in our views of the proper use to be made of a redskin devil as we do in the proper use of a French waiter or Italian barber. You believe in making unmentionable uses of the two latter while I believe in keeping the one to skip around a dining room, like a fly in a hot skillet, and employing the other in all the legitimate arts tonsorial. You believe in taming the "fast expiring" race and making them a source of profit to the *unpolluted* (in a horn) Indian Department officers; I believe in making coyote feed of the whole brood . . .

I believe that it is possible after a long course of sin for that attribute of man called a soul to become disgusted with its earthly tenement and to take its departure to some far-off bourne from whence it never returns . . . for the sake of that spark, hasten at once to Washington and resign the trust you are so incapable of filling. Tell Andrew Johnson that the same flag that waves over the palace of the White House and secures him in life, property and power should cover with its starry folds the pioneer upon the most remote frontier . . . Tell the President to send us an Executive who is a *Man*, we care not what his politics may be, so long as he is a man uncontaminated with the dishwater philanthropy of the age . . .

Dear old Volute!—you must not mind my calling you pet names, for if I was only proficient in the vocabulary of Billingsgate, or fish-market, I would apply them all to you that are therein found, for you would deserve them all.

Your very affectionate and humble servant,
   Sam'l P. Duzan

—*Owyhee Avalanche*
Ruby City, I.T.
March 17, 1866

Lo! the poor Indian, whose untutored mind,
Sees God in the clouds and hears Him in the wind.

Isn't that beautiful? How sublimely poetical it sounds to a settler over on Jordan Creek, or a traveler just in from Humboldt. Care must be taken to pronounce the last two lines in perfect rythm. Hill Beachey reads the whole poem every day, with the addition of *"Hiawatha"* on Sundays. Says it soothes his nerves and compensates very much for the loss of an occasional double span of stage horses . . .

—*Idaho Statesman*
Boise City, I.T.
March 21, 1866

INTERESTING PUBLIC DOCUMENT

The following document fully explains itself. Those who have a personal acquaintance with Senator Nesmith can best appreciate the practical matter of fact way in which it is his habit to attack an incompetent official. His long experience in Indian Affairs make him the best authority in the Senate or even in the United States upon such matters:

WASHINGTON, D.C., March 16th, '66.

EDITOR, IDAHO STATESMAN—Dear *Sir:* The following is a

verbatim copy of a letter filed in the Interior Department by Senator Nesmith, of Oregon:

College Hill, (near Cincinnati) Ohio
October 23rd, 1865.
Hon. James Harland
Secretary of the Interior

Sir: Having just returned by the Overland route from the States and Territories of the Pacific where I spent the last summer in investigating the condition of Indian affairs, I deem it my duty to call your attention at once to the condition of Indian affairs in Idaho Territory. As you are aware the Governor of Idaho is Ex-Officio Superintendent of Indian Affairs—one Caleb Lyon of Lyonsdale— and has, for some time, been the nominal incumbent and has drawn the salary of that office.

For more than six months he has not shown himself within the Territory, while everything pertaining to the office of Superintendent has been most shamefully neglected. The Nez Perces, who are the most powerful tribe of Indians on the Pacific coast, are within the boundaries of Idaho Territory. Our Government has a treaty with them by the stipulations of which they are entitled to certain annuities to be paid annually. I find that not a dollar's worth of annuities has been paid to these people for more than two years, and a portion of the tribe are threatening to resort to hostilities in retaliation for the bad faith with which the government and its officers have treated them.

I was unable to find any records in the Governor's office showing what disposition had been made of the appropriations made by Congress to fulfil the treaty stipulations with this tribe; indeed, I was unable to find any records in the Governor's office in any way pertaining to Indian affairs, and the person who had been employed by the Governor to act as Clerk or Secretary for the Superintendency, and who had received a salary for that duty, informed me that no records of any sort had ever been kept.

Supt. James O'Neill, Esq., agent in charge of the Nez Perce reservation, is a competent officer and seems to be doing everything in his power to pacify the Indians and protect the interests of the Government, but he is without a dollar of funds with which to defray current expenses. The wages of the persons employed upon the reservation in pursuance of the treaty stipulations have not been paid for nearly two years, and they are forced to sell their vouchers at from 50 to 60 cents on the dollar in currency.

The money disbursed by Governor Lyon's order while he was pretending to discharge the duties of Superintendent of Indian Affairs has been totally and grossly misapplied and squandered (by the Governor's orders) for objects which were neither authorized by the treaty or desired by the Indians. Under this state of facts and as a member of the Committee, authorized by Congress to inquire into the condition of Indian affairs, I would earnestly recommend that some person be appointed to discharge the duties of Governor, and Superintendent of Indian Affairs in Idaho, who has, at least, some claims to common sense and common honesty. The change cannot be made too soon for the protection of the government and the preservation of peace among the Indians.

I regard "Caleb Lyon of Lyonsdale" as an improper person to be permitted to run at large amongst the Indians or to be entrusted with public funds, and would recommend that any funds intended for the Nez Perce Indians be sent direct to agent James O'Neill.

I am, very respectfully,
Your ob't serv't.
W. Nes'mitb.

The Secretary of the Interior and the Commissioner of Indian Affairs coincide fully in the opinion of Governor Lyon, entertained in this letter by Mr. Nesmith, and have made such statements officially to the Secretary of State, while the President declares that he never thought Lyon fit for the office, but left him where he found him temporarily. Yesterday Dr. Ballard, of Oregon, was nominated to the Senate for Governor of Idaho, with Caleb removed . . .

Yours truly,

H. Cummins.
—Idaho Statesman
Boise City, I.T.
April 17, 1866

COME AND GONE—A PARTING WORD.—Caleb Lyon of Lyonsdale entered Idaho twice as Governor and was received with tooting of horns and the usual amount of credulous assurance of distinguished consideration; and now twice has he departed amid a big cloud of unparalleled disgust. His first reception was given because of his position; his second was given because a Governor was needed and to encourage him to *be* one by overlooking his former failure and disgrace . . .

Of all the political mountebanks that ever attained position, Caleb stands at the head of the gang. As a shrewd humbug, he doesn't approach mediocrity; as a willing schemer, he lacks ability to succeed; as an executive, he does not possess the primary elements; and, as a man always giving hollow caresses for expected favors, he is the basest of ingrates . . .

God in His providence has a way of scourging the people, which is doubtless right. With what pestilence He will next inflict us is uncertain, but can hardly be worse. Cholera, small-pox, yellow fever, diphtheria and poisonous simoons may be coveted in comparison to such granny governors. These visitations would at least benefit doctors, undertakers, sextons and probate courts, but the other would be a blight upon the Territory.

—Owyhee Avalanche
Ruby City, I.T.
May 5, 1866

GOVERNOR BALLARD arrived on the western stage last night.

As he followed the Lyon controversy in the Territorial newspapers, Andy Hale mused that if as much time, energy, and passion had been applied to solving the Indian problem as to ridding Idaho of its governor peace would have come to this part of the country long ago. As their winged duck fluttered lamely out of range, charges of editorial buckshot continued to spatter in his direction from the pens of Jim Reynolds and Joe Wasson. But the final potshot at Lyon came from an unexpected source. Some months after the governor had left Idaho, the New York *Tribune* printed the following item:

ROBBERY ON TRAIN.

Upon his arrival in Washington D.C. yesterday, Caleb Lyon, formerly Governor of Idaho Territory, reported to police that $47,000 had been stolen from him. The money was being carried on his person, he said, in a money belt secured about his waist under his clothing. It was taken from him by a person or persons unknown while he slept. The money belt itself, he said, was not disturbed. Although not directly confirmed by ex-Gov. Lyon, it is assumed that the large sum of money which he reportedly was carrying was a part of the Federal Government funds for whose accounting he had been summoned to Washington. Earlier, in New York, he had stated: "I can account for every dollar I spent in Idaho . . ."

Also without confirmation is his alleged statement to a friend that he intends to appeal to Congress for relief of paying over the stolen sum, whose loss was, he says, an "Act of God" and no fault of his own . . .

Chapter Twelve

"Pray, excuse a bit of sarcasm," said Smith to Jones, "but you are an infamous liar and a scoundrel."

"Pardon a touch of irony," replied Jones to Smith, knocking him down with a poker.

—*Owyhee Avalanche*
Silver City, I.T.
December 1, 1866

The cross he carried through life, Joe Wasson had once confessed to Andy when slightly in his cups, was that he had too great a love for putting words down on paper and too great a dislike for the purely mechanical process of reproducing those same words in print. Words could sing like meadow larks in the dew-fresh dawn when a man of *his* indisputable talent strung them together on a sheet of fresh paper with a pen, he said immodestly; but setting those same words up in metal type possessed no more thrill for him than picking graybacks off a Digger Indian's greasy skull.

He hated the confinement of the print shop, hated dead-lines, hated advertisers, subscribers, and collecting and paying bills. Most of all, he hated people who came into his office when he was daydreaming of becoming a roving free-lance writer and lecturer like Mark Twain and wasted his precious time telling him why he *must* give special coverage to some hum-drum local event in which he had not the slightest aesthetic interest.

"No, Mr. Murphy," he told today's unwelcome caller firmly, "I will *not* write up next Sunday's prize-fight. To me, the mere thought of two grown men clumsily attempting to beat each other's brains out for pay is revolting, degrading, and obnoxious."

"'Tis a grand sport, prize-fightin' is, Mr. Wasson. Half the town will be there. What will the lads say, Mr. Wasson, if you offend them by givin' no mention to the greatest prize-fight ever held in Owyhee?"

"Why should the lads care whether or not it's reported in my paper? They'll see it with their own eyes, won't they?"

"Ah, but you don't understand, Mr. Wasson. 'Tis not just watchin' a prize-fight that's sport to the lads; 'tis debatin' it round by round and blow by blow after the affair's over and done with. Why, that's half the fun of it, sir! How else will they know exactly what happened if a reliable eyewitness ain't there to write it up for the paper?"

Joe Wasson sighed. "Are you an expert on prize-fighting, Mr. Murphy?"

"I've seen a few rum goes in my time," Mr. Murphy admitted modestly. "I know a left-lifter from a right-hooker."

"Good! I'll make you a proposition, Mr. Murphy. *You* go to the fight as official correspondent for the *Avalanche*. Write a detailed report, review, critique, or whatever such things are called of who bloodies whose nose and how and when—and I'll publish it."

Mr. Murphy's round red face lighted with pleasure. "Now that's a fair proposal, Mr. Wasson. Though it may be a wee bit rusty for lack of use, I do have a small talent with words. You must promise me one thing, though."

"What's that?"

"That you will publish my report just as I write it, Mr. Wasson, without puttin' it into fancy, high-falutin' words. After all, as you yourself admit, sir, you're not an expert on prizefightin'."

"Mr. Murphy, I shall not decapitate a single semi-colon," Joe Wasson said earnestly. "Now, if you'll excuse me, I have a paper to get out . . ."

PRIZE-FIGHT BETWEEN PATSY FOY AND JAMES DWYER, ON SUNDAY SEPTEMBER 30.

Reported by T. G. Murphy,
by Request of Parties Interested.

This was the first prize-fight in Owyhee. It occurred about two and a half miles above Silver City, near Bloom & Herd's Sawmill. The day was pleasant and between 400 and 500 were in attendance. Admission $2.50 and $5.00.

The bets were $500 a side, in addition to the ring money, which amounted to about $1100. Long before the fight came off Foy was the only one on whom bets could be made, but the day before the fight considerable money was bet on Dwyer.

The ring was the usual size; the ground inside the ropes was well arranged, and everything inside the ring was got up regardless of expense.

At 5 minutes to 2 o'clock, P.M., Dwyer made his appearance, followed by his second, Hugh Kelly, when he shied his castor into the ring, which was hailed with some cheering; and at 20 minutes past 2 o'clock Patsy Foy threw his cabeen inside the ropes, which was hailed with much cheering. Foy's second was Barney Green.

Green and Kelly tossed up for choice of corners; Green won, which gave Foy great advantage over Dwyer, as the sun was shining bright and had a blinding effect on Dwyer, who had to face it.

After some delay the Judges, John McMahon and M. Short, were selected, and J. P. Gabriel was appointed Referee.

When Foy entered the ring he held a purse in his hand and offered to bet its contents, besides his share of the ring money, but got no takers.

Foy's colors were white silk, bound around with green, with a green star in the center; while Dwyer's was a purple reach with white spots.

All arrangements having been made, at 3 minutes to 3 o'clock, the parties came up to the scratch, shook hands, looked smiling and seemed evidently spoiling for a beating, and before leaving both of them got a good dose of the same.

Dwyer's weight was 149 pounds, while Foy's was 159. Between the build of the two men but little difference, if any, was visible.

1st Round. Time being called, both came up smiling, began to eye each other and get true measure, when at it they went, squaring and sparring, when Dwyer landed a lefter, followed up by Foy's right, then his left, which told on the boy, and some sparring then commenced, each watching his chance to give a lander; at last both clinched and fell, Dwyer under, with cries of the first fall and blood for Foy. Time, 1 minute and 30 seconds.

2nd. Time being called, both jumped at the word and looked as smiling as though it was his intended he was meeting, but to the astonishment of Foy he got a lifter on the right peeper, then another under his listener, when both clinched and fell, Foy under, and cheers for the boy. Time 1 minute.

3rd. Both came to time with clinched snatcher; they done some good sparring among much cheering, and after punching each other right lively for some moments, both clinched and fell, Foy under.

Time, 1 minute and 2 seconds.

4th. The men came up sparring and some good sparring and hard blows were exchanged, when both clinched and fell, Foy under. Time, 2 minutes and 5 seconds.

5th. Both came to time; Foy made a feint, when Dwyer countered on the right ear, dealing a lefter, then one with a right, leaving a mouse under Foy's left blinker; both clinched and fell, Foy under. Time 2.2.

6th. Both men came to the scratch and squared off; the blow came too careless around Foy's frontispiece, and to get in safer quarters he dropped under and kissed the sage. Time 1.5. Cries of foul from Dwyer's seconds, which the Referee could not see.

From the 7th to 15th rounds but little punishment was given, but Foy went under with each round, with loud cheering for Dwyer.

16th. Some fair sparring set in, with both men striking right and left, when Dwyer sent a teller which hit off Foy's smeller, then another on his listener, besides a smarter which busted his air—taker, that landed him square on his back. Great cheering for Dwyer, he winning the first square knockdown of the fight. Time, 1:32.

17th & 18th. But little punishment was given; Foy dropped to avoid punishment each round.

19th. Foy came up looking weak, but showing good pluck, and by accident, it would seem, got a teller right in his breadbasket, which disarranged the whole concern and sent him in the grass, amid great cheering for second square knockdown, which was won by Dwyer. Time, 18 seconds.

20th. Dwyer met his man, but began to look weak, showing good spunk, but Foy landed a teller on his right vision, which drew the claret, then on his snuff-taker, which brought the red, then both clinched and fell side and side. Time, 25 seconds.

From the 21st to the 24th rounds there was hard striking, Foy dropping each time to avoid punishment and claiming foul, but no go.

25th. Time called, Foy looking fresher and giving Dwyer some hard punishment, when both hugged, went to mother earth, Dwyer under. Cheering for Foy and two to one offered on him. Time, 1 minute.

26th. This was a short one, Foy dropping on his knees and claiming foul.

27th. Time being called, both came up chafing, when Foy received a right hander, going down. Cries of foul and great excitement arose in favor of Foy's having won the fight, but to no purpose.

From the 28th to 31st round Foy dropped and received some fouls, which was claimed by his friends, but the Referee decided against him.

32nd. This was the hardest round of the fight, Dwyer wilting, but to save himself went in to spar, then hard striking became the order, and for a time the rights and lefts were numerous and hard, and not being satisfied, Foy went on his knocker. Time, 36 seconds.

From the 33rd to 35th round but little punishment was given to either.

36th. This round almost ended the fight, as Foy punished Dwyer badly; both clinching, Foy fell on Dwyer, who was carried to his corner, whence his moans could be heard all over the ring, and had the time-keeper been prompt in calling time, Foy would have won the fight.

Between the 37th and 45th rounds but few blows were exchanged to cause much suffering, but lots of points were offered, and a desire by both to show their skill in the P.R., and Foy, in almost every round, expecting a foul to gain the fight, but to no purpose, although he went on his knees or fell each round.

46th. Both came up trying to kill time; after some hard hits, both clinched and Foy threw Dwyer. Cheering for Foy. Time, 54 seconds.

From the 47th to the 53rd rounds neither was able to give much punishment, and Dwyer having the best tripper Foy generally went under.

54th. Both men were weak, but Dwyer gaining his second wind, administered some hard blows, and to avoid them Foy dropped, when his friends claimed a foul, but it was not allowed. Time, 1.2.

Between the 55th and 80th rounds, Foy, to save himself, went down, and neither were anxious to come to time, when called.

81st, 82nd and 83rd rounds. Foy could hardly stand on his pins, but showed good grit and kept a lookout to save being hurt, always going on his knees to prayers.

84th, and last round. Foy came up slow and showed a bold front; being hardly able to stand he threw himself into the friendly embrace of Dwyer, who hugged him like a bear, then both fell, Dwyer on top; Foy was carried to his corner so used up that when time was called for the 85th round his second threw up the sponge, which was the signal of Dwyer's victory and end of the fight.

There were about 500 persons present in the ring, and a more orderly crowd of men never met together. All present seemed to favor fair play, which was carried out to the letter. From the beginning to the end of the fight everything was conducted on the square, showing that the men of Owyhee, even at a prize-fight, do not forget that they are gentlemen. The Judges and Referee, without exception, acted in their capacity in such a manner as to give general satisfaction to all parties.

Patsy Foy has fought several ring-fights before, while this was Dwyer's maiden effort in the P.R. Dwyer is quite a young man, not yet 21 years of age, and although he proved himself to be a good sparrer and able to endure much punishment, he cannot do better than to turn his attention to some more honorable profession than that of a bruiser. As to Foy, he too would do much better to make up his mind that he was never intended for a boxer, for last Sunday he proved to all present that he could give but little punishment, although he can endure any amount of it.

Considerable money was bet on the result of this fight, and both the men who won and those who lost seemed well satisfied with the result of it, as it was pronounced, and as I think justly, to be one of the best prize-fights that ever came off on this Coast. From the commencement of the fight to its end, Foy's points and aim to win the fight was for Dwyer to strike him when he was down, and many of those present, who were Foy's friends at the commencement of the fight, turned against him and were friends with Dwyer, who showed good judgment and acted fairly from the first to the last of the fight. The fight lasted 2 hours and 5 seconds.

Patsy Foy now proposes to fight Dwyer, six weeks from now, for eight hundred dollars, and whether we shall have another bruising match will simply be a question of agreement. Go in, boys!

True to his promise, Joe Wasson published Mr. Murphy's critique of the fight without cutting, editing, or putting it into "fancy, bighfalutin' words"—and received much favorable comment from his paper's readers for his thorough coverage of this important sporting event.

But deep in his secret literary soul, he told Andy, he wept.

CHAPTER THIRTEEN

The fund raised by public subscription to arm, mount and supply a group of volunteers to go Indian-hunting now totals $3000. At a recent meeting, the name "Ada County Volunteers" was chosen; Dave C. Updyke, former sheriff, was elected Captain of the group, Chas. Ridgely Lieutenant. Within the week, some 25 well-armed, well-mounted men will head for the Snake country under Captain Updyke's leadership.

Good hunting, boys!

—Idaho Statesman
Boise City, I.T.
February 27, 1866

As a matter of policy and civic good will, the law firm of Kimball & Creed donated $100 to the Indian-hunting fund. Though Councilman Creed privately told Armand Kimball they might just as well fling the money out of the upstairs office window, so far as killing Indians was concerned, the fact that they were being public-spirited in a generally approved cause might bring their firm some business and himself some votes. Yes, it was ridiculous to assume that a handful of untrained, undisciplined volunteers could in one brief expedition solve a problem that for three years had continued to worsen despite all the time, effort, and money the Federal government had expended upon it through its troops stationed in this part of the country. But the point was, public sentiment had been roused to such a fever pitch by Indian outrages in southwestern Idaho Territory action was demanded, a plan for action had been proposed, and any person objecting to it might as well go on record as also being against low taxes, hard money, and motherhood.

"This Dave Updyke," Kimball said. "Wasn't he arrested a few months ago and charged with misappropriating some Ada County funds?"

"He was. A thousand dollars of tax money he collected as Sheriff went into his pocket and never come out. He resigned his job, the District Attorney asked the court for a *nolle prosequi,* and Judge Kelly granted it. After all, the way our Territorial officials have been absconding with public funds the past few years, making off with a mere thousand dollars is too small a matter to bother with."

"He's a Democrat, I take it?"

"Naturally. Did you ever know a rough that wasn't?"

"It seems odd to me that a group of public-spirited volunteers would elect a man you call a 'rough' to lead them against hostile Indians in dangerous country."

"Your choice of words is not very apt, Armand," Creed said with a sardonic smile, "In the first place, these public-spirited volunteers are most all roughs themselves. They have been promised that in return for their services they will be given the horses, arms, and supplies with which they are being equipped. And those supplies, I'm told, include a substantial quantity of whisky. In the second place, you may be sure that their esteemed captain will give all hostile Indians a wide berth. In the third place, you may be positive he will stay clear of dangerous country."

"Well, if that's the case, why are the Volunteers being given such enthusiastic public support?"

"Because Captain Updyke's plan of campaign sounds like it will get results. He intends to ride south, he says, cross Snake River and bring the hostiles to battle in the Reynolds Creek area where they've been raising so much hell lately. With any luck at all, he brags, he and his bully boys should be able to kill forty or fifty redskins. Then they'll swing upriver and make a clean sweep of everything from Reynolds Creek to the Bruneau Valley, round up two or three hundred captives, and our Indian troubles will be over. Who would be skeptic enough to fail to contribute a few dollars to such a well-planned campaign as *that?*"

"You've attended all their meetings, I notice. Do you plan to go with them?"

"Oh, God, no!" Creed said, rolling his eyes at the ceiling in mock horror. "They've got my money. What would they want with me?"

According to reports appearing in the newspapers during the next three weeks, Armand Kimball noted with the concern of an interested investor, the Ada County Indian-Exterminating Expedition was getting along swimmingly. Captain Updyke had led his well-armed, well-mounted, well-supplied fighting men south to Snake River, crossed it, then had wisely camped for a few days while he taught his troops discipline by intensive drilling, marksmanship by grueling shooting sessions, and horsemanship by prolonged hours in the saddle. Ready now for any enemy, he had headed his column eastward with the firm intention of giving battle to the Bruneaus; however, messages hastily sent by Governor Lyon (who was trying to negotiate a peace treaty), Major Marshall (who with one hundred soldiers was guarding him), and by a man named Jennings (who was said to possess a petition signed by a large number of Owyhee district citizens begging the Volunteers *not* to shoot their peace-abiding Bruneaus), had persuaded Captain Updyke to turn his column in a southwesterly direction, toward the Malheur country, where it seemed more likely that *really* hostile Indians could be found.

The Ada Volunteers had ridden as far as the new Army post of Camp Lyon, it was reported, seeing no Indians, but had found Captain Walker and a contingent of Regular Army troops stationed there, who claimed they had things well in hand. Being refused a replenishment of ammunition and supplies by the penurious quartermaster, the brave but weary Volunteers had had no course left them but to turn about and come back to Boise City.

"The Ada Volunteers returned this week after being out twenty-four days without finding any Indians," reported the *Statesman*. "At present, all the Indians appear to be gone from the area . . . this is no fault of the Volunteers . . ."

Indeed, it was not, Councilman Creed agreed with a chuckle, and wondered aloud to Armand Kimball if Dave Updyke and his brave lads would take editor Jim Reynolds' sly comment straight or read a double meaning into it as he did.

As the days passed, indignant denials of Captain Updyke's recent war dispatches began to filter back to Boise City and tarnish the glory of the intrepid Volunteers. The expedition had never even *looked* for Indians, Reynolds Creek settlers claimed; there had been no messages sent from Major Marshall or Governor Lyon; there had been no petition signed by the Owyhee district citizens and delivered by Jennings; nor had the war party ever even moved off the sagebrush flat south of Snake River, upon which it had first camped, until it started the return trip to Boise City.

What actually had happened, it now appeared, was that the men had made camp, cleared a race track grounds on the sage-covered flat, and then had spent the next two weeks racing horses, shooting at marks, eating, drinking, and having themselves such a high old time that no hostile Indian could have bought himself a fight unless he had offered to pay them by the hour for it in gold. And then, when ammunition, food, and whisky were at last exhausted, they had come home.

"The rascals!" Kimball said indignantly. "They ought to be jailed!"

"Well, that's the way these things usually turn out," Creed said with a fatalistic shrug. "But Charley Davis is mighty sore. He gave them a good horse as his public-spirited contribution to the fund, he says. Now he's trying to get it back."

"Won't they give it to him?"

"No. Dave Updyke claims the deal was that all horses, rifles, and gear contributed were to remain the property of the Volunteers—win, lose, or draw. But Charley says there was no contest. He says he'll be damned if he'll stick to his end of the bargain when they didn't stick to theirs. He's bringing suit to get the horse back."

"I hope he wins."

"The cards are stacked against him, Armand. Outside of 'Honest' Rube Raymond, every man jack that was in that war party will swear to the truth of any story Dave Updyke asks them to tell. And Rube is only a kid. Sure, he'll tell the truth if given the chance—as he did to me last night—but what's his word worth against that of twenty-four grown men? He'll be scared to talk, I imagine."

Councilman Creed was wrong. Barely eighteen years old and so inexperienced in the ways of the adult world that he still believed all the simple maxims he had been taught at his mother's knee, "Honest" Rube Raymond was a lamb fallen by accident into a pack of wolves. He liked excitement; he had thought Indian-fighting would *be* exciting; he had volunteered and been chosen because he was always good for a laugh, for, no matter how outlandish a statement was made to him, his invariable reaction was to open his blue eyes wide, stare at the speaker and say naively, *Honest?*"

Thus his nickname, "Honest" Rube. Always good for a belly laugh.

But what he did in the justice of peace court did not strike the Ada Volunteers as very funny, for, when asked, he told the plain and simple truth, flatly contradicting the bald-faced lies of his former comrades. Oddly enough, the judge believed him and Charley Davis recovered his horse.

When Creed told Kimball what had happened, Kimball smiled and said, "'Out of the mouths of babes . . .'"

"Oh, hell, Armand! Don't you see what the poor boob has done? That crowd has no sense of humor. They'll tear him limb from limb, wait and see."

Shortly after nine o'clock in the morning, the day following the trial, Kimball was working alone in the upstairs law office when he heard voices raised in argument on the street outside. Getting to his feet and crossing to the window, which was open to admit the warm spring air, he saw a knot of men gathered on the boardwalk in front of a saloon on the far side of the street. One was Reuben Raymond;

another a professional gambler, Johnnie Clark, who also had been a Volunteer; the others all of the Updyke crowd.

". . . son-of-a-bitch . . . turn on me . . ."

"I just told the truth, Johnnie! The judge said he *wanted* the truth—!"

"You made liars of all of us!"

"But you fellows *were* lying, Johnnie! I was there and I know it didn't happen the way you told it! When the judge said tell the truth, what else could I do?"

"You stupid, wet-nosed bastard! You could of said you didn't remember—"

"But I *did* remember, Johnnie!"

"Then remember this, goddam you!"

Drawing back his right hand, Johnnie Clark slapped young Raymond sharply across his left cheek.

Kimball saw Raymond stumble backward against the saloon's front wall. The men in the crowd laughed. But their laughter ceased as suddenly as it had begun. For "Honest" Rube had clumsily pawed his Navy Colt out of its holster and was holding it leveled in a shaking, uncertain hand.

"Leave me alone, Johnnie! You've got no call to hit me—"

From his vantage point, Kimball saw Johnnie Clark hesitate as he stared at the gun, which Raymond was making no effort to cock, as if trying to decide whether the white-faced youngster would shoot or not. Apparently he decided in the negative.

"Pull a gun on me, will you!" he sneered. "Well, go ahead and shoot."

"No, Johnnie, I won't shoot. I just don't want to be hit no more."

Johnnie Clark pulled his own gun out of its holster, cocked it and aimed it at Raymond's chest. "Shoot, damn you!"

"No, Johnnie—"

"Well, if you won't shoot, I will—"

Armand Kimball told his law partner afterward that he heard Johnnie Clark's gun snap once, possible twice, as it misfired, with Raymond even then making no effort to cock and fire his own weapon. Then, taking deliberate aim, Johnnie Clark cocked and fired yet another time, the sound of an explosion shattered the morning quiet—and young Raymond sagged to the boardwalk.

Vaguely, Armand Kimball recalled exclaiming, *"Oh, my God!"*, wheeling away from the window, running down the stairs and crossing the street. By the time he reached its far side, the crowd of men gathered around the fallen youngster blocked off his view. He heard somebody calling for a doctor. He heard another man say, "Here's Eph Smith—let him through, boys, let him through." He heard Johnnie Clark saying plaintively, "He drew on me. You all seen that, didn't you? He drew on me. Didn't you see that?"

The crowd opened up to admit Dr. Ephraim Smith, a well-liked local surgeon, who bent down and examined young Raymond. It was only then that Kimball realized that his law partner, Councilman Creed, was the man who was down on his knees cradling Raymond's head in his arms. Creed's eyes as he looked up to meet Kimball's gaze were sick with shock.

After a moment, Eph Smith stood up, shaking his head. "He's mortally hurt, I'm afraid. Gentlemen, this is a dastardly outrage."

"Did you hear what he said before he passed out, Eph?" Creed said huskily.

"Yes, I heard."

"He said, 'It's a hard thing to be shot down like a dog for telling the truth.' Did you hear that, Eph?"

"Yes, Art—I heard. Give me a hand, boys. Let's get him inside. I'll save him if I can."

As the unconscious young man was carried away, angry mutterings against Johnnie Clark ran through the crowd. But before hands could be laid on him, a constable appeared, arrested him, and, surrounded by a number of his friends, hustled him off upstreet. Seeing his law partner still down on his knees, his trousers and hands stained with blood, his face white, his eyes blankly staring at nothing, Kimball went to him, put a hand under his armpit and said gently, "Come on, Art. You'll want to wash up."

Unresisting, Creed let Kimball help him to his feet, lead him across the street and up the stairs to their law office.

"Sit here, Art. I'll get you some water and a towel."

"He's only a kid, Armand," Creed said brokenly. "Johnnie Clark knew he wouldn't shoot. The bastard—the cowardly bastard!"

"Would a drink help?"

"No." Arthur Creed suddenly lowered his head and clasped his temples with both hands, a convulsive sob wracking his body. After a moment, like a man waking from a nightmarish dream, he straightened and said, "If that boy dies, Armand, Johnnie Clark will get what's coming to him. I'll take oath to that."

Without ever regaining consciousness, Reuben Raymond passed away a little before dark that day, which was Tuesday. Because of the intense feeling of the townspeople against Johnnie Clark and the rumors of vigilante action that were being heard in all quarters, the gambler—charged with murder—was hastily taken to Fort Boise where, with the commandant's permission, he was confined to the post guardhouse.

Not once during the next three days did Councilman Creed mention the shooting to Armand Kimball. Not once did he speculate upon the outcome of the gambler's upcoming trial. On one occasion when he, Jim Reynolds, Dr. Eph Smith, and Kimball were having supper together in the dining room of the Overland House and Reynolds bitterly remarked that no jury of tried and true Idaho men could be expected to convict a man whose victim had drawn his own gun first, Councilman Creed quietly put down his fork and leaned forward as if about to say something. Then his lips compressed, a veil dropped over his eyes, he lowered his head, and resumed eating.

Thursday morning, Creed told Kimball that he had to ride up to Idaho City and confer with a client there. He would likely be gone until Sunday, he said.

Saturday morning, while eating breakfast, Kimball heard that Johnnie Clark's body had just been found suspended from an improvised gibbet of three poles not far from the fort. Pinned to one of the poles, Jim Reynolds told him, was a notice which read:

No. 1.

Justice has now commenced her righteous work. This suffering community, which has already lain too long under the bane of ruffianism, shall now be renovated of its THIEVES and ASSASSINS. Forbearance has at last ceased to be a virtue, and an outraged community has most solemnly resolved on SELF PROTECTION.

Let this man's fate be a terrible warning to all his kind, for the argus eye of Justice is no more sure to see than her arm will be certain to strike.

The soil of this beautiful valley shall no longer be desecrated by the presence of THIEVES and ASSASSINS. This fatal example has no terror for the innocent, but let the guilty beware, and not delay too long, and take warning.

XXX

Councilman Creed returned to Boise City late Sunday afternoon. By then, the peak of the excitement had passed. Dave Updyke and his friends, who all day Saturday had been marching up and down the streets and in and out of the saloons swearing terrible oaths that *somebody* was going to pay for this, by God, when they found out who the right somebodies were, had decided that they needed a change of scene and had ridden eastward into the mountains near Rocky Bar.

The town had not been put to the torch, as threatened, though it had been deemed advisable by the authorities to double the number of night watchmen patrolling the streets and keeping an eye out for fires.

Creed told Kimball that he had advised his Idaho City client to settle his complaint out of court. He did not say who the client was, nor did Kimball trouble to ask him.

Tuesday morning, the *Statesman* published an account of the lynching. It read:

> . . . John C. Clark was confined in the post guard house with three other county prisoners. Between the hours of one and two o'clock Saturday morning a party of men, numbering from fifteen to twenty-five, attacked the guard on the outside and entered the guard house at the same moment, then threw them down, smothered and pinioned them, threatening them with death if they resisted, while others entered the cell where the county prisoners were and took Clark away. After all were gone, one of the guards loosened himself and then his companions and gave the alarm at the garrison, but it was too dark to learn what direction had been taken by the captors. All the men were disguised so that they could not be recognized by the guard or by the remaining prisoners in the cell. No other disturbance whatever occurred, and nothing unusual was observed in town till daylight, when Clark was found hanging as before mentioned. Sheriff Duvall took charge of the body and buried it during the day.
>
> From all the circumstances attending the case, there can be no doubt but there is a most effective and determined organization of "Vigilantes" in the community. The idea of taking the chances of overpowering the sentinels and guard at the post was a bold one, though at that time the men were all detailed on different expeditions, the officers all absent and not a sufficient number of men to do garrison duty . . .
>
> In regard to the crime of Clark, there is but one opinion in the community and that is he was guilty of cold blooded murder. Saturday morning there were some rather intemperate "threats" indulged in by certain parties, particularly about burning the town and the like, but nothing more has transpired . . .
>
> The threats with which grand juries and trial juries have been menaced in the investigation of criminal matters in this county, have been such that no good citizen felt it to be safe for him to act in that capacity, while easy escape or Executive clemency set at defiance the execution of the law, even in the few rare cases of conviction. In this case a careful attention to the proceedings upon the preliminary

examination, leaves no room to doubt that there was a settled purpose on the part of a few to prevent his conviction, though as we have said before his guilt was undeniable . . .

If the Boise City readers of the *Statesman* sensed a certain firmness and warning in Editor Jim Reynolds' account of the Clark lynching and its aftermath, they were most discreet in their public comments. In Idaho City, the Democratic *World* published an editorial deploring "lawless stranglers," but carefully avoided mentioning Clark or Updyke by name. It was common knowledge around Boise City, Kimball knew, that before riding off toward Rocky Bar, Dave Updyke and his friend Jake Dixon had sworn that they could name at least ten "stranglers" and that before the week was out they intended to return and "get even." But it was also common knowledge that a group of men in no way connected to the Boise City Vigilante Committee had been watching Updyke and Dixon with suspicious eyes for a long while now, and, though he would make no comment regarding the Boise City Vigilante Committee, Councilman Creed was quite articulate in speaking of the other group.

"It's the Ben Holladay Stage Company people," he told Kimball. "Last summer, a band of road agents held up a Holladay stage in the Portneuf Canyon on the Salt Lake road, killed four men and made off with $75,000 in gold. The Holladay people kill their own snakes. They've got good reason to believe that Updyke and Dixon were in on that Portneuf affair. And that fool Updyke set fire to some stage company hay, a while back, just out of sheer cussedness. He knows they're after him. If he's got a lick of sense, he'll run fast and far."

But Dave Updyke had started running too late. Exactly one week after the *Statesman* reported the Clark lynching, the Boise City paper relayed the following to its readers:

MORE OF THE VIGILANTES—
UPDYKE AND DIXON HUNG

Mr. Dover and another gentleman arrived in town from Rocky Bar Sunday afternoon bringing the news that D. C. Updyke and Jake Dixon were hanging at Syrup Creek. Mr. Dover and his companion camped at Syrup Creek about dark on Saturday night, and had occasion to go down to the house, a short distance, and were surprised at finding no one living there, but Updyke suspended in the shed between the two houses. On the body was pinned the following card:

DAVE UPDYKE,
 The aider of Murderers and Horse Thieves.
XXX

The discovery had the effect to make their camp a lonesome one for that night. Coming on the next morning they learned that Jake Dixon was also hanging to a tree a few miles down the creek. They could not tell how long the bodies had been there. Justice Kline started yesterday for Syrup Creek for the purpose of properly disposing of them. Monday morning the following card was found posted on Main street, written in the same hand-writing as the one found on Clark a week ago:

DAVE UPDYKE,
Accessory after the fact to the Port Neuf stage robbery.

Accessory and accomplice to the robbery of the stage near Boise City in 1864.

Chief conspirator in burning property of the Overland Stage line.

Guilty of aiding and assisting West Jenkens, the murderer, and other criminals to escape, while you were Sheriff of Ada County.

Accessory and accomplice to the murder of Raymond.

Threatening the lives and property of an already outraged and suffering community.
Justice has overtaken you.
XXX

JAKE DIXON,
Horse thief, counterfeiter and road agent generally.

A dupe and tool of Dave Updyke.
XXX

All the living accomplices in the above crimes are known through Updyke's confession and will surely be attended to.
The roll is being called.
XXX

Purely as a matter of abstract speculation, Armand Kimball mused, he would have enjoyed the mental exercise of assembling all the bits of evidence which were common knowledge, adding to them a few more shreds possibly known to himself alone, applying to them practical formulas of space, time, and rates of travel, and then sitting down with his law partner and a bottle of brandy on an evening when they had nothing better to do and attempting to figure out by deductive reasoning exactly what had transpired and who had been involved in it.

But he never did so. Abstract speculation, he gathered, was a mental exercise that Councilman Creed abhorred, these days.

Chapter Fourteen

LETTER OF RECOMMENDATION
FOR A TRAMP PRINTER.
He is too lazy to earn a meal and too mean to enjoy one. He was never generous but once, and that was when he gave the itch to an apprentice boy. Of his industry, it may truthfully be stated that the only time he ever worked was when he mistook castor oil for honey.
—Joe Wasson
Owyhee Avalanche
Ruby City, I.T.
October 28, 1865

To endure life in a western mining town, Joe Wasson firmly maintained, a sense of humor was a vital requirement for survival to any newspaper editor. If that were so, he certainly was well equipped to survive, for no event that occurred in the Owyhee district was so trivial or so important that it could not be turned into an outrageous pun or a barbed quip by his facile pen.

When a subscriber three months in arrears complained that his paper had been delivered at his doorstep too damp to be read, Joe Wasson blithely replied: "That's because there's so much due on it."

"Crime seems to be catching," he wrote, in needling the laxity of local law enforcement, "but our officers are catching less of it than they should."

"A strong wind caused some damage up in the Flint district last week," he solemnly reported. "Our correspondent says it was so violent it blew away a basement, a mine shaft and two wells."

When Lewiston citizens, disgruntled over the loss of the Territorial capital to Boise City, threatened to join up with equally unhappy eastern Washington residents and form a new Territory of their own, he applauded, saying: "If they can stand a Territorial government of their own, let them have it.

In dull times, he conducted a Social Etiquette and Problem Advising Service, offering to answer any question or solve any problem sent in by his readers in the columns of his paper. These were typical:

Question: "What does the polite host say when the Christmas goose he is carving slips off the platter and lands in the lap of the lady to his right?"

Answer: "Madam, I will thank you for that goose."

Question: "How does one make a realistic duck decoy out of a block of wood?"

Answer: "Whittle away from you."

He was an apt literary mimic, dashing out fake articles in the style of Horace Greeley, Mark Twain, Josh Billings, Petroleum V. Nasby, Artemus Ward, and other prominent literary lights of the day which sounded so genuine that readers never detected the forgeries until Joe Wasson himself chose to admit them. Once, when invited to fill in as guest editor for two weeks on a Nevada paper whose vacationing publisher was a rabid Republican, Wasson wrote a final editorial entitled: **WHY I AM SWITCHING TO THE DEMOCRATIC PARTY,** signed the absent publisher's name to it, left town, and, from a safe distance, chuckled fiendishly over reports of the near-riot with which the formerly loyal subscribers greeted his publisher friend upon his return.

At times, his editorial comments stung more than they amused. Men chuckled when he wrote: "Stolen from Jim Reynolds' desk, one loaded pistol; if the thief will return same, he will be given its contents, Jim says, with no questions asked." But neither the outraged judge nor the offended jurors smiled when; in reporting prolonged deliberations following a local trial, Joe Wasson wrote: "At press time, it is rumored that the jury has agreed—to send out for another half gallon."

Well acquainted with the editor's wry sense of humor as he was, Andy Hale did not know whether Joe Wasson's cryptic note, dropped off by a northbound stage one day in mid-February, was in jest or in earnest. It read:

Dear Andy: Toot the whistles, ring the bells—your Indian problems are about to be solved! A "War Meeting" of all tried and true "Redskin Renovators" is scheduled for Wed. Eve, next, 7 p.m., Challenge Saloon, Silver City. Come early, come empty—and verily, ye shall be filled! Don't fail me, friend.

Yrs.

Joe.

Deciding that if there was one thing in this world that Joe Wasson would not joke about it was the Indian problem, Andy decided to go up to Silver City and see what was in the wind. Leaving Levi behind to keep an eye on the ranch, he rode up the trail, next day, finding it clear of snow on the lower slopes following the recent spell of mild weather, muddy but passable across the ridge, and, higher up, a sloshy, messy mixture of sodden, packed snow and ice the rest of the way on to the mining settlements, which he reached in time to share a drink and an early supper with Wasson before going to the meeting. As they ate, he asked the editor why the meeting had been called and who had called it.

"Some of the boys got to talking," Wasson answered. "Times are dull, spring is just around the corner, a man feels an itch he can't get at to scratch—so why not go chase some Indians?"

"If that's all it amounts to," Andy said disgustedly, "I'm wasting my time here. We've lost thirty head of cattle to the thieving devils since last fall. I don't want them chased—I want them caught."

"Badly enough to go after them yourself?"

"Under certain conditions, yes. But I'll not ride off on a wild goose-chase with a bunch of saloon roughs, Joe. Chasing an Indian is easy. So is killing him, once you drive him into a corner and wear him down. But the thing in between—catching up with him so that you *can* corner him—that's what takes some doing. And time. And horseflesh. And guts. How well equipped in these things are the bully boys that are meeting tonight?"

"A fair question, Andy. Let's go find out."

The only thing they had found out at the first War Meeting, Andy and Joe agreed over a late nightcap afterward, was that the bully boys knew how to organize. In admirably democratic fashion, Mr. Miller called the meeting to order, Mr. Tregaskis was elected president, and Mr. Whitcomb was chosen secretary. A committee of five men was appointed to collect money and provisions; another committee of five was appointed to collect arms; still a third committee, this one of twenty-five men, was appointed to collect horses to be used in the expedition; Mr. Sinclair and Mr. Lytle were appointed enrolling officers; Mr. Bloom was appointed treasurer; and Mr. Bohannon was named special emissary to Boise City, where his primary duty would be to solicit aid, comfort, approval, and support from the governor.

As an afterthought, it was unanimously resolved that Boise City and Idaho City residents be invited to cooperate with the company.

During the meeting, Andy had made no comment, even though, as the only ranch owner present, he might have been expected to make one when it was resolved: ". . . that any one who has lost stock of any kind can have it by going out with this company and capturing it, but not otherwise . . ." Puzzled by his silence, Joe Wasson asked him afterward why he had not spoken.

"My cattle are my cattle," Andy said grimly. "When I run into a man herding along a steer with my brand on it, I'll shoot him if he stole it or thank him if he's bringing it back to me. I'd expect him to treat me the same way. But for a bunch of townspeople to say I've got to join their party to get back what's already mine is a thing I won't swallow."

"You're not enthused by what you saw and heard tonight?"

"Sounds to me like they've got their minds set more on loot than they have on Indians, Joe. But I'll give them the benefit of the doubt. Let them talk it up around town tomorrow, like they say they want to do. We'll go to their meeting tomorrow night and see what develops."

A few minutes after 7 P.M., next evening, President Tregaskis called the meeting to order. "The first order of business," he announced, "will be the treasurer's report. Mr. Bloom, are you prepared?"

"I am, Mr. President."

"Read your report, please."

"Well, what it amounts to," Mr. Bloom said, squinting down at the sheet of paper in his hand, "is we've got a lot of people that say they will help. What it foots up to, in round numbers, is 'leven hundred and forty dollars."

"In cash, Mr. Bloom?"

"Oh, no, Mr. President! What I've done is to get the merchants to promise fifty dollars worth of flour, say, a hundred dollars' worth of rifle cartridges and so on. Even the Chinks offered blankets—"

"Be sure an' git mine fumigated first!" a voice called from the back of the room. "Damned if I want my native Idaho graybacks mixin' with heathen Chinese lice!"

"Order, please!" President Tregaskis said sternly. "So you have translated the subscribed supplies into terms of retail prices, Mr. Bloom. Is that what you're saying?"

"Yes, Mr. President. It comes to 'leven hundred and forty dollars."

"Thank you, Mr. Bloom. It's good to know that the community is so solidly behind us."

A general round of polite applause was given the community, then the meeting got down to the serious business of discussing how the Indian-fighters would be chosen and what their rewards would be. Each man present, it appeared to Andy, had definite opinions on these two subjects and meant to make himself heard if it took all night. After a great deal of loud, sometimes rowdy discussion, the following resolutions were adopted:

1. That three men be appointed to select twenty-five men to go

Indian hunting ... and that all chosen shall receive a nominal sum for all scalps that they may bring in ...
2. That for every buck scalp be paid one hundred dollars, and every squaw scalp fifty dollars, and twenty-five dollars for anything in the shape of an Indian under ten years of age.
3. That the Chair appoint three men to pick out the twenty-five ... the Chair appoints Messers. Massey, Brown, and Mills.
4. That each scalp shall have the curl of the head, and each man shall make oath that the said scalp was taken by the company.
5. That Mr. Massey act as temporary Quartermaster.
6. That this meeting adjourn to meet at 7 o'clock tomorrow night."
—(Signed) G. O. Whitcomb, Sec'y.

From the Challenge Saloon in Silver City to the office which housed the *Owyhee Avalanche* in nearby Ruby City, the distance was a mile or more, the night was dark, the air cold, and the trail filled with frozen slush so chopped up by heavy traffic that walking was difficult. But neither Andy nor Joe Wasson minded the walk; both felt a need for some fresh clean air and exercise after the smoke, stuffiness, and noise of the crowded meeting room. Opening the door of his office and lighting a lamp, Joe Wasson pulled a bottle of whisky and two glasses out of a desk drawer, poured drinks, then sighed and shook his head.

"Sorry, Andy. I'm afraid that wasn't a very productive meeting."

"Did you expect it to be?"

"One can always hope. One shouldn't. But one does."

"I'm no Indian-lover, Joe—you know that. But I'm not going to kill a man just because he's red. If he's a thief and stealing my property, all right, I'll shoot him down. But to my way of thinking, any white man that would put a bounty on *all* Indians and ride out collecting scalps is pretty good for nothing."

"It made me sick to my stomach, too. But what are we going to do, Andy? What are we going to do?"

Andy shook his head and admitted he did not know.

In the columns of the *Avalanche,* Joe Wasson dutifully reported the continuing meetings, resolutions, and doings of the Owyhee Indian-hunting party, even as Jim Reynolds was relating the activities of the Ada Volunteers, which were now reported heading for Snake River, but in his own inimitable way Wasson made it clear he did not approve. "We've not talked with any one," he wrote, "who believes the present 'ebullition of unfriendly temper' of the whites will produce a single scalp ..."

Down in the ranching country just over the ridge from Andy and Levi's cabin, fifteen Indians attacked a group of white men, wounded one of them seriously, burned ten tons of hay and made off with thirty-nine head of cattle and horses. Lieutenant Pepoon, stationed at Camp Lyon, immediately set out with a detachment of infantry in pursuit of the raiders but saw nothing of them but their tracks. A few nights later, a band of Indians said to number twenty-five attacked the Osgood and Inskip ranch on Cow Creek, besieging the owners and several travelers that chanced to be stopping there overnight from eight P.M. until three o'clock the next morning before setting fire to everything burnable and driving off a number of horses and cattle. Judging from the length and ferocity of their barrage, the Indians seemed to be well supplied with rifles and ammunition; it was believed that a loud-mouthed chief, whose voice had suddenly been stilled during the exchange of shots, had been wounded or killed during the fray, though no body had been found afterward. Captain White and thirty soldiers arrived at the scene, next day, "too late to effect any efficient pursuit."

A day later, David P. Brown and Moses Mott, driving a wagon pulled by two yoke of oxen up the long grade northeast of the Owyhee River ferry, were suddenly attacked and killed by an undetermined number of Indians.

"Brown's whiskers were cut off," the *Avalanche* reported, "and his head mashed with rocks. Mott's head was beaten into a jelly and his heart cut out and carried off . . ."

Meanwhile, Andy noted as he followed the wanderings of the scalp-hunting party of whites through accounts of its movements in the weekly paper, its efforts were producing just about as many topknots as Wasson had predicted they would:

". . . the volunteers arrived at Osborn's Ranch on Cow Creek on the 20th. Remained till the 23rd, when they moved to Lockwood's Ranch. Next day to Hall's. By shrewd rustling they secured six horses to pack their grub and blankets, and next morning started for the Forks of the Owyhee. Reached and crossed the North Fork just above the junction of it and the Middle Fork. Followed up eighteen miles to the mountains. Crossed back to the North Fork and scoured the country up to the mountains in that direction. Would have crossed to the Bruneau, but could not pass over the snow. Found where eighteen to twenty cattle had been killed. Returned by nearly same route as traveled out, saw and pursued some redskins, but could not reach them on foot . . .

". . . each morning by 8 o'clock scouts were sent in advance and occupied eligible sites to view the country, and everything was done that could be done to find the rats. Captain and men were all anxious for a fight. The boys campaigned two weeks on foot. They waded streams of icy temperature and had no luxurious time. That they killed no Indians was not their fault. They are anxious to return—if horses can be obtained . . ."

Stopping off to spend the night at Andy and Levi's cabin on his return from a trip to Boise City, Joe Wasson said the situation was growing grimmer and more desperate every day. The expedition of the Ada County Volunteers had turned out to be even more of a farce than had that of the Owyhee Indian-hunting party. Major Marshall, the commandant at Fort Boise, seemed to be spending more time attempting to make treaties with already peaceful Indians than he did in chasing hostiles; there were ugly rumors floating around now that he was lining his pockets with money in the form of bribes from civilian hay, grain, and supply contractors, even as Boise City merchants were making a nice profit by surreptitiously selling arms and ammunition to the hostiles through so-called friendly Indians.

As spring faded into summer, it became increasingly evident that "Old Lady" Marshall, as the settlers now were contemptuously calling him, intended to continue in the same bumbling course he had been pursuing, despite any good advice he might receive. In late May, two traveling companies of Chinese, bound for the Idaho mines along the overland route from California, were attacked by a large band of Indians near the southwestern border of the Territory; of the one hundred unarmed Orientals that comprised the two companies, only five terror-stricken survivors escaped to tell the tale of their comrades' butchery. Near the scene of the massacre, a pair of Mexican packers also were killed. Emboldened by these successes, the Indians turned their attention to the Army itself.

"Major Marshall found the Indians five hundred strong on last Sunday at the Forks of the Owyhee," a field dispatch to the *Avalanche* reported. "Had a four hour fight, he on the west and the enemy on the east side of the river. Indians kept up a continuous fire with rifles— not an arrow was shot. Was at least two hundred and fifty armed warriors. Major is confident seven were killed and twelve wounded . . .

". . . military stock, grub, blankets, etc., were captured by the Indians; and one soldier, named Phillips, was killed, scalped, and dragged up a hill by a rope around his neck . . ."

"We threw five shells into the wickiups—could not say with what effect. Tried to cross the river with the howitzer; boat was capsized and went to the bottom, where it now lies. Will get it again. Would have crossed the river, but the Indians were so well armed 'twould have been madness and murder to have made the attempt, as the enemy were so numerous, well fortified and armed. Major's command lost one man next day; none wounded. Says he'll go after them continually; if he can't wipe them out this Summer, will go after them in the Winter and keep doing so till the job is completed. Says the party had about one thousand head of good horses which were driven up the middle fork of Owyhee . . ."

As Andy expected he would, Joe Wasson now went after Major Marshall with no holds barred. Addressing his editorial to the Commandant of the Northwest District, General Steele, in San Francisco, Wasson pointed out the folly of "keeping ineffective detachments of men from year to year at exposed points on the frontier, for it only emboldens the savages without accomplishing anything . . ."

"Major Marshall is now making a raid after the Chinamen murderers on the west side of the Owyhee," he went on in a none too subtle effort to show his contempt for the Fort Boise commandant while not condemning the troops under him. "If the Major overtakes them and is not overpowered, may the Lord have mercy on their souls—if they have any—for the troops will have none . . ."

Major Marshall and his troops did not catch up with the Chinese murderers, it developed, and soon quit the chase. When word drifted down to Owyhee that Major Marshall and Captain Collins had recently journeyed northward to Idaho City and were "spending a few quiet days" in the Boise Basin, Joe Wasson's fury knew no bounds. In an earlier interview with the major or and a fellow officer, one of them had made the statement that, while it was true the Army had not been successful in its recent campaign, it now had been "shown the road" to be followed toward eventual victory and soon would embark upon it. The officer who made that statement unfortunately possessed a speech defect which forced him to turn "r's" into "w's" in his anger, Wasson pounced on that as typical of the effeminate way the Army was pursuing its Indian policy. In a scathing article, he wrote:

"BULLY—'SHOW US THE WOAD'.— . . . it is so comforting to know that these two "Melican Chiefs" are spending a few quiet days in Idaho City while horses are being stolen by the score and men ruthlessly murdered in Owyhee. It is dangerous over this way and great captains should not imprudently expose themselves. The Major and Captain are sufficiently prudent. The former exhibited his caution in one of those celebrated retreats from the Owyhee, leaving a portion of his men and baggage behind, while the Indians were going the other way with greater alacrity. From a three weeks' careful inquiry, we are forced to the conclusion that the evening after the fight the battlefield lay midway between the contending armies—say from twenty to fifty miles from either. Lieutenant Pepoon was imprudent enough to want to go after the retreating savages . . . but the great design of the campaign was to "find the woad" and the Lieut. could not be gratified . . .

". . . the howitzer was safe at the bottom of the Owyhee River; could get that any time. The men who rashly rushed among the Indians could come back at their leisure—so they could. They found "the woad into the Indian country" and certainly could find it back again—reasoned the Major . . ."

Belatedly learning of the speech defect of the officer with Major Marshall, Joe Wasson apologized in print for having made fun of him. But he did not apologize to Major Marshall; instead, he implied that the major had been so frightened by the Indian fight, even though conducted at long range, that he had hastened as far from the scene as he could get and had sought protection behind the lines of the Boise City Vigilantes, whose hanging of Johnnie Clark, Dave Updyke, and Jake Dixon he had previously denounced so righteously.

In Ruby, in Silver, in Flint—in all the towns of the Owyhee district—the citizens now were roused to a fury of indignation and anger that demanded action. Hearing that the Army had sent sixty infantrymen equipped with thirty days rations to Flint, from whence they were about to embark on yet another Indian-hunting expedition, Joe Wasson caustically commented: "We have bought a big rooster cut on purpose to stick at the masthead when we record a victory over the Indians. Have not had an opportunity of using it yet. Would as soon trot it out in honor of a victory by Marshall as anybody. Let us hear of the victory."

Of all the ranchers, farmers, miners, and townspeople living in the Owyhee district, none had a better reason to cry out for revenge and do something tangible to bring it about than did the Chinese residents, of which there was now a sizable number working as menials in the towns and mining the less productive claims. Though regarded with contempt by the whites, the Chinese were intensely loyal to their kind. When a Catherine Creek rancher, Isaac Jennings—a man experienced in Indian-fighting and an able leader—offered to head a force of volunteers which would go after the Indians and "settle their hash once and for all," the Chinese were among the first to respond.

"... the Chinamen wanted to equip and send thirty of their countrymen," Wasson wrote approvingly, "but they were not accepted. They are, however, willing to aid all they can and have furnished thirty to forty good horses . . . Considerable money, equipment, and nearly a hundred men with thirty days rations are being assembled. Success and glory attend them . . ."

Andy knew and respected Isaac Jennings. Talking it over with a group of his rancher neighbors, he said, "Ike deserves our help. We can't all go with him, that's clear, for there'd be nobody left behind to look after our property and stock. But I'll go—"

"Me, too," Levi said.

Though his first notion had been that the Delaware should stay behind to mind the ranch, Andy nodded. The party could make good use of Levi's skills as a tracker, and their neighbor to the east, a family man, could keep an eye on their place as well as his own.

"Well, I guess you can count me in," another neighbor said. "Since the bastards burned my hay and stole most of my stock last week, I'm pretty much out of the ranching business anyhow."

"I'll go," a fourth man said. "I ain't got much left to lose, either."

Of the fifteen men present, six volunteered to join the Jennings party, while the others promised to do all they could to protect the community's property and stock while they were gone. Among this group of men as they rode up-trail, next day, Andy heard no boastful talk of collecting scalp bounties or sharing in the proceeds of the sale of captured stock and guns. Loot did not interest them, nor were they driven by any great desire for revenge. All they desired was to put an end to what had become an intolerable nuisance.

The towns of Ruby and Silver City had taken on the appearance of armed camps, Andy saw as they rode into them that warm early summer afternoon. An unusually large number of hard-faced men carrying rifles and wearing six-shooters filled the streets, suspiciously eying one another as they met and passed; on the higher ground along the foot of War Eagle Mountain he saw what appeared to be breastworks or forts, constructed in such a manner that they faced each other across an intervening space of several hundred yards, each manned by wary-eyed watchers.

"My God, are they scared of the Indians jumping 'em *here?*" a rider beside Andy said. "The red bastards must really be getting cocky!"

The forts and the heavily armed men had nothing to do with hostile Indians, Andy learned from Joe Wasson. This show of latent hostility was strictly between white men; but it was apt to explode into bloody warfare at any moment.

"It began as a squabble between two mining companies over a rich chimney of almost pure silver," Wasson said. "God knows who's right—the Poorman company or the Hays & Ray people. Lawsuits and injunctions have been flying right and left. Two months ago the court declared a ninety-day truce. Both companies were supposed to work their claims peacefully during that time; but both have imported paid gunmen, built forts around their mine shafts, and hired batteries of lawyers."

"I ran into Armand Kimball and Arthur Creed a little while ago. They seemed to be too busy to stop and pass the time of day."

"They've been retained by the Poorman people, I understand. Kimball tells me they're hoping to settle the fight out of court. But with all those gunmen around, anything could happen."

"Where is Ike Jennings?"

"He and his boys are outfitting in Flint. They'll head out from there tomorrow or next day. You're planning to go with them, I hope?"

Andy nodded. "Six of us are, yes. What kind of a crew has he got?"

"A capable one, from what I've seen of it."

"There's a company of Regulars camped near town, I hear. Will they go with us?"

Wasson shook his head. "I doubt it. Governor Ballard sent up several deputy marshals last week to try to keep order. My guess is he asked the Army to supply some soldiers to lend them a hand if it's needed. There's said to be millions of dollars at stake in this mine squabble, Andy. One side swears the other is trespassing; the other swears it isn't. One says it intends to take the law into its own hands if the court decision goes against it; the other says it's ready to fight, too."

"Sounds to me like we'll be safer chasing Indians than we would be hanging around here," Andy said dryly.

"You well may be," Wasson answered. "Good luck to you, anyhow."

It was the country itself that whipped you, Andy was beginning to realize; that, and the sheer cussedness of human nature. In the ten days that had passed since the Owyhee Volunteers assembled in Flint, one hundred strong, the casualty rate had been sixty percent, without a shot being fired. Ten days ago, one hundred men had answered roll call; this morning, only forty had responded. Well, maybe there hadn't really been one hundred ready, able, and willing Indian-fighters to begin with. Maybe a dozen or two of them had been bragging or drunk or both when they enlisted in Ruby, in Silver, and in Flint. Finding themselves riding into a rough, broken country shy on saloons and filled with trees and rocks behind which murderous Indians might be hiding, they were not long in discovering their horses were going lame, their guns were out of order, or their out-of-condition bodies were wracked by old ailments or incapacitating injuries that forced them to turn back now, much as they truly desired to go on.

Ike Jennings told Andy he was not in the least surprised. Hunting Indians in this kind of country punished the butt a sight more than it stimulated the spirits. It took patience; it took grit; it took time; it took a special kind of man.

"Ever hear of George Crook?" Jennings asked Andy.

"He was a Union general during the war, I understand."

"A damned good one, too. But when I first met him, ten, twelve years ago, he was just a young peckerwood lieutenant fresh out of the East. Odd sort of fella, for an Army officer. Didn't drink, didn't smoke, didn't swear, didn't chase women, didn't even drink coffee. But, Godamighty, how he wore them Indians out!"

"Where was this?"

"In the Rogue River country down along the Oregon-California border. It's got more water than this country has but the mountains are just as bad as the Owyhees. So were the Indians, till Crook took after them. He just plumb wore 'em out."

"How?"

"Well, he went after 'em, stayed after 'em, and never gave 'em no rest. None of this damn foolishness of taking a week to ride out from a fort to where the Indians were, chasing around over the hills after 'em for a week, then riding back to the fort to resupply. He stayed right on their backs. Day after day, week after week, month after month—that was his style."

"What did his troops do for supplies?"

"Had 'em sent out to 'em. It was hell on his quartermaster, I tell you, and hell on the men and horses. But it was worse hell on the Indians."

"Is that the sort of thing you're hoping to do?" Andy asked.

"More or less," Jennings said, nodding. "We've got rations for thirty days. If we knock off a few Indians and recover some stolen stock, I'm hoping the people back in Silver, Ruby, and Flint will be encouraged enough to send out reinforcements and enough food and ammunition to keep us going for another month or two."

Give Ike Jennings credit, Andy mused, he was bulldog-tenacious and tough as the heel of a boot. What he said made good sense. But even with the braggarts, the weak-spined and the slackers gone from the ranks, grumblings were increasing among the Volunteers.

In ten days of the hardest kind of riding, the company had managed to exchange long-range shots with only two small groups of hostile Indians. Each time, the Indians had gotten away unscathed, and the only stock captured from them had been half a dozen sore-backed, sore-footed, scrawny ponies. The Volunteers were getting discouraged. But Jennings was not.

"Where there's bees buzzing, there's bound to be a hive near. Come mornin', we'll cross the divide and head down toward the Owyhee River. That's where the main camp is likely to be, I'm thinkin'."

Acting as advance scouts for the party were a white trapper named Daniel Pickett and an Indian called Bruneau Jim. The afternoon following the company's second exchange of shots with a small group of hostiles, Dan Pickett hurried back to Jennings to report that the trail of a large party of Indians had just been sighted.

"Seems to be a village on the move," he said. "Men, women, kids—the whole caboodle."

"Which direction are they headed?" Jennings asked.

"South. Bruneau Jim says there's a good camping spot about a mile ahead of us. They may be holed up there—he's checkin' now. If they ain't, he figures they'll cross the Owyhee at a ford just down the ridge, then head upriver into the mountains southeasterly."

"How many would you guess are in the band, Dan?"

"Godamighty, Ike, there's a hell of a lot of 'em. Four, five hundred, maybe. We'd best go easy."

Earlier in the campaign, Andy recalled, the campfire arguments among the Volunteers had dealt not with the question of whether one white man could whip one Indian in a fair fight but whether it was not reasonable to assume that *any* white man could take on five, ten, or even fifteen Indians any time, any place, and come out winner. But no such arguments were heard now.

"Five *hundred!*" a Volunteer muttered hoarsely. "Why, hell, boys, this must be the bunch that whipped Major Marshall's ass!"

Yes. And Major Marshall's command had been made up of Regulars. It had possessed a howitzer. Yet a soldier had been killed, scalped, and dragged up a hill, Army stock and supplies had been captured, and the soldiers had suffered a stinging defeat. At least two hundred and fifty of the Indians had been armed with rifles, it was said, whose fire had been "murderous . . ."

Jennings halted the company and ordered the men to dismount, spread out, and seek whatever cover they could find while further reports from the advance scouts were awaited. Presently Bruneau Jim rode back with word that the Indians had camped at Twin Springs Basin last night, then had moved on down the slope to the Owyhee ford and crossed the river. The sign, he said, was only a few hours old. He suggested that the Volunteers camp at the springs, which were located in a good defensible position on high ground surrounded by broken lava rock, until a more thorough scout could be made of the country ahead.

"Good idea," Jennings said, nodding.

A ride of a mile or so brought the Volunteers to the Twin Springs Basin campsite. It was indeed a place well adapted to defense, Andy noted approvingly. Surrounded by a slightly higher rim of jumbled volcanic rock, the circular, sunken basin contained two springs of pure, cold water, a hundred or so feet apart, each of which was screened by clumps of willows. In all directions, the terrain sloped downward away from the rise of land on which the basin set, was devoid of trees, and offered little cover to an attacking force.

While Dan Pickett, Bruneau Jim, and Levi prowled the flat plateau and the rock-strewn slope which lay between the camp and the Owyhee River ford—which was the only feasible crossing place for miles upriver and down—the Volunteers rested in the welcome shade of the twin clumps of willows. The men were too tired to move about or indulge in their usual horseplay. One of them, a tall, thin, quiet-mannered man named Tom Caton, sat near Andy with his feet folded under him Indian-fashion, intently writing in a notebook. Andy teased him good-naturedly.

"Keeping a diary, Tom?"

"Sort of."

"What do you write about?"

"Oh, just the usual things. What the country looks like, how far we come, what we do and see."

"Going to make a book of it some day?"

"Lord, no," Caton said with a smile. "I don't expect anybody to read it but me and my children—if I ever have any."

The afternoon was warm and Andy was feeling drowsy. "Well, if we catch up with those Indians tomorrow," he said with a yawn, "maybe you'll have something really exciting to write about."

It could be seen plainly enough, Dan Pickett, Bruneau Jim, and Levi agreed, next morning, that the main body of Indians had ridden down the slope to the river and crossed it early the previous day. From the search the three scouts had made over the near slope yesterday afternoon, they were confident that no Indians had been concealed there then; still, it behooved the Volunteers to move cautiously now, for any number of hostiles could have recrossed the river during the night.

"Oh, hell, I'll bet we don't see another Indian this whole trip!" a Volunteer grunted skeptically. "Come on, boys, let's ride down to the ford."

Followed by two companions, the man boldly spurred his horse and led the way down off the high bluff upon which the company had halted. Jennings made no effort to stop them. The truth was, Andy knew, Jennings was getting tired of giving orders to men as independent-minded as these were, for they obeyed them only when they felt like it.

The morning was quiet; too quiet. Taking a pair of field glasses out of his saddle bag, Andy lifted them to his eyes and scanned the steep slope on the river's far side. It lay in shadow; a shadow intensified by the darkness of the lava rock. His searching eyes, adjusting to the dim light, caught a flicker of movement among the scattered bushes and rocks covering the far slope. A bird, perhaps, or an animal. No, by God, it was a man!

"Ike!" he said urgently.

"Yeah?"

"That slope yonder! It's crawling with Indians!"

"I see 'em, Andy. My God, they're thicker'n fleas on a Digger's dog!" Cupping a hand to his mouth, he shouted down at the three riders, "Git back here, boys, git back! There's Injuns—"

Rifle fire suddenly crackled from the far side of the river. Slugs kicked up gouts of dust below and above the riders. In sudden panic, they spun their frightened horses around; a hail of bullets sought them out as the horses clambered frantically up the slope to the bluff upon which the rest of the company had paused. Miraculously, neither horses nor riders was touched.

Howls of derision came from the hostiles hidden among the rocks and bushes of the far slope. Turning to Bruneau Jim, Jennings asked, "Is that Paiute jabber?"

"Yes."

"Can you talk it?"

"Sure."

"Well, tell 'em they're yellow-bellied bastards! Tell 'em to come across the river and we'll give 'em a fight they'll never forget! Tell 'em—"

Inviting the Indians lying on the far slope to cross the river and fight proved to be a completely unnecessary courtesy, Jennings suddenly learned. For the Indians themselves had planned this party—and planned it well. Now that the force lying in ambush on the far slope found its presence discovered, a second force—this one numbering seventy or so hostiles—came pouring out of the ravine on the near slope, in which it had been lying hidden, and charged the Volunteers in a flank attack.

Jennings kept his head. So did the Volunteers. At their leader's order, the men slid out of their saddles, turned their horses over to previously designated holders, knelt behind what sheltering rocks they could find and unloosed a volley of rifle fire that forced the charging band of Indians to swerve aside while still beyond effective range.

"We can't make a stand here!" Jennings cried. "Fall back to the springs! You horse-holders lead the way! Stay between them and the Indians, boys! Keep movin' but don't break and run!"

It was a fortunate circumstance that the terrain lying between the bluff and the site of last night's camp was reasonably flat and open, Andy realized, for, as the small group of whites moved across it, they were able to protect the horse-holders and keep the shouting, circling band of Indians a comfortable distance away. On the several occasions when the hostiles did venture too near, well-placed rifle slugs made them regret their boldness.

Without serious casualties, the company successfully made its way back to the previous night's camp site, secured the horses in the shelter of the willow clumps, then hastily began strengthening defensive positions by piling up loose rocks in front of improvised rifle pits. By now, the Indians that had been lying in ambush on the far side of the Owyhee had forded the river and joined the siege of the sunken basin. Ike Jennings had chosen his spot well. His men and animals would not suffer for water here. This being the highest point of land in the vicinity, there was no way the Indians could get above the Volunteers to fire down into their camp. All the same, the situation was grim, Andy realized, for the hostiles numbered in the hundreds, seemed to be well supplied with rifles and ammunition, and help for the whites was far, far away.

After posting riflemen around the interior rim of the basin to ward off attacks from all quarters, Jennings directed that the saddle and pack horses be crowded into the larger of the two clumps of willows, while the smaller be utilized as a storehouse for the company's provisions and a shelter for its cook. To his warning to all the men that they must lie prone and move only on their bellies, the cook—a Dutchman—wryly responded it was "Gotdam liddle cooking" he could do lying flat on his stomach. But food, right at this moment, was the least of the Volunteers' worries.

As the day slowly passed, the Indians appeared content to make a prolonged siege of it, sniping from long range at anything that moved, concentrating their fire on the willow clump containing the horses in hopes of picking them off one by one. By evening, two of the animals had been killed and several others wounded. Of the Volunteers, one had been shot in the neck, another in the hip, and others had suffered superficial flesh wounds.

When darkness fell, Jennings withdrew the men from the rifle pits around the basin rim and put them to work building up a four foot high wall of rocks around an area sufficiently large to accommodate half the company, while at the same time three smaller fortified stations were constructed at strategic spots. Building a small fire, the cook prepared coffee and a meal. The men slept in shifts. By dawn, the outposts on the basin rim were again manned.

As daylight came and the Indians saw what had been accomplished during the night, they immediately opened up with a heavy volley of firing, again concentrating on the horses, but the strategically placed pickets on the basin rim answered in kind, keeping the hostiles at extreme range, and the bullets did little damage. By noon, the firing had dwindled down to sporadic sniping by both sides.

But the whites knew now that the Indians were in no mood to let their quarry slip out of the trap. In mid-afternoon, Jennings held a conference with Dan Pickett, Bruneau Jim, Andy, Levi, and the other Volunteer leaders. The way he sized things up, he said, the company could be pinned down here for as long as the Indians chose to maintain the siege. The Volunteers had plenty of food and water, but if the firing kept up at its present rate their ammunition would be exhausted within a few days. By his reckoning, Silver City lay at least fifty miles away to the north; few whites traveled through this part of the country; and the chance that friends or soldiers would hear of the company's plight and come to its aid was so remote that it need not be considered.

"We got to have help," he said bluntly. "Which means we got to slip a messenger through the Injun lines tonight. Dan, do you think it can be done?"

"Come dark, we can try."

"Afoot or a-horseback?"

"Got to be afoot, Ike. A horse'd make too much noise."

"Fifty miles is a mighty long walk, Dan."

"Well, a man can't make fifty yards a-horseback if he's dead."

Jennings nodded. "All right, afoot it'll be." His worried gaze circled the group. "I ain't ordering anybody to make the try. I'm asking for volunteers. Who'll go for help?"

"Me," Dan Pickett said. "I'll go."

"Me," Bruneau Jim grunted. "I'm a heap good walker."

"Me," Levi said.

"And me," Andy murmured.

"Two men's enough," Jennings said. "Dan, Jim—it'll be up to you. May the good Lord guide your feet."

To make sure that the men defending the basin stayed alert, Jennings had adopted the sensible system of having each rifle pit manned by a pair of Volunteers during the daylight hours, relieving them periodically with rested men. Around four o'clock the second day of the siege, Andy and Tom Caton, who had been napping in the shelter of the main fort, were wakened and ordered to spell the two riflemen stationed at an outpost some two hundred yards distant.

"Be careful," Jennings warned them. "There ain't much rock to hide behind up there."

Indeed, there was not, Andy agreed after he and Tom Caton had wormed their way up the incline to the rifle pit through the hot dust and sent the tired, thirsty watchers there snaking their way back to the main fort. Lying prone behind the foot-high pile of rocks, a man had shelter enough, but the rifle slugs that frequently whined past uncomfortably close overhead or thudded into the rocks in front gave ominous warning of what might happen if a person raised up. Two hand-sized gaps had been left in the pile through which rifle barrels could be thrust and fired, but with a long siege expected and ammunition limited, Andy and Caton agreed there was no sense in shooting unless they were sure of hitting a live target.

Save for occasional quick looks through the peep-holes to make sure no Indians were working their way up the slope, the two men lay quietly behind their shelter, too engrossed in the task at hand to waste breath in idle talk. The day was hot. Not a whisper of breeze stirred, not a cloud marred the sharp blueness of the sky, and the sun, though dropping downward now toward the western horizon line, seemed to be losing none of its heat.

For the past half hour or so, the hostiles besieging this quarter had not fired a shot nor had Andy or Tom Caton seen any suspicious movement on the slope below. Rolling over on his left side, Tom Caton stifled a yawn.

"Do you think they've given up?"

"Likely they're just resting."

"Well, sing out if you need me," Caton said, fishing his notebook and pencil out of his pocket. "I might as well put my time to some use."

A cool customer, Andy thought as he watched Caton open his notebook and begin writing in his neat, precise hand. He asked curiously, "What are you writing now, Tom?"

"A story I heard one of the boys telling about Chief Big-foot."

"Oh, hell, you don't believe *that* nonsense!"

"Nonsense?" Caton asked, glancing up. "Don't you believe there is such a person?"

"A lot of people swear they've seen him. He's a giant, they say, strong as a bull and big as a barn. They say he's organized all the hostile Indians in this part of the country and is going to keep them fighting till he's wiped out the whites to the last man. They say he's part white himself but turned renegade because another man stole his sweetheart."

"Interesting, if true," Andy said, shaking his head. "But I won't believe there is such a person till I see him with my own eyes."

"Why not?"

"Because I think I know where that Chief Bigfoot fairy tale started," Andy answered. "And I'm reasonably certain that the man who inspired it has been dead for three years."

"Was he Indian or white?"

"Something of both. He called himself Will Starr. He came west with us in—"

In the late afternoon stillness, a sound beyond the protecting rock barrier made him suddenly break off and gaze out through the peephole. Something had moved out there. Something . . .

Beside him, Tom Caton rolled over, came to his hands and knees, then raised his head and gazed curiously down the slope. It was purely an unconscious act, Andy felt sure, the unthinking act of a man untrained for warfare who momentarily had forgotten where he was. Andy reached out to pull him down. But before he could do so a rifle shot sounded. And Tom Caton, shot squarely in the center of his forehead, dropped face down on the open notebook in which he had been writing.

There was nothing to be done for him, Andy saw. Nothing at all. Taking the blood-soaked diary out from under the dead man's face, he wiped its pages as clean as he could on his trouser leg, put it in his pocket, turned the corpse over so that it faced away from him, then resumed his place at the peep-hole, seeking but not finding the Indian that had fired the fatal shot.

Poor Tom! Who'll keep your diary now?

As twilight fell, Levi crawled up the slope bringing orders from Ike Jennings to abandon the outpost for the night. No sense taking a chance of being cut off, Jennings said. What will we do with Caton's body? Well, it would be a chore to drag it two hundred yards while snaking along on our bellies. A corpse in camp would not be a cheering thing to the besieged men there. And Tom Caton is past being hurt now.

"All right, we'll leave him here for the time being," Andy said. "Let's go."

FIFTY MILES FROM SILVER CITY
July 3, 6 P.M.

Messers. Tregaskis, Minear, and other friends:—We are in a very critical condition. Now, gentlemen, if you can relieve us, in the name of God, do so. We shall intrench tonight. Indians have us completely surrounded. Five of our men deserted us in the morning before we saw any Indians. We have had one of our men killed and two wounded. Thos. B. Caton was killed while holding a rifle-pit. Aaron Winters was shot in the neck. Charles Webster received a flesh wound in the side. The most of the men have been shot through the clothing. We have fought two hundred and fifty well mounted Indians for two days and one night. We have but a meager amount of ammunition left. Bring Henry rifle cartridges and lead. We had two horses shot and several wounded. We have given up nothing to the Indians, but have captured ten horses from them. If we had one hundred and fifty good men, we could walk through this country.

Now, gentlemen, in the name of Heaven, send us assistance within 36 hours—if possible. There are but thirty-two of us all told. We have killed and wounded at least twenty Indians. Send us out some horseshoes and nails.

Unless you send the force required, not one of us can escape. Mount the men at Flint.

(Signed) *I. Jennings.*

PERILOUS SITUATION OF THE OWYHEE
VOLUNTEERS—CITIZENS GONE TO THE RESCUE.

—We were aroused at two o'clock yesterday morning by the steam whistles of the various mills, the ringing of bells, beating of drums and blowing of horns. Simultaneously with these alarms, Capt. Hinton, of the post at Flint District, and 0. R. Johnson made their appearance, bearing the fearful intelligence that Jennings and party were surrounded by Indians on the 3rd, and had been for two days, and that unless relief be at once afforded they must all perish. Ruby, Silver and Boonville, with one accord, sprung to arms and by eight o'clock some two hundred well armed and mounted men, with four or five days' provisions, started to the relief of their unfortunate fellow citizens.

Mr. Dan'l. Pickett, the messenger who brought the note from Capt. Jennings (published elsewhere), stole out of the lines on the night of the 3rd, in company with another, and were harassed by Indian scouts on the way, and thereby detained some twelve hours—otherwise relief would ere this have reached the brave little band of citizen soldiers.

May the God of battles rule in their favor and enable them to hold out until the rescuers come. And woe betide the red devil that lurks near the battle-field when they do come . . .

—*Owyhee Avalanche*
Silver City, I.T.
July 7, 1866

How many of the paid gunmen guarding the property of the two squabbling mining companies joined the rescue party was a fact he never accurately ascertained, Joe Wasson told Andy later. But this much he did know: a lot of their rifles and pistols went to battle with the citizen army whether the men themselves went or not. Public feeling saw to that. And public feeling forced Judge Cummins to declare a ten-day adjournment of the Poorman-Hays & Ray suit, which had reached a crucial point in court, so that attorneys, jurors, and witnesses could join the citizen group in attempting to relieve the besieged Volunteers. When the group left town, Wasson noted, there were no more than a dozen firearms left behind—a fact which greatly worried the stay-at-homes who feared an Indian attack but which must have contributed considerably to the efforts of the men working behind the scenes to effect a peaceful settlement between the feuding mining companies.

At any rate, by the time the excitement ended the Poorman and the Hays & Ray people had reached an amicable agreement.

But there was nothing at all amicable in the charges and countercharges that flew for weeks between rescued and rescuers, followers and leaders, civilians and soldiers, suppliers of arms, horses, and equipment and the men who had used them. Captain Hinton, who had marched the sixty soldiers under his command to succor the Volunteers, was ridiculed because he had taken only three days' rations along; thus, had been forced to forego chasing the fleeing Indians and had returned to his post without firing a shot. Captain Baker, at Camp Lyon, was praised because he had given the Volunteers every possible assistance, but no praise was directed toward Major Marshall, who still appeared to be spending "a few quiet days" far from the scene of battle.

As a group of fighting men, the Volunteers were generally lauded, though Joe Wasson did comment caustically:

". . . a very few experienced a weakness in the abdominal regions which resulted in giving their garments anything but a rose-water perfume. This occasion, like all others of the kind, only illustrated the old saw that 'the poorest wheel in the wagon makes the most noise . . .'"

With the siege broken, the Indians gone, and the Volunteer ranks swelled to one hundred and thirty men, Isaac Jennings insisted on continuing the campaign. Andy agreed to stick with him to the bitter end, though the truth was, he admitted to Levi, his heart wasn't in it.

"Criticize the Army all you like," he said, "fighting Indians is no job for amateurs. Sure, Ike Jennings is a good man. But he's got no hold on the people under him. Hell, how can you fight a war when every soldier insists on being a general?"

Ike Jennings played out his hand to the very last. For three more grueling weeks, he kept the Owyhee Volunteers in the field; but day by day he saw his command disintegrating as the men grew bored, grew weary, went home, argued over which trail to follow or which direction to ride, split up, quit—until at last he had no troops left to lead.

"Col. Jennings arrived from the Indian country yesterday," Wasson wrote in late July, "having been on the war-path since June 23rd. He has had from thirty to two hundred men with him, and no doubt has accomplished all that as many men could do in such a country with such a foe. They killed thirty or forty warriors and drove the remainder to the vicinity of Warner's Lakes, one hundred and twenty-five miles west of here . . . the recent expeditions have unquestionably been valuable to this region generally . . ."

If that were true, Andy mused bitterly upon returning home to find his cabin looted, his privy tipped over, his fences torn down, his haystacks burned, and a dozen head of his cattle missing, the "region generally" was demonstrating its gratitude in one hell of a nasty way. Because this was not the work of Indians; this was the work of white men.

"They've hit us all, Andy," the neighbor who had promised to look after his place said wearily. "Some say they're roughs just passing through; some say they're an organized band of looters and thieves. All I know is if I manage to catch 'em, they won't live long enough to make no long-winded explanations."

Andy felt dispirited and weary. Godamighty, what a pee-poor country this was to live in! He must have been out of his mind that day three years ago when he decided that here was the spot where he would put down his roots. Sure, the grass was here. But one winter out of every three, a man lost a goodly portion of his cattle to deep snow and bitter cold; every third summer or so a range fire destroyed a piece of his best grass. If a man planted a patch of garden, swarms of crickets moved in to devour it down to the last green sprig. Cattle got hurt, got drowned, got snake-bit, got bloated, got the scours, or just plain up and died out of sheer contrariness. When you had beef to sell, the bottom dropped out of the market; when you needed hay to pull your herd through a tough winter, its price soared out of sight.

If you stayed home to tend your ranch, murdering Indians took pot-shots at you. If you rode off hunting them, white roughs stole you blind—and pushed over your privy. Embezzling country officials made off with public funds; idiotic governors wasted Federal money; corrupt Army officers lined their pockets with the help of grafting contractors and dollar-grabbing town merchants; Legislators ignored the needs of the people who had put them in office and sought only personal gain...

"A pee-poor country!" he muttered aloud. "The pee-poorest country I ever saw!"

"Oh?" Levi grunted. "So what're you gonna do about it?"

"Go to bed," Andy answered. "Then tomorrow morning we'll set up that privy . . ."

CHAPTER FIFTEEN

Pity he has gone . . .!
—*Idaho World*
Idaho City, I.T.
July 28, 1866

"W. J. MCCONNELL.—This gentleman, who has been acting for nearly a year past as U. S. Deputy Marshal in this Territory, has left Boise City by stage for San Francisco. He plans to go East for an extended visit to his old home in Michigan. Marshal McConnell is a young man of talent, has made an excellent officer and possesses the confidence and respect of all who know him. He is an uncompromising Union man and we regret to lose such an estimable citizen. May his trip be prosperous and pleasant."
—*Idaho Union*
Idaho City, I.T.
July 26, 1866

"THE *UNION'S* SYMPATHIES.—A year ago when the Stranglers were making their raid upon the jail, W. J. McConnell was one of their leaders. Every Democrat then was only fit to be shot at. Mr. McConnell has left for the East and the *Idaho Union* cannot refrain from giving him his letters of recommendation . . .
He was indeed making an EXCELLENT OFFICER when he was organizing a band of horse and cattle thieves, bogus dust operators, abolitionists, Loyal Leagueists, etc. into a vigilante band for the purpose of hanging and shooting Democrats simply because they were Democrats . . ."

Publishing a frontier newspaper, Armand Kimball had come to realize, was a dangerous occupation. When a reader took offense at something the editor wrote, he never bothered to employ an attorney and seek financial balm for his wounded feelings by means of a suit for slander. He simply grabbed up his cane, horsewhip, or gun, headed for the newspaper office, and sought satisfaction in blood. Usually these affairs turned into confused brawls whose outcome both parties claimed as *their* victory; usually the insult given was intended and the reaction expected; and usually the parties involved were content to let the matter drop after tempers had cooled.

Still, on occasion, repercussions could be serious.

Councilman Creed liked to tell the story—perhaps apocryphal—of the newspaper editor over in Walla Walla who received a brutal horse-whipping from an indignant husband simply because he inadvertently left one little word out of a perfectly innocent news item. A Mr. and Mrs. Dunn, who lived a few miles from town, raised wheat on the dry land portion of their farm and strawberries on a small patch of bottom land down along the creek near their house, it being Mr. Dunn's task to take care of the grain-raising, while Mrs. Dunn tended the strawberries. Because of an extremely dry spring, the wheat crop had been an almost total failure, while the strawberries— which had been irrigated—produced abundantly and sold at a very good price. Justly proud of his wife, Mr. Dunn had bragged about her achievement to the newspaper editor; but when he saw the story in print, he picked up his horsewhip and headed for town. For the item's final line read:

". . . so Mrs. Dunn made more money off her little piece of bottom than her husband did off the whole farm."

The error made by H. C. Street, editor of the *Idaho World,* was not as innocent as accidentally omitting a four-letter word such as "land." His mistake was in assuming that by the time his attack on Billy McConnell was put into print, the Deputy U. S. Marshal would be hundreds of miles away. Instead, McConnell was still in Boise City, having been detained there several days past his originally scheduled departure time by lack of space on the San Francisco-bound stage. And his good friend, Rube Robbins, angered by Editor Street's blast at a man presumably too far away to defend himself, wasted no time in galloping downtrail from Idaho City and placing a copy of the paper in Billy McConnell's hands only minutes before the young man *was* due to get into the stagecoach and head south.

Billy McConnell reacted exactly as those who knew him well anticipated he would, Kimball heard later. His face turned red, then white; his eyes burned hot, then cold. He ordered his luggage removed from the stagecoach. He went to the Boise City office which he maintained as Deputy U. S. Marshal of the Payette District, wrote out a letter of resignation and handed it to Judge Milton Kelly. He secured a stout horsewhip, made sure his pistol was in good working order, saddled a horse, mounted, and then, accompanied by Rube Robbins and several other friends, headed up-trail for Idaho City.

His announced intention, so Kimball heard, had been to confront H. C. Street in the office of the *Idaho World,* demand an apology in person and in print, and, if not given it, to lash the editor from one end of town to the other and back again. But Street's friends made sure he knew McConnell was coming. Though the editor was far from being a coward, he raised no strenuous objection when a group of his loyal supporters armed themselves, appointed bodyguards to watch over his safety day and night, and swore that they would meet McConnell and his cronies in pitched battle in the Idaho City streets, if need be, to preserve the high principle of freedom of the press.

Observing how matters stood, Billy McConnell withdrew his forces to the Warm Springs Resort, just south of town, and, by courier, dared H. C. Street to meet him man-to-man and receive the horse-whipping he had so richly earned. Street politely declined. McConnell then sent a message asking if the editor were such a craven as to deny him satisfaction of any kind. Street replied that he was perfectly willing to give McConnell satisfaction; let each man name a representative, he suggested, who would discuss such matters as weapons and grounds.

After a prolonged period of negotiation, the weapons agreed to by both parties were single-shot Derringers at ten paces; the grounds, a sandbar on More's Creek downstream from Warm Springs; the hour, four a.m. of an August morning. Because both men knew that dueling was forbidden by law in Idaho Territory, it was further stipulated that strictest secrecy would be kept; that, in addition to the principals, only a second for each man, a friend of each man, a referee, a surgeon, and a gunsmith, who would load both weapons, would be present; and that, whatever the outcome of the duel, the matter would end there.

But, inevitably, the word got out. Hardware stores and gunsmith shops in Idaho City did a brisk business the day preceding the duel as Street's friends replenished their supplies of ammunition and made sure that their weapons were in tiptop condition. By midnight, at least a hundred determined, grim-eyed men had taken positions in the timber and on the higher ground along Moore's Creek, from which they could observe the duel, make sure fair play was done, and, if they thought their principal wronged, take appropriate action against the offender.

McConnell's friends were no less foresighted. In order to "avoid attention," the young ex-Deputy Marshal spent the night at the Warm Springs Resort, which, having recently gone into receivership, was now in charge of his friend, Deputy U. S. Marshal Rube Robbins. Long before dawn, the spa was surrounded by a hundred determined, grim-eyed Union men, who were also prepared to observe, make sure, and, if need be, take appropriate action.

Included in the list of overnight guests were two frightened, trembling young married ladies, who—despite their fears—managed to be up, dressed, and in a good vantage point on the resort's veranda thirty minutes before the fated hour.

Dawn was only a faint glow in the eastern sky when Billy McConnell stepped out onto the veranda. Noting the vague bulks of the uninvited watchers, he turned and called to the barkeeper inside the main room: "George!"

"*Yes,* Billy?"

"Better wake up the porters."

"Why, Billy?"

"Because you're going to do a landslide business in baths today," McConnell answered, chuckling. "The customers are lining up out here already!"

Down on the sandbar below the resort, the seconds were pacing off the grounds in the growing light, arguing heatedly with the referee over the way the land lay. As McConnell strolled in that direction, a friend called to him urgently, "Billy! Oh, Billy!"

"Yes, Dan?"

"I'm making you a gift of this horse. He's the fastest thing on four legs in Idaho Territory. There's a lunch and two loaded pistols in the saddlebags. If worst comes to worst, you hop on him and scoot—"

"That won't be necessary, I'm sure, Dan."

"Just in case, Billy, just in case. Look out for the point of timber a mile down the road. A dozen of the worst roughs in the country are waiting for you there. The sons-of-bitches have sworn to kill you, if you get out of this alive. Stay clear of that point of timber, Billy, and ride like hell—!"

Daylight had come by now, though the sun itself had not yet topped the hills bounding the east bank of Moore's Creek. Editor Street was waiting on the sandbar, backed by a second and a friend, and as McConnell approached with his own second and his own friend, the two antagonists nodded stiffly to each other. The surgeon was there with his black satchel of instruments and bandages; the gunsmith was there with the box containing the two identical single-shot Derringers, the powder, the bullets, the primers, and the loading tools. Although both weapons had been loaded the previous evening in the presence of the seconds, it was customary to fire the weapons in the presence of both principals, the gunsmith pointed out, just to make sure they were in working order.

"Very well," Street said, looking a trifle pale. "Fire away."

"By all means," McConnell murmured. "Shoot them off." The gunsmith raised the Derringer which Street had chosen, pulled the trigger, and the gun fired perfectly. He raised the weapon chosen by McConnell, pulled the trigger—and nothing happened. McConnell's second immediately protested that the Derringer had been tampered with; McConnell's friend hinted strongly that the duel should be called off, if the other side were going to indulge in such underhanded play as this. The gunsmith inspected the faulty Derringer, discovered that it had not been properly primed, drew its charge, reloaded both weapons, then announced that he was positive both Derringers were in perfect working order now.

It was now four-thirty and the sun had cleared the hills to the east. Position would be a matter of vital importance, the seconds saw, for the sandbar ran in an east-west direction, and whichever man faced the sun would be greatly handicapped, for he must stare directly into it. Well, there was only one way to settle the matter, McConnell and Street agreed. Flip a coin.

The coin was tossed. Street won. Naturally, he chose the position toward the east end of the sandbar. As McConnell took his place toward the west end of the sandbar, he squinted experimentally at his opponent, blinked, then looked away, shaking his head.

"Can you see him?" his second called anxiously.

"Not very well."

"Here," the surgeon said, stepping forward. "Wear my hat. It's got a big brim."

"Ah, that helps."

"Ready, Mr. Street?" the referee inquired.

"Ready."

"Ready, Mr. McConnell?"

"Ready."

"You will fire, gentlemen, when I count 'three.'" There was a long pause. "One. Two. Three!"

Mr. Street fired.

Mr. McConnell fired.

The seconds rushed forward to see if the principals had been hit. The friends rushed forward to assist the seconds. The surgeon stood ready to aid whichever man needed him.

"Are you hit, Mr. Street?" the referee asked politely.

"No."

"Are you hit, Mr. McConnell?"

"No. I suggest we reload and try again."

That was out of the question, both seconds protested. The friends of each antagonist agreed. So did the referee. An alleged insult had been given, he pointed out; satisfaction had been demanded; an opportunity for satisfaction had been supplied. That ended the matter. After all, gentlemen, it's foolish for two honorable men to stand on a sandbar shooting at each other interminably. Someone might get hurt.

"Shake hands, gentlemen, and let bygones be bygones."

The antagonists did.

Later that day, both Street and McConnell were arrested, charged with dueling, then released on bond. That their quarrel had ended quite differently than the Ferd Patterson-Sumner Pinkham affair of a year ago might have been attributed to the fact that a .41-caliber Derringer at ten paces was not a very dangerous weapon. Or it might have been that each man had deliberately aimed wide of his target. Neither would admit having done so, of course, even to his closest friend. Street did say he was glad no blood had been shed. And McConnell observed that the editor had conducted himself like a gentleman.

Then, next day, Billy McConnell rode downvalley toward Boise City.

During that ride, his friends said later, Billy McConnell thought long and he thought deep. Since coming to Idaho, he had wronged no man, he told them. He had done what he felt he had to do. But he had made many enemies, he knew, and, though he did not fear them, he realized that they would kill him if he ever once let down his guard.

He was weary of having to be forever alert. He was sick of violence. At the age of twenty-eight, bachelor life had lost its charms for him. There was a young lady in western Oregon with whom he had long had an understanding; he was lonely without her. He had hoped to bring her to Idaho, but he could not ask her to face what he knew *he* must face if he stayed.

The answer?

Yes, he was going away—for good. Not running away, mind you. Just going.

When Billy McConnell had disposed of the last of his property, he announced for the benefit of any of his enemies that might wish to drygulch him on the trail that he was heading east by stagecoach at a certain hour on a certain day. Instead, he rode west under cover of darkness the night before, bound for the Willamette Valley and a certain young lady . . .

Months later, word drifted back to Boise City that Billy McConnell had gotten married and gone into the ranching business down in Nevada. Would he ever return to Idaho? No, he said firmly, never.

"Don't you believe it," Rube Robbins said. "He'll come back some day. And he'll be a big man in Idaho, just you wait and see."

Chapter Sixteen

Down in Colorado, a Mrs. Throckmorton lately eloped from her husband, taking their three youngsters with her. She was thoughtful enough to leave him a note urging him not to mourn over the loss of the children, as none of them were his, anyway.

—Idaho Statesman
Boise City, I.T.
March 30, 1867

The woman sitting in Armand Kimball's private office was thin, plain, severely dressed in black, and obviously under great emotional strain. He had closed the door, as she had asked him to do, partially lowered the blind so that the mid-morning sun would not strike her veiled face, and placed her chair directly across from his desk so that she could speak without raising her voice. Yes, he said politely, he remembered her from wagon train days. Mrs. Smith, was she not? From Iowa. And her husband's name was . . . ah, Frank? Joseph?

"Jonathan," she answered, her lips a straight, tight line through the veil. "Jonathan W. Smith."

"Yes, I remember now. And you have four children, don't you?"

"Three. One died last winter."

"I'm sorry, Mrs. Smith. Now—what can I do for you?"

"Get me a divorce."

It was on the tip of his tongue to say that he never took divorce cases. In the first place, there was no money in them. In the second, the squabbles, the washing of dirty personal linen in public, the emotional turmoil in which an attorney inevitably became involved, were things he wanted no part of—for any fee. But this poor woman appeared to be under such a great strain that he found himself unable to give her a blunt refusal.

"Mrs. Smith, you're a deeply religious woman, I'm sure—"

"Don't preach to me, Mr. Kimball. Just get me a divorce. I'll pay whatever fee you want."

"It's not the fee, Mrs. Smith. What I was about to say was, have you talked this over with your minister?"

"No."

"I suggest you do."

"No. There's nothing to talk over. I just want a divorce."

"On what grounds?"

"He left me."

"When?"

"Three weeks ago."

"How do you know he won't come back?"

"Because he said he wouldn't. And I wouldn't take him back if he did. Not when he's become such a . . . such a monster."

Right here was the place to cut it off, Kimball mused wearily. He remembered Jonathan W. Smith from wagon train days; during the three years that had passed since the train had disbanded in Boise City, he had run into the man now and again on the street. A quiet man, a gentle man, a gaunt, stooped, somewhat sad-eyed man who always appeared to be a little tired and dispirited. He had told Kimball that he was farming ten miles west of town and barely managing to get by. There was so much to do and the children were too young to help. Ditches sprung leaks, fences fell down, cattle strayed, wind blew away the seed, a plague of grasshoppers came. But he worked on, a quiet man, a tired man, doing his best to get by.

That, at least, was the kind of man he appeared to be on the outside, and that was all Kimball cared to know about him. But in his wife's eyes he was a monster, and, if required to, she seemed prepared to prove it.

"Mrs. Smith, an absence of three weeks can hardly be called evidence of permanent desertion on the part of your husband. Even if he told you verbally in the presence of witnesses that he was leaving you and did not intend to support you and the children any longer, it would be months before you could obtain clear title to his property—which I assume you must have, if you and the children are to get by. My suggestion is that you wait a year—"

"I won't wait, Mr. Kimball. I want the farm. I want the children. I want a divorce—and I want it now."

Kimball sighed. "Did he go away with another woman?"

"No. It was worse than that."

"What *did* he do?"

"He went to town and got drunk. Then he . . . then he . . . then he wrote a letter, saying he was leaving for good."

"May I see that letter, Mrs. Smith?"

"Do you have to see it?"

"No. You can wait a year, as I've suggested. During that time, of course, you will not be able to sell the farm, which is in his name. If you feel you can stick it out for a year—"

The woman sitting stiffly upright on the far side of the desk betrayed her feelings only by the trembling of her hands as she opened the bag on her lap and took out a white envelope. She hesitated a moment, then gave it to him, saying in a choked voice, "I swore to God, Mr. Kimball, that no eyes but mine would ever read how this man has shamed me. I loved him once. He's the father of my children. But now . . ."

Feeling both pity and distaste, Armand Kimball took the envelope, withdrew the single sheet of lined paper, and read the pencil-written message scrawled upon it;

My Dearest Wife:
This is the hardest thing I've ever had to do in my life. I'm going away. By the time you get this letter, I'll be far away from you and you won't ever see me again.

I've done a terrible thing. You know how hard I've worked on the farm and how nothing ever seems to go right. It was getting me down more and more lately, working from daylight till dark, never catching up, never getting anywhere, but I kept on doing the best I knew how.

Last Saturday when I came to town, I met some friends and we started drinking. We drank all afternoon and evening and I guess I got awful drunk. Anyhow, that night, I went to a place where there were some women, and I spent the night there.

Now I've got a loathsome disease that I know will rot away my mind and body and kill me sooner or later. Knowing I have it, knowing what a terrible thing I've done, I can't come home to you and the children. So I'm going away and will never bother you again.

Take good care of the children.

Goodbye,
Jonathan

In silence, Armand Kimball folded the sheet of lined paper, replaced it in the envelope and handed it across the desk to Mrs. Smith, who quickly took it and put it out of sight in her bag. Without realizing he was doing so until too late to stop, Kimball took a handkerchief out of a coat pocket and wiped off his fingers, which suddenly felt grimy. He got to his feet.

"I'm sure the divorce can be arranged without any further embarrassment to you, Mrs. Smith," he said gently. "It should take no more than a week."

She stood up. "And your fee, Mr. Kimball?"

"There will be none."

"Thank you. I won't forget your kindness."

When she had gone, he went into the washroom adjoining his private office, poured water into a basin, soaped, scrubbed, and dried his hands, returned to his office, raised the window shade and stood for a long while gazing down at the traffic on the street below. Good God, he thought, what messes some people make of their lives! Yet they go on getting married, getting drunk, fathering children they can't support, whoring, squabbling, moving on, seeking pleasure in careless haste and repenting in miserable leisure.

Isaac Shelby and Beulah Baker were getting married next month, Beulah's father had told him last night. Well, that one might work, for Isaac apparently had settled down. A week ago, Melinda Belford and Sergeant Patrick O'Neil had finally tied their nuptial knot, though there had been some pride-swallowing involved on the part of Cornelius Belford, Kimball gathered, for he had long sworn that he would rather see his daughter dead than married to a man that was a foreigner, a Catholic, and a Yankee soldier. Kimball smiled. Poor Cornelius! He had never understood his daughter. Nor had he understood redheaded, hot-tempered Patrick O'Neil.

What had triggered the whole affair, apparently, was Belford's order to his daughter that O'Neil never come calling upon her again. If he did, Belford threatened, he would take a buggy whip to him and drive him from the house, for no foreigner, no Catholic, no Yankee soldier was good enough for *his* flesh and blood. This threat, of course, Melinda had quickly passed on to her boy friend—whom she had been coquettishly dangling on a string for a long while now—and he had reacted explosively.

Stalking into the Belford home during the supper hour without even bothering to knock on the door, he told Cornelius in no uncertain terms that: (1) he was not a foreigner but a naturalized American citizen; (2) he was not a Catholic, he was a Presbyterian; (3) he *was* a soldier, a damned *good* soldier, and damned proud of it; and (4) he hoped there was plenty of cream and sugar in the house and Belford's digestion was good because, by God, if Belford tried to use that buggy whip on him, he intended to break it into little pieces, cram it down his throat and make him eat it.

There was nothing Cornelius Belford could do but back water and say that this was all an unfortunate misunderstanding. But Sergeant O'Neil did not wait for apologies. Turning to Melinda, who was staring at him in open-mouthed awe, he declared that he was sick and tired of her shilly-shallying, that she was of age to get married, that if she couldn't make up her mind and say "yes" to him immediately, he intended, by God, to do his courting elsewhere—beginning right now.

And that had been that.

Well, Kimball mused, she got herself a real man. Which is what she's needed all along, whether she realized it or not. He'll make her toe the line.

Kimball's thoughts turned to his own wife. Every month or so Martha wrote him a long letter, filling page after page with tedious accounts of her dull, petty, endless social and church doings, passing on gossip about relatives and acquaintances he had never had the slightest use for, with only now and then a querulous question as to his doings and why he was staying so long away from St. Louis. Lately her questions had become more frequent and sharper. Cousin Robert had told her that he had disposed of a great deal of St. Louis property. Why? Was it true he had sold a waterfront warehouse and put the money into mining stock? Uncle Jack said mining shares were risky investments, these days. And the last time she'd been in New York, her brother Walter had told her . . .

Perhaps I should end it now, Kimball brooded. Simply, straight-forwardly, honestly. Give her enough property to keep her in a style not quite up to the style she lives in, so that she'll squeal a bit but not really be in want. Tell her I've left the Church. Oh, *that* will make her rave! Tell her I've divorced her. Tell her I've become completely heathen and Godless—no, by Heaven, I'll tell her I've turned Mormon and taken to bed three wives, all young, all pretty, all desperately in love with me—and all pregnant.

No. Even as he chuckled to himself, Kimball knew he could not do it that way. He did not hate Martha that much. He simply felt sorry for her in a vague, dispassionate way, even as he felt sorry for Mrs. Jonathan W. Smith. Somewhere along the course of years something had gone wrong. A man not cut out to be a farmer had become a farmer; a man not cut out to pioneer in a new land had attempted to do so; a man with no head for drink had gone into town on a Saturday afternoon and taken a few drinks with the boys to lift his spirits . . .

We wanted children once, Martha, but they did not come. That was long, long ago. And then we parted ways. You found your interests, I found mine—and they did not touch at all. We're past understanding each other now. So I take my pen in hand to write you a farewell letter:

My Dearest Wife:

This is to tell you I won't be coming home—ever again. You see, I went West with the boys one day and I met this wh—

No, I can't call her that, though in some respects she has all the attributes of the trade. She's blowsy, crude, rough and has a heart of gold. Silver, too, though it takes a lot of expensive crushing and separating equipment to refine that.

She can be brutal at times. She breaks men's bodies and spirits and doesn't give a good goddam. She's not intelligent, not cultured, not polished—not anything a real lady in your world should be. But, Lord, Martha, she's got a vitality, a fascination to her that grips a man and just won't let him go.

Her name is "Idaho."

So I won't be coming home, Martha. I went West with the boys one day, you see, and met this lady . . .

Shaking his head and marveling at his own foolishness, Kimball turned away from the window. No, he couldn't write a letter like that, either, even though it would be closer to the truth than any other he might send his wife. Well, let things ride on as they were for the time being. Some day he'd think of a better way . . .

Chapter Seventeen

MILITARY CHANGE.—Gen. Crook, formerly from Siskiyou County, California, arrived from the East last Saturday to supercede Major Marshall and take command of this military district. We are assured by those who are acquainted with him that he is well calculated to manage the military situation of Idaho . . .

—*Idaho Statesman*
Boise City, IT.
December 11, 1866

If the ladies belonging to what passed for high society in Boise City expected their dinners, parties, and balls to be graced with blue dress uniforms that holiday season, they were doomed to be sadly disappointed. For George Crook was not a high society man. He did not drink whisky, coffee, or tea; he did not use tobacco in any form; and, instead of a braid-embellished dress uniform, he much preferred a black slouch hat, a canvas hunting jacket, heavy brown wool trousers, and thick-soled, moderately low-heeled boots that were as serviceable walking as riding. When mounted, his taste ran to a steady, sensible mule rather than a high-spirited, handsome horse. And, where duty was concerned, he had a one-track mind.

"From what I have observed of this country," he told a reporter shortly after his arrival in Boise City, "it is in a state of siege. My job is to settle the Indian problem once and for all. That is what I intend to do—by extermination, if necessary."

Although he did not openly criticize the district commander that had preceded him, he was appalled by what he saw. The hostile Indians seemed to experience no difficulty in obtaining modern arms and ammunition; yet the Army was equipped with obsolete pre-Civil War rifles. Troop mounts were in short supply; care of the pack mules was so indifferent that few of the sore-backed animals were in shape to carry aparejos; discipline was lax among the enlisted men, morale low, and habitual drunkenness a shockingly common thing among the officers.

In his firm, quiet way, General Crook undertook to remedy the situation. He was no stiff-backed martinet. An honest mistake, an occasional slip from sobriety or an error in judgment could be forgiven the first time and merely reprimanded the second; but the third time it happened the guilty party found himself tossed into the discard forever.

Winter came early that year and promised to be cold and bitter. Exactly a week after his arrival in Boise City, General Crook received word that a band of Indians had stolen some stock and shot at some settlers in the lower valley, twenty miles west of town. Taking along a toothbrush, a single change of underwear, and Captain Perry's company of the 1st Cavalry, General Crook left Fort Boise within an hour of receiving the report, determined to have a firsthand look.

"Sir, the men are wondering how long we will be gone," Captain Perry said as they rode west under the leaden, threatening sky. "With Christmas coming next week—"

"Oh, we'll be back by Christmas, I imagine."

"May I tell them that, sir? Just to raise their spirits . . ."

Crook shook his head. "Let's wait, Captain. Just in case we get interested after the Indians . . ."

Early the next day, the company reached the area raided by the Indians. While Captain Perry sent Cayuse George, chief of scouts, and ten friendly Boise Indians casting about for sign of the vanished hostiles, Crook talked to the farmers and ranchers of the neighborhood in an attempt to assess the damage done, the amount of stock stolen, the number and identity of the raiders. Snow was falling intermittently now and the wind was bitingly cold.

"Sir, Cayuse George says there were only a dozen hostiles," Captain Perry reported. "Their trail leads northwest, he says. It would be foolish of us to attempt to follow them, he thinks, for by now they'll be well scattered."

"Oh?" Crook said skeptically. "From what the local people tell me, there were at least thirty hostiles. And they headed southwest, not northwest."

"I'm only relaying what Cayuse George said, sir."

"Fetch him. I'd like to hear it for myself."

When brought into Crook's presence, Cayuse George was sullen and evasive. After questioning him sharply, Crook said, "This man is a lazy, worthless liar. He doesn't want to chase hostiles. All he wants to do is go back to the fort. Can't you see that, Captain?"

"Major Marshall thought highly of him, sir."

"Well, I don't. In my opinion, those Indians headed southwest and will hole up somewhere along the Owyhee. We're going after them."

"In *this* weather?"

"We're as well clothed as they are."

"But we have only a week's supplies, sir."

"Send back to the fort for more. We're not going to quit a hot trail."

Cheered by the fact that an Army officer was willing to pursue hostile Indians in any kind of weather, two white settlers who knew the country to the southwest volunteered to go along as guides. Crook accepted their services. After establishing a rendezvous point to which fresh supplies would be sent from Fort Boise a week hence, Crook led the cavalry company southwest to Snake River, ferried it near the mouth of the Owyhee, then, moving cautiously, resting during the daylight hours, riding only at night, tracked the band of hostiles to its camp in a sheltered canyon of the Owyhee and attacked without warning in the early hours just after dawn.

"We killed a good many, demoralizing the others," Crook wrote laconically in reporting the engagement to his superior in San Francisco. "That ended any more depredations from that band."

Since Cayuse George and the Boise Indian scouts under him had proved themselves utterly undependable, Crook discharged them as soon as the company reached Snake River, lingered there a few days while fresh supplies and a new batch of scouts were obtained from the fort, then, disregarding the grumblings of the enlisted men, who had been forced to pass up their Christmas drunk, made ready to celebrate the New Year holiday season with a cold, comfortless ride westward up the Malheur River. Again, he insisted that the company remain holed up during the daylight hours and travel only at night. Again, a close approach was made to a camp of unsuspecting hostiles, but before a surprise dawn attack could be mounted the careless behavior of the Boise Indian scouts, who did not appear to understand this kind of warfare, gave the alarm to the hostiles, who quickly broke camp and fled.

Angry though he was, Crook took the reverse philosophically. "Discharge those scouts, Captain Perry. And find me some friendly Indians with intelligence enough to obey orders."

"Sir, I'll do my best. But an Indian is an Indian, after all."

"Nonsense! That's like saying a white man is a white man. It's a generalization that simply isn't true. I've known a lot of Indians that could be trusted. The problem is to find them."

"Well, sir, the settlers tell me that this half-breed, Archie McIntosh, is a fairly intelligent man," Captain Perry said hesitantly.

"Is he a Boise?"

"No, sir. He comes from the Warm Springs reservation in central Oregon. But I must warn you, sir, he has one bad fault. He drinks."

"We'll give him a try, just the same."

If it struck the officers and enlisted men as strange that a teetotaler like General Crook and a moody, non-communicative, habitual drunk like Archie McIntosh should establish a mutual respect and trust that would last a lifetime, it was because they did not understand their commander. Being a completely practical man, Crook required only one thing from a scout: accurate information. If he got that, sobriety could go hang.

Whatever demons controlled the half-Scotch, half-Indian soul of Archie McIntosh and forced him to drink himself into complete oblivion whenever the opportunity offered itself, he had a memory that retained every image imprinted upon it, a shrewd intelligence that weighed impressions precisely and realistically, and an inborn instinct for direction, time, and space that was as infallible as that of a wild animal. If sober enough to talk, his information could be relied upon. If sober enough to ride, he could lead Crook where he wanted to go.

"A blizzard was howling when we set out that day," Crook wrote in one of his reports, "and I could tell from Archie's attitude that he thought us foolish to travel. But he made no objection, for he never gave me advice unless asked for it. We traveled all day and for several hours after dark, with Archie leading us. His route never deviated one foot to either side of the trail we wanted to follow, though the snow was falling so thick we could see no landmarks of any kind. Late at night we arrived safely at our previous camp. What was truly remarkable was that Archie had been in that place but once previously—and on that occasion had been so drunk he could barely ride."

Now that he had a scout and guide he could depend upon, General Crook got "interested after the Indians" in earnest. Moving on up the Malheur, his command brought the hostiles it was pursuing to bay in a slough-slashed section of river bottom half a mile or so in width, where sharp ridges of sand and dense growths of willow trees formed a network of natural fortifications. Here, the hostiles holed up and prepared to make their stand.

Crook ordered a cautious attack to test the defenses. The trees, bushes, and sand ridges behind which the Indians had dug in proved to be so impregnable that, after a brief foray, Crook ordered his soldiers to fall back.

"Any casualties?" he asked Captain Perry after the company had regrouped on open ground well out of rifle range.

"Private Schultz was shot in the chest, sir," Captain Perry answered. "He told me the shot came from a rifle not twenty feet away from him."

"You mean he's still alive?"

"Very much so, sir," the captain said with a smile. "He was carrying a horseshoe in his shirt pocket, it seems. It was the horseshoe the bullet hit."

"Dumb Dutch luck!" Crook muttered. He scowled at the Indian stronghold. "In all my experience fighting Indians, Captain, this is the one time I wish I had a few pieces of artillery. A frontal assault will gain us nothing. Run up a flag of truce. Station snipers on the high ground covering the edges of the thicket so they can pick off any hostiles that try to break and run. But if those Indians act like they want to come into our camp and talk, we'll let them."

"From the way they've been yelling at us, sir, they appear to believe they've won the fight."

"I know. But we'll talk, just the same."

As darkness fell, the Boise and Warm Springs Indians employed by the Army as scouts kept up a running gabble of conversation with the entrenched hostiles, bragging about the amount of food available in the soldier camp, the good treatment they could expect if they laid aside their arms, and the willingness of the soldiers to make profitable trades with them. Jeers and boasts were the only replies at first, then, motivated by greed and cunning, the hostiles changed their tone and began to express a desire to make peace.

"Don't trust them, sir," Captain Perry warned his commander. "They think they've got us whipped."

"Let them keep on thinking that, Captain. If my scheme works, they'll be singing a different tune presently."

When daylight came, Crook and the leaders of the hostiles agreed to a truce. By twos and threes the Indians came out of hiding, walked over to the camp of the soldiers, were fed and made to feel at ease. Yes, they told Crook arrogantly, they were willing to make peace—on their terms. They would remain where they were. The soldiers must go home and promise to molest them no more. No, they would make no promises themselves. And before they let the soldiers leave, they must be given presents.

"The saucy red bastards!" exclaimed one of the white settlers that had accompanied the expedition. "You know what I'd do to 'em, General? I'd let a whole mess of 'em come into camp, stuff 'em with food till they was so goggle-eyed they couldn't wiggle, then I'd kill 'em right down to the last man!"

"No," Crook answered shortly. "There's a better way."

By the middle of the morning, as many of the soldiers—acting under strict orders from their thirty-eight-year-old commander—had sifted into the hostile camp as Indian visitors had crossed over to the camp of the bluecoats. The soldiers made a great show of stacking their rifles and leaving them behind. But under their blouses they were wearing their pistols. When General Crook judged the time to be right, he quietly sent an order into the hostile camp, sidearms were suddenly displayed, a new firmness came into the manner of the whites, and, too late, the Indians saw that what they had meant to be a false truce must now become genuine or they would suffer the consequences.

"Their whole demeanor changed at once," Crook wrote, "and they got ready to go with us. Their stronghold was much more impregnable than I had any idea it could be. I thanked my stars that affairs terminated as they did."

Through the bitter winter of deep snow and punishing cold, Crook stayed "interested after the Indians," remaining in the field, leading his chilled, weary command back and forth across the bleak high desert country of eastern Oregon, northern Nevada, and southwestern Idaho, flushing bands of hostiles out of their camps in the sheltered canyons, fighting them when they chose to stand their ground, pursuing them when they scattered and ran, accepting their surrender when they became too weary to resist any longer.

In a private note to Governor Ballard, Crook wrote: "I cannot tell you when I shall be in Boise again, as my future movements depend so much on circumstances that I cannot form any idea where I may be a month hence. The fact is there is so much to do in this district and so few to do it that it is enough to discourage one just to look at the prospect . . ."

But his actions revealed determination rather than discouragement. For once, the fumbling bureaucracy in the War Department had placed the right man in the right job at the right time, Joe Wasson wrote approvingly; let us pray, gentlemen, that they do not discover their happy error and correct it by recalling the only efficient Indian fighter Idaho Territory has ever seen.

In late February, Crook's command made a surprise dawn attack on a large village camped at the base of a range of mountains in eastern Oregon, killed some sixty bucks and took a number of women and children prisoner. One of the captured squaws told Crook that the Indian leader, Chief Bigfoot, had been killed during the battle, but he put no stock in her story.

"If such a person exists," he said, "I'll believe it only when I see him—alive or dead."

Crook himself had two close brushes with death during that battle. Before it began, he gave specific orders to the soldiers, the civilian scouts, and the fifty Warm Springs and Boise Indians under Archie McIntosh's command not to fire a shot until the sleeping village was surrounded and the main body of troops was within its borders. As commander, he intended to remain in the rear to make sure that the attack was properly carried out. But because the mule he customarily rode had turned up lame that morning, he mounted himself on a spirited, nervous horse. When the order to charge was given, the horse lost its head.

"Taking the bit between his teeth, he led the charge," Crook wryly admitted in a report to his superior. "Instead of obeying my injunctions, the troops behind me began firing at once. The balls whistled by me, and I was in much more danger from the rear than I was from the front. My horse ran through the village, and I could not stop him until he reached some distance beyond . . ."

Jumping off the overly ambitious animal, Crook ran back afoot toward the village, where the battle now raged violently. Directly ahead of him, a completely naked Indian armed with a bow and a quiver of arrows slung over one shoulder knelt on one knee, calmly singing his death song as he notched arrow after arrow to the bowstring and let fly at the blue-coats closing in around him. An arrow whistled past Crook's cheek, missing him by the narrowest of margins. Then a number of rifles barked simultaneously and the Indian collapsed, his body riddled by half a dozen bullets.

A white civilian named Hanson, who had joined the command as a guide, fell in beside Crook as they ran toward the outskirts of the village, which consisted chiefly of brush wickiups. As the two men neared one of the shelters, Crook called, "Stay clear of the entrance, Mr. Hanson! You go on the right side, I'll go on the left, and we'll smoke the devil out."

"Oh, hell, the thing's empty!" Hanson muttered recklessly.

"Look, I'll show you—"

As the man went running toward the entrance of the wickiup, a rifle shot sounded from within. Hanson pitched forward, shot squarely through the heart. A volley from Crook's own rifle, which riddled the shelter from wall to wall, silenced the Indian within.

Only two full-grown male hostiles had survived the attack, Crook learned; this pair had been outside the encircling lines at the moment the charge had been made and had been seen fleeing toward the hills. Within the village, not a single adult male prisoner had been taken, for, in the heat of battle, it had been impossible to control the blood lust of the troops, who had many old scores to avenge. Archie McIntosh proudly displayed half a dozen fresh scalps which he claimed he had taken in hand to hand combat. Whether he had actually done so or had merely killed and scalped unarmed hostiles that were attempting to surrender was a question Crook knew there was no point in pursuing. As a scout and guide, Archie had no peer. As a fighting man, he had his faults. And the truth was, explaining the niceties of civilized warfare to Indian allies was a task Crook had long since written off as hopeless.

The weather played freakish tricks in this country. Following a week of sub-zero cold on the high plateaus of eastern Oregon, Crook led his frozen command down into a sheltered canyon along the Owyhee in late January and found the sun so warm and the temperature so mild that grasshoppers were seen bouncing about. A month later, while the command was making a scout through the Dunder and Blitzen country to the southwest, a raging blizzard left powder-dry snowdrifts fifteen feet deep in which the horses sank almost out of sight. Temporarily camped on the shores of Warner Lake because deep snow and bitter cold had made travel impossible, the command was awakened in the middle of a March night by the eerie sighing of a Chinook wind, which, in minutes, raised the air temperature sixty degrees, and, by morning, so rapidly melted the snowdrifts that the camp had to be hastily moved to higher ground for fear of being flooded out.

To a passionate sportsman like Crook, the lake and marsh country of south-central Oregon was a veritable paradise. Swan, geese, ducks, cormorants, and coots nested by the thousands among the tules and bullrushes. Getting a skilled Indian craftsman to fashion him a dugout canoe from a pine log, Crook spent many hours exploring the lakes, which seldom were more than four to six feet in depth. He discovered that when the weather was growing colder, a well concealed hunter could get in several shots before the wildfowl would take alarm and fly, for the swan, geese, and ducks mistook gunshots for the sharp reports of ice freezing and cracking, a sound they were accustomed to hearing. In one day, he reported, he collected sixty-seven dozen cormorant and coot eggs and brought them back to the camp cooks to supplement the troops' meager diet.

"The coot eggs were good eating," he noted, "being about the size and color of a guinea fowl egg. But the white of the cormorant egg was bitter and strong when cooked, and the eggs were not healthy."

With the coming of April and milder weather, Crook went after the hostile Indians with renewed vigor. Under his direct command he now had some two hundred men; at Camp Smith, Camp Lyon, Camp McDermit, and the other Army posts strategically located in the heart of the Indian country. The campaign which he planned for the coming months was a simple one: go where the hostiles were, fight them, chase them, and wear them down until they got so sick of war they would sue for a permanent peace. But thanks to the carelessness of the camp guards, the campaign got off to a bad start. Displaying a daring and cleverness that he had not thought them capable of, a band of hostiles made a surprise raid on Crook's main camp one dark night in mid-April, stampeded the horse herd, got away with several hundred Army mounts, and, in a matter of minutes, turned his cavalry into infantry.

Though he knew that security measures had been lax, General Crook wasted neither words nor energy bewailing the loss of the horses. Marching his chastened troops afoot through deep mud and melting snowdrifts from the shores of Warner Lake to Camp McDermit— a punishment well-calculated to instill alertness in any cavalryman— he mounted what men he could, scoured the countryside for miles about for the stolen horses, and then, recovering only a few, ordered his quartermaster to run advertisements in the newspapers of northern California for 450 well-broken saddle horses, eighty pack mules, and forty draft mules. This summer's campaign, he promised, would be a big one.

It was two months before the badly needed horses and mules arrived. By then, Crook's command had acquired more soldiers, three separate companies of Indian allies, and a newspaper correspondent.

"My name is Joe Wasson," the man said in introducing himself to General Crook. "Perhaps you've seen my paper, the *Owyhee Avalanche?*"

"Yes."

"And have used it for other purposes than reading, no doubt," Joe Wasson said with a wry smile. "Well, General, my motto has always been: 'The press must serve its readers' ends.'"

Ignoring the outrageous pun, Crook said, "What can I do for you, Mr. Wasson?"

"First, I should tell you I'm no longer editor of the *Avalanche.*"

"I'm sorry to hear that, Mr. Wasson. You write very well."

"Thank you, sir. But I had to get out of the print shop or die. I had to get out into the world where things were happening."

"Very little is happening here at the moment, Mr. Wasson. We're awaiting remounts from California. As soon as they arrive, perhaps we'll see some action."

"So I understand. Would you have any serious objection, sir, against my going along with your command as a correspondent?"

Joe Wasson looked thin and tired and his face had the unhealthy pallor of a man too long indoors. Crook said dubiously, "Fighting Indians is no lark, Mr. Wasson."

"I'm sure it isn't, General. But I'll be no burden to you, I promise you that. If I can't keep up, just let me lie where I fall."

"Well, if you want to come along, I suppose there's no harm in it. But don't expect to be pampered."

Crook had thought that two weeks of soldiering would be more than enough for Joe Wasson. But he had misjudged his man. Irrepressibly curious, perpetually enthusiastic, and possessed of a sense of humor that made wry jokes of the worst hardships, Joe Wasson took to campaigning as if he had been born for it.

"I came on this trip in search of new life," he wrote the new *Avalanche* editor, William Hill, jubilantly, "and I certainly found it. Last night, while sleeping in the tent assigned to me, I had no more than rolled into my blankets when I felt new life creeping upon me from all directions. These Oregon graybacks have no abiding loyalties; they like white meat fully as much as red . . ."

Before the command left Camp McDermit, the remounts, pack and draft mules arrived from California. But somewhere along the line there had been a slight error. The animals had not been broken to the saddle, aparejo, or harness and were as wild as deer. The command had recently been strengthened by two companies of infantry, made up chiefly of German, Dutch, and Irish emigrants, who had never ridden, packed, or harnessed a four-footed animal in their lives. Determined to mount his entire command, Crook gave the foot soldiers and the unbroken animals just forty-eight hours to get acquainted.

"Put a Dutchman who's never ridden on a horse that's never carried a thing on its back but hair," Wasson wrote, "and they're both bound to learn something new right away. For a while around here, it literally 'rained' soldiers."

Now four hundred strong, the command set out in midsummer on a sixty-day campaign whose ambitious purpose was to cover all the desert, lake, and mountain country of southeastern and south-central Oregon, into whose immense, sparsely populated area the hostile Indians that had been terrorizing southwestern Idaho, northern Nevada, and eastern Oregon were accustomed to retreat when the pressures against them became too great. In his continuing dispatches to the paper he had formerly published, Wasson admitted he yearned for a big battle, a decisive major engagement in which a large body of Indians could be brought to bay and forced to fight the now formidable forces arrayed against them.

But General Crook had no illusions about the kind of war he was fighting. In the clear air of this flat, treeless, sage-covered country, Indian lookouts stationed on the high buttes and sharp peaks, which occasionally rose like islands in a vast sea, could spot a traveling column hours and miles away, accurately judge its strength, and advise the leaders whether to flee or fight on terms and grounds of their own choosing.

In an effort to counteract this disadvantage, Crook broke his command into several components. Twenty miles or so in advance of the main column rode a company of Warm Springs Indians under Archie McIntosh. Ten miles to the right and left, companies of Snake and Boise Indians under Captains Darragh and McKay rode as flankers; thus, the command could sweep a wide swath which General Crook could be assured was cleared of hostiles whether they were brought into battle or not. When word was sent back from McIntosh, Darragh, or McKay that the hostiles moving before them appeared to be in a mood to halt and make a stand, the main column ceased traveling during the daylight hours and moved forward only at night, hoping to close in, make a surround and a kill. Now and again the advance and flanking parties of Indian allies encountered small bands of hostiles or caught up with stragglers whom they ruthlessly killed and scalped with little regard for age or sex. But the main column seldom saw action.

Crook was not dissatisfied. His basic strategy was to keep the hostiles moving, for he knew that an Indian on the move could not hunt, fish, dig roots, rest, or properly care for his old people, his women, his children, or his horses.

Though he was careful not to impose his puns, his practical jokes, and his stock of "medicinal" whisky upon the General himself, it did not take Joe Wasson long to make friends with the officers under Crook. McKay, Darragh, Perry, Madigan, and Parnell soon became bosom comrades. But before the campaign was three weeks old, Wasson blundered his way into the commanding officer's disfavor. Blithely forgetting his noncombatant status, he joined Captain Darragh's Indian scouts uninvited one day and went galloping merrily off with them in pursuit of a band of hostiles. When the Indians were brought to bay at the edge of a marsh, Wasson started banging away at them with his new Henry rifle in such a reckless, enthusiastic manner that friend clawed for cover as frantically as did foe. Hearing about it, Crook sent for him.

"Mr. Wasson, didn't you tell me you were a newspaper writer by trade?" Crook asked sternly.

"Yes, sir."

"Do you believe in the old adage: 'The pen is mightier than the sword'?"

"Old adages must be taken with a grain of salt, General. To an educated person, the pen can be very potent. But to an unlettered savage, the sword is all powerful."

"From what I've heard," Crook said dryly, "a pen or sword would do a great deal more damage to an Indian than a Henry rifle—in your hands. Captain Darragh tells me you nearly shot two of his best scouts."

"That's an outright slander, sir!"

"Indeed? Lieutenant Madigan says he offered to bet you five dollars you couldn't hit an Army tent at twenty paces."

"Yes—so he did."

"But you wouldn't accept the wager?"

"Sir, I felt you would not approve of my damaging government property," Joe Wasson answered self-righteously. "Besides, it was a very small tent." Observing that not even a ghost of a smile had come to General Crook's face at that feeble attempt at a joke, Wasson added contritely, "Sir, I was only trying to help—"

"I know. But in the future, Mr. Wasson, you will confine your help' to writing accurate, factual stories about this campaign and leave the fighting to the professionals. Is that clearly understood?"

"Yes, sir."

The truth of the matter was, Joe Wasson wryly confided to his friend, Lieutenant John Madigan, George Crook did not possess much of a sense of humor. He never told jokes. Unlike most men in this country, he would not even smile at any remark that was in the least degree off-color or at any happening whose amusing angle was related to the differences between the sexes.

For example, Wasson said, Crook had not been in the least entertained by Archie McIntosh's graphically illustrated tale of how he and his scouts had captured a band of a dozen hostiles the other day, decided to kill all the males and take the females prisoner, then, as the blanket-wrapped captives danced about in a desperate attempt to conceal their sex, had seized them one by one and ascertained what kind of cat they were by the most direct means possible—with one clever, supple young fellow putting on such a great show in protection of his secret that the scouts had laughed uproariously and let him live.

On another occasion, Wasson told Lieutenant Madigan, he had

been present when General Crook was discussing the food-gathering talents of Indian women. Quite solemnly, Crook had said, "Squaws have an amazing instinct for finding food. Even though she can't see a sign of it, an Indian woman always knows where to dig for the biggest root."

A smile spread across John Madigan's face as he eyed Joe Wasson. "And you said . . . ?"

"Exactly what you would have said, my evil-minded young friend. That I've known a lot of white women with that same talent."

"But the general didn't laugh?"

"Lord, no! He just froze me with a look. Then he went on talking like I wasn't even there."

Back East, George Crook had a wife, Lieutenant Madigan told Wasson, whom he hadn't seen since he'd sailed for the West Coast late last fall. Rumor had it that she was due to arrive in San Francisco shortly. Did her husband plan to join her for the winter there when this summer's campaign was ended? No, just the opposite. The way Crook talked, he was planning to establish a permanent post in the heart of the Indian country of south-central Oregon—probably near Warner Lake—from which spot operations could be kept up through all but the very worst weeks of the winter. Mrs. Crook was to join him there.

"Lord!" Wasson muttered admiringly. "She must be made of rawhide and iron—just like he is!"

Much as he respected the single-minded efficiency of the expedition's commanding officer, Joe Wasson—now that he was restricted to words as weapons—could not refrain from getting in a sly dig at the Army now and then in his dispatches to the *Avalanche*. After admitting that the volley of shots fired from his Henry rifle probably had missed its target, he wrote: "Army statistics say it requires 272 lbs. of metal to kill a man—so I should be satisfied with my effort, it being a new business to me . . ."

Though he still yearned for a major battle to report, he took a measure of satisfaction in passing on the information that, by the end of July, the campaign figures totaled ". . . thirty-five Indians killed and captured—all ages and sexes; just about one-half were warriors . . ."

On the grimmer side was the recently compiled Army estimate that in the Pacific Northwest since settlement had begun, over one thousand whites had died at Indian hands, excluding soldiers killed in combat.

Among the three companies of Indian allies a lively rivalry had sprung up, Wasson noted, as to which one could kill or capture the most hostiles and acquire the most loot, the latter practice being one Crook left to their own consciences, which were not "overly tender." Wasson called this "fighting the devil with fire . . ."

". . . three fires, I may say, for yesterday three Indians had to be literally burned out of the rocks—one being cooked almost white; they would not yield on more favorable terms . . ."

When hostiles were captured, Wasson explained, they were turned over to the care of the Indian allies—Crook's experience having proved that they did better with their own kind. "Among the seven captured Wednesday last are one or two papooses whose complexion suggests a mixed origin. It may be that when they are washed out of their savage tints, the physiognomies of some of the past Legislatures of Nevada and Idaho may be developed; during such assemblies, members frequently become very hard up in more ways than one . . ."

". . . some of the little imps take capture as a matter of course, while others frown like young hyenas for several days. The change of diet, I am told, acts violently upon the papoose system for about a week, but after the first clean-up (a mining phrase, you will recollect) and the interstices get filled, the animal organs continue operation . . ."

The captured squaws were either put to work around the camps of the Indian allies, he wrote, or taken out with scouting parties to help locate others of their tribe.

Resting during the daylight hours and traveling mostly at night as the main column had done, Wasson had found the weather so uniform that he "failed to notice it"; even the mosquitoes—a chief source of annoyance in camp life—were so few and "so badly disciplined" he found himself compelled to put in a good word for them.

But August had come now. Displeased with the results of the campaign's first thirty days, General Crook called in the scouting parties, abandoned the practice of moving the main column only at night, and headed back toward Warner Lake, which was located in a grassy, sheltered valley in southern Oregon a day's ride north of the California and Nevada borders. Now the mid-summer heat made itself felt. After being forced to ride ten miles over a bare, black, lava-strewn mesa, Wasson wrote: "It was so hot at noon yesterday I was reminded of a story told me by an officer who had recently served at Fort Yuma, Arizona. A soldier died of sunstroke, he said, went to Hell, and slept badly his first night in that place. When Old Scratch caught him trying to sneak out the gate, next morning, and asked him where he was going, the soldier answered: 'Back to Fort Yuma to get my blankets.'"

Leaving the main body of his command encamped at Warner Lake to rest and await fresh supplies, General Crook took twenty-five men on a two-week scout of the high desert and and marsh-edged lake district of south-central Oregon. He was seeking answers to three perplexing questions. First, he wanted to know the present whereabouts of the hostile Indians whose main forces had so persistently eluded him. Second, he wanted to identify beyond doubt their source of firearms and ammunition, which never seemed to dry up. Third, he wanted to make a final decision as to the proper location for the Army's main winter quarters so that the necessary buildings could be constructed while good weather lasted.

The truth was, he admitted to Joe Wasson, he put little faith in a summer campaign. The most he had hoped for in this one was to keep the hostiles moving, to wear them down, and to pick up a few stragglers. But in the eight months that had passed since he had left Fort Boise with a toothbrush, a change of underwear, and a single company of cavalry, he had gained a knowledge of the country, had learned what must be done, and had made considerable progress toward putting together the forces required to conquer the Indians. Now, all he needed were the answers to these three simple questions and the time in which to get the job done.

"How much time?" Wasson asked.

"A year. If the authorities will just leave me alone for one more year, the Indian problem will be settled—I promise you that."

"The papers and people of Idaho are solidly behind you, sir, if that's worth anything."

"Thank you, Mr. Wasson. But in my trade, there's no substitute for a victory won in battle."

Thirty days of campaigning with Crook had completely restored Joe Wasson's health and good spirits. Gone was his indoor pallor. By eating only what he could chew, drinking only what he could swallow, sleeping only when there was nothing more interesting to do, bathing infrequently, and having absolutely nothing to do with medicines or doctors, he had become as tough and calloused as a cavalryman, he boasted. Yes, he had suffered privations. For example, one dry, dusty, blisteringly hot day he had ridden thirty-five miles with a detachment of Army packers driving a string of laden mules across the desert between Owyhee Ferry and Camp Smith. Earlier, he had generously shared his limited supply of whisky with the soldiers; now it was gone, he was perishing of thirst, the cargo on the pack mule directly ahead of him was two kegs of lager beer, and it seemed only logical to assume that past favors would be returned. But his hints, his suggestions, and, finally, his abject pleas, had fallen on stone-deaf ears.

"Confound such discriminating discipline!" he moaned to Editor

Hill. "They would not sacrifice one drop of lager, were I to die for the lack of it! So I was compelled to continue the journey 'beholding Heaven yet feeling Hell.' Had my companions been American graduates from West Point, such as I have met more recently, the trip would have been rendered comparatively pleasant."

In this current trip with Crook, he complained, the detachment had been forced to ride forty-five miles one scorching day with but a single drink of water from an alkali puddle "as palatable as second-hand soap-suds." Shortly thereafter he had experienced a briefly hopeful moment when being introduced to an Army officer encountered on the trail.

"The General said something that sounded like 'good ale.' I quickly replied that I did indeed enjoy 'good ale.' But, sad to say, it turned out that the Lieutenant's *name* was 'Goodale.' A very likeable man, I must admit, but I would have much preferred the two syllables split, well chilled, and with a different sort of head."

CHAPTER EIGHTEEN

The two-week scouting trip had answered at least one of General Crook's questions. The most strategic spot for a permanent post, he now was sure, was Warner Lake. Being relatively low in elevation, this valley had a fairly mild winter climate; water, grass, and game were plentiful; in the nearby mountains there was timber; and supply lines to the towns of northern California and western Oregon were not excessively long. Contracts for the construction of log buildings to house officers, men, and animals were let to civilians; arrangements were made for the cutting of hay and the hauling of grain; and Crook now let it be known that he had decided to extend the campaign an additional thirty days, which meant that the troops would not be returning to this place until late in October.

"As I have heard of no order commanding me to leave the camp, I expect to make the round trip," Wasson wrote. "If I can keep the officers from seeing what I have said about them till I can get away, I expect to get out of this adventure alive. The only orders Crook ever gives me is *to help myself;* I'll bet he never saw a more willing subordinate . . . I have no guard duty to perform, unless a sort of general blackguard duty, which is rather a pleasure . . ."

Among the officers, a lively, critical interest in the newspaper reports of their exploits made Wasson hastily correct any writing errors he had inadvertently made. ", . . it was Captain McKay, not Darragh, who killed the five Indians in the scrap coming over from The Dalles. The mistake was mine. In fact, the only thing I am never mistaken in is my appetite . . ."

A great variety of human nature was represented in this command, Wasson noted. "My good neighbor, Lieutenant Parnell, was one of the 'Six Hundred' at Balaklava. Nearly all the officers and men here were through the ups and downs of the Civil War. I get many interesting things from these veterans—things that never saw type—that knock the gloss off incidents in print and accepted as history . . ."

One of the Army surgeons, Dr. Tompkins, had recently received several pamphlets from an Eastern friend employed at the Smithsonian Institution and a letter urging him to secure a collection of Indian skulls, birds, insects, reptiles, etc. and instructing him as to how this should be done. Being otherwise occupied, Dr. Tompkins passed on the material to Wasson, suggesting that he do what he liked with it. One quiet, hot Sunday afternoon, Wasson devoted a few hours to what he called "philanthropic purposes."

He could understand and sympathize, he wrote, with the Smithsonian professor's statement that "among the first of the *desiderati* is a full series of the skulls of American Indians." General Crook desired such a series, too. However, obtaining it would require a bit of "skullduggery." As to the "geographical position" of the Indians, Wasson observed, that "is just what I'm afraid we'll find one of these days when we ain't looking for it." He then proceeded to answer the professor's specific questions concerning the Indians of the region:

Q: Ordinary duration of life?
A: Extraordinary—say the settlers.
Q: Can photographs be taken of individual Indians?
A: Yes—if the camera is mounted on a Henry rifle.
Q: Type of food?
A: Spontaneous.
Q: Do they practice agriculture?
A: Mostly they raise settlers—hair and all.
Q: Type of dwellings?
A: Remarkable for their skylight.
Q: Religious beliefs?
A: Great Spirits—liquid, that is.
Q: Do they indulge in burnt offerings?
A: Frequently. Haystacks, houses, cattle, settlers—
Q. Type of government?
A: He-red-itary.
Q: Do they practice scalping?
A: Don't need to. They've got it down perfect.
Q: Do they retain the bow and arrow?
A: No, they let the arrow slip.
Q: What kind of medicine do they practice?
A: They are expert at blood-letting.
Q: Have these Indians, so far as you know, always lived in their present territory?
A: So far as *I* know, few of them have ever *died* in their present territory.
Q: What changes have been introduced among them by their intercourse with the whites?
A: That's a leading question, Professor. But the change usually

shows for itself.

Q: What are they called?
A: Usually they come without calling.
Q: Are there antiquities such as earthworks in their countries?
A: Along the emigrant roads, yes; they're built by the whites—who call them "graves."

A section of the instructive pamphlets that particularly intrigued Joe Wasson was the one in which the Smithsonian professor had written: ", . . a great obstacle in the way of making alcoholic collections while on the march is the escape of the spirits and the friction of the specimens . . ."

Indeed, Wasson commented, this was a knotty problem.

". . . a fourth proof whisky will be found best suited for collections made at permanent stations," continued the pamphlet, "but the specimen must not be crowded . . ."

On the contrary, Wasson begged leave to differ, around many permanent stations in this part of the country he had seen a number of "specimens," fuller than a tick with fourth proof whisky, who hadn't minded the friction of being crowded the least bit.

"Skins of reptiles may be stuffed with either sand or sawdust," advised the pamphlet, "or they may be simply flattened out . . ."

It had been his own experience, Wasson observed, that the reptiles he came across kept better flattened out.

". . . eggs are emptied with the least amount of trouble at one hole . . ."

Verily, this was so, Wasson agreed.

". . . minerals and samples of rock are also desired at the Institution."

With that, Wasson gave up in disgust. "I've heard of nothing but minerals and samples of rock for five years," he wrote, "and I came on this trip to get rid of the accursed sound. All I'm interested in these days is quarts (z) of coffee."

During the latter part of August, the rested, resupplied command moved out of Camp Warner and headed in a southwesterly direction toward Goose Lake. An advance scouting party of eighteen Warm Springs Indians, led by Archie McIntosh, had a sharp encounter with a larger force of hostiles in the mountainous country east of the lake, captured two squaws, killed three braves, but finally had to fall back on the main command.

"Archie lost one of his best men," Wasson wrote, "a tall, rash cuss called Copinger. When the fight began, the scouts all chose a rock or bush and got behind them, but Copinger climbed on top of a rock and started saucing the hostiles—said they couldn't shoot much anyhow; but the sequel was they put a bullet through him while there—and he is *there* yet . . ."

It was Archie's opinion that this particular group of Indians had fought Crook's men on at least three previous occasions; this was the fourth time they had come out winner and they were getting mighty cocky about it. Their chief, Archie claimed, was an Indian named "Chee-oh," a warrior so successful against the whites that he had become a legend among this kind.

"Oh, damn Chee-oh!" Wasson moaned in a dispatch to Editor Hill. "In sounding his name, incidentally, you must accent the *'chee'* part with a good sneeze—the rest will naturally follow. I am loth to believe in his corporeal existence. I *hear* about all these great Indian chiefs but I never *see* one. Chee-oh, We-ah-we-wa, Bigfoot, Winnemucca—I wish they all were dead or would stay on the Reservation without any mental reservation . . ."

"I'm tired of writing about someone I don't see and am eternally hearing of. I do hope if Bigfoot (?) is 'killed and carried off by his friends' you folks up there will say no more about it. I want a hero worse than Byron ever did—but one that will show himself in flesh tights occasionally; not 'tight in the flesh' (for I see that now and then and would not mind being exposed to it myself) . . ."

"If Archie's scouts could exchange their weapons for some others nor bearing the brand of 'Harper's Ferry, 1845,' and get revolvers swung to them also, their confidence would be enhanced and better accounts rendered in these skirmishes . . ."

"P.S.—WEDNESDAY, 28th.—Several of the Boise wagons arrived here last night, and among other things brought Spencer carbines for Lt. Parnell's Co., and today Archie's men got the best of the Sharp's guns. He has done the most of the rough work so far with the poorest tools, and it is time that his outfit be improved . . . All the reliable indications point to the country south and west of this as the general rendezvous of the hostiles . . ."

When the news reached Joe Wasson that the final details of transferring ownership of the *Avalanche* had been completed, he found time to pen a letter of sympathy and advice:
South Fork Darragh Creek, Oregon,

August 28th, 1867

FRIEND *HILL.—Dear Sir:* News today to the effect that you are installed in the *Avalanche* . . . Hill, you're pretty well muscled—an excellent qualification in an editor—and I hope to hear of your having knocked down and dragged out several indignants or intruders the first week; nothing I can think of would bode more good to your future welfare.

You must never pay any attention to flying assertions on the street (unless accompanied by a brick-bat), as it would occupy all your time; you will doubtless feel huffy at being characterized every day as a male descendant of Cain-ine, but never descend to notice it. After a few months' experience, should you manage to get one-half of the community to severely hate you, without being able to assign any reason for it, and the other half to respect you more through fear than favor—it will be good evidence that the paper is running about right and is bound to be a success.

In this age of more brass than brains, soft-soap, however strong, will do more for you than the best of logic or lore, but the application of the article requires skill or it may smart the hands of the applicant and many a promising point "by lost in the wash."

Gruff old Dr. Johnson, who "loved a good hater," said that "vituperation is the safety-valve of an honest man," but I think the ingredient should be held in reserve as long as possible in newspaper infelicities, as in most instances the editor cannot do the subject justice. When anything occurs that is melancholy or malicious, you must appear sad or mad as occasion requires, but you will learn to relish such things in the sanctum, and finally pray for a fire or funeral to come about six times a week. Such are the proper food for an itemsman. Then, if the subject is caused by any fault of the opposite creed, corporation or party, is the time to cut loose at length.

You must cultivate charity and generosity at home by pleading poverty on the part of yourself. But in the meantime, preach that advertising is the only salvation of business men and that to obtain it costs a contemptible per cent of their profits. You will frequently be called upon to write a puff where you would much prefer to insert a funeral notice, but you must shut your eyes, keep a stiff upper lip, etc., and go in; conscience will gradually cease to harass you, till you finally become as cold as a lizard and as callous of fellow-feeling as the backbone of an alligator—your tears crockodilish—after which you will be fitted for a lifetime of usefulness in the sanctum-sanctorem . . .

But go right along, doing the best you can, and if you don't think you are in Hell in less than six months, the fact that you are on the right track will fully appear, and then you can govern yourself accordingly.

Thus far the *Avalanche* has been a sort of wet-nurse for Owyhee during the infantile pains of cutting teeth; but the cutting of eyeteeth by this proprietor will not be forgotten by the undersigned for several revolving moons. To stand up to the metal-rack like a beast to stake-oats and die by inches had become my lot, or else the alternative of regaining health by taking my chances in adventure; I'm on the latter now, and I don't care to take a formal farewell of Silver City. Opportunities to "go below" from here are frequent, and I'm liable to steal a horse and head for the hallowed waters of the Sacramento ere winter comes. What the sequel to this campaign will be, I expect to tell you from somewhere . . .

If the readers of the *Avalanche* will but condescend a moment from cussing it for what it *did* say and think of what it *didn't* but *could* have said, I'll willingly throw up the sponge. The politician's cry is eternally for saving the country, but in the case of Owyhee some people thought it necessary to first make a country worth saving.

Hill, I hope you have struck it in the stage of coming to its "second wind"—as I really believe you have—and that the new firm may come out as well at least as the old one started in. Be happy if you can't be virtuous, and may the Lord have mercy on your soul—a tender thread, but everlasting things are hung thereupon. Keep up the idea that everybody pays "in advance," whether you see a dollar in a month. In my case, the world is all before, where to choose, etc., but I expect to act on the old injunction—

Trust to luck, trust to luck,
Stare fate in the face,
Sure your heart must be 'aisy,'
If it's in the right place.

P.S.—Remember me to "Big Nick," Somercamp and the balance of "the boys," and I remain, & etc.,
Joe.

By his own admission, Joe Wasson was appalled at the way he developed "diarrhea of the pen" whenever he sat down to write an account of the campaign. "I never discover the difference between scribbling for a newspaper and a running, rambling conversation with 'the boys' until I see the blasted stuff in print," he confessed to Hill, "and then I am astonished to observe what an amount of human cussedness and conceit a single individual under no restraint can produce. I will faithfully promise to be more concise from this out . . ."

Included among the 360 soldiers, scouts, and packers that comprised the command was an "old stager" called "Dad" Wilson whom Major Perry had picked up that summer and employed as a scout. The superstitious, bumbling, garrulous old fellow so mistrusted modern firearms that he still carried a muzzle-loading rifle, vintage 1820. He claimed it was "the truest shootin' gun thar ever wuz" but Joe Wasson had yet to see him hit a blessed thing he shot at with it.

Near Goose Lake, Darragh and his scouts found fresh moccasin and horse tracks; the fact that remains of seventeen campfires were seen in one camping place showed that the band of hostiles was a sizable one. Now the problem, as Wasson put it, was to determine:

"Whether the Snake that made the track
Was going north or coming back . . ."

General Crook immediately dispatched Darragh and his band of scouts north to the Abert Lake country, while McIntosh and McKay, with their Indians, went in a westerly direction to make a search of the mountains bordering that shore of shallow, partially dry Goose Lake.

"During the night of September 4th the main command left the prairie," Wasson wrote, "came out through a canyon to the northwest seven miles to Goose Lake Valley, crossed over to the mountains west and camped in the timbered valley of Kelly's Creek. Twenty miles altogether on this night's march . . ."

Two mornings later, Archie McIntosh and Donald McKay returned with their scouts and four fresh scalps, taken, Archie claimed, from stragglers that had fallen behind the main band of hostiles, whose present whereabouts he was sure he knew. If he were given more time . . .

"Take two more days," Crook said. "As soon as it gets dark, we'll pull out of here and move on up the creek after you. If you find the hostile camp, don't disturb it—just send word back to me."

"Sir, at the risk of making a nuisance of myself," Joe Wasson said eagerly, "may I ask permission to go along with Archie on just this *one* scout?"

Crook gave the self-appointed correspondent a coldly appraising look. "Will you behave yourself, Mr. Wasson, and do what you're told to do?"

"Word of honor."

"All right. But don't get yourself killed."

"If I do, sir," Wasson said earnestly, "I'll never ask you to let me go on a scout again. That's a promise."

Much to Joe Wasson's disappointment, the only interesting things he saw during his two-day scout with Archie and his Indians were ". . . fine mountain scenery and considerable game . . ." Archie did find evidence that the hostiles had camped where he had guessed they would. But the nest was empty and the birds flown; likely they had taken alarm from the scouts' killing of the four stragglers a few days ago.

"Which way did they go?" Wasson asked.

"South," Archie grunted. "We'll get 'em by and by."

Sorely tempted by the numerous deer seen during the return trip, Wasson tried to persuade Archie, now that the hostiles had vanished, that there would be no harm in downing a fat buck and taking the general some fresh venison. If Archie would let him attempt just *one* shot with his Henry . . . In reply, the head scout turned in his saddle and grunted an order to one of the Indians riding behind him. Without a word, the Indian swung out of the column and rode over a ridge to the left, stringing his bow as he went. An hour later, he rejoined the scouts packing the carcass of a freshly killed and dressed deer. Archie grinned at Wasson.

"No bang, no boom. But we get meat."

During their absence, General Crook had moved his troops some fifteen miles up Kelly's Creek. Darragh and his scouts were back. They had trailed a band of hostiles as far north as Abert Lake, Darragh said, then had spent two frustrating days trying to flush them out of the tule marshes.

"Muskrats!" Darragh said in disgust. "That's what they are! We saw their trails, we knew they were in there, and we thought where they could go we could go. So we tried—and all of a sudden we were up to our rumps in mud."

Abandoning the futile hunt, he had brought his scouts back to the main command with nothing concrete to report except the discovery of two sizable lakes that were not shown on the Army maps. As a matter of fact, Wasson wrote, the only reliable feature about the maps Crook possessed—most of which had been drawn by the Frémont exploring expedition—was that they could be depended upon to be wrong.

"On the 10th, the entire command marched together northwest through the mountains," Wasson wrote, "passing through a beautiful valley six miles in length, with as fine a stream of water running through it into Abert Lake as I ever saw; it was swarming with brook trout . . ." After a short march of six miles the next day, fresh Indian sign was seen, tending off to the southeast. A detachment of Darragh's scouts was given several days' rations and ordered to follow it, while the main body of the command moved southwest into the mountains.

"The General had become satisfied by this time that the Indians he had 'lost' had gone south," Wasson wrote, "but he concluded to split his command and go in opposite directions."

On the morning of the 13th, Crook ordered Major Perry to take Darragh, McKay, their scouts, and two companies of Regulars and make an extensive sweep northward, then east, eventually ending up at Camp Harney. He himself would take one company of cavalry, another of mounted infantry, Archie McIntosh, and his scouts, and go south.

"The General remarked that if his venture on this southern tour failed in any way to meet public expectations," Wasson wrote, "the blame should fall upon him alone."

Crook's patience was wearing thin, Wasson could see; his normally even temper was growing short. Though he confided in no one, Wasson could make a good guess at the worries troubling his mind. He had been in the field nine months now in command of an operation constantly increasing in size, scope, and expense. From his original station at Fort Boise, he had wandered a long way: into Nevada, into Oregon, and now soon would be moving south into California. "Public expectations," as well as his superiors in the War Department, were obviously putting increasing pressure upon him to produce some tangible results.

Though the newspapers of southwestern Idaho were solidly behind Crook, Wasson knew that the Portland and San Francisco editors were overlooking no opportunity to play up the Indian unrest in the interior country and the ineffectiveness of the Army's campaign against the hostiles. They wanted to maintain their monopoly on the freight and passenger traffic to Idaho; thus, had no scruples against distorting the truth if it would aid the merchants whose advertising supported them.

"Why risk lives and goods on the long, dangerous, Indian-infested desert route from California to Idaho?" they asked over and over again in their editorials, "when such a safe, sure, comfortable sea and river route to Idaho exists?"

A further source of irritation to Crook, Wasson knew, was the ill-conceived reservation system, which placed bands of Indians that had never really been conquered or tamed on refuges run by incompetent civilian appointees—refuges which loot-hunting bucks could ride away from at will, their bellies full of government-supplied food, their horses fattened on government-owned grass, and their arms and ammunition government-supplied. Frequently, those firearms were more modern than the ones issued to the soldiers whose duty it was to keep the hostiles in line. Ostensibly, the Indians left the reserves seeking wild game; but their definition of "game" was an extremely broad one.

It was Crook's firm conviction that trouble-making Indians never committed depredations near the borders of their own reservations; instead, they traveled far afield—perhaps two or three hundred miles. It was not unreasonable, therefore, that he should attempt to solve Idaho's hostile Indian problem by tracking down and soundly trouncing a band of savages holed up in the mountains of northern California. But if he were to justify this past summer's campaign, he badly needed a rousing fight and a clear-cut victory—soon.

Now, in mid-September, the weather turned bad. "Equinoctial influences made marching very disagreeable," Wasson wrote, "and the 14th was passed in camp. On the 15th, we continued south across a valley so strewn with cinder-black rocks it should have been included in the Infernal Regions. We rode twelve miles through a blinding storm of rain, snow and hail, the rockiest going so far."

The next few days the command remained in camp, resting the sore-footed, tired horses and pack animals. On the 21st it marched eight miles over sharp lava rock; on the 22nd, it made fifteen miles. And here, Wasson wrote, "the trouble commenced . . ."

"Archie with some of his Indians were sent ahead in the evening to look for sign. Dad Wilson was entrusted with six Indians to go in a southwest direction for the same purpose—and to join Archie in the night. This was only the second time during the summer that Wilson had been allowed to go on a responsible errand—the General takes no stock in a person who is always talking about how many years he has 'fit' Indians and how many 'sculps' he has taken. But good horseflesh was scarce, Dad Wilson had two sound animals, so General Crook sent him out . . ."

"About nine o'clock at night the old fellow displayed his scouting knowledge by building a large fire on an exposed peak in full view of our camp and the camps of any hostiles that happened to be in the country. Very shortly, his fire was answered by another from a peak in the Warner Range, twenty-five miles away. But this was nothing compared to what happened the next day . . ."

Next day, Wasson wrote, Dad Wilson ran puffing and sweating into camp headquarters with the story that early that morning he had run into a nest of fifty hostiles, had charged and "fit" them to a fare-thee-well, and would sure have massacred the whole bunch if those no-good, cowardly scouts of his'n hadn't broke and run away.

Crook was furious. By this time, seven or eight Indian signal fires were visible atop peaks for ten miles ahead of the command. "Why in the name of Heaven didn't you report back to me, as I ordered you to, instead of attacking those hostiles?" Crook demanded.

"Jest forgot, I reckon," Dad Wilson mumbled.

"Why did you build that big signal fire last night?"

"Well, you said find Archie—and that seemed t'be the best way. . . ."

As the old man dropped his head in embarrassment, turned and slunk away, General Crook for the first time since Wasson had known him looked like he heartily wished he were a profane man.

"Two weeks," he muttered. "Night and day, foul weather and fair, for two weeks I march my company over the most infernal ground imaginable, for the sole purpose of keeping under cover and closing in on those hostiles undetected. We get within one night's march of where we want to be . . . and then . . . and then . . ."

The disgust exhibited around headquarters, Joe Wasson observed dryly, was "the most expressive" he had ever seen.

Well aware now that the element of surprise had been lost beyond recall, General Crook swung his command over to the wagon road next morning, and, in broad daylight, marched it twenty miles due south, as if bound for the Sacramento. Striking a well-used Indian trail that led southeast, the command followed it through a rough, rock-strewn canyon, making a hard fifteen miles on the 25th. Knowing that the hostiles were already alerted, Crook released two Indian captives that had been captured a few days ago and did not molest the women and children that had lingered behind in the wickiups of a small camp lying in the route of the day's march, from which the adult males had fled at the approach of the troops.

"The General's cup of indignation was more than full tonight," Wasson wrote, "and to add to the gloom the clouds were black and it was raining. He sat off by himself under a pine tree roasting his feet, trying to whittle and whistle, his face longer than this report with two veto-messages added. He considered the campaign 'all up.' Archie's horses were about on their last legs for scouting; all the stock was weary and much of it sick; and the country around was alive with hostile Indians on the alert. I never wanted to make a suggestion so bad in my life . . . but I was afraid to indulge . . ."

CHAPTER NINETEEN

On the 26th, Wasson wrote, the command moved eastward, climbing out of the canyon and crossing several miles of high, open tableland; the hostiles had made no effort to conceal their trail—in fact, the fresh sign was abundantly clear, as if there had been a great deal of riding back and forth during the preceding night. The command was now in the vicinity of the South Fork of Pit River, in northeastern California.

"Turned north along the foot of the bluffs," Wasson reported, "and when about five miles north of a place Williamson's map calls 'Camp S. F. Meadows,' Archie came galloping down off the high bluffs with the word that he had tracked Indians into the rocks but could only guess at the number . . ."

If General Crook disliked fighting the hostiles in a place and time of their choosing, he showed no sign of it. "He ordered Parnell to dismount half his men and form a line across the south side of the occupied rocks. Madigan was to act on the same order with regard to the north side. Under the circumstances, the Indians would hardly try to escape to the plain below. Archie got the remainder of his boys and returned to the high bluffs. I went along with him, satisfied that a good view of the performance could be obtained up there . . ."

By one o'clock in the afternoon, Wasson reported, he and Archie's scouts reached the higher ground overlooking the lava-strewn, basin-like depression into which the hostiles had been tracked. ", . . just as Madigan's men got in line, not understanding the disposition of the troops as yet, they gave us a volley of Springfield rifle balls. Some blasphemous remarks in the American language fixed that matter. No one was hurt, I'm glad to say . . ."

Taking out his opera glasses, Wasson was starting to make an inspection of the rocks into which the hostiles had disappeared when several shots from their direction whistled past him uncomfortably close and made him claw for better cover. "I got a place that seemed tolerably comfortable, and a birdseye view of the enemy's works appeared in outline about as follows:

"A perpendicular lava wall three hundred feet high and a third of a mile in length forms the west side; on the north, running down towards the valley, is a ridge of great lava boulders; on the south is a canyon; from the valley to the east it is a gradual rise till within about four hundred yards of the high wall, where it forms a low, sharp ridge with loose boulders along the crest—this forming the eastern side, and giving the whole a basin-like appearance.

"Running into this basin from the southeast side are two promontories of rock one hundred and fifty feet in length, fifty wide and thirty high, and walls perpendicular; the two points are parallel with each other and thirty feet apart—thus making an impassable gorge between. On the north end of the eastern point is a circular artificial fort twenty feet in diameter, breast-high, with port-holes; on the western point are two forts on a larger scale. Between the forts and the bluff, the canyon on the south and the ridge on the north, it is a mass of shapeless lava boulders from the size of an 'A'-tent up . . ."

Even to a man as unschooled in warfare as Joe Wasson was, it was clear that the hostile Indians had chosen their defensive position with great care. "The only practicable approach is from the eastern slope; they seem to be making the fort covering it their headquarters at this time, 2 P.M. When Parnell approached the canyon from the south, he got a volley from fifteen or twenty Indians, who then fell back into the forts—making defiant gestures and exclamations. Parnell's men were then enabled to get a position within fifty yards of the forts under the rocky crest, but in attempting to reconnoiter in advance of this, a volley from the fort mortally wounded Sergeant Barchet, killed Private Lyons and wounded Privates Clancey and Fisher . . ."

Realizing that a siege was inevitable, Crook ordered Lieutenant Eskridge, who was in charge of the herders and stock, to unsaddle the horses, take the packs off the mules, move the animals back to the valley floor to the eastward out of harm's way and make camp. Meanwhile, the troops surrounding the stronghold of the hostiles ", . . poured a constant stream of bullets into the forts; with the sound of the firing, mashing and glancing of the balls and the yelling from both sides, the occasion was interesting, to say the least."

"One old chief or 'medicine man,' from a safe standpoint, kept up an almost ceaseless 'talk' in a loud voice, the burden of which no one on the outside could or cared to interpret—it was but too evident that a large number of the Lo faction had centered here and were waiting, in true Donnybrook style, for the soldiers to 'tread' on the tails of their coats. Which the latter at once proceeded to do . . ."

Now that he had at long last pinned down a band of hostiles,

General Crook appeared to be ready to settle for nothing less than complete extermination or surrender. Armed with a Spencer carbine which he did not hesitate to use when he thought he glimpsed a likely target, he spent the rest of the afternoon scrambling from rock to rock, personally directing the fire of the troops and scouts, making a complete circuit of the defensive positions and trying to discover their weak spots. In truth, there appeared to be none. Of the hundreds of rifle shots poured down from the heights into the rock-strewn basin and the hundreds more slanted up at the three forts, not one injured a hostile, so far as Wasson could see.

"We did capture two loose horses that came down the gorge through our lines," he wrote. "One slippery Indian cuss made his way through the junipers past Madigan, but by the time he was seen on open ground he had too much of a start to be headed. He made some saucy gestures, gave a whoop, and scooted off down a canyon to the north. Archie gave him a good chase, but he got away . . ."

In venturing too close to one of the forts, Lieutenant John Madigan suffered a slight flesh wound in his right forearm. On several occasions, Crook himself had to dive for cover as the hostiles caught him crossing open spaces between rocks. A squad detached from Parnell's company, sent by Crook to reinforce Archie's scouts, at first mistook friend for foe, making Wasson fleetingly regret not having retreated to the camp of the packers, where Crook had suggested he go. ", . . after being persuaded it was improper to shoot us from the rear," he wrote wryly, "they helped us throw lead down at the forts . . ."

As the afternoon waned ". . . the General came up for a final observation, ordered Archie's command to supper and the soldiers to watch the bluffs until further orders. Parnell was ordered to keep up a strong picket. About dark all the available men were ordered to crawl up as near the forts as possible and prevent any escape. Archie's men were to occupy the ridge between the soldiers. For good reasons, I chanced the night with the scouts. Nothing ever looked so damned ridiculous to me as their 'war dance' after supper—as much as to say the show couldn't go on without some of that sort of thing . . ."

". . . we crawled up within one hundred feet of the east fort. As soon as darkness set in, the besieged devils turned loose with their Paiute tooth-picks (arrows) and what with these and throwing stones we had no occasion to go to sleep. The bodies of Barchet and Lyons were recovered early in the night. One of Madigan's men—Carl Bross—was killed accidentally. He had crawled too far ahead, and the soldiers couldn't distinguish him in the dark . . ."

All night long, Wasson wrote, he could hear rocks being moved and tumbled about, as if the Indians were busy building up the walls of their fortifications. Every once in a while the surrounding pickets would pour in a volley of rifle fire, directing it by sound alone. In reply, the Indians would howl insults, the tones muffled and echoing hollowly, as if coming from within deep caverns. About nine o'clock, a thunder and lightning storm began roaring and flashing; it lasted until midnight, and, combined with the sporadic rifle fire from the pickets, the tumbling of rocks, the fluttering of unseen "Paiute toothpicks" and the defiant howls of the penned-in hostiles, "added considerable interest to the scene."

At suppertime, Wasson had gotten an inkling of what was to come, he wrote. First, General Crook said, he intended to continue the siege until the red devils were all killed or starved to death; second, he regarded it as most important that the Indians learn right here and now that *his* bluecoats would not run them into their holes, besiege them briefly, then go off and leave them, as other soldiers had invariably done in time past; last, he was seriously considering taking the forts by storm.

"He feels that this would heighten the effect on the Indians," Wasson wrote approvingly, "besides saving the men. . . ."

Crook was up by daylight, next morning. After hearing the reports from the commanders of the various units surrounding the stronghold, he ordered Parnell and Madigan to bring all their available men and form up at the base of the slope to the east. Each officer had about twenty soldiers fit for duty. Archie and his scouts were to man the high ridge to the west of the basin.

"The storming parties were ordered to crawl up the slope as far as possible without discovering themselves, and halt," Wasson wrote. "One Lawrence Traynor, a civilian, took Private Lyons' carbine, and he and I offered to go with the 'boys in blue . . .'"

"All right," Crook said curtly. "It's your funeral."

"We joined Madigan's company," Wasson continued. "The General talked to the men like a father. He told them that at the word 'Forward' they should rise up quick, go with a yell and keep yelling and never think of stopping until they had crossed the ditch, scaled the wall and broke through the breastworks . . ."

"About sunup (of the 27th) the word was given. We had gone about twenty yards when a volley of all sorts of slugs and arrows knocked eight of Madigan's men out of line—killing the Lieutenant himself, badly wounding Corporals McCann, Fogarty and Firman, wounding Privates MeGuire, Embler and Baybes—the two latter with arrows— and badly wounding Traynor. The remainder of the boys kept going, a canyon or natural ditch, wide and deep to cross, notwithstanding.

"There were but two points along the wall that seemed like practicable ascents, and the men immediately commenced the climb—on the left, Sergeant Russler of Co. D, on the right, Sergeant Meara and Private Sawyer of Co. H; these men leading at the different places. About twenty-five feet up, the wall receded into a natural parapet, six feet wide and continuing around the east and north side of the artificial fort.

"Meara jumped across, looked over into the fort and exclaimed:
'Come on, boys, we've got 'em!' Then he instantly fell on the parapet dead—his head, with a bullet hole in it, striking about a foot to the left of me.

"At the same moment, Russler put his gun through a port-hole, fired, and, looking over, said: 'Get out of that, you sons-of-bitches!' I went around the parapet to the north side of the fort to get a shot as they came out, but they dropped their empty guns, slid over the west side and disappeared in the gorge in an instant like so many lizards.

"I found Sawyer, who had preceded me but a moment, stretched out on the parapet—the brains oozing out of his left temple. Saw James Shea (of Co. H) down under the wall to the right waiting for them to come out, but could see no other live human being round about or in the gorge beneath—except, through a port-hole, I could see the soldiers getting into the fort.

"But an instant afterwards a volley of arrows and bullets came across from the west forts and apparently from the natural rocks below—one slug striking the guard-iron of Shea's carbine, splitting the breech wide open, and wounding him (not seriously) in three places. The prospects for continuing in the good state of health of which I had been boasting, were not now very bright, and I went back to the southeast end of the parapet, by which time Parnell had all the soldiers up and the fort full of them.

"Inside, lay a big buck with two dead shots through him—some of the men on the left had caught him, or the General himself, who shot twice at the retreating devils from the ridge where Madigan fell. He makes few mistakes with that Spencer of his. While a number of us were lounging around outside the fort on the south side, taking observations, another of those mysterious volleys came from the west, most of it ranging up and over us, only cutting clothes and scratching a few men, but strongly indicative that in taking the fort we had got hold of something we couldn't let go . . ."

Now a quiet fell. Search though they would over the broken surface of the basin, not a single live hostile could be found. None of the Indians had escaped through the lines of the surrounding troopers and scouts; Crook was positive of that. From the intensity of the firing—which Lieutenant Eskridge swore had been thicker than any he had ever faced during the Civil War—it was obvious that a far larger number of hostiles had been entrenched among the rocks than had been found dead or wounded after the battle. So the puzzling question was: Where in God's name had they gone?

"Down," Crook muttered grimly. "That's the only way they could have gone. There must be all sorts of holes and caves under the surface that they can crawl into."

"Which means they're still down there?" Wasson asked.

"Yes."

"How do we root them out, crawl in after them?"

"You're perfectly welcome to try that technique, Mr. Wasson, though it's not one I would recommend."

"Pity you don't have a few pieces of artillery, sir."

General Crook shook his head. "Artillery wouldn't touch them, Mr. Wasson—they're too well protected overhead. Greek fire, hand grenades or nitro-glycerin would do the trick. But we haven't got them. All we can do is sit on their holes and starve them out."

As the day slowly passed, only an occasional shot from a hidden Indian trapped above ground or too badly wounded to move broke the quiet. One of those shots gave Private Kingston a dangerous wound in the right temple; as he was carried to the dressing station, Wasson heard a trooper exclaim: "Good God! That's a jinxed gun, if ever I seen one! First Lyons, then Traynor, now Kingston. Damned if you'll catch *me* touching that Spencer!"

It was true, Wasson learned, that all three men had been carrying the same carbine when shot. To a fighting man, it was but natural, he wrote, that they discard their long, heavy, single-shot rifles the moment that the lighter, breech-loading, seven-shot repeating Spencer carbines became available. But it would be a while before any trooper in the command nerved himself to use this particular gun again.

"The curious quiet of the afternoon was rendered more singular during the night," he wrote, "by the squawling of papooses. The night was very dark. We could not be sure where the sound came from, though it seemed to come from both the front and rear of our lines . .

. About eight a.m., next morning, a young squaw was permitted to come out through the lines. Her story was that all of the bucks had escaped—leaving behind only the squaws and the papooses . . ."

It seemed impossible. Yet it was true, Archie and his scouts learned after a thorough search of the area. "Running from the fortified promontories to the canyon to the southwest," Wasson wrote, "is a deep strata of lava threaded with fissures and subterranean passages. The slippery devils wormed out under the very feet of the pickets, emerged beyond the canyon some distance away, and then fled in such a demoralized state that their trail was littered with the bows, arrows, guns and ammunition they had cast away in their panic . . ."

Now that it had been established that the main body of hostiles had fled, troopers and scouts began gingerly exploring the passage-honeycombed area underneath the basin, each man venturing according to the extent of his fearlessness and curiosity. On his part, Wasson admitted he was content merely to record descriptions obtained by braver men.

". . . in this ten acre area, ten thousand men could be stowed out of sight in fifteen minutes," he wrote. "Five hundred men unacquainted with the place could never capture five well posted, armed and supplied defenders. Regular hatchway holes run down through from the artificial forts, many of which are worn smooth from the climbing up and down. In scaling the walls and overrunning the fissures, a man could be shot from three feet and never know what did it. That this place is an old but lately active volcano is probable."

"To thoroughly explore these caverns, which very likely still contain wounded and armed savages who know all the exits and entrances and can hide in darkness while the stranger must carry a light to see his way, is too much to demand of the officers and men. The General permits each one to use his own discretion in the matter . . ."

One of the troopers let his boldness overcome his discretion. ". . . about eleven o'clock, Jas. Carey (of Co. H) started down into a dark den head foremost and six-shooter in hand; he reached a shelf with a bullet through his heart. In recovering the body, one of the men said he got sight of a cave in which 'you could camp the command . . .'"

A cautious exploration of the underground passages revealed no supply of drinking water, but their coolness, dampness, and the fact that deposits of ice were often found in lava-field caves such as these made it reasonable to assume that a water supply did exist. In the east fort, it was found, the hostiles had carefully gathered the battered leaden balls thrown down into their stronghold by rifles on the heights; no doubt many had been re-used. A large store of powder and caps, still in brand-new boxes such as those stocked in the stores of the white settlements in California, Nevada, and Oregon, was discovered, along with a number of new guns of the American half-stocked pattern.

"I know the exact source of those arms," General Crook said grimly. "But how does a mere soldier persuade the politicians to cut it off?"

Acutely aware as he was of the tendency of fault-finding editors to treat any fight in which soldiers suffered severe casualties as a stinging defeat for the Army, Joe Wasson put his pen to use in an eloquent defense of Crook's management of the campaign.

"The hostiles had no idea of the soldiers' staying with them," he wrote. "Whether they ever again attempt to make a stand in such a place remains to be seen. I heard no man complain of the charge; all felt that the siege was conducted and finished on the cheapest plan. The only expressed regret was that the Indians knew about the passages under the rocks and we didn't . . ."

"The estimate of their dead is fifteen, though only five bodies were found among the rocks. One was that of an old chief who apparently had been in on the massacre of the Chinamen on the Jordan Valley road some months back. He was wearing a fur cap tasseled with the queues of murdered Orientals . . ."

"The young squaw captured by the scouts told us some palpable lies at first, but when Archie and his crowd took her to a tree and threatened her in a way an Indian could quickly understand, she talked freely enough. She said there were about seventy-five Paiutes in the fight, thirty Pit River Indians and a few Modocs. Some of them had been in on the horse-stealing up Dunder and Blitzen way. They had eaten some of the horses, she said, and traded the rest off for things they wanted to Indians living on the Pyramid Lake and Truckee Reservations. There is a big trade, she says, between the northeastern California and Nevada Indians and the white settlements, and large bands of Indians go north every so often to raid in eastern Oregon and Idaho . . ."

"When General Crook came to Idaho last winter, he set about whipping the Indians and learning their haunts, meeting with much success and some vexatious losses. He soon became satisfied that, from the impudent character of the depredations on the Humboldt Road and the Owyhee settlements, the perpetrators had some far-off place of retreat where they lived in apparent innocence. He is now convinced that it is the Palutes instead of the Snakes who are doing most of the deviltry . . ."

"This campaign should convince the most incredulous of the correctness of his reasoning. The General will take a pleasure in fighting the devils this winter, if he can get the reasonable means he asks for at Camp Warner . . ."

The six enlisted men that had been killed during the battle were buried on the river flat a mile or so north of the scene of the fight. Gathering what sketchy information he could from their comrades and officers, Joe Wasson wrote their pitifully scant obituaries:

Charles Barchet, German. Served through the War with 7th Vermont Vol's, has relatives in Texas.

Jas. Lyons, father and brother living in Place Dale, Rhode Island.

Michael Meara, born in Galway, Ireland; has been in the U. S. Army eighteen years, relatives in Boston, Mass.

Willoughby Sawyer, native of Canada West.

Jas. Carey, for a long time a resident of New Orleans.

Carl Bross, German, family in Newark, New Jersey.

After the men had been buried side by side in separate graves, the earth was tramped in, the surplus dirt was removed and fires were built in an effort to eliminate all sign.

"Bad enough to be killed by savages," Wasson wrote grievingly, "but there is additional horror attendant on knowing one has to be left hundreds of miles in the wilderness, without so much as a little lumber to designate the line of demarkation between human and mother earth; yet the greatest respect that can be afforded is to have every trace obliterated . . ."

Unable to bear letting their gay, witty, life-loving friend John Madigan go without some more fitting ceremony, his fellow officers and the enlisted men of the company he had commanded insisted on taking his body along for a day's march on the homeward-bound trip. Two-mule litters were made for the wounded unable to ride. Reaching the juncture of the South Fork with the main branch of Pit River in late afternoon, September 29th, "Lieutenant John Madigan, Co. 'H', 1st U. S. Cay., was buried with extra ceremony—of its kind . . .

"He was born and brought up in Jersey City, N.J., served through the War with the Army of the Potomac, and for gallantry therein received a commission in the Regular Services. His friendship was of the genuine sort. Possessing a droll originality and humor, his presence at the campfire had become almost indispensable with Crook's officers. No one could more regret his taking off in the prime of life than the General himself."

"Alas, poor Madigan!" Wasson added sadly. "'Where are your oddities now? Hushed amid the yells of fiends and no sound but the bugle call of Judgment can awake you to glory again . . .'"

Although General Crook kept an alert rearguard trailing the weary command on its slow journey north, ready and eager to get in a final lick against any hostiles that might be wishing more action, the trip home proved to be an uneventful one. October had come; the wild plums were ripe; autumn frosts had splotched the hills with patches of crimson and gold.

"On the 4th we traveled six or eight miles," Wasson wrote, "and Camp Warner was reached again. The soldiers were truly glad to see a chance to rest—especially the wounded, who seemed to get along finely . . . Among the letters awaiting Madigan was a promotion. Lt. Small reports killing and capturing thirty Indians in the tules of Abert Lake; I think Capt. Darragh helped him to 'that bowl of blood . . .'"

On the 7th the General started to Camp Harney, from which point I expect to furnish you a few items. Incidents of interest occurred every day of the campaign that must go by the board. I have endeavored to give you a plain statement of how a month's operations developed from day to day.

Had a bully time and have no excuses to make.
Joe.

As a veteran war correspondent and a seasoned Indian fighter, Joe Wasson seemed reluctant to say farewell to Crook's command and seek more gainful, though less exciting, employment. His loyalty to his Army friends had become absolute. In the General's absence, he wrote indignantly, construction of the new buildings at Camp Warner—which had been left in charge of civilian contractors—had slowed to a snail's pace. Profiteering hay, grain, and lumber dealers were running up fantastic bills which they insisted must be paid in hard money. Carpenters and craftsmen were drawing wages as excessive as their work was incompetent. And, as a special homecoming greeting, a Department order awaited General Crook transferring

CROOK'S CAMPAIGN 1867

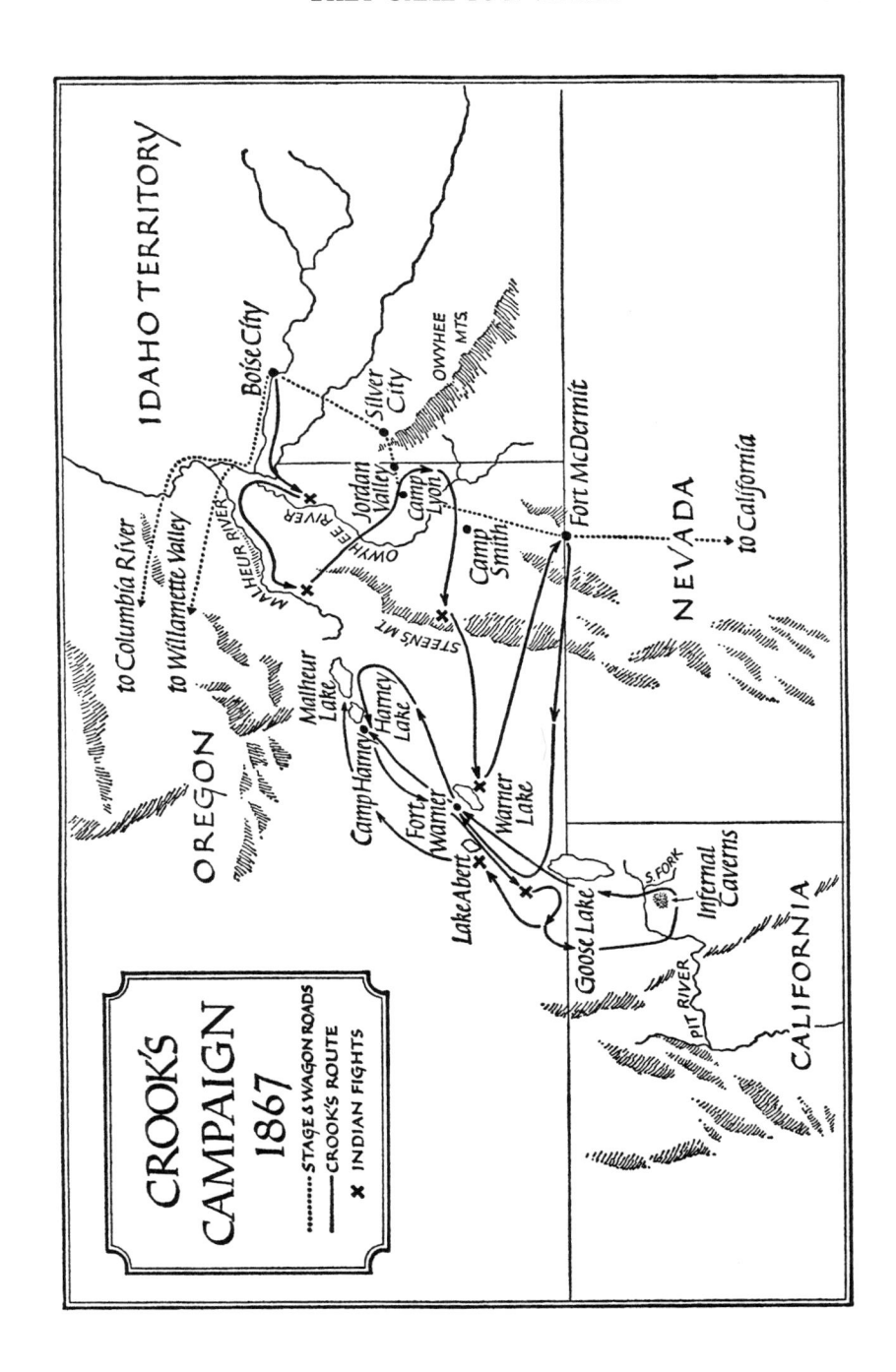

.... STAGE & WAGON ROADS
—— CROOK'S ROUTE
✗ INDIAN FIGHTS

Major Perry and Company "F" to Fort Boise, in Idaho Territory, and Captain Parnell and Company "H" to Camp Smith, in eastern Oregon, where they would be of no use to him in this winter's campaign against the hostiles.

"If this order is not revoked," Wasson wrote bitterly, "the General will be left with so few forces he might just as well spend the winter sitting in his quarters 'issuing orders,' as the 'Desk Generals' do in San Francisco and Washington City."

But Crook was not ready to resign himself to becoming a "Desk General" just yet. Immediately after completing his inspection of Camp Harney, which was situated a hundred miles or so northeast of Warner and was to be an important auxiliary post in this winter's campaign, he dispatched Lieutenant Eskridge to Department Headquarters in Portland with letters detailing his future plans and urgently asking that Companies "F" and "H" be retained where he could put them to their best use.

"There are 'powers behind the throne' which boast that they 'can buy Department Headquarters for a horse,'" Wasson wrote acidly. "And the fact is, the General anticipates more trouble from them than he does from the Paiutes. To ask for tough mustang stock and receive an indifferent makeup of unacclimated, gangling horses that one day's march will play out, is not very flattering to men willing to risk their lives in a service where the pay and promotion will increase as rapidly sitting in comfortable quarters as fighting in the field. And to know that contracts are so let that no man of integrity ever gets a hearing, is not a pleasant state of affairs . . ."

"Men engaged in this species of robbery are a set of chronic thieves, who, like Falstaff's pimps:—

"'Will steal anything, and call it—purchase.'"

The hay contract at Camp Harney, for example, was being filled by a civilian contractor who was supplying "old door-mats" at $40 (coin) per ton. To add insult to the indignity, the so-called hay was being hauled two miles and stacked by soldiers whose pay was $16 (greenbacks) per month. But with Crook's arrival, Wasson reported jubilantly, the atmosphere changed rather suddenly.

". . . those civilian mule teams suddenly commenced hauling two loads instead of one per day; some nine or ten fancy carpenters got eternal leaves of absence and were replaced by one practical old man, who, in four days, did more toward building the quarters at Camp

Harney with a little soldier help than had been accomplished for four weeks previously . . ."

Not content with speeding up the lazy and firing the dishonest, General Crook issued the following order and required that it be posted in several conspicuous places:

". . . for the purpose of protecting all honest and industrious citizens—horse-thieves and other disreputable persons being known to be in the vicinity—all citizens not in the employ of the Government or having no visible occupation, will leave this Military Reservation at once . . ."

Joe Wasson heartily approved of the order. "It was a sight to see the scattering caused by the foregoing bull," he wrote. "Pack trains returning to the settlements had back loads in passengers, and many adventurers left camp afoot with blankets on their backs. Major Perry swore that I came under the special ban and wanted to know when I intended leaving."

"The truth was, I replied, the only horse I ever contemplated stealing died a natural death near the site of the recent unpleasantness down in the Pit River country. 'Old Buster,' as I called him, was about the last of the Oregon Cavalry—he had webbed feet and only lacked wings to make him a complete Swamp Angel. He carried me about twelve hundred miles, but got the 'California fever' and died like a hero. He could keep fat on greasewood with the bits in his mouth . . ,"

Furthermore, Wasson informed Major Perry, the contractors had left nothing *to* steal. But if it would make the major's anticipation of the coming winter's social events more pleasant, the time was rapidly approaching when ducks, geese, newspaper correspondents, and other forms of migratory wildlife must spread their wings and point their beaks southward to a sunnier clime.

"There will be quite a number of married ladies at Warner," Wasson wrote, "if no other arrangements are made to the contrary. Mrs. Crook, Hinton, Parnell, Eschenberg, Jack, Lewis and Cosby all are expected to arrive soon . . ."

From the vast store of knowledge he had acquired during the past few months of campaigning, Joe Wasson generously offered a final paragraph of advice to the War Department brass regarding the future conduct of the war against the hostiles in this part of the country.

With two companies of cavalry at Harney, and Archie's scouts increased and well mounted, the General intends to scout the Owyhee and Malheur during the first of the winter; and then—with two companies of cavalry at Warner—start for the Paiute headquarters. He believes that one more winter will "settle their hash" and "close out their business." Archie's band possess much independence of character, mind their own business, are fat, jolly and contented (because they are treated justly) and the soldiers rather like to see them around. Donald McKay and his scouts are invaluable, too . . .

If I have talked pretty plain about many things seen and learned while "swinging around the circle" the last four months, there has been nothing said which the public should not know, and nothing that need offend except in the right places . . .

If I have not said enough already to make the General wish the devil had me, I would say he was one of "God's own men" in the right place—thoroughly in earnest regardless of fear or favor from any source.

Yours truly
Joe

Chapter Twenty

"Back East, a Dr. Bryant claims he can cure rheumatism by the laying on of hands. That's nothing. Out here in Idaho, we cure horse-stealing the same way."

—Idaho Statesman
Boise City, I.T.
October 3, 1867

To Melinda Belford O'Neil, mirrors had lost much of the fascination they once held for her. Four years of Idaho sun, dust, wind, and heat had taken the rosy bloom of youth from her cheeks; maturity, marriage, and the grim realities of living on a noncom's pay had dimmed the sparkle of her eyes; and six months ago Sergeant Patrick O'Neil had completely ruined her once-slim figure by making her pregnant.

She cried a great deal, these days. She complained of feeling unwell. Bad as barracks life at Fort Boise had been during the early weeks of their marriage, it had grown intolerably worse during the long, dull, dreary summer which she and Patrick had been forced to endure at the comfortless outpost of Camp Lyon, in Jordan Valley, just across the Oregon line from the southwestern corner of Idaho Territory. At Fort Boise, at least, there had been a city, her family, and her pre-Army friends nearby. Here, there was nothing but heat, dust, wind, and soldiers, and not a blessed thing of interest to do.

Oh, the officers managed to have a social life of sorts between patrols and Indian-hunting expeditions, for now and again a few of them brought their wives into camp for brief visits. Every once in a while a bachelor officer or a married officer whose wife was far away smiled at Melinda, spoke to her, or looked at her in a way that made her feel sure that, if a meeting could be discreetly managed, he would not mind helping her pass the time during Patrick's frequent absences. But she knew she dared not risk it, innocent though such an interlude might be.

"You're Sergeant Patrick O'Neil's wife," her husband had warned her sternly. "Don't you never forget that, Mellie. Say 'sir' to the officers, just like I do, and don't give the enlisted men the time of day.

Where women are concerned, mix only with your equals—and be goddam careful what you say to them."

"How do I know who my equals are?" Melinda asked petulantly.

"By the stripes on their husband's sleeve, by God. Take Sergeant Grogan's wife, for instance. She's our kind. A plain, sensible, hardworking woman— "

"Olga Grogan? Oh, Patrick, I wouldn't dream of associating with her!"

"Why not?"

"She's as big and ugly as a cow, for one thing. She's got a Dutch accent so thick I can't begin to understand her, for another. She takes in laundry, just like a common Chinaman. Worst of all, she used to be a hurdy-gurdy in one of those awful Boise City dance halls!"

Sergeant O'Neil threw back his head and roared with laughter. "Sure, and what's so terrible about taking in laundry to make a few extra dollars? It's clean, honest work. As to Olga being a hurdy-gurdy, sure, she was that for two whole years before she married Mike Grogan. But she saved her wages, Olga did, bringing a right handsome dowry to her husband, which is a sight more than *you* did for me."

"Is Mike Grogan *proud* of that?"

"Why shouldn't he be? She was virgin goods on their wedding night, you can bet on that. Many's the time I've seen her box a man's ears for laying a hand on her the wrong way or whispering an improper word to her when in his cups. Oh, and didn't she pack a mule-kick in that hefty meat-hook of hers!"

"Well, *you* would know, I'm sure," Melinda said peevishly. "But she certainly isn't *my* kind of person."

"Who is, love?" Patrick chuckled. Putting an arm around her waist, he gave her a hug that took her breath away. "You and your foolish airs and daydreams, Mellie! The world ain't made of moonbeams and music, satin and fine manners, you know. You'll learn that by and by. Take the world for what it is, make the best of it and be grateful for what you've got."

The sad truth was, Melinda had learned, Patrick O'Neil was content with his lot and saw no reason why she should not be satisfied with hers. Her father had had a trade by which he could earn a living for his family whenever he chose to work at it; his father had had none. Her father had moved discontentedly from one ill-producing farm to another; his father had never even owned a square foot of ground. Her father had supplied the table with few luxuries but the family had never gone hungry; his father, mother, and many of his relatives had died in a brutal famine. In the Missouri hills, her father had never found the opportunity for advancement that suited his peculiar talents; in the Ireland from which Patrick O'Neil had fled, there had been no opportunity at all.

A week after setting foot on the docks in New York City, penniless, illiterate, sick, and starving, he had enlisted in the United States Army, he told her. Ten years later, here he was, able to read and write, healthy, well-clothed, well-fed, a sergeant in the United States Cavalry and an American citizen. He had climbed a long way up the ladder of success from the peat bogs of Ireland, he felt, and was damned proud of it.

Well, he *was* handsome, Melinda admitted. Even after seven months of marriage, it still gave her a tingle of pleasure to see him lift his hand in a nonchalant salute of farewell as he went riding off on a scout with his captain and his company. He possessed a tremendous masculinity in the way he sat his horse, in the way he walked, in the way he issued orders to his men, in the way he smiled at her and embraced her, a virility that no young woman could fail to respond to—even if he did smell rankly of dust, sweat, leather, and horses. There had been many moments in the early weeks of their marriage when she felt she was wildly in love with him and that he was indeed everything she wanted in a man. But lately—especially since her pregnancy had brought her these frequent sick spells—she had begun to have doubts . . .

Ah, what has happened to the girl I used to be? The girl who had only to walk in a certain way, smile in a certain way, and toss her head in a certain way to make the mirror-eyes of every man that saw her grow luminous with admiration? Didn't that girl deserve better than what she got?

You're very beautiful, Miss Belford. Are you aware of that?
Oh, please, Mr. Warren, you mustn't say such things!
Why not? I'm an artist and an expert on beauty, you know . . .

Before their marriage, Patrick had been wildly jealous of every man that looked at her, and it had been great fun to tease him with vague references to the horde of handsome, charming, well-off suitors which she claimed had constantly pursued her. Now, he did not appear to care how many beaus she had had before she met him, just as long as she remained a faithful, obedient wife. Irritated by the way he would sit dozing in their shabby quarters through the long summer evenings, his shirt off, his unwashed feet bare, his face unshaven, his trouser braces drooping to the floor, she would try to stir up his old fire by reminiscing about the men she had known.

"Poor Will!" she would sigh. "He was *so* attentive to me. In a way, I suppose, I was responsible for the awful thing that happened to him . . ."

Patrick would open his eyes, blink sleepily at her, and grunt indifferently, "Oh? How so?"

"He wanted to marry me. But when Mr. Warren joined the train at Fort Hall, Will got *so* jealous of him. It was silly, really, for I never gave Will the least little bit of encouragement. The trouble was, Mr. Warren was an artist and wanted to paint my picture. I *did* like him. He was such a gentleman and had such nice manners. And he was rich, too . . ."

Along about then, Patrick's eyelids would sag, his head would drop and he would begin snoring softly. Even when she became angry enough to shake him back to consciousness and accuse him of rudely ignoring her—as she did do a few times—he would merely grin at her and say, "Sure, Mellie, and you're a fine story-teller. But it happened years ago, didn't it now, when you were a mere slip of a girl and saw things through daydreaming eyes? Go on talking, Mellie, the sound soothes me. It's been a long, hard day . . ."

No, she could strike no spark in Patrick O'Neil by talking about old beaus, real or imagined. He was a practical-minded man living in a world of hard realities and he would spare neither time nor interest for anything but his life as a soldier. Only once did her wistful remembrances of wagon-train days get a rise out of him. That was when, in talking about Will Starr, she said, ". . . and there are *some* people that believe he's Chief Bigfoot . . ."

"What's that?" Patrick demanded, opening his eyes, dropping his feet to the floor and sitting suddenly erect. "Who do you say is Chief Bigfoot?"

"Will Starr. *I* don't say it, mind you. But some of the people that came to Idaho in our wagon train do."

"Ah, they're full of horse manure!"

"Patrick, how many times must I tell you I won't stand for stable talk under my roof!" Melinda exclaimed indignantly. "Maybe I can't make you wash your filthy feet or change your filthy underdrawers, but I simply *won't* put up with your filthy language!"

"Sure, Mellie, and it's sorry I am," Patrick said with a genial smile. "But this Chief Bigfoot nonsense—"

"Don't you believe there is such an Indian?"

"Not till I see him with my own two eyes."

"Sergeant Grogan believes in him. Didn't I hear him talking to you about Chief Bigfoot the other evening?"

"Ah, Mike Grogan was in his cups, Mellie. As you should know by now, an Irishman in his cups sees everything from little men sitting on mushrooms to pink elephants walking the ceiling."

"But he didn't say *he* saw him—he said Archie McIntosh claimed *he* saw him."

"Poor Archie! Let *him* get drunk and he'll people the earth with ten-foot giants and hundred-foot snakes speckled with green polka dots. General Crook himself will tell you that."

"Well, all I know is *some* people say Will Starr and Chief Bigfoot are the same person," Melinda pouted. "*I* don't say it, mind you. Still, I'm bound to wonder . . ."

Patrick eyed her thoughtfully. "He was a big fellow, this Will Starr?"

"Yes."

"And part Indian?"

"Mr. Warren thought he was—Cherokee, maybe, or Creek. And he was *terribly* strong. Even after Mr. Warren shot him in the chest, Will managed to choke him to death, get on his horse, swim the river and ride off into the desert."

"Did anybody try to track him down?"

"Andy Hale and his Delaware friend Levi did. They followed him as far as the mountains north of Silver City, they said, found his horse where it had fallen dead, and saw some tracks that showed Will Starr had been captured by the Snakes."

"In that case, he'd be a goner for sure. The Snakes wouldn't take in a total stranger."

"Not even if he were an Indian?"

Patrick shrugged. "Not likely, Mellie. But it's your tale—go on and finish it."

"Well, what people say is suppose the Snakes that found him *did* recognize him as an Indian?" Melinda said eagerly. "Suppose they took him in, nursed him back to health and he became their leader? He would hate all white people, wouldn't he? He would be so much bigger, so much stronger, so much smarter than the Snakes that he would soon gather a large band of hostiles around him. He would know the ways of the whites. He would know how to send spies into the settlements. He would know how to get guns and ammunition . . ."

"And then he would declare war," Patrick said, smiling tolerantly, "and try to wipe out the whole cursed white race living in this part of the country. Ah, Mellie, it's a fine tale to scare children with of a windy winter night, but it's got too many holes in it to convince *me*."

"I'm not saying *I* believe it, either," Melinda admitted. "Still, *some* people do."

Patrick laughed good-humoredly. "Just let me meet the booger face to face, Mellie. After I've emptied my Spencer into him, I'll tell you how real he is. Just let me meet the booger . . ."

The commander of Patrick's company, a bachelor, did not regard Camp Lyon as a proper place for a white woman's first child to be born in. In mid-October, Patrick came home one afternoon with the welcome news that he had been ordered to pack their belongings into an Army ambulance, take Melinda back to Fort Boise and remain attached to that post until after the baby arrived. Melinda was overjoyed.

"Oh, Patrick!" she cried, throwing her arms about his neck and kissing his dust-grimed cheek. "Everything will be fine now!"

"Sure, love. Let's start packing."

Sergeant Mike Grogan was to go with them, Patrick said, then drive the ambulance back loaded with special purchases made in Boise City for the private use of the officers and noncoms stationed at Camp Lyon. What the nature of the special purchases was to be, Patrick laughingly refused to tell her, but from the number of greenbacks stuffed into his wallet—$1200 worth, he admitted—she guessed that the major portion of them would be whisky.

By eight o'clock, next morning, they were on their way. There had been a light sprinkle of rain during the night, not nearly enough to settle the dust, but sufficient to clear the air of its early autumn haze, cool it considerably and give it a refreshing zest. While Patrick drove the four horses and Sergeant Mike Grogan sat on the front seat beside him, chatting amiably, Melinda lounged in a half-reclining position on a blanket-padded wooden bench set lengthwise along one side of the ambulance. She felt unusually well this morning. The ambulance top shaded her from the sun and the canvas sides could be lowered to protect her against dust and wind later in the day, although right now the morning was so pleasant she had insisted that they be left rolled up, so that she could see out.

Not that there was much to see, she mused ruefully. This was a bleak, depressing piece of country, with nothing to look at but gray-green sagebrush along the roadside, jumbled brown rocks on the canyon rims in the near distance, and, beyond, gray, monotonous, treeless space stretching off in all directions to horizons broken by mountains. But the breeze was pleasant and the air was fresh. With Patrick's capable hands holding the reins, the ambulance moved along at a steady but not uncomfortable rate, and the knowledge that she was going home lifted her spirits.

Going home? Well, at least Fort Boise would be better than Camp Lyon. But, oh, if only she *were* going back to the home she had once known, the soft, green, gentle Missouri hills, where fine trees grew, where rain fell in the summertime, where no ugly sagebrush, no harsh brown rocks, no stifling dust, no vast reaches of frighteningly empty space offended the eye or sickened the soul! Where one's world was contained, known and peaceful. Where her youth had been forever left behind . . .

Glancing down at the swollen bulk of her once-trim waist, she felt a sudden wave of loathing for her husband. James Warren would not have done this to me. Not so abruptly, anyway. He would have taken me back to his family home in Virginia, whose hills, he once told me, were the greenest, softest, most beautiful hills on earth. He would have taken me to New York, London, and Paris. He would have shown me the world I so wanted to see.

"A woman as beautiful as you are, Mellie, can have her pick of men. Marry a rich man, Mellie, and let him show you the world you deserve to see . . ."

Well, perhaps those weren't his *exact* words, but that was what he had meant. And he *was* in love with me; I realize that now. He would have married me eventually. I know he would have. If only Will Starr hadn't seen the painting and accused James of making him look like a . . .

Poor Will! He was so considerate, so thoughtful, so humble. Why, he worshipped the very ground I walked on! Yes, he was dark-complexioned. But terribly handsome, too. He *could* have had French or Spanish blood in his veins, to make him look that way, with no Indian blood at all. And certainly James was wrong about the . . . the other. If James had not been at Fort Hall, if he had not joined the wagon train, if Will had taken Lafe Perrin's map and found the gold . . .

It *was* there, you know; why, only months later a rich strike was made in the Owyhees in that very same location. Or near it, at least. If Will had struck it rich, if we had gone on west to the Willamette Valley, if we had built a fine house in the green, soft hills near Portland, if we had married . . .

No, Will would not have done this to me. He loved me too much. Why, I always was able to wrap him around my little finger! Will, you must be patient, I would have said. You must wait a while. You must be a gentleman and treat me like a lady . . .

Oh, I had so many opportunities to marry well! There was Andy

Hale, for example. Yes, I'll admit he did not make much of a play for me. With Will and James both courting me so avidly, how could he? But I caught him looking at me now and then and I could tell what he was thinking. That evening when he read the map for Will and me, I deliberately leaned on his shoulder, squeezing his arm, pressing myself against him, just to see what he would do. Don't tell me he breathed faster because he had a sudden attack of asthma!

Oh, yes, my dear, I could have had Andy Hale if I had wanted him bad enough, in spite of Sally Lynn and her coy, simpering, schoolgirl tricks. They say she's still got her cap set for him. And they say he's dying to marry her, if ever he's able to support her. Well, good luck to him. From the shabby, down-at-the-heel way he looked the last time I saw him in Boise City, I'm better off with Patrick . . .

"You're a *femme fatale,* Miss Belford. You're a woman who makes things happen. While empires crumble and blood runs ankle deep in the streets, you walk serenely on . . ."

Melinda sighed. She did not feel like a *femme fatale* now.

She felt like a dull, stodgy, shapeless married woman, and she feared she looked like one, too.

The ambulance was moving now along the floor of a twisting, narrow canyon whose steep sides were covered with a jumble of dark brown rocks. There was no breeze here, no sound but the dust-padded thudding of hoofs and the rumbling of wheels. Closing her eyes against the sun glare, she daydreamed on . . .

What a strange man Armand Kimball is! So polite, so obliging when asked for favors, yet so distant. They say he's not interested in women but I don't believe that. *Every* man is interested in women to some degree. He enjoys going to dances, dinners, and parties. He's charming at small talk. And one Christmas Eve at the Overland House when he'd had quite a bit to drink, he held me so close dancing I could hardly breathe.

Pa would have been pleased if I had married Armand. Which was exactly the trouble. No well-to-do gentleman like Armand Kimball will endure having a girl thrown at him by her own father. Inexperienced as *I* was then, I knew being brazen and pushy would only scare him off. That was why I pretended to be so interested in Patrick. But poor, foolish, ambitious Pa had to go and spoil it all . . .

Well, Armand still hasn't married and I'm still a great deal younger than he is. Suppose something should happen to Patrick. Suppose something should happen to the baby. Oh, no, I wouldn't *dream* of wishing for either, but a body has to be practical, has to look ahead, has to plan, doesn't she? Soldiers *do* get killed, my dear; that's part of the risk one takes in being an Army wife. And an attractive young widow could hardly be expected to live alone all the rest of her life . . .

From another world, far removed, there came the sound of an explosion. Shocked into a numbed awareness of her present surroundings, Melinda heard more explosions, wild yells, and angry buzzings as the air around her seemed suddenly filled with vicious, invisible insects. She tried to scream. Her paralyzed throat could utter no sound. On the driver's seat ahead of her, she saw Mike Grogan bend over and snatch up his rifle. She heard him shout.

"Indians! Drive like hell, Pat! I'll hold the bastards off!"

The ambulance lurched into violent motion. Thrown off the bench, Melinda rolled over, clawed her way up to her hands and knees and stared dazedly at the two men on the seat ahead. Mike Grogan, sitting on the left hand side, lifted his rifle and began firing at the rocks above him. She saw Patrick frantically lashing the rumps of the horses with the tag end of the reins. She saw him turn his head toward her.

"Get down, Mellie! Get—"

Dust spurted from the left side of his blouse. She saw him wince, saw him sway. She heard him grunt harshly, "My God, I'm hit . . ."

A scream of pure horror forced itself through her lips as she saw his body toppling toward the right hand edge of the seat. Mike Grogan, whirling around, dropped his rifle to the floorboards, reached out with his right hand to catch Sergeant O'Neil and prevent him from falling out of the ambulance, while with his left he grabbed for the lines of the panicked horses, which now were running full tilt.

He missed both.

Through the clouds of dust raised by the speeding, jolting wagon, Melinda got a fleeting glimpse of a blue-clad figure lying sprawled on the ground behind. Seizing her by the shoulders, Mike Grogan was shouting something into her ear that she could not understand and was trying to force her to do something that she had no power to do. From behind the rocks on either side of the canyon, half-naked, dark figures were scrambling now, some mounted, some afoot, heading toward the unmoving body of her husband.

"No!" she screamed. "No, no, no!"

"Lie down, Mellie!" Mike Grogan shouted. "There ain't a thing we can do for him!"

She fought him. Unable to take her eyes off the patch of blue lying on the canyon floor, she struck him, scratched him, elbowed him, kicked him. An abrupt sideward lurch of the ambulance sent them both sprawling full length. By the time she managed to push him off and struggle again to her hands and knees, the patch of blue and the dark figures had been lost from sight beyond a turn in the canyon.

Mike Grogan crawled forward to the driver's seat. Lying full length, leaning far out, he reached down for the lost lines, trying to grasp them and bring the runaway horses under control. Suddenly there was a squeal of panic from a terror-stricken horse, a sound of wood splintering, a skidding of the ambulance.

"Look out!" Mike Grogan shouted. "We're going over!"

The next thing Melinda knew, she was lying full length on the ground, her mouth and eyes full of dirt. She struggled to her feet. Mike Grogan had her by one arm, his rifle held in his free hand, and was urging her to go somewhere with him.

"No!" she screamed. "No, no, no!"

"For God's sake, Mellie, c'mon! We got to hide out in the rocks!"

"No, I'm going back to him!"

"Mellie, come on!"

"No! No! I'm going back!"

Now she was free of the restraining hand. Her panic was gone. Now she was in complete control of herself. Now she was slim and young and brimming with health and good spirits. Now she was a little girl again, with no cares, running barefoot, free and happy down a soft, grass-covered hill near home to a cool, clear, remembered stream whose tree-shaded secret haunts only she knew. My, how light on her feet she was! One more turn in the path and she would find the mischievous playmate that had been hiding from her.

There you are, Patrick! Game's over, love! Don't think you can hide from me by sprawling there on the ground. I see you. Turn over, sweet! Aren't you ashamed of yourself, getting your nice blue uniform so dirty! Get up, darling! Open your eyes and get up!

There was something sticky and dark on her hands. No, Patrick, you're not hurt. You're only pretending. Because this is just a game. We're young, young, young, and I'm getting awfully put out with you for playing possum so long . . .

She was surrounded by dark, half-naked figures, she vaguely realized. She could hear them grunting to one another. She could smell them. All right, so it isn't a dream. Patrick is dead. These are Indians, real Indians, and I am alone in a wild and awful land. But they won't hurt me. Not me . . .

Hands jerked her roughly to her feet. She forced her gaze upward from the patch of blue lying in the dust. Her breath was failing her.

The day was growing dim. She felt sick and faint. Standing before her, staring at her unblinkingly, was a bronzed, nearly naked man.

How dark he is! How huge! How implacably evil!

He grunted something and stepped toward her.

She knew no more . . .

Late that afternoon, Sergeant Mike Grogan staggered into Carson's ranch on Sucker Creek, some miles down the road, and told his horrible story. Yes, he said, he was sure Sergeant O'Neil was dead. Likely he'd been dead or dying when he fell out of the ambulance; if not, the Indians had wasted no time finishing him off, for, from his shelter among the rocks, he had seen the devils dragging the stripped, naked corpse off to one side of the road. No, he hadn't seen them kill Mrs. O'Neil. She'd run back maybe half a mile, he said, thrown herself down on her husband's body, then he'd seen the bastards jerk her to her feet.

"She fainted, I think. Then I saw one of the boogers—a big one, he was, a hell of a big one—pick her up and carry her off. What he done to her, I can't say. But I can guess, God help me . . ."

No one found fault with Sergeant Grogan, who obviously had behaved as well as any man could have behaved under the circumstances. Poor Mrs. O'Neil had panicked, that was clear. Young, newly married, and pregnant as she was, the shock of seeing her husband shot down before her very eyes had driven her out of her mind with grief.

The attack had occurred on a Monday. That same day in that same canyon, nine miles east of Camp Lyon, three other groups of white travelers had been set upon by Indians, it was learned, but had managed to fight their way to safety with no losses other than a saddle horse shot out from under one of them. After a night's rest at Carson's ranch, Sergeant Grogan went on to Boise City by stage, made his report to the military authorities, and then was permitted to tell his story to Jim Reynolds. Following an account of the tragedy in the October 24 issue of the *Statesman,* Reynolds wrote a bitter, strongly worded editorial headed:

RECORD OF BLOOD.—Almost every issue of this paper since its existence tells a story of some dark and bloody deed committed by Indians . . .

Down in Silver City, a group of white volunteers was organized as soon as word of the attack reached the mining settlement. On October 26, the *Avalanche* reported:

IN PURSUIT.—The party that went out from Silver to bring in the body of Sergeant O'Neil found it only a short distance from the scene of the murder, stripped and mutilated. His wife was carried off by the Indians alive. Her track was plainly distinguished with those of five or six Indians. Eight picked men—brave and true and armed to the teeth—started in pursuit, determined not to return without bringing her back or ascertaining her fate.

They are what the philanthropic would call "cruel and barbarous," and mean business—and business means scalps, of which article we hope they will come back each with a fresh string.

The whole community is in deep suspense in regard to Mrs. O'Neil, and await with breathless anxiety tidings of her fate. She was in feeble health, and not in condition to keep pace with her merciless captors. The unfortunate woman is probably murdered ere this, or given into the hands of the squaws, who in the exquisite torture of their victims, exercise the ingenuity of demons.

The eight picked men—brave, true, armed to the teeth and determined though they were—found nothing, and presently were forced to give up the search. From Fort Boise, Camp Lyon, and Camp McDermit, Army patrols were sent continuously into the desert, canyon, foothill, and mountain country of southwestern Idaho and eastern Oregon despite the worsening November weather. Their luck was no better. No trace of Mrs. O'Neil could be found—alive or dead.

In Boise City, Cornelius Belford had become a tragic, pathetic figure as he pleaded daily with the governor, the Legislators, the military authorities, the newspaper editors, and the townspeople to do *something* for his beloved daughter. She was still alive; he was positive of that. To her rescuers, he would pay any amount of money they might ask; to her captors, he would pay any ransom they demanded. Yes, he *was* a poor man; but he would raise the money somehow.

"Poor old Corny!" Levi murmured after reading the letter Belford had sent Andy begging him to enlist a large company of volunteers and go in search of his daughter. "He won't face the truth, will he?"

"Meaning she's dead?"

"Sure. Them Snakes ain't gonna haul no pregnant white woman around with 'em for long."

"Well, I haven't got the heart to tell him that. Let him hope as long as he can."

"You gonna hunt for her?"

"No. That's a job for the Army."

As the weeks passed, rumors spread; some hopeful, some despicably cruel. One nameless white braggart, while half drunk in a saloon, claimed that he had talked to an Indian eyewitness present in the hostile camp the night of Mrs. O'Neil's capture. With obscene relish, he related the details of what the Indian had supposedly told him: how Mrs. O'Neil had been stripped, abused, turned over to the squaws, tortured, then finally burned to death at the stake in the most fiendish way. Nobody recalled the white man's name, for he had been a drifter, but the story he'd told spread and was generally believed until the *Avalanche* indignantly scotched it in its November 9 issue:

. . . we conversed with a Sergeant from Camp Lyon, who says the story about Mrs. O'Neil being burned is untrue in every particular. It was the invention of some "smarty." So far as is known, Mrs. O'Neil is still alive . . .

. . . a squaw told our informant that the captured woman has "gone to Winnemucca to be traded off." Everything should be done to ascertain the truth of the matter. If she is gone to the headquarters of Paiute-dom, it is only additional evidence that the deviltry along the Owyhee is done by the savages two or three hundred miles away . . .

On December 17, the *Statesman* passed on an item that offered the missing woman's parents and friends a faint glimmer of hope that she still might be alive:

Hill Beachey says a party of scouts from Camp Lyon last Saturday found a camp of about twenty Indians on the Owyhee. The soldiers immediately attacked the Indians, killing five and taking five or six prisoners. Among the latter were three squaws, one of whom it was said wore the stockings of Mrs. O'Neil.

One of the horses that was hitched to the ambulance in which Mrs. O'Neil and her husband were riding was also captured at or near the Indian camp. The captured squaws were taken to Camp Lyon, and a messenger was sent for McCandless, the interpreter, to see if the percise fate of Mrs. O'Neil can not be ascertained.

McCandless was over on Catherine Creek and it would take two days for him to reach Camp Lyon. Nothing can be learned till he arrives. It is understood that there were two bucks among the captives; if so, let rope be administered to them until they will "talk," and then hang them for good.

Interpreter McCandless, when he did arrive, was unable to decide whether he was being told the truth or not. He suggested that the captives be taken to Fort Boise, where the chief of scouts, Sinora Hicks, could have some time alone with them. Mr. Hicks knew this breed of Indian. And Mr. Hicks was a most persuasive man . . .

On February 6, 1868 the *Statesman* reported:

The fate of Mrs. O'Neil seems at last positively decided. The Indians captured on the Owyhee several weeks ago and brought to Fort Boise by Mr. Hicks and his Indian scouts, were, according to their own acknowledgment, a portion of the band which captured and killed her. Since their arrival here, they have told the Boise Indians that they killed Mrs. O'Neil.

The squaws had many portions of her wearing apparel, and a revolver was captured with the band that is recognized as belonging to O'Neil. So the question stands about thus: This was the party that murdered O'Neil and captured his wife. They admit that she is dead, if not by violence then by cruelty and exposure.

The query naturally arises whether there is not sufficient evidence to convict them of murder, and whether all the bucks in the party ought not to be tried, and, if adjudged guilty, executed.

The captured Indians were not brought to trial, for by now they were in Federal custody, held and protected first by the Army, then by the agent in charge of the nearby reservation upon which they had been placed. As government wards, they were out of reach of civil court procedure. *A rotten miscarriage of justice!* swore more than one civic-minded white citizen. *Let me catch one of the red bastards off the reservation* . . .

Chapter Twenty-one

A man can always go back to Kansas. Lord, Levi mused as he put down his hammer, filled his pipe and leaned against the corral fence he was repairing for a few minutes rest in the mild March sunshine, it had been nigh onto five years since he told Andy that. And here he was, still hanging around . . .

Helping out . . .

Passing time . . .

Living out his days . . .

He was content. He liked ranch work and he liked this part of the country. Now that the Army had gotten after the wild Indians in earnest and the vigilantes had hung a few of the white roughs, this section of Idaho was beginning to know more peaceful days. Andy seemed happy. Twice during the past winter he had gone up to the Payette Valley for visits with the Lynns; and, since then, weekly letters had arrived from Sally, which Andy read with a pleased, reflective smile.

Well, it was high time this bachelors' nest had a mistress. When the spring chores were done, he would nudge Andy a bit, Levi brooded. Go marry the gal, he would say. Knock a wall out of the cabin and build on a couple of decent-sized rooms. What about me? Hell, I'll move out to the barn. But you go marry the girl; she won't wait forever.

No, Levi mused, maybe a better way to nudge him would be for me to just up and leave. Tell him I got a yen to go back to Kansas. I wouldn't go back there, of course. But I would pull out, spend the spring and summer wandering around northern Idaho, Washington Territory, and western Oregon. Make him think I'd left for good. Just let him spend a month alone here, he'd get married quick enough, I'll bet. Then, come fall, I could drift back through for a visit. If he said he needed a hired hand, I could say, "Well, I'll help out for a while . . ."

Gazing into the distance, Levi smiled. He had never agreed with Andy's suggestion that they be partners in the ranch. It simply would not work. But once Andy got himself a wife, once she took over as mistress, once they started raising a family, nothing would suit Levi better than living out his days working on the ranch as a hired hand.

On the road to the south of the cabin, a lone rider appeared. It was not Andy. This man was mounted on a gray horse, which, as it drew near, looked winter-thin, badly cared for and about ready to drop in its tracks. As the man let the weary animal come to a stop in the yard before the cabin, Levi studied him through veiled eyes, noting first that he was a stranger, then that he wore a holstered Navy Colt and carried a short-barreled shotgun in a homemade leather sheath fastened to his saddle.

"Howdy," the man grunted. "You live here?"

"Yes," Levi answered.

"Mean to say you own this place?"

A week's reddish-brown beard stubble covered the man's face; his eyes were bleary and bloodshot; his voice harsh and ugly. Trash, Levi decided. Vigilante bait. But a white man.

"No," Levi said carefully. "I just work here. This is Andy Hale's place."

The stranger's eyes flicked to the open cabin door, then back to Levi. "Is he home?"

"Sure. He's working just over the ridge yonder."

The low swell of ridge which Levi had indicated with a jerk of his head was a mile or so west of the cabin. After a glance in that direction, the stranger's nervousness vanished, he gave a derisive laugh and swung out of the saddle. "He must be to hell and gone away or I'd of seen him as I come down the hill. Well, it don't matter. You got anything to eat?"

"Andy'll be coming home for dinner soon. You better ask him."

"Christamighty! I'm starved! Well, what about whisky—you got a jug stashed away in the cabin?"

"No. But if you'll wait till Andy comes—"

"You're an Injun, ain't you? A goddam filthy Paiute! What're you doin' runnin' loose?"

"I told you. I'm working for Andy Hale."

"Well, it's a piss-poor white man that can't find any better help than a murderin' Paiute, that's all I got to say! Now, you listen to me, you ignorant red bastard—I don't give a damn if your hair is cut short and you can speak English and you do work for a white man—you're scum to me. I want food and I want whisky and I want it right now! Do I get it or not?"

Levi was unarmed. But in the cabin, he reflected coldly, a holstered, loaded pistol hung from a gunbelt on a wooden peg on the wall. And just inside the door, leaning against the wall, was a loaded rifle. If he could lay hands on either weapon, he'd bet that the stranger's manners would show a vast improvement.

"Sure, mister," he said politely. "You wait right here while I see what I can rustle up."

He was within two strides of the cabin doorway when the stranger, who had been eying him suspiciously, jerked the short-barreled shotgun off the saddle of the jaded horse, waved it at him and grunted, "Whoa, now, not so fast!"

Levi stopped. "But you told me—"

"Never mind what I told you, you sneaky bastard! That sorrel horse in the corral—is he sound?"

"Yes."

"All right, I'll do my own rustling for whisky and grub. Take my saddle and bridle off the gray and put 'em on the sorrel. I'm gonna trade horses with your boss."

"You're making a mistake, Mister. When Andy gets home—"

"I'll be long gone from here by then, Injun. Jump, damn you, 'fore I fill your red ass with buckshot!"

Letting his face show no expression save resignation, Levi shrugged, walked to the gray, stripped off its bridle and saddle and carried them into the corral. Out of the corner of his eye, he saw the stranger enter the cabin. As he opened the corral gate, he noted the position of the hammer he had recently put down, and, without breaking stride or appearing to glance at it, managed to scoot it along the ground with his foot toward the center of the corral. Not much of a weapon with which to face a sawed-off shotgun, he mused. But if he could take the stranger by surprise . . .

After putting the bridle on the sorrel, he laid the blanket and the saddle on its back, then stooped—his back to the cabin—and picked up the hammer and the dangling cinch with the same gesture. He took several moments to fasten and adjust the cinch; when at last he turned to lead the sorrel out the corral gate, he held the hammer, head down, alongside his right leg and slightly behind it.

The stranger stood watching him from the cabin doorway. In his left hand, he held a half full bottle of whisky which he had hastily snatched off a shelf; in his right hand, he held the sawed-off shotgun.

"To hell with the food! I'll settle for whisky! Tell your Injun-lovin' boss I'm sorry I can't stay for dinner."

"All right," Levi said impassively. "I'll tell him."

"You're a cool bastard, you know that?" the man sneered, moving toward him. "What makes you so cocky? Do you think a bunch of your Paiute cronies are gonna come whoopin' up and lift my hair?"

Levi did not answer.

"You'd like that, wouldn't you?" the man persisted. "If the odds were right—twenty of you, say, and me without a gun— you'd have yourselves a gay old time strippin' me naked, stakin' me out on the ground, and then peelin' my hide off inch by inch? Wouldn't that be fun?"

Levi did not speak.

"'Course, it'd be a hell of a lot more fun if I was a woman, wouldn't it? Then you and your buddies could treat me the way you treated that poor Army woman. You dirty red bastards—if I'd been there, you'd never have got away with *that!*"

Levi continued to stare at him. *If he'll only keep talking . . . If he'll only drop his eyes . . .*

The man laughed. "All right, you dumb Injun, stand aside. When your boss shows up, tell him I traded horses. If he wants boot, tell him I'll give it to him when he catches me—right in the rear!"

"Why don't you tell him yourself?" Levi said quietly, turning his head toward the ridge to the west. "He's coming yonder now."

The stranger's head jerked around. Levi's right hand rose, his wrist cocked, and the hammer sailed through the air. But it was not a weapon made for throwing. Instead of its metal head striking the stranger between the eyes, as Levi had intended that it do, the head struck him where his left shoulder joined his neck, while the handle, spinning over, caught him a glancing blow on the cheek.

He let out a howl of pain and rage. Dropping the bottle of whisky, he swung the barrels of the scattergun in Levi's direction and his finger tightened on the twin triggers. Even as Levi dove for the stranger's knees, hoping to go under the blast, he knew that he would not make it.

The bright spring day went dark . . .

Running into Andy Hale on a Boise City street, Armand Kimball smiled and shook his hand. "It's certainly good to see you, Andy. How are things at the ranch?"

"Bad, Armand. Levi is dead."

"What!"

"He was murdered yesterday. By a white man."

From his haggard, unwashed, unshaven appearance, Andy had not rested nor eaten for quite a while, Kimball guessed.

He took him by the arm. "You need a drink and a square meal."

"Later. Right now, I'm looking for Rube Robbins."

"He left town two days ago, Andy, and hasn't got back yet. Come along with me and tell me about Levi."

A stiff drink of whisky relaxed Andy and loosened his tongue enough that he could talk about it. He had returned to the cabin at noon yesterday, he said, and found Levi sprawled just outside the door, dead. He had been shot in the face with a shotgun fired by a person standing no more than ten feet away.

"It had to be a white man," Andy said. "Levi was outside, fixing fence, where he could see the road in both directions. If he had seen an Indian coming, he would have gone into the cabin and gotten a gun."

"Do you suppose he knew the man?"

"I doubt it. The neighbors all liked Levi. He didn't have an enemy in the world."

"A white rough, then? A drifter? A drunk?"

Andy shook his head. All he knew was that a sorrel horse was missing from the corral, with a worn-out gray left in its place. He had followed the tracks of the sorrel north to the ferry, and the ferryman had given him a description of a burly, bleary-eyed, bearded white man who had crossed Snake River a few hours earlier and then had ridden on in the direction of Boise City.

"There were too many tracks for me to make sure he came on to Boise City," Andy said, "and after it turned dark I lost the sign completely. But my guess is he's here. I want him found, arrested, and tried for murder. Where did you say Rube Robbins went?"

"Down toward the mouth of the Payette. We had a murder of our own a few days ago. Rube is after the men that did it."

"Who was killed?"

Kimball toyed with the drink he had ordered to keep Andy company. He had not particularly wanted it; now he suddenly did. Lifting the shot glass, he drained it, set it down, took a swallow of water from the taller glass beside it, then said, "A man you know, Andy. An Indian. People call him Bruneau Jim."

"Oh, for God's sake! Who would want to kill him?"

"All we know now is that there were four of them. White men. Bruneau Jim and a couple of Indian women ran into them on the trail a few miles east of town. They were drunk, apparently—"

"The Indians?"

"Lord, no! The whites. According to the story the women told Rube later, the white men tried to run Bruneau Jim off so that they could have some fun with the squaws. He wouldn't go. He tried to tell them who he was, how he'd always been a friend of the whites, how he'd scouted for the Owyhee Volunteers, how he'd gone for help when they got trapped—"

"I remember, Armand. I was there."

"But they wouldn't listen. One of them made a grab for a squaw. Bruneau Jim objected. So they killed him."

"And then raped the women?"

"All of them. Several times."

Andy stared down at the plate of food which had just been placed before him, his thin face pale under the dust-grimed beard stubble, his eyes hurt and sick. Hoarsely, he said, "This is a pee-poor country, Armand."

"Well, it's got some pee-poor people living it in, I'll agree with you there. But that's a fault a few legal hangings will cure in a hurry, now that our courts have finally found nerve enough to order the death penalty."

"No Idaho jury is going to hang a white man for killing an Indian, Armand, you know that."

"We hung Anthony McBride a few weeks ago, Andy. Which shows how times are changing."

Andy shook his head. "McBride killed a Chinaman, not an Indian."

"I know. But his defense was he shot the poor devil because he *thought* he was an Indian. Progress is slow where justice is concerned, Andy. But now that our courts have finally learned that they *can* hang a man for murder, let's hope it becomes habit-forming."

Levi's murderer never was found. But a week after the killing of Bruneau Jim and the raping of the two squaws, Deputy U. S. Marshal Rube Robbins returned to Boise City with four prisoners, which he took to the fort guardhouse for safekeeping. Their names were Brady, Sullivan, Hayden, and Jacobs, they said. When questioned by Judge Cummins, they claimed they were strangers to this country and greatly concerned about its reported Indian dangers. Yes, they had been drinking that day, they admitted; in fact, they had been so drunk they weren't sure *what* had happened. No, they hadn't known that Bruneau Jim was a harmless, friendly Indian; fact was, he'd seemed mighty hostile to them. And after all, he *was* an Indian . . .

The leader of the group, John Brady, swore that Sullivan, Hayden, and Jacobs had done the actual killing. Sullivan, Hayden, and Jacobs claimed it had been John Brady who had fired the fatal shot. As to the raping of the squaws . . . *well, your Honor, like we told you, we'd been drinking and the women were Indians* . . .

Though Judge Cummins made no secret of the fact he thought they all deserved to be hanged, he was a practical-minded man. No white jury in Idaho would convict a countryman on a rape charge when the victims were Indians, he realized, so the rape charges were dropped.

Only one Indian had been killed; thus, it seemed fair to try only one white man. In lieu of $700 cash bond, Sullivan, Hayden, and Jacobs were jailed as witnesses; John Brady was indicted on a charge of first degree murder.

Kimball's law partner, Arthur Creed, said cynically, "Ten dollars of my money to five dollars of yours Brady never stands trial."

"He'll be tried," Kimball answered, shaking his head. "But I'll bet you a dinner he gets that first degree murder charge reduced—and then goes free."

The wave of indignation that had swept over the community immediately following the unprovoked killing soon subsided; the dead Indian was forgotten and the live white man behind bars was extended sympathy by many people of his kind. *Poor John Brady! He was drunk, wasn't he? And all he done was shoot an Indian . . .*

After an escape attempt arranged by Brady's friends had been frustrated by Marshal Robbins, the defense attorney entered a plea that the charge against him be dropped. The court denied it. The defense then requested that the charge be reduced. Reluctantly, the court took the request under advisement. Six weeks after the killing, Brady was re-arraigned, new arguments were heard by the bench, and the charge was reduced to manslaughter. A jury panel was drawn and a trial date set. A week later, a spirited, emotional defense put up against a dull, lackluster prosecution resulted in a hung jury. Following a second trial five days later, another jury disagreed, six and six, Judge Cummins gave up, and the prisoner was discharged.

As he ate the dinner he had won from his law partner, Kimball said ruefully, "The truth is, this was one wager I wanted to lose. I really hoped they would hang John Brady—as they did Anthony McBride. It would have proved that Idaho justice can be consistent."

"Hell, Armand, justice had nothing to do with McBride's hanging—don't you realize that?"

"What do you mean?"

"McBride was a rough, a drunk, a murderer, and a tough customer all around. But the reason why the jury put him away was he had poor eyesight. When a trigger-happy rough can't tell the difference between an Indian and a Chinaman in broad daylight, he becomes a menace to the community. What else can you do with him but hang him?"

Chapter Twenty-Two

Six months after Sergeant O'Neil's death and his wife's disappearance, the *Statesman* reported in an issue dated May 2, 1868:

MRS. O'NEIL AGAIN.—We learn from parties just in from Camp Harney that some Indian prisoners at that post report Mrs. O'Neil yet alive and a prisoner among the Indians, although her whereabouts has not been ascertained. It is hoped that this is true and that the unfortunate woman will be rescued from the hands of the savages.

An hour after the newspaper came off the press, Cornelius Belford climbed the stairs to Armand Kimball's office, a copy of the *Statesman* in his hands. Thrusting it across the desk and indicating the item with a trembling finger, he said eagerly, "Did you see this?"

"Yes, I was just now reading it."

"Do you realize what it means, Armand? Melinda's alive! She's still alive!"

"Sit down, Cornelius," Kimball said gently. "I know how you feel, but you musn't let wild rumors like this upset you."

"But it isn't a rumor!" Belford exclaimed excitedly. "It's true! It's absolutely true! I've known in my bones all along that they wouldn't harm Melinda! I've hoped, I've prayed, I've told everybody that would listen to me—"

Time had not been kind to Cornelius Belford, Kimball mused sorrowfully. His once thick, dark hair had become gray and thin; his once wiry, erect body had become frail and stooped; his once powerful, compelling voice had become shaky and weak. Though no strong bond of affection had ever existed between father and daughter that Kimball had seen, it was only natural, he supposed, that her loss had shaken the poor man. He could talk of nothing else. He claimed he was too worried to work. Although the townspeople pitied him, they were avoiding him more and more of late, for in his eternal harping on his daughter's tragic disappearance he was beginning to make a pathetic but wearisome nuisance of himself.

"Well, there's no law against hoping," Kimball said patiently. "If there's any truth to the story, we'll know it soon, I'm sure.

General Crook feels he'll be rounding up the last of the hostiles this summer."

"I have no confidence in General Crook," Belford said. "But I do trust you, Armand. I trust you more than any man I've ever known."

"Nice of you to say so," Kimball said warily. "Will you do me a favor, Armand?"

"Certainly—if I can."

"I want you to act as chairman of a ransom committee."

"To ransom Melinda?"

"Yes. To be effective, your committee should have at least a dozen prominent Idaho people on it—people like Arthur Creed, H. C. Street, Jim Reynolds, Daniel Lynn, Ed Holbrook—people belonging to all trades, all religions, all political parties. First, we'll raise a fund by public subscription. Next, we'll petition Governor Ballard for a contribution in the name of Idaho Territory. Then we'll make up a telegram signed with a thousand names and send it to President Johnson—"

Staring across the desk at his visitor, Kimball got a sudden uncomfortable feeling that he was listening to a demented man who cared more for organizing projects than he did for his own flesh and blood. He raised his hand and interrupted.

"One moment, Cornelius. What's the point in doing all that when we have no evidence that Melinda is still alive to *be* ransomed?"

"She is! I know she is!"

"Have you received any demand for ransom money?"

"No, but I'm expecting one any day, now that the truth is out." Getting to his feet and leaning over the desk, Belford lowered his voice to a husky whisper. "Of course, money is only a part of what he'll demand of me. He'll want favorable peace terms, too. That's why we can't trust General Crook, who's interested only in making himself a big reputation as an Indian-killer—"

"Hold on! *Who* will demand ransom money? *Who* will want favorable peace terms?"

"Why, Chief Bigfoot, of course," Belford answered, sitting down. "He's the Indian who captured Melinda, you know. But he's not really a Snake or Pajute, as most people think. He's half Cherokee and half white. He's the man we knew five years ago as Will Starr . . ."

No, this was not a demented man, Kimball mused as he leaned back in his chair and wearily listened to Belford's involved theory of why his daughter had been taken by the Indians and what must be done to get her back; this was merely a pompous, frustrated little man who had brooded so long on one subject he now accepted his own fevered imaginings as facts.

Yes, Kimball admitted, he had heard of Chief Bigfoot. No, he had no absolute proof that Will Starr was dead. Yes, if one accepted the premise that Starr had survived it *was* possible that the giant Indian long rumored to exist in southwestern Idaho could be the huge young man that had killed James Warren and fled into the desert. But to believe that he now commanded all the hostiles in this country, had deliberately abducted Melinda, was holding her prisoner and soon would ask a large sum of money and favorable peace terms—well, somewhere along this chain of reasoning, the links of credibility fell apart.

Keeping his doubts to himself, Kimball patiently heard Belford out. When at last Belford was done, Kimball got up, went around the desk, eased his visitor up from his chair and steered him gently toward the door.

"You've given me a great deal of food for thought, Cornelius. Let me brood on it for a while, will you? I'll see you again in a day or two . . ."

The organization of a ransom committee, the public solicitation of funds, the appeal to Governor Ballard and the telegram to President Johnson never got past the talking stage. For on June 11, 1868, the *Statesman* published the following item:

REMAINS OF MRS. O'NEIL FOUND.—Sinora Hicks, the scout, returned on Monday from a twenty day run through the mountains. He reports the discovery of the remains of Mrs. O'Neil, although he was unable to gather them together in any decent shape, the wolves having scattered the bones so much.

The Snake Indian guide with whom he started took him directly to the place where the O'Neil party were attacked, and showed him where they killed Mrs. O'Neil. The Indian pretended to say that he was the one who killed the poor woman. After stripping her, they dragged her by the neck some distance, he said, and then laid her head upon one stone while they took another and beat it into a jelly.

The place where they committed the atrocious deed was within half a mile of where they attacked the party. After showing Hicks where they killed Mrs. O'Neil, the red devil, who appeared to glory in killing her, endeavored to make his escape. He was riddled by bullets from Sinora Hicks' Indian scouts . . .

In New York City, an *Avalanche* editorial sarcastically noted, a society had just been organized whose aim was to be the "protection and elevation of the Indians of the Territories." Society missionaries, wrote the *Avalanche* editor, were cordially invited to begin their good work in Idaho, where he would attempt to arrange that they be "scalped just a little" so that they could report their good works "understandingly..."

Armand Kimball put down the newspaper. Leaning back in his chair, he clasped his hands behind his head as he gazed out the window overlooking the street, along which the shadows of the warm June afternoon now were lengthening. *Understanding? No, my friend, not in this time, this place, this country, this world. **it** is too much to ask of human beings.*

Poor Melinda, who was so beautiful...

Poor Cornelius, who has no cause left to organize...

Poor Patrick O'Neil, an Irishman, who was a good soldier...

Poor Levi, an Indian, who harmed no man...

Poor Andy, a white man, who drew no color line...

Poor Bruneau Jim, an Indian, who was always a friend of the whites...

Poor nameless Chinaman, who died because he was mistaken for an Indian...

Poor Anthony McBride, an Irishman, who made a mistake, deserved to die, and did...

Poor John Brady, an Irishman, who made a mistake, deserved to die, but didn't...

Poor Joe Hatley, who tried to swim a river to save seven dollars, and died...

Poor James Warren, who loved no one but himself, and died...

Poor Will Starr, who loved Melinda, pretended to be white, wasn't, and died... or became a monster...

Poor Sumner Pinkham, who died because he was a Union man...

Poor Ferd Patterson, who died because he was a Rebel...

Poor Rube Raymond, who died because he told the truth...

Poor Johnnie Clark, Dave Updyke, and Jake Dixon, who died because they were liars and thieves...

Poor one hundred nameless Chinamen, massacred by Indians on the Jordan Valley road...

Poor hundreds of white settlers and travelers, killed by Indians...

Poor hundreds of Indians, dead or dying now of hunger, bullets, or exposure as General Crook and his soldiers remorselessly keep after them...

Poor John Madigan, Charles Barchet, Jas. Lyons, Michael Meara., Willoughby Sawyer, Jas. Carey, and Carl Bross—killed in action and buried far from home...

God in Heaven! Kimball mused, *it's a long, long list! They all 'were searching for something in Idaho but found only suffering or death.*

What we need out here is not a society to protect and elevate the Indians but one which will save us all from our blind, stupid crimes against one another. Five years ago, there was a war on back East. We wanted to get away from it. We did not want to get involved. So we came West where there was space, free land, gold, grass, and no laws, war, or government to pester us. We had a chance to start from scratch. We did. And, by the Almighty, haven't we made a great job of it . . . ?

Dusk was at hand. Steps sounded on the stairs, deliberate, precise, slow. Even before Arthur Creed reached the top landing and opened the office door, Kimball knew that his law partner would be a little drunk. Councilman Creed always moved deliberately when he'd been drinking.

"Hey!" Creed said from the doorway. "Anybody here?"

Kimball got up and lighted a lamp. "Yes, I'm here."

"Working?"

"No."

Creed dropped into the chair on the far side of the desk, took off his hat and ran his long, thin fingers aimlessly through his hair. Though his face was flushed, he did not appear to be very drunk. In fact, he looked rather subdued. "Did you hear about Mrs. O'Neil?"

"Yes."

"I talked to Sinora Hicks a while ago. He told me some details that didn't get into the paper. With gestures." Kimball shivered. "Fix us both a drink, Armand, then I'll tell you the whole story."

Getting up, Kimball fetched a bottle of whisky, two glasses, and a pitcher of water. As he poured, he said, "Skip the details, please. My imagination has been working too much as it is."

"Lord, what the devils can think of to do! Hicks sweat the truth out of that Snake before he killed him, he said. The bastard told it in sign language—"

"*Please,* Art!"

"All right. It makes me sick, too."

Crossing the room to the window, Kimball stood gazing at the steep hills rising from the valley floor north of town; the grass upon their slopes was a fresh, soft shade of green in the last rays of the sinking sun; higher up, the peaks were covered with dark green pine. Without turning, he said, "I'm curious about just one thing, Art."

"What's that?"

"Chief Bigfoot. Was he in on this?"

"Well, Sergeant Grogan said the Indian he saw pick her up and carry her off was a big booger—a hell of a big booger—"

"Which doesn't mean he *was* Bigfoot. Or that such a monster really exists."

"No, I guess not."

"What does Sinora Hicks think?"

"You can't pin him down. He's heard a lot of squaw talk, he says, but who's to believe a squaw? He's talked to men who claim they've actually seen Bigfoot, but they may have been lying. He did see some awful big tracks once, he admits, but he thinks they were made by pranksters."

"Indian pranksters?"

"Yes."

"I didn't realize Indians had that sort of sense of humor."

"Oh, hell, yes! There's nothing they like better than making a fool of a white man, Hicks says. If a white man is looking for a monster, they'll oblige—whether they've got one handy or not."

Likely that was the size of it, Kimball mused wearily. Likely the big Indian Mike Grogan had seen had been only that—a big Indian—and not anywhere near the size of Will Starr. Likely Will Starr was five years' dead. Likely there was no such person as Chief Bigfoot . . .

And yet . . .

Impatiently, he turned away from the window. "Let's go eat. Poor Cornelius will want to bury Melinda decently, I imagine, though he hasn't got a dime to his name. I'll go talk to him after supper and help him arrange the services . . ."

Chapter Twenty-Three

PEACE WITH THE INDIANS.—We take pleasure publishing General Orders No. 24, signed by Gen. Crook, containing stipulations of peace with the bands of hostile Indians infesting the vicinity of Malheur River, Castle Rock, Owyhee and Steen's Mountain . . . . . . we hope this order may be generally read, understood and acted upon by all travelers through their country . . .

—*Owyhee Avalanche*
Silver City, I.T.
July 25, 1868

Andy Hale paid the Lynns a visit in early November and stayed three days. He had the grim, quiet, bleak look of a man who had brooded long and hard over a disturbing problem and had finally made up his mind. Daniel Lynn thought he knew what was troubling Andy and feared he knew what Andy had decided to do. But he did not press him. Sooner or later, he guessed, it would come out.

Henry, too, noticed an oddness in Andy's manner, and asked, "What ails him, Pa?"

"Well, for one thing, he's thirty years old—and suddenly realizes it."

"That's not old."

"No. But when a man feels like he's getting nowhere, it *seems* old, Henry. For another, he misses Levi. He's lonesome."

"He can move to town or get himself another partner, can't he?"

"If he makes a move, son, it'll be a sight farther than to town. And I have a notion he'll never try to replace Levi. He's got a look in his eye . . ."

Andy did not mention Levi, those three days. He did not mention his ranch. Times were slow in the Owyhee mining settlements, he said, because of the shortage of water in the creeks, the replacement of white prospectors by penny-pinching Chinamen, and the curtailment of hardrock operations by the Eastern-controlled companies due to a slump in the silver market. Beef prices were falling. Some of his neighbors were giving up, he said, selling their cattle for whatever they would bring and moving out of Idaho Territory.

"Seems a shame they're pulling out now," Lynn said. "With the Indian trouble settled, things ought to be peaceful down your way."

"For a while, maybe. But there are still a few Indians around."

"According to the paper, General Crook claims the Army has killed, starved, or froze out at least half of the hostiles in this part of the country. And the rest have surrendered."

Yes, Andy agreed, Crook had done a good job. And he had laid down terms that made sense. The hostiles that wished to do so could go live on the established reservations; those that did not could remain free so long as they kept the peace. White settlers who had lost livestock were not to attempt to retrieve it themselves but were to leave that chore to the Army. No treaties had been signed with the hostiles and no promises had been made them. They were to keep the peace; if they did not, the Army would resume its war of extermination against them.

"It's not just my neighbors puffing out that bothers me,"

Andy said. "But there comes a time when a man wonders . . ."

"If someplace else would be better?"

"Yeah."

"Well, Andy, that's a thing a man has to decide for himself. Sometimes he's right, sometimes he's wrong."

"Did you ever wonder, Daniel?"

"I left Iowa and came out here, didn't I?"

"Since then, I mean. Since settling in Idaho. Did you ever wonder, Daniel? Did you ever have any doubts?"

"Sure. But I'm still here."

Daniel Lynn would go no further than that, much as he was tempted to do so. He liked Andy. He wanted him to stay. But if he'd made up his mind to give up and go, Lynn had no intention of attempting to argue him out of it.

When supper was finished the third evening, Andy helped Sally carry the dirty dishes out to the kitchen, stayed there with her for some time, then returned alone to the living room, where Lynn sat reading the *Idaho Statesman* by lamplight while Henry played with a black and white kitten on the hearth in front of the fireplace. As Andy paused before him, Lynn sensed that he was ill at ease.

"Listen to this," Lynn said, his gaze still on the paper. "'Forest fires burning in the Cascades and the Coast Range are so bad that their smoke impedes navigation on the lower Columbia, even in broad daylight. Friday last, below Portland, one ship captain reported that the sun could not be seen even at high noon . . .'" Shaking his head in amazement, Lynn glanced up. "Imagine that!"

"Guess the forest fires are bad all over this year," Andy said stiffly. "It's been a mighty dry fall."

"Hasn't it rained yet down your way?"

"No." Andy cleared his throat uneasily. "I've been talking to Sally, Mr. Lynn—"

"*What* did you call me?"

"Daniel, I mean. I told her how poor my prospects are. I told her how bad the cattle market is, how a lot of my neighbors are leaving, how risky a place mine is to live in because of the Indians and white roughs—"

"Oh? And then you told her goodbye?"

"No. I asked her to marry me."

Lynn folded his paper and laid it aside. "What did she say?"

"That I should talk to you."

"She's of age now, you know."

"Yes, sir. Still, she thought I should give you a chance to say whatever you want to say."

"Well, in the first place," Lynn said dryly, "she's only known you five years—"

Sally, who had quietly appeared in the doorway between the kitchen and the living room, moved forward beside Andy and took hold of his arm. "Please, Pa, don't tease us. We're serious."

"So am I. Like Andy says, his prospects are poor, the cattle market is down and he lives in a dangerous neighborhood. Is that any kind of life to ask a new bride to share?"

"It suits me, Pa."

"Or are you both thinking of leaving Idaho?" Lynn persisted. "Is that in your mind?"

"Whatever Andy wants to do will be fine with me," Sally answered. "If he wants to go, I'll go."

"Now, look here, Daniel," Andy said angrily. "A man's got a right to wonder, hasn't he? But wondering isn't the same as going. Sure, my prospects look poor. But I'm not ready to give up yet. If Sally is willing to risk it, what I thought I'd do is buy up some of those cheap cattle from my neighbors that are pulling out, try to carry them through the winter and hope for the market to pick up next spring—"

"We could make our place a lunch stop for the stage," Sally said eagerly. "I like to cook and it would be an easy way to make a little cash money—"

Lynn smiled. Getting up out of his chair, he shook Andy's hand, gave his daughter a hug and said, "There's nothing I'd like better, Andy, than to have you in my family. Take her and welcome to her."

"Oh, boy!" Henry moaned in mock agony, rolling his eyes at the ceiling. "If he only knew what he was getting!"

"Henry!" Sally exclaimed, her eyes suddenly moist.

"Aw, Sal, I was only joshing, you know that!"

"This calls for a celebration," Lynn said. "Sally, do you suppose you could dig up something to drink?"

"There's fresh cider."

"Fine!"

When the glasses had been filled and the proper toasts had been drunk, Daniel Lynn sat for a moment gazing into the fire, then said reflectively, "You asked me if I'd ever had any doubts about Idaho, Andy. Yes, I have had. Many times. Sally doesn't know this. Neither does Henry. But two years ago I tried to sell the farm."

"Pa!" Sally exclaimed. "You didn't!"

"It was right after Billy McConnell sold out and left," Lynn said, still staring into the fire. "It had been a bad year all around. Roughs, crickets, poor crops, poor prices, dust, heat—they piled up on me till I was mighty discouraged. When McConnell left, I wondered if I shouldn't give up and leave, too. The War was over, back East. I got to thinking how nice it would be to go back to Iowa and live like we used to live there, before the war. So I drove over to Boise City and told Armand Kimball if he could find a buyer who'd pay me four thousand dollars in cash I'd sell out."

"But you didn't," Andy said soberly. "What changed your mind?"

"Simple bull-headedness, Andy. The best offer I got was twenty-five hundred dollars. It made me mad. It made me so mad I took the place off the market, said to myself I was going to stay—and that ended that." He chuckled. "Here's the queer thing about it, Andy. Next year, the roughs moved on, the crickets quit pestering, the crops were fine, the dust and heat didn't bother me anymore—and I took in more cash money that one season than I'd been offered for the whole farm." He shook his head in wonder. "Maybe there's a moral in that, Andy. Maybe the Lord likes to test us. When He finally sees we won't give up, He relents, smiles, and gives us His blessing."

"Well," Andy said dryly, "if that's so, Sally and I sure will give Him a fair chance to relent, smile, and cast some blessings our way."

Lynn looked at his daughter. "Set a wedding date yet, Sally?"

"Andy says the sooner the better. But I was just thinking. If I could have a couple of weeks to fix up a dress and let a few of the neighbors know, it would be nice to make a *little* ceremony of it. And there are some good friends in Boise City I'd like to invite—the Duncans, the Hocketts, the McCalls . . ."

"Don't forget the Weavers up in Idaho City," Lynn said. "They'd be hurt if you left them out. And I sure want Rube Robbins to come." He frowned. "Wonder if Rube knows how to reach Billy McConnell down in Nevada? I'll bet Billy and his wife would love to come up, if they knew about it in time."

"If it's going to be that big an affair," Andy said, "I'd like Matt Miller to come. He always thought a lot of Sally. And Armand Kimball. They could drive out together."

"Hey, I got a wonderful idea!" Henry said gleefully. "Why don't we invite everybody that was in our wagon train? Kids and all! Make it a real big shindig! Dancing, horse races, fireworks—"

"Oh, Henry, be serious, please!" Sally scolded. "All we want is a few old friends."

"Wait a minute, that's not such a bad idea," Lynn murmured, nodding approvingly. "Sure, we've scattered and lost track of one another, but I'll bet if we put our minds to it we could run down thirty or forty families that were in our wagon train. Not just Iowa people. Missouri people, too. We could make it a First Settlers Reunion. The Belfords, the Pences, the Frasers, the Dilworths. Everybody. How would three weeks from next Friday be?"

"Fine with me," Andy said. "Sally?"

"Certainly." She pursed her lips, did some mental figuring, then suddenly exclaimed in horror. "Oh, no, that won't do at all! That's the day after Thanksgiving. With people coming from so far away, they'd have to travel on Thanksgiving day and that just wouldn't be right."

"Well, then, we'll set it a week earlier," Lynn said.

"Oh, no!" Sally protested. "If it's going to be such a big wedding, I'll need at least three weeks to get ready."

"All right. We'll make it a week after Thanksgiving."

Andy shook his head. "That'll put it into December, Daniel. We may run into bad weather. Come an early snow in the hills, a lot of people won't be able to make it."

Henry chuckled fiendishly. "Poor Sally! Guess there'll be no wedding this year. Well, next Fourth of July will do fine! *Then* we can have fireworks for sure!"

Lynn scowled at his son. Sally looked like she was about to cry. Andy looked like he was sorry he'd ever brought up the subject. A firm decision seemed required, and, as head of the household, Lynn knew he must make it.

"Now listen to me, everybody. I've got the answer." He paused to make sure he had their undivided attention, then said with a smile, "Lately I've been thinking I'd like to throw a party for my neighbors and friends, just to show them how glad I am we came to Idaho and stayed here. So why not make this affair a Thanksgiving dinner, a party, a reunion, and a wedding all rolled into one? We'll invite all our Payette Valley neighbors and all the wagon train people to come over the last Wednesday in November. We'll have a dance that evening, have church services Thursday morning, eat a big Thanksgiving dinner together, and then have the wedding the next afternoon—"

"With horse races, fireworks and *another* party afterwards!" Henry chortled. "Boy, that *is* an idea!"

"Be quiet, son, I'm in dead earnest."

"Oh, Pa, it's a wonderful thought!" Sally said gratefully. "But we couldn't possibly handle all those people for that long a time—"

"Why not?" Lynn demanded. "We traveled out to Idaho together and managed to put up with one another for months on end, didn't we?"

"Yes, I know—"

"Then leave the details to me. Just leave them to me . . ."

This was one Thanksgiving celebration that Daniel Lynn would remember for the rest of his days. But the details of arranging it and seeing that it went off without a hitch were taken out of his hands by the first neighbor lady he mentioned it to, next morning.

"Land's sake!" Ruth Shelby exclaimed, when he rode over and told her about it. "If that isn't just like a man, thinking up such an affair! It's impossible, Daniel! It just can't be done at all! Now, let's see, here's how we'll have to arrange things . . ."

It was like old times, Daniel Lynn mused as he made his way slowly through the crowd toward the parked wagon from whose bed it would soon be his privilege to announce that the Thanksgiving dinner was ready. Which was about the only thing the ladies were letting him do, he thought ruefully. Lord, how they did love to run things!

"Now, first, Sally is not to do one blessed thing but get ready for the wedding. Two ladies will help her, keep her quiet, and see to it that she gets her rest . . ."

"Yes, we'll need a committee to meet the people from outside the valley as they arrive. No, we won't let them sleep in their wagons. We'll distribute them around. Let's see, the Lynns have room for four adults in their house. No children, though; they'd be noisy and disturb Sally. Well, yes, some of the older boys and men can sleep with Daniel and Henry in the barn. But we'll parcel the other families out among the Payette people . . ."

"The Wednesday night dance? Yes, the Ben Shelby barn is the place for that. We'll have services in the church at nine o'clock Thursday morning. Then we'll eat dinner at two. On tables set outside at the Lynns if the weather is decent; in the house and barn if it's not . . ."

Daniel Lynn's notion that this was to be *his* party had received an overwhelming veto very early in the planning stages. Let him butcher and roast a few steers over outdoor pits and boil up a few pots of beans? That's no Thanksgiving dinner, Daniel! No, it won't do at all. All the ladies will cook and bring something. Turkeys, geese, ducks, hams, vegetables, pies, cakes. If you feel you simply must provide something, Daniel, a little cider would be nice. Soft cider, mind you. We don't want this celebration spoiled by the men's drinking . . .

No, Lynn silently agreed, we don't want that. But a host has to be a host, by golly! If the cider he thinks is soft turns out to be hard, if he buys a few barrels of beer to slake the dust in the throats of thirsty travelers in case the day is warm, if he has a few bottles of whisky around to warm up chilled friends should the day be cold—well, what's the harm of that?

The weather cooperated beautifully. The snow held off in the high country. The roads stayed good. The sky this Thanksgiving afternoon was cloudless, the air was invigoratingly brisk but not uncomfortably cold, and, though a few light rains had fallen in the mountains to the north and east during the past week, seasonal forest fires still burned in places, hazing the yellow-brown lower slopes of the foothills with a soft blueness that made them look unreal.

Five years.

Lord, it doesn't seem that long since we stopped in the Boise Valley in August of '63! Matt said Boise City was "kind of a passing-through place." And I said that was what I intended to do, "pass through it, the quicker the better." Yet here I am.

And I've got a lot to be thankful for. Sally's grown up; tomorrow she's marrying a good man. Henry's nearly grown; he's taking hold like I'd never dreamed he would. Queer, kids are, these days. Used to be, I'd get awful exasperated with him because he wouldn't do farm work the way I told him to do it but was forever trying to find ways to do it easier. A sitting-down farmer, that's what I told him he'd turn out to be. A gadget-fancying farmer. A lazy-way farmer. But lately, I'm beginning to wonder if he isn't smarter than I am about some things.

If a new piece of machinery will let a man plough three furrows with less effort than his father used to plough one the old way, that's progress, isn't it? If he can mow, rake, and stack more hay in one day sitting down than his father could do in a week on foot, why shouldn't he do it his way? Of course, a youngster Henry's age is bound to have some wildly impractical ideas—like replacing horse-power with steam-power, which Henry says is bound to come some day—but you've got to let youngsters dream, got to let them learn which ideas will work and which won't . . .

Farming is different out here and a man has to think differently about it. Back in Iowa when the corn needed moisture during a dry spell in July the only thing a man could do was peer at the sky and mutter a pious prayer for rain. Out here, knowing good and well there'll be no rain between mid-June and late September, he has to figure out a way to water his crops during the dry summer months before he even breaks his land. A spring, a dug well with a bucket on a windlass, or a drilled well with a hand-powered pump, will do for household water and a small garden patch. But to raise crops a man needs a lot more water than he can raise by hand. A windmill-powered pump is no good because there's seldom any wind. A man has to ditch-irrigate, which means gravity-flow water, gates, canals, valley-wide planning and cooperation with one's neighbors.

Yes, in Idaho a man learned different ways. And the younger he was, the quicker he seemed to learn them.

Passing the table where Matt Miller sat talking with a group of friends from wagon train days, Lynn paused and put a hand on the old man's thin, bony shoulder.

"You making out all right, Matt?"

"Tol'ble, Dan'l." With a shaky hand, he lifted the tin cup of whisky he was holding, a glint of humor in his tired eyes. "Ain't had a celebration like this since Fourth of July in South Pass, have we, Dan'l? D'ye mind that brawl?"

"Sure do, Matt. I remember it well."

"Mighty ornery bunch, them ridge-runners were," Matt muttered with a chuckle. "Gonna be some big heads and queasy bellies amongst 'em, come mornin', I said. Tell you what we'll do, Dan'l, I said—we'll git up 'fore dawn an' hit the trail."

Squeezing the old man's shoulder, Lynn smiled and moved on, a tightness in his throat. Of the fifty-five families that had traveled west from South Pass together and parted near Boise City that August day five years ago, only thirty-one had come here for the reunion. Of the missing, some had moved on, some had returned to their former homes, some had died, some had dropped out of sight. Of those that were here, some had prospered and some had not; some seemed to have aged greatly, others seemed not to have aged at all.

"Daniel, I wanta shake your hand. Wanta tell ya what a great idea this here reunion was . . ."

Phil Duncan, with his vague blue eyes, his weak chin, his puppy-like amiability, was one of those persons that time had treated kindly, Lynn mused as he shook hands. Maybe alcohol preserved a man. Or, more likely, having a wife like Beth Duncan—solid, practical, good-humored, loving—was what helped her husband keep his youth.

"Thanks, Phil. Sure glad you and Beth could come."

"Next time you're in town, drop in and see me, you hear? Drinks're on the house fer *my* friends. Any ol' time . . ."

Lordy, Lordy, how time does fly, Lynn thought as he passed by the table where Isaac Shelby, his wife, Beulah, Obidiah, Benjamin, Ruth, and their families sat visiting with one another. Naomi, a toddler with a penchant for getting into trouble when the wagon train left Fort Laramie five years ago, sprouting up tall and lanky as a colt; David, born on the trail, a sturdy child now, baby fat lost and muscles beginning to show. Isaac and Beulah had a toddler of their own to keep track of now, and, from BeulaH's shape, another one well on the way . . .

And Ike came within a 'whisker of being hung as a horse-thief. Which proves that good raising will tell, if you give it time.

"Can you spare me a moment, Daniel?" a voice said at his elbow. "I have a business proposition for you."

"Oh, hell, Armand!" Lynn said, shaking Kimball's hand. "You know this isn't the day for business propositions!"

"No?" Armand Kimball said gently, his eyes twinkling.

"Well, all I want to tell you is that I believe I can find a buyer for your place who would top the offer I passed on to you a couple of years ago. If you would give me a price to quote—"

"You go to the devil!" Lynn said with a smile. "Enjoying yourself, Armand?"

Kimball's eyes roamed over the crowd; for a moment as he watched a group of children playing a boisterous game of tag between the tables, a shadow seemed to pass over his face, then it was gone. Quietly he murmured, "We're all sort of a family, aren't we? We came so far together, lived through so much . . ."

As he walked on, Lynn saw Rube Robbins and Billy McConnell engaged in what appeared to be a rather one-sided argument. Rube had hold of McConnell's arm, was shaking an admonishing finger in his face and was lecturing him sternly, while McConnell smilingly gazed at him. As Lynn came up, Rube turned.

"Damn it, Daniel, help me talk some sense into Billy!"

"Sense about what?"

"Getting rid of that ranch of his down in Nevada and moving back here where he belongs!"

"Well, Billy," Lynn said. "Why not?"

"Someday, maybe," McConnell said. "Someday . . ."

"Listen, you darned fool," Rube persisted. "Idaho is your kind of country. If you'll move back, I'll guarantee we'll put you in the governor's chair . . ."

Yes, Lynn thought as he strolled on, likely that very thing would happen if Billy McConnell came back to Idaho. And he would come back, someday. Because Idaho was changing . . .

Up in the high country of the Boise Basin, Rocky Bar, and Owyhee, the free and easy days when pick-shovel-and-pan prospectors could make their pile and move on to another strike were done. A lot of these men had moved on, and with them had gone the roughs. The boom days were finished. But the grass still grew on the benchlands, the soil still lay deep and fertile in the valleys, water still flowed in the rivers, towns still existed, people still came West. And there was talk now of a railroad from Salt Lake City to Portland, which of course would come through Boise City . . .

In contrast to Phil and Beth Duncan, Cornelius Belford and his wife were a couple whose faces clearly showed the ravages of time. Poor Cornelius, Lynn mused. All he could talk about these days was his lost daughter. He looked tired, he looked old, he looked ill. Observing him now where he sat on a bench shivering in the autumn sunlight despite his heavy coat and the relative mildness of the day, Lynn found it difficult to recall how deeply he had once disliked this man. All he felt toward him now was pity. On a sudden impulse, Lynn paused and put a friendly hand on Belford's shoulder.

"Cornelius . . ."

"Yes, Daniel?"

"We're ready to eat dinner. For old times' sake, would you say Grace?"

Belford looked childishly pleased. Getting shakily to his feet, he said, "I'm not sure they'll be able to hear me. Weak as my voice is these days—"

"They'll hear you," Lynn said quietly. "I'll help you up onto the wagon."

Hoisting Cornelius Belford up to the wagon bed, Lynn climbed up beside him and signaled to Henry, who was standing near the corner of the house. When his son's vigorous beating of an iron bar against the metal triangle hanging nearby had gained the crowd's attention, Lynn raised his hand.

"Welcome to the First Settlers Reunion. You didn't come here to listen to a speech by me, I know. You came to eat. The ladies tell me the food is ready. But first let's have a word of Grace from Mr. Belford."

Lynn stepped down off the wagon. There was a rustle of movement as the people got to their feet, quieted the children, bared their heads and lowered their eyes. As he dropped his own gaze to the ground, Lynn felt a moment of doubt. *That was a fool thing for me to do!* Frail though he is, he won't let an opportunity like this pass without doing it justice. Once he's started, he'll pray forever. He'll ramble. He'll moralize. He'll mumble for tune on end, while the food gets cold, the children grow restless and the adults stand with glazed eyes . . .

In the silence, Lynn stole a quick glance upward. Cornelius Belford had removed his hat, closed his eyes and was standing with his head lifted slightly, facing the afternoon sun. His stooped shoulders were squared; his body was erect; his bearing was proud and full of dignity. When he spoke, his voice, though far from strong, possessed a remarkable carrying quality.

"Let us pray together as our Saviour taught us," he said simply. "'Our Father, Which art in Heaven . . .'"

He paused for a moment, then went on as all joined in: "'. . . hallowed be Thy Name. Thy Kingdom come. Thy will be done, on earth, as it is in Heaven. Give us this day our daily bread . . .'"

OTHER BOOKS FROM CAXTON PRESS BY BILL GULICK

Snake River Country

ISBN 0-87004-215-7 (cloth) $39.95

12x15, 195 pages, maps, 104 color photos

Manhunt: The Pursuit of Harry Tracy

ISBN 0-87004-392-7 (paper) $18.95

6x9, 250 pages, illustrated, maps, index

Chief Joseph Country
Land of the Nez Perce

ISBN 0-87004-275-0 (paper) $39.95

9x12, 316 pages, 231 illustrations, maps, index

Outlaws of the Pacific Northwest

ISBN 0-87004-396-x (paper) $18.95

6x9, 216 pages, photographs, maps, index

Traveler's History of Washington

ISBN 0-87004-371-4 (paper) $19.95

6x9, 560 pages, illustrations, maps, index

The Moon-Eyed Appaloosa

ISBN 0-87004-421-4 (paper) $12.95

6x9 1xx pages

For a free Caxton catalog write to:

CAXTON PRESS
312 Main Street
Caldwell, ID 83605-3299

or

Visit our Internet Website:

www.caxtonpress.com

Caxton Press is a division of The CAXTON PRINTERS, Ltd.

WC